THE
STOLEN THRONE

THE
STOLEN THRONE

DAVID GAIDER

TOR®

A TOM DOHERTY ASSOCIATES BOOK
NEW YORK

BioWare™

This is a work of fiction. All of the characters, organizations, and
events portrayed in this novel are either products of the author's
imagination or are used fictitiously.

DRAGON AGE: THE STOLEN THRONE

Copyright © 2009 by Electronic Arts, Inc.

All rights reserved.

A Tor Book
Published by Tom Doherty Associates, LLC
175 Fifth Avenue
New York, NY 10010

www.tor-forge.com

Tor® is a registered trademark of Tom Doherty Associates, LLC.

ISBN 978-0-7653-6371-8

First Edition: March 2009
First Mass Market Edition: September 2012

Printed in the United States of America

0 9 8 7 6 5 4 3 2 1

For my Oma

ACKNOWLEDGMENTS

First off, a big thanks to my cheerleaders Jordan, Steph, Danielle, and Cindy. Without you I would not have persevered. Also thanks to my parents for being so certain that all those games would never lead to anything useful yet letting me get away with playing them anyhow. You encouraged my imagination, and that's more important than anything. I will always be grateful to you both.

Thanks cannot be said without acknowledging the hard work that the Dragon Age team has put into bringing this world to life. Each day I spend in the company of such visionary and creative people makes me more proud of what we're creating. You guys have made my job that much easier.

Also, one last thank-you to BioWare for giving me such a fantastic opportunity, and for being the kind of game company that believes writing is something worth investing in.

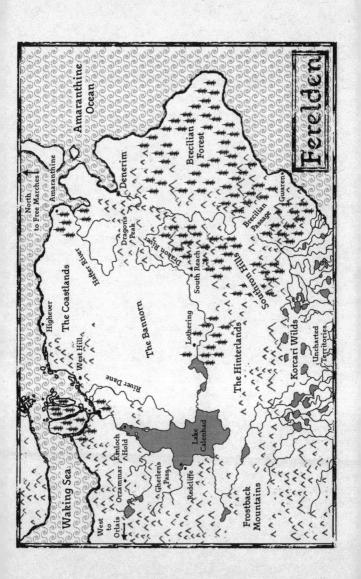

1

_____

"Run, Maric!"

And run he did.

His mother's dying words whipped him into action. The image of her grisly murder still burning in his mind, Maric reeled and plunged into the trees at the edge of the clearing. Ignoring the clawing branches that scraped at his face and clung to his cloak, he blindly forced his way into the foliage.

Strong hands grabbed him from behind. One of his mother's men, or one of the traitors who had just orchestrated her death? He assumed the latter. Grunting with effort, Maric shoved back, struggling to dislodge the hold on him. He succeeded only in getting a few more branches striking him in the face, the leaves blinding him further. The hands attempted to haul him back into the clearing, and he dug his boots into the ground, gaining a bit of purchase on gnarled tree roots. Maric violently shoved back again, his elbow connecting with something hard . . . something that gave way with a wet crunching sound and a startled grunt of pain.

The hands loosened, and Maric leaped forward into the trees. His cloak resisted, jerked him back. Something had caught on his long leather coat. He twisted and fought frantically, like a wild beast caught in a trap, until he somehow wriggled himself out, leaving the cloak torn on a branch. Maric gasped, launching himself into the darkness beyond the clearing without risking even a glance behind. The forest was old and thick, allowing only the faintest beams of moonlight through the dense canopy. It was not enough to see by, only enough to turn the forest into a maze of frightening shadows and silhouettes. Tall twisted oaks stood like dark sentinels, surrounded by dense bushes and recesses so black, they could have held almost anything.

He had no idea where he was going; only his urge to flee guided his feet. He stumbled over roots that jutted out of the uneven ground and bounced off solid tree trunks that kept springing out of nowhere. Wet and slippery mud made his steps treacherous and his balance so precarious, it seemed the ground might give way beneath him at any moment. The woods were completely disorienting. He could have been running in circles, for all he knew. Maric heard men shouting as they entered the woods behind him, giving chase, and he could clearly make out the sounds of fighting as well. Steel blade ringing on steel blade, the cries of men dying—his mother's men, many he had known his entire life.

As he frantically ran on, images kept whirling

through Maric's mind. Moments ago, he had been shivering in the cold forest clearing, convinced that his presence at the clandestine meeting was more a formality than anything else. He barely paid attention to the proceedings. His mother had informed him earlier that with the support of these new men, the rebellion would finally become a force. These men were willing to turn on their Orlesian masters, she said, and that made it an opportunity she wasn't willing to pass up after so many years spent running and hiding and only picking what battles they could win. Maric hadn't objected to the meeting, and the idea that it might be risky never even occurred to him. His mother was the infamous Rebel Queen; it was she who had first inspired the rebellion, and she who led the army. The battle had always been hers and never his. He, himself, had never even seen his grandfather's throne, never understood the power his family had possessed before the Orlesians invaded. He had spent his entire eighteen years in rebel camps and remote castles, endlessly marching and forever being dragged along in his mother's wake. He couldn't even imagine what it might be like to not live that way; it was a completely foreign concept to him.

And now his mother was dead. Maric's balance was ripped from him, and he tumbled in darkness down a short hill covered in wet leaves. He slid awkwardly and slammed his head against a rock, crying out in pain. His vision swam.

From far off came a muffled answering cry of his pursuers. They had heard him.

Maric lay there in the moonlit shadows, cradling his head. It felt like it was on fire, a raging inferno that blotted out reason. He cursed himself for being

so stupid. By sheer luck if nothing else, he had managed to run some distance into the forest, and now
he had given away his location. There was a thick
wetness on his fingers. Blood was caking in his hair
and running down around his ears and neck—warm
in sharp contrast with the frosty air.

For a moment he shook, a single sob escaping his
lips. Maybe it was best just to lie here, he thought.
Let them come and kill him, too. They had already
killed his mother and earned whatever lavish reward
the usurper had surely promised them. What was he,
besides an extra body to be slaughtered along with
the too-few men Mother had brought? And then he
froze as a terrible realization settled at the edge of his
consciousness.

He was the King.

It was ridiculous, of course. Him? The one who
elicited so many impatient sighs and worried looks?
The one for whom Mother always had to make excuses? She had always assured him that once he got
older, he would grow into the same easy authority
that she evinced. But that had never happened. It
was no great offense, either, as he had never taken
seriously the idea that his mother might actually die.
She was invulnerable and larger than life itself. Her
death was a hypothetical thing, something that had
no actual bearing on reality.

And now she was gone and he was supposed to be
King? He was to carry on the rebellion on his own?

He could just imagine the usurper upon his throne
in the capital, laughing uproariously when he received
the news of Maric's succession. Better to die here, he
thought. Better that they put a sword through his gut,
just as they had done to his mother, than to become

the laughingstock of Ferelden. Maybe they would find some distant relative to take up the banner of rebellion. And if not, then it was best to let the bloodline of King Calenhad the Great die here. Let it end with the Rebel Queen falling just short of her goal— rather than petering out under the leadership of her inept son.

There was a certain amount of peace in that thought. Maric lay there on his back, the damp coldness of the leaves and mud almost comforting against his skin. The irregular shouts of the men drew nearer, but it was almost possible for Maric to blot them out. He tried to focus solely on the rustling of the leaves in the wind overhead. The tall trees stood all around him, like giant shadows peering down at the tiny figure who had tumbled at their feet. He could smell the pine, the tartness of nearby tree sap. These forest sentinels would be the only witnesses to his death.

And as he lay there, the pain in his head dulling to an insistent throb, the thought rankled. The men who had lured his mother here with promises of aid were nobles of Ferelden, the sort who had bent knee to the Orlesians so they could keep their lands. Rather than finally live up to their ancestral oaths, they had betrayed their rightful Queen. If no one escaped to inform those who had remained with the rebel army about what had actually happened, they might never know the truth. They would guess, but what could they do without proof? The traitors might never pay for their crime.

Maric sat up, his throbbing head protesting fiercely. Aching and shivering, he was wet and chilled right to the bone. Getting his bearings was difficult, but he guessed he was not far from the edge of the forest.

He had stumbled only a short ways in, and the men chasing him were not far away, searching and calling out to each other. Their voices were getting fainter, however. Maybe he should just remain still? He was in some kind of a depression, and if he stayed there long enough, these men could pass him by, giving him enough time to catch his breath. Perhaps he could find his way back to the clearing and see if any of his mother's men had survived.

A sudden crunch of twigs nearby made him stop again. Maric listened carefully in the darkness for an agonizing moment, but heard nothing. The noise had been a footstep; he was sure of it. He waited longer, not daring to move a muscle . . . and heard it again. Quieter, this time. Someone was definitely trying to sneak up on him. Maybe they could see him, even if he couldn't see them?

Maric cast about desperately. The far side of the hollow he was in opened up into a downward slope. It was difficult to tell the general terrain with so little moonlight coming through the canopy. There were also trees in that direction, roots and thick bushes that would prevent him from crawling out of sight. He had to either stay where he was . . . or climb out.

A squelch of wet leaves nearby forced Maric as low to the ground as he could go. Listening closely was difficult given the muted shouting in the distance and the sound of the wind blowing high in the trees, but he could ever so faintly detect the soft steps of someone passing nearby. He suspected they couldn't see him at all. In fact, it was dark enough that his pursuer would likely end up doing exactly what Maric had done and fall right into the hollow.

Maric didn't exactly relish the idea of his enemy

falling on top of him, so he cautiously tried to get up onto his feet. Sharp pain lanced through his knees and arms. There were cuts on his face and hands from the branches, and he was sure there was a gash on his head . . . but it all felt distant, as if someone else were experiencing the pain. He tried to control his movements, making them slow and quiet. Smooth. And he continued to listen for more footsteps, anxiously biting his lower lip. It was difficult to hear anything over the desperate thumping of his heart. Surely it was obvious to whoever was out there. Perhaps they were closing in for the kill even now, laughing at his terror.

Breathing deliberately, sweating despite the chill, Maric slowly pulled himself upright enough to get both his feet underneath him. His right knee spasmed, shooting lightning-sharp agony up his leg. This injury he felt very clearly, unlike the others. In shock, he hissed through gritted teeth, nearly gasping out loud.

Immediately he clamped his mouth shut and closed his eyes in silent reprimand at his idiocy. Crouching there in the darkness, he listened carefully. The footsteps had stopped. Someone else, farther out among the trees, shouted in Maric's direction. He couldn't quite hear what the man had said, but there was definitely a question to it: calling out, asking if they had found anything. But there was no response. The source of the footsteps nearby had probably heard Maric and was not willing to give his own position away by answering.

With the utmost care, Maric crawled up the side of the depression. He squinted into the shadows, trying to pick out anything that might resemble a human form. He imagined his pursuer doing the same thing, playing a cat-and-mouse game in the dark. The first one of them to spot the other would win the prize. Belatedly, Maric realized that even if he did see this man, there might not be much he could do about it. He wasn't armed. An empty sheath dangled at his waist, his belt knife lent to Hyram not two hours earlier to cut some rope. Hyram, one of his mother's most trusted generals and a fine man he had known since childhood, most likely lying dead at his Queen's side, their blood cooling in the midnight air. Maric cursed himself for a fool and tried to put the image out of his mind.

Just then, Maric noticed a glint in the shadows. Narrowing his eyes helped him just barely discern a sword, its polished blade reflecting the faint moonlight. In the mass of dark shadows and bushes, he still couldn't see the form of the man holding the weapon, but it calmed him to finally know where his opponent was.

Gaze locked in that direction, Maric raised his hands to grasp the edge of the depression and quietly heaved himself up. The pain that shot through his arms was considerable, but he ignored it and never for one second took his eyes off that sword. As he got over the edge, the sword moved. A dark shape began lumbering toward him, raising the sword up high and growling with menace.

Without thinking, Maric launched himself forward and charged. The sword slashed down by his ear, narrowly missing his arm. He rammed headfirst into the man's midsection, knocking the wind out of him. Unfortunately, the pursuer was wearing a heavy chain hauberk, and Maric's head exploded with pain. He may as well have head-butted a tree trunk.

The world spun around him wildly. He would have careened out of control had his momentum not carried the two of them backwards, knocking the man off his feet. They fell on hard uneven ground, with the swordsman taking the brunt of the impact. His weapon arm swung out to one side, causing the sword to fly out into the shadows.

Almost delirious and barely able to see, Maric pulled himself back up and grabbed the man's head in both hands. He felt a strong whiskered jaw, and the man flailed wildly with his free hand, trying to push Maric off. He tried to shout, possibly call on his fellows for help, but all that came out was a muted bellow. Maric used the benefit of leverage to pull up the man's head and then slam it down hard. The man grunted when his head hit an exposed root.

"You bastard!" Maric snarled. The man's desperation intensified, the hand reaching for Maric's face, slapping and clawing. Finding purchase, it pushed hard against Maric's nose, one finger digging into his eye. Maric pulled his face away as he shoved down hard on the man's head, grinding it back into a root. The man grunted and tried to buck Maric off, but the heavy hauberk worked against him. He writhed and pushed with that one hand against Maric's face, but none of his efforts were enough to get him free.

Maric's throbbing head was torture, and his neck was stretched to its limit, trying to pull away. When Maric let go of the man's head to battle the pushing hand, the bearded man made an attempt to kick Maric off. Maric lost his balance for a moment and the enemy's hand turned into a fist, thumping him solidly across the face. Light-headedness came over Maric, and he saw stars. He fought against swooning, reached down, and grabbed as much of the man's long hair as he could, pulling him upward. This time the man bellowed loudly, his head yanked up at an awkward and painful angle. Letting out his own cry of effort, Maric crashed the man's head down on the tree root a third time. Even harder.

"You killed her!" Maric shouted. He picked up the man's head by the hair yet again to slam it down. "You bastard, you killed her!" He smashed the head down again.

And again.

Tears welled up in his eyes, and he choked on his words: "She was your Queen, and you killed her!" He slammed the head again, still harder. This time the man stopped fighting back. A cloying, meaty smell assaulted Maric's nostrils. His hands were covered with thick, fresh blood that wasn't his own. Almost involuntarily, he fell off the body and scrambled back, his bloody hands slipping on the cold leaves, and pain shooting anew through his legs. He half expected the man to rise up and charge at him again. But he didn't. The body lay there in the shadows, a vague shape resting awkward and still upon a clump of tree roots. Maric could barely make out the great oak behind him, thrusting up into the overhead canopy like a gravestone.

He felt physically ill, his stomach twisting in knots and his body shaking. Almost involuntarily, he brought a hand up to his mouth to keep his bile down, smearing fresh blood onto his face. There was gore on his hand, clumps of skin and hair. He convulsed, vomiting onto the muddy ground what little lunch he had eaten earlier in the day. Despair threatened to overwhelm him.

You're the King, he reminded himself.

Maric's mother, Queen Moira, was a tower of strength who could lead armies of battle-hardened men to victory. She was every inch her grandfather's daughter; that's what everyone said. She had inspired some of the most powerful noblemen in Ferelden to rise up in her name and fight to put her on the throne simply because they knew beyond a shadow of a doubt that she belonged there.

And now she's gone, and you're the King, he repeated to himself. It felt no more real now than it had before.

In the distance, the sounds of the pursuit were getting louder again. The traitors might have heard Maric's struggle with the bearded man. He needed to leave. He needed to run, to keep going. Yet he could not will his legs to move. He sat in the dark forest, his bloody hands held out in front of him as if he had no idea where else to put them.

All Maric could think of was his mother's voice the last time she had returned from battle. She was in full armor, covered in blood and sweat, and grinning madly. Maric had been dragged in front of her by his trainer for brawling with a commoner boy. Even worse, Arl Rendorn had been with his mother, and he asked if Maric had at least won the fight. Burning with shame, Maric admitted to being soundly beaten, causing the Arl to snort and ask what sort of king Maric could possibly make.

And then his mother had laughed merrily, a laugh that could dispel anything serious. She had taken Maric's chin in her hand and looked in his eyes, and with a gentle smile told him not to listen to the Arl. *You are the light of my life, and I believe in you.*

Grief brought Maric close to laughing and crying at the same time. His mother had believed in him, and yet he had gotten lost in the woods in less than half an hour. Should he somehow elude his pursuers, make it out of the forest, and obtain another horse, he still needed to find a way to locate the army. He was so used to being led around, being told where to go and where to ride, that he hadn't paid attention to any route they'd taken. He had followed as he was bidden. Now he couldn't even guess his location.

And thus passes the last true King of Ferelden, he thought with bizarre amusement. *He wanted to be a good king, but he didn't know his arse from a hole in the ground.*

Mad giggling threatened to overtake his tears, but Maric shut down both reactions. Now wasn't the time to be thinking of the past, or grieving. He had just killed a man with his bare hands, and there were other enemies nearby. He needed to run. He took a deep, ragged breath and closed his eyes. Deep down inside of him there was steel. He embraced it, tasted its bitter edge and let it shut out the whirlwind inside of him. He needed to be calm, even if only for a moment.

When he opened his eyes again, he was ready.

Maric cast about calmly for any sign of the sword that had flown out of the other man's hand. Everything around him was somehow moving very slowly, none of it seeming quite real. There were too many bushes, too many odd dips and clumps of trees where the sword could be hiding. He couldn't find it. Then he heard another man's voice, this one calling out from somewhere close. There was no more time.

Standing gingerly, Maric listened for where the

voices were coming from. As soon as he ascertained their source, he headed in the opposite direction. It was an awkward hobble at first. His legs were bruised and cramped and he might have broken some bones, but he ignored the pain. With effort, he grabbed on to low-hanging branches and pulled himself farther into the darkness.

They would pay for what they had done. If he did only one thing as King, he would make them pay.

"Something's happening," Loghain muttered, frowning.

He stood at the edge of the forest, absently wiping mud off his leathers. The effort was pointless, as his clothing was as worn and as filthy as one might expect from a poacher. The Orlesians, of course, had less kind names for him and the others like him: *criminals*, *thieves*, and *bandits*, too, though only when desperation forced their hand.

Not that Loghain much cared what the Orlesians called him, since it was their fault his family had been forced off the farm. The Orlesians didn't believe in anyone owning land but their fancy, painted-up nobility, so it came as no surprise that they didn't look favorably on Ferelden's freemen. An extra "tribute" tax was concocted by the Orlesian Emperor, and any freemen who couldn't afford it had their lands confiscated. Loghain's father had managed to scrape together enough to pay the tax the first year, so naturally it was decided the tax could stand to be even higher. The next year, his father refused to pay, and when the soldiers came, they determined that not only was the farmhold forfeit, but his father should also be arrested for tax evasion. Loghain's family resisted, so now they lived out in the Ferelden wilds, banding together with other desperate souls to eke out a living however they could.

Loghain might not have cared what the Orlesians thought of him, but he did very much care to avoid being arrested. The local constable over in Lothering was a Fereldan man, and so far he had been tolerant of their band. So long as they didn't prey on travelers and restricted their thefts to the petty sort, the constable made only token efforts to track them down. Loghain knew that the man was going to be forced to hunt them in earnest someday, and hopefully he would be decent enough to let them know about it in advance. They would move on, as they had already done many times. There were enough forests and hills in Ferelden to hide an entire army, after all; even the Rebel Queen knew that. But what if the constable didn't warn them? That thought worried Loghain now and had him staring into the forest. Men didn't always get to do as they'd prefer.

A cold wind blew across the field, making him shiver. It was late, and the moon shone down from a cloudless night sky. He wiped the black curls out of his eyes, resigned to the fact that his hair was no doubt as dirty as his hands, and pulled his hood up. The spring had been more of a lingering winter that had refused to let go. The cold nights he and his band had spent in their makeshift tents had been less than comfortable, to say the least, but the accommodations were preferable to some of the alternatives.

Dannon, a big brute of a man with an untrustworthy air, walked up behind him. Loghain suspected that Dannon had once been a thief, the dedicated sort who lived in the cities, picking pockets and robbing travelers, and that he was here with them now because he wasn't a very good one. Not that Loghain was in much of a position to judge him. They did what they could, all of them, and Dannon pulled his weight. That didn't mean Loghain had to feel comfortable around the man.

"What's that you're saying? You saw something?" Dannon scratched his beak of a nose while he adjusted the carcasses he was carrying. There were three rabbits slung over his shoulder, the prize of the evening's work, poached from the fields of a lord known for his Orlesian sympathies. Hunting in the dark was never easy, especially when one took more care to avoid being spotted than to actually hunt, but they had been fortunate for once.

"I said that something's happening," Loghain repeated irritably. He turned and glared at Dannon, and the man backed away a step. He had that effect on people. Loghain had been told before that his blue eyes lent him an icy, intense air that could put people off. And that was fine by him. Loghain was still considered young by most in the camp, Dannon especially, and he preferred that the man didn't get any notions about trying to give him orders. "Are you telling me you haven't noticed?"

Dannon shrugged. "There's some tracks. I think maybe there's some soldiers about."

"And you didn't think that was of any interest?"

"Agh!" He rolled his eyes. "Karolyn down at the village already told us that there'd be soldiers, didn't she? Said she saw Bann Ceorlic marching through the north field with some of his fellows just this morning."

Loghain frowned at the name. "Ceorlic is a lick-spittle. Desperate for favor with the Orlesian usurper, everyone knows that."

"Yes, well, Karolyn said he was marching well out of sight, and didn't even stop at the inn. Like he didn't want to be seen." Loghain gestured at the rabbits Dannon carried. "Look, whatever he's up to, it doesn't have anything to do with us. Nobody saw us hunting. We're good. We should go." He smiled, a nervous, friendly smile meant to be reassuring. Dannon was afraid of him. Which was as Loghain preferred it.

He looked back into the forest, his hand grazing the sword belted at his side. Dannon's eyes followed the motion, and he grimaced. Dannon was skilled enough with a knife, but hopeless with anything larger. "Aw, come on, now. Don't go making trouble," he groused.

"I'm not interested in making trouble," Loghain insisted. "I'm interested in avoiding it." He advanced toward the forest's edge, crossing over a ridge that led him downhill a ways. "Nobody has to have seen us hunting to know that we're here. You know as well as I that we may have overstayed our welcome."

"That's not for you to decide," Dannon said, but he followed quietly after that. It was Loghain's father who would decide, after all, and even a man like Dannon knew that Loghain and his father were seldom of different minds when it came to such matters. *As it should be*, Loghain thought to himself. His father hadn't raised a fool.

The pair of them descended into the dark forest, pausing only once to let their eyes adjust to the patches of moonlight that managed to snake through the canopy above. Dannon grew increasingly agitated by the treacherous ground, even though he had sense enough to stay quiet. For his part, Loghain was beginning to think Dannon might have the right of it.

He was just about to turn them both around when Dannon stopped short. "You hear that?" he whispered.

Good ears, Loghain thought. "Animal?"

"No." He shook his head, uncertain. "Sounds more like shouting."

The two of them stood still, and Loghain tried to be patient and listen. The breeze rustled the branches overhead, a significant distraction, but after a moment he heard what Dannon was referring to. It was faint, but in the distance he could pick up the sounds of men calling to each other, engaged in some kind of search. "It's a foxhunt."

"Huh?"

Loghain restrained the urge to roll his eyes. "You were right," he said tersely. "They're not here for us."

Dannon seemed pleased by the news. He shifted the rabbits on his shoulder and turned to go. "So let's not wait around, then. It's late."

But still Loghain hesitated. "You said Bann Ceorlic passed through. How many men did he have with him, you think?"

"I don't know. I didn't see them, did I?"

"What did your bar wench say, exactly?"

The big man shrugged, but his back stiffened in quiet rage. Loghain noticed with a vague interest that he had hit a sore spot. A dalliance, then? Not that Loghain truly cared, but it was better to avoid provoking the big man needlessly. "I don't know," Dannon gritted out. "She didn't say. It didn't sound like a lot."

Loghain figured there must easily be twenty men out there. Surely if Bann Ceorlic had brought that many men near Lothering, it would have caused more comment. So what was going on, exactly? The fact that it involved one of the Fereldan noblemen most notorious for his open allegiance to the Orlesian tyrant did not sit well with him. Whatever Ceorlic and his men might be up to, it was undoubtedly not good for the band—even if it didn't involve them directly.

As Loghain stood there, trying to ignore Dannon's impatience, he conceded to himself that there might be nothing he could do either way. The political goings-on of Ferelden were none of his concern. Survival was his concern, and anything political was important only when it affected that survival directly. He sighed irritably, staring off into the shadows as if they would provide the answer to his mystery.

Dannon harrumphed. "You sound like your father when you do that."

"That may be the first compliment I've heard from you."

He snorted derisively, glaring at Loghain. "It wasn't intended." He spat down between them. "Look. This doesn't involve us, like you said. Let's *go*."

Loghain didn't like being challenged. He met Dannon's glare with his own, and for a long moment he said nothing. "If you want to go," he stated quietly, "then go."

Dannon stood his ground, though Loghain saw the man shift nervously. Dannon didn't want to be in this position. Loghain could almost sense him thinking about his knife there in the dark, wondering if he would need to use it, wondering how he would get back to camp if he did so. Loghain was tempted to push it further. He wanted to step right up in front of Dannon's face and take his measure. Maybe Dannon had the guts to knife him and be done with it. For all Loghain knew, he was a murderer, the sort who liked to cut people just to hear them scream, and that was the past he had fled. Maybe Loghain was being foolish by not going along with his suggestion.

But he doubted that.

The silence between them was long and tense, intruded on only by the sound of the wind in the trees and the far-off shouts of the hunters. Loghain narrowed his eyes, not even touching his sword hilt, and was inwardly pleased as Dannon was the first to look away.

The moment was broken by the sound of someone approaching.

Dannon leaped at the interruption, letting the urgency of the new threat cover up the fact that he had just backed down. As though their standoff had never happened. But Loghain knew.

Something was coming toward them, fast and clumsy. Whatever it was, it scrambled madly through the bushes, heedlessly pushing branches away in a panic. The fox, Loghain surmised. Of course it would end up right in their lap, wouldn't it? If there truly was a Maker up in the heavens, as the priests said, He had a troublesome sense of humor indeed.

Dannon retreated a few feet, nervous and agitated, while Loghain drew his sword, waiting. Their guest suddenly fell into view, deposited out of the shadows like an unwanted gift, and then stopped short, staring at the two of them with wide, fearful eyes.

It was a young man, Loghain's age or perhaps younger. His fair hair and fairer skin were obscured under scratches, leaves, dirt, and a healthy dose of blood. He certainly wasn't dressed for a run in the woods, wearing only a tattered shirt and enough mud to make one think he had escaped whoever he was running from by crawling around on his belly. The blood covered his face as well as his hands. Probably not all his. Whoever this man was, he had likely killed to get away, which told Loghain just how desperate the intruder might be.

The new arrival crouched before them in the shadows like a caught animal, frozen between fight and flight. Behind him, the shouting drew near. Loghain slowly raised a hand, carefully showing his palm to the fugitive to demonstrate that he meant no harm. And then he put his sword back in its scabbard. The blond man didn't move, only narrowed his eyes suspiciously. His attention darted nervously behind him as more muffled shouts came through the trees.

"Let's get out of here!" Dannon hissed behind him. "He's going to lead them right to us!"

"Wait," Loghain whispered, not taking his eyes off the fugitive. Dannon bristled, and Loghain caught a glimpse of the knife now in his hand. Holding out his hands to calm both of them, Loghain turned back to look at the blood-covered man in the shadows. "Who's chasing you?" he asked slowly.

The blond man licked his lips, and Loghain saw calculation in his eyes. "Orlesian dogs," he said evenly. Still he didn't move.

Loghain glanced at Dannon. The big man was grimacing, but Loghain could tell he wasn't without sympathy for the fellow's situation. No doubt he was interested only in his own hide, but finally he relented with a grunt.

"Good answer." Loghain took a step back and half turned as if to leave. "Come with us."

Dannon swore unhappily, refusing to look at anything but the ground as he sheathed his knife and stalked off. Loghain made as if to follow him, but watched to see if the fugitive would fall in, too. For a long moment, the blond man was visibly torn. Then, without further hesitation, he sprang up from his crouch and ran after them.

The three proceeded quietly back the way Loghain and Dannon had come, the blond man trailing and Dannon staying ahead as if he were close to leaving them behind. The set of the big man's shoulders said he was angry and resentful. Loghain didn't care.

They kept up a brisk pace, and after a short time, the shouts of the blond man's pursuers were left behind. The stranger seemed relieved, and appeared even more at ease as they approached the edge of the forest and moonlight could be seen more clearly overhead. Getting a better look at him, Loghain couldn't help but be a bit mystified. The man's clothes, while torn and dirtied, were plainly of quality if not fancy. The boots in particular seemed solid, made of fine leather, the sort that Loghain saw templars wear on occasion. So no pauper, certainly. He was also shivering and jumped at every strange forest sound, so this hike was no normal event for him. Not by a long shot.

"Dannon, wait," Loghain called out as he came to a halt. Dannon stopped only reluctantly. Loghain turned to the blond man, who now edged back with renewed suspicion, his eyes darting between them as if wondering who was going to come after him first. "This may be as far as we can go," Loghain reluctantly acknowledged.

"Thank the Maker!" Dannon muttered under his breath.

The blond man considered for a moment, looking around as if to judge his location. The field outside the forest could be seen from where they were. "I can find my own way from here."

Loghain couldn't place the young man's accent, but from the way he spoke it was clear he was educated. A merchant's son, perhaps? "Is that so?" He gestured at the blond man's tattered clothing, noting he didn't even have a cloak. "You look more likely to freeze before you even reach town." He raised an eyebrow. "If that's where you intend to head, with those men after you."

"Why *were* they after you?" Dannon demanded, shoving his way up beside Loghain.

The blond man paused, glancing between Loghain and Dannon as if uncertain to whom he should be responding first. Then he looked down at his hands and saw the dark stains of blood in the moonlight as if for the first time. He was clearly repelled, despite his efforts to fight down his reaction. "I think I killed one of them," he breathed.

Dannon whistled appreciatively. "They won't give up easily, then."

Loghain's brow furrowed. "These were Bann Ceorlic's men, I take it?"

"Some of them," the blond man agreed reluctantly. "They killed . . . a friend of mine." The pain that crossed his face told Loghain that the last statement

was true enough, at least. The blond man closed his
eyes, shivering again and trying vainly to wipe some
of the blood from his cheek. Loghain glanced at Dannon, and the big man shrugged in response. Whatever the full story was, Loghain doubted they were
going to get it. And perhaps it wasn't necessary to do
so. This stranger wasn't the first person they had encountered who had crossed the Orlesians. And if
Loghain was in this man's shoes, he wouldn't trust
them either. There was definitely more here than met
the eye, but Loghain's gut told him that whatever this
was, it wasn't a trick. And his gut was seldom wrong.

"Look." Loghain sighed heavily. "We don't know
for sure who's hunting you back there. You say they're
working with the Orlesians, I'm willing to take your
word for it." The blond man looked about to object,
but Loghain held up a hand. "Whoever they are, it
sounded like there's quite a few of them. They're going to figure out soon enough that you got out of the
forest. First place they're going to look for you is in
Lothering. Do you have somewhere else to go?"

The blond man hung his head, looking grim. "No,
I . . . suppose not. Nowhere I can get to easily." Then
he set his jaw and looked up at Loghain. "But I'll
make do." For a moment, Loghain actually believed
he might try. No doubt he would fail, but he would
try. Whether this was a sign of stubbornness or fool-
ishness or even something else, he couldn't tell.

"We have a camp," Loghain offered. "It's hidden."

"You both . . . You didn't have to help me, I know
that. I'm grateful." His look was reluctant. "It's not
necessary."

"If nothing else, I'm sure we could find an old

cloak for you. Get you cleaned up and . . . less conspicuous." He shrugged. "Or you can go your own way. Up to you."

The fellow squirmed, shivering again in the cold as a breeze blew in from the field. For a moment Loghain thought he looked lost, adrift in his own little free fall from whatever life he had led. Fate could hand you a poor hand when you least expected it, that Loghain knew very well. He recognized the signs, even if his sympathy was minimal. This offer was all the blond man was going to get, after all.

Dannon snorted. "Maker's breath, man! Will you look at yourself? What else are you going to do!"

Loghain eyed the big man dubiously. "You changed your tune rather quickly."

"Bah! You're the one who dragged him along. Now that he's here, he may as well just come." He turned on his heel and stomped off. "If it'll get me back to a fire any faster, I'm all for it."

The young man stared at the ground, uncomfortable and shamefaced. "I . . . don't have anything valuable." And then he added: "To repay you, I mean."

To steal was what he'd really meant. But it was hard to be offended when he and Dannon were indeed thieves, after all. "It certainly doesn't look that way, does it?"

There wasn't much else the blond man could say. He nodded lamely.

Loghain motioned his head toward Dannon, who was already long gone. "We'd better catch up to him then, before he manages to fall in a hole somewhere." He stepped forward and extended a hand. "You can call me Loghain."

The blond man hesitated a fraction before taking Loghain's hand and shaking it. "Hyram."

It was a lie, of course. Loghain wondered for a moment if he would regret doing this. His gut had never been wrong before, but there was always a first time. Still, the die had been cast. Nodding to Hyram, he turned, and the two left the forest together.

2

When Maric awoke, he was certain he was back at the rebel camp, the victim of some terrible nightmare brought on by bad stew. Surely his mother was about to sweep into his room, reprimanding him for sleeping so late. But even as he felt a wave of palpable relief, he knew it wasn't true. The blanket covering him was threadbare and moldy-smelling, the room around him tiny and unfamiliar. Cuts and bruises suffered the previous night were announcing their presence. Slowly he began to remember everything.

Several times during the trek, the one called Loghain had become certain they were being followed. It vexed the big fellow, Dannon, when Loghain insisted on taking lengthy detours off their route. Maric didn't begrudge the extra caution, but by the time they reached the foothills, his legs had been ready to give out. They had spent two hours trudging in the dark, frozen to the core, with barely a word exchanged among the three of them. He only dimly remembered reaching the camp itself and being surprised by the number of filthy tents scattered amid the rocks and bush. He had expected maybe a handful of outlaws, but here was an entire community hidden in the cliffs. He remembered a blur of suspicious eyes and whispered accusations greeting him. By then, Maric no longer cared whether they decided to lock him up or cook him for dinner. The sleep he needed desperately had at some point reached up and claimed him.

A gentle sound of splashing drew Maric into the present. He made the mistake of opening his eyes to bright afternoon sunlight shining through a small window, making him wince. His vision was blurry, and his head throbbed with an insistent and unpleasant pounding. Blinking, his eyes adjusted enough to see, but there wasn't much to look at. He remembered one permanent structure in the camp, a tiny log hut that couldn't have consisted of more than a single room, and he assumed this was it. The furnishings were sparse: the rickety bed he occupied, a single table, and a few piles of what looked like dirty rags. The only adornment was a wood carving hung above his bed: a blazing sun within a circle. A holy symbol.

Maric flexed his shoulders, trying to cope with the pain. In the back of his mind, he registered the surprising fact that underneath the blanket he was wearing little more than his smallclothes.

"Did I wake you?" a voice came from beside his bed. He craned his neck and realized that a woman had been kneeling next to him the entire time, soaking a rag in a bowl of water. "I apologize. I am trying to be as gentle as I can." She sounded matronly and kind, and she wore red vestments that marked her as a priest of the Chantry. He'd had few opportunities to step into a proper house of worship since the Chantry had come down in favor of the usurper long ago, but Mother had still insisted on his education in such matters. He believed in the Maker and honored the sacrifice of His first wife and prophet, Andraste, as any other Fereldan might. Maric certainly knew a priest when he saw one. What was she doing here in a camp of outlaws?

"Your . . . Reverence?" His voice came out as a hoarse croak, and he coughed, intensifying the pounding in his head. He groaned out loud and laid his head back down to stop the spinning room from making him nauseated.

The woman chuckled ruefully. "Oh, dear me, no. Nothing so grand as that." Maric now saw her more clearly. Age had weathered her, but gracefully. Her blond curls had given way to gray, and her weary eyes were heavily lined. It was easy enough to see the beauty she had no doubt once been, long ago. Aside from the vestments, she wore a gold medallion emblazoned with the image of Andraste's cross and its wreath of holy flame. She noticed his gaze and smiled. "My days within the Chantry hierarchy are long behind me, I'm afraid."

She finished wringing out the stained cloth and then returned to wiping his face. The water was cool and refreshing, and so Maric closed his eyes and allowed her to minister to him. When she finally stopped, he touched her hand. "How long have I . . . ?"

She paused, studying him with those weary gray

eyes. There was compassion there, he saw, but also suspicion. "Most of the day," she finally answered. Then she smiled reassuringly and stroked the hair from his forehead. "Not to worry, lad. Whatever you've done, you're safe enough here for now."

"And where is here, exactly?"

"Loghain didn't tell you?" She sighed and soaked the cloth again, creating an impressive bloom of scarlet in the water. "No, he wouldn't have, would he? It would take a dragon to pull more than two sentences in a row out of that boy. He's his father's son." The amused look she gave him seemed to say that should be all the explanation required.

"These are the Southron Hills, just outside of the Wilds ... though I expect you've gathered that much." She gingerly wiped the back of his head, prompting a new jolt of pain to lance through him. The source of his throbbing headache, he assumed, and tried not to think too closely about how badly he might have hurt himself. "There's no name for this place. It's where we've settled for the moment, nothing more. The people in the camp have slowly banded together over time, out of necessity. Mostly they're just trying to survive."

"Sounds familiar," Maric muttered. He wondered, however, how much his life really compared to theirs. Even on the run, he and his mother had decent accommodations wherever they hid. Remote castles, abbeys tucked away in the mountains ... There was always some nobleman willing to take them in, or someone willing to provide a spacious tent on the march. He always complained about it bitterly, about the limits he endured, the boredom and the lack of freedom. Judging from the squalor he saw here on his arrival, these people would probably consider him privileged. He probably was.

"It's Gareth that we follow. He keeps us safe, and with each passing year there seem to be more and more of us. There is never any shortage of desperate souls with nowhere else to turn, it seems." She dabbed at his head again, frowning with concern. "That's Loghain's father, if you haven't met him."

"I haven't."

"You will." She wrung the cloth out again; this time the swirls were dark and ominous. Maric wondered if his head looked as much of a mess as it felt. "I am Sister Ailis."

"Hyram."

"Yes, so I hear." The sister nodded toward his hands. "You'll want to wash those."

Maric glanced at his hands and saw that they were still filthy, stained practically up to his elbows with dried blood and dirt. He accepted the wet rag without comment.

"That is a great deal of blood on your hands," she said pointedly.

"It's not mine. Mostly."

Her gaze was even, calculating. "And how do you feel about that?"

He wiped his hands slowly, keeping his own eyes firmly on the task. He knew what she was asking. His first instinct back in the forest had been to keep his identity secret, and it was probably the correct one. After all, Sister Ailis had said it herself: these people were desperate. Maric had no idea what the usurper would pay for him, but it was probably more than these people had ever known. You didn't have to be poor to know that the promise of wealth could corrupt anyone. He wondered how many gold sovereigns it had taken to put that sword through his mother's gut.

"He attacked me. I was defending myself." His voice sounded hollow and fake, even to himself. "They killed my mother."

Saying it out loud didn't make it feel any more real.

The sister watched him a moment longer, her eyes sharp. "Maker watch over her," she intoned, relenting.

Maric hesitated. "Maker watch over her," he repeated, his voice husky with grief. Sister Ailis placed her hands on his, a gesture of understanding. He jerked his hands away more roughly than he intended, but she said nothing. For a long, awkward pause he stared at his half-cleaned hands. She took the bloodied rag from him and soaked it again.

Lamely, he changed the subject. "So if you are a priest, what are you doing here?"

The sister smiled, nodding as if this were a question she had heard many times before. "When the Maker returned to the world, He chose for Himself a bride that would be His prophet. He could have looked to the great Imperium, with its wealth and its powerful mages. He could have looked to the civilized lands of the west, or the cities of the northern coasts. But instead He looked to a barbarian people on the very edge of Thedas."

"*And thus fell the eye of the Maker upon Andraste,*" Maric promptly intoned, "*she who would be raised up from outcast to become His bride. From her lips would fall the Chant of Light, at her command would the legions of righteousness fall upon the world.*"

"An educated man?" The sister seemed impressed, but Maric cursed his need to show off. She cradled the golden holy symbol around her neck, regarding it as one might an old friend. "People forget that Ferelden wasn't always as it is now, the homeland of the Maker's prophet. Once it was reviled by the civilized world." She smiled gently, her eyes twinkling. "Sometimes that which is most precious can be found where you would least expect to."

"But aren't these people . . . ?"

"Criminals? Thieves? Murderers?" She shrugged. "I am here to guide them and help them with their struggle, as best I can. The things that each of them has done shall, in the end, be judged by the Maker and no one else."

"The magisters judged Andraste in the end, after her crusade. They burned her on the cross for her troubles, you know."

Her chuckle was amused. "Yes, I seem to recall hearing that somewhere."

They were interrupted as Loghain marched into the hut. He was cleaner than Maric remembered, and now wore armor fashioned from studded leather straps. It looked heavy, and the great bow slung over his shoulder was intimidating. Unusually good equipment for a poacher, Maric thought to himself. Perhaps sensing the scrutiny, Loghain glared at him. Unlike with the sister, there was nothing guarded about the suspicion in his eyes. Suddenly self-conscious, Maric pulled the blanket up to cover his lack of clothing.

"So he's decided not to sleep the entire day away," Loghain commented dryly, not taking his gaze away from Maric.

"He is doing better," the sister noted. She picked the water bowl off the floor. "His injuries were not inconsiderable. You did well in bringing him here, Loghain."

His eyes flicked toward her. "We'll see about that. Has he said anything to you?"

Maric raised his hand. "Err . . . I'm right here. . . ."

Amused, Sister Ailis arched a brow at Loghain. "Indeed. Why don't you speak to him?"

"I intend to." Then, to Maric: "My father wants to see you." Not waiting for a reply, he spun on his heel and marched back out into the sunlight.

The sister motioned toward a pile of clothing in the corner of the room next to the small table. "Your boots are under the table. I'm afraid I had to burn everything else. There is nothing fancy in the pile, but I'm certain you will find something suitable." She turned to leave.

"Sister Ailis," Maric called out. She paused at the door, looking back, and suddenly he found himself at a loss for words.

"I wouldn't keep Gareth waiting," was all she said. And then she was gone.

Maric stepped out into the camp. In the bright afternoon it almost seemed like any other bustling village. Clothes were being beaten on rocks in the nearby stream, rabbit meat was being smoked at several central fires, tents were being mended by clutches of chattering women, small children were scampering underfoot. They might have been thinner and filthier than he was accustomed to, but it was not all that different from other places in Ferelden. The Orlesians were hardly the kindest rulers. There was plenty of refuse about, enough to tell him they had camped here for months. Long enough to build the hut he had just walked out of, at least. Several tough-looking men garbed mostly in rags marked Maric's appearance and openly stared at him with chilling, calculating looks. Loghain's fine leather armor was definitely the exception here.

Looking around, it was easy enough to spot Loghain standing not far away and speaking to a larger man that Maric assumed must be his father. The man was dressed in the same kind of studded leather armor and had the same stern glower and same black hair, though there was far less of it and far more gray at his temples. Even had he been in the same rags as the others, there would be no mistaking who led these people. Maric had known men like this all his life—the sort of men who were commanders in his mother's army, the sort of men who breathed and lived discipline their entire lives. Odd that he should find such a man here.

Loghain finally noticed Maric standing amid the bustle and nodded so his father could see. That suspicious glare didn't let up for a second, and Maric wondered just what he had done since last night to earn such hostility.

It's because you lied to him and still are, he reminded himself, *and also because you're an incompetent boob.*

The pair of men crossed the camp while Maric

waited for them, squirming as he felt himself being sized up from afar. Right then he felt about as far away from being a king as he imagined he possibly could, cold and sore and awkward. He found himself wishing for his mother to ride in to his rescue. The Rebel Queen would have looked magnificent with her golden armor, blond hair and purple cloak fluttering in the breeze. It had always been easy to see why people loved her. These poor sods would all have fallen instantly to one knee if she were here, Loghain and his father included. But she wasn't going to come to his rescue any longer, and fanciful wishes wouldn't make it so. Maric firmed his jaw and did not avoid the two sets of icy blue eyes looking his way.

"Hyram." Gareth offered a friendly hand in greeting. Maric shook it and was immediately aware just how strong the man was. Gareth was hardly young, but Maric was certain Loghain's father could have folded him in half and tossed him about like a small child, and would hardly have worked up a sweat doing so.

"Umm, yes," he gulped. "Hello. You must be Gareth?"

"That I am." Gareth scratched his chin, staring down at Maric as if he were a curiosity. Loghain stood a step behind, his expression now decidedly neutral. "My son tells me you ran into a bit of trouble near Lothering. You were being chased by Bann Ceorlic's men."

"There were others, too, but yes."

He nodded slowly. "How many were there, exactly?"

"I'm not sure. It seemed like a lot."

"All in the forest? Bann Ceorlic's not even from these parts. Do you know why they were there?"

"No," Maric lied. The lie hung there while they stared at him, Loghain's eyes narrowing further. Apparently Maric could add "terrible liar" to his list of flaws. Not something he would consider a very kingly virtue, had his mother not constantly told him that the complete opposite was true. Suddenly his throat felt dry and scratchy, but he stood his ground. "They chased me after they killed my friend."

Gareth pounced quickly. "Your friend? Or your mother?"

Of course Sister Ailis had told him. Maric's mind was suddenly awhirl, trying to remember what he had and had not said so far. The effort made the lump on the back of his head throb. "My mother is my friend," he explained lamely.

"And why were you and your mother in the forest? You've no more business there than the Bann, surely."

"We were just . . . traveling through."

Gareth and his son exchanged a significant look that Maric couldn't read. The elder man sighed and scratched his chin thoughtfully. "Look, Hyram," he began, his tone completely reasonable, "with our situation here . . . we have to be very careful, always. If the King has soldiers out there, we need to know why."

Maric said nothing, and Gareth's expression darkened with anger. He turned and gestured at the other people in the camp, some of whom had begun to gather around. "You see these people?" Gareth stated evenly. "They are my responsibility. I aim to keep them safe. If those soldiers are coming this way—"

Maric looked around nervously, increasingly aware of the growing crowd he was attracting. He swallowed hard. "I wish I knew."

"I shouldn't have brought him," Loghain swore.

Gareth barely heard his son, however. Instead he stared at Maric with a mystified expression. "Why would they be after you?" His brows furrowed. "What have you done?"

"I haven't done *anything*."

"He's lying!" Loghain seethed. He drew his belt knife and stepped forward menacingly. The crowd of onlookers murmured excitedly in response, smelling blood. "Let me kill him, Father. This is my fault. I should never have brought him here."

Gareth's expression was unchanged. "He's not lying."

"What does it matter? We need to get rid of him, so let's do it now." Loghain lunged forward at Maric, but Gareth interposed an arm between them. Loghain stopped short, staring at his father with surprised confusion, but Gareth was still looking intently at Maric.

Maric stepped back uncertainly, but several men with deep frowns blocked his path. "Look," he said slowly, "I can just leave. I didn't mean to bring any of you harm."

"No," Gareth stated. It was the sort of tone that left no room for argument. He glanced at Loghain. "How certain are you that you weren't followed?"

Loghain considered the question. "We lost them halfway back. No doubt about it." He grimaced.

"That doesn't mean they can't find us. We've been here too long. How many locals know we're out here by now?"

His father nodded, accepting the answer, and then looked back at Maric. "I've sent men out, and they'll find out what's going on soon enough. If we're in danger, I'd appreciate knowing it now. Are we?"

Inside, Maric quailed. Bann Ceorlic and the others would surely keep looking for him, and eventually they would track him down. For a single moment, he considered telling them everything. But would they even believe him? And if they did believe him, would that be better or worse? "Yes," he finally blurted out. "Yes, I . . . You're in danger if you keep me here."

Loghain snorted derisively and turned to Gareth. "Father, we'll find out if we're in trouble soon enough. We don't need him here to make it worse. We should kill him to be safe."

Several of the nearby men nodded, their eyes shining dangerously. Gareth, however, frowned at Loghain. "No. We won't be doing that."

"Why not?"

"I said no." Father and son locked glares. The crowd was dead silent, not eager to get involved in what was evidently an old argument. Maric kept quiet. He wasn't an *idiot*.

"Fine." Loghain finally relented, rolling his eyes. "Then let's pull up. Let's not wait."

Gareth considered it. "No." He shook his head. "We'll wait for the men to return. We still have time." He then spoke to one of the burlier men standing nearby. "Yorin, take Hyram—or whatever his name is—back to the sister for now. Watch him." The man nodded as Gareth raised his voice to address the many others who had gathered around the spectacle. "Everyone! We may need to pull up soon! I want everyone alert!" The decision had been made and they knew it. Already the crowd was dispersing, though their looks and whispers were agitated. They were frightened.

Loghain shot a dark look at Maric, who was taken by the shoulder and led away. Behind him, he heard Loghain speak to his father. "I bet I could get the truth out of him. The whole truth."

"It may come to that. For now, we treat him as he appears to be: a frightened young man who needs our help."

Gareth's tone was final and Maric heard nothing more of the exchange—Yorin was steering Maric back toward the log hut, and he didn't struggle. Overhead, above the tall trees, dark clouds were already obscuring the afternoon sun. It was going to rain, and hard.

"Well, who do *you* think he is, then?"

Loghain ignored Potter's question as he restrung his bow. One of the small contingent of elves who traveled with the camp, Potter could be counted on to do little more than laze about and spread idle gossip, and Loghain didn't want to contribute to the growing panic any more than he already had. It would have been far better for everyone if his father had let him force "Hyram" to spill whatever secrets he was withholding. And he was withholding something—Loghain could almost smell it. For a moment there it had seemed that Hyram was going to tell them, but then nothing. And Father had let him walk away.

"Well, come on!" Potter insisted, kneeling beside Loghain. "You must know something! You were walking with him all night, weren't you?"

The elf was missing most of one of his long delicate ears, making his head look decidedly lopsided. He also had a nasty scar down his face, leaving one empty eye socket and a permanent sneer. That these had been "presents" from an Orlesian lord was all Potter had ever let out about it.

A slaver, Loghain guessed. In most cities, elves lived freely enough in their slums, the poorest of the poor. Their enslavement had ended long ago at the hands of the prophet Andraste, but the practice still secretly flourished in the more remote corners of the Empire. Potter had come close to speaking of his ordeal one night when they had been deep into the drink, the bitterness threatening to spill out of him like so much poison. But then he had swallowed it all down even further, flinching from company until he had successfully numbed himself into oblivion.

Everyone had their secrets. Loghain sighed and forced himself to give Hyram the same benefit of the doubt as his father had. It was not easy.

"Don't you have work to do?" he snapped at Potter. The elf sighed and ran off. He knew better than to continue pestering Loghain, or he really would be put to work.

Still, Potter's question was a good one. If this Hyram was a spy, then he was either a terrible one or better than any Loghain had ever heard of. Perhaps he was actually what he seemed, as his father suggested. Gareth had always allowed his compassion to rule him. Nobody was perfect. But there was surely something they were missing, some puzzle piece that

Hyram wasn't giving them, and it gnawed away at Loghain. Like most of the others in the camp, he had developed a sense over the years of when to run, and right now it was going crazy. Just looking around, he could see it in everyone's eyes. They hurried their steps and jumped at every strange noise coming out of the forest. Some of them were already picking up their tents, packing up what little provisions they had in expectation of Father's call to move on.

Loghain steered clear of Sister Ailis's hut once he was finished with his bow, not wanting to tempt himself. The sister had her own way of questioning new arrivals to the camp, and he respected the fact that she was often able to elicit information when neither he nor his father could. Many saw the sister as being the camp's leader almost as much as his father was, and certainly his father had relied on her advice for many years now. There had been a time when Loghain hoped the affection between the two of them might grow into something more, for both their sakes. Sister Ailis, however, had her calling, and his father had never been the same since they fled the farmhold. It had taken Loghain a long time to realize it, but a part of Gareth had been broken that night. Sister Ailis knew what his father needed better than Loghain ever would, and he had to be content with that.

Padric was on watch at the edge of the camp, perched on a rock that allowed him to keep an eye on the valley below without being easily spotted himself. The lad was a couple of years younger than Loghain, but a skilled shot with a bow and could usually be counted on to show some sense. On the other hand, Dannon was standing next to Padric now, which didn't bode well. The pair abruptly stopped whispering as he drew close.

"Any sign of the men my father sent out?" Loghain asked Padric, making no comment about what he had interrupted.

"Not yet," Padric offered shyly. He turned and scanned the hillside below. "There's been no sign of anything."

"There's some talking about leaving," Dannon announced. He crossed his arms and glowered at Loghain. "Tonight, maybe, if nothing's said."

"It's stupid." Padric kept his eyes on the valley. "Even if someone knows that blond fellow's here, so what? They going to come all the way out here for one man?"

"I agree." Loghain turned and stared at Dannon. "But if you want to join the cowards, Dannon, why don't you go ahead and do that? Assuming you aren't the only one."

"You said yourself that boy's dangerous."

"I said we don't know who he is. We will soon enough. And if my father thinks it's worth us leaving, then he'll say so."

Dannon squirmed. "This was your doing," he groused. "You're the one that wanted to bring him, not me." With that, he hurried off.

Padric looked relieved to see Dannon go. He smiled his thanks to Loghain and turned back to his watch duties. "He's right, though. It's odd."

"What is?"

"Well—" He nodded out to the valley. "—the men who got sent out, some of them should have come back by now."

"How overdue?"

"An hour. Maybe two. It hasn't rained yet, so I don't know. . . . I was thinking Henric would have come back, at least. He's been worried about his girl, with the baby and all."

Loghain's stomach felt like it sank. "You let anyone know?"

"Just Gareth."

He nodded and headed down the trail on his own. He wanted to take a look for himself, and it would do no good hanging around the camp while his father tried to keep a lid on the hysteria—justified or not. Loghain thought it was understood that the outlaws traveled together under a purely provisional basis. His father kept them organized and fed, and Sister Ailis kept them united—and it also didn't hurt that few of them had anywhere else they could go—but they were on the run, each of them for their own particular reasons, and people that desperate didn't hold any loyalties. His father believed differently, and maintained that it was in the worst of times that people needed to cleave together the strongest. Whenever Gareth would say that, Sister Ailis would smile at him and get all teary-eyed. For that single moment that faith of his father's would seem like it could almost be true. But Loghain knew better. If things ever got bad enough, Dannon wouldn't be the only rat to abandon the sinking ship.

Loghain was gone most of the afternoon, hoping to put his worst fears to rest. First he backtracked along the path the three of them had taken the previous night, confirming they indeed had not been followed. He returned to the Southron Hills and followed three of the trails he knew, hoping to run into one of the men his father had sent out, or anyone, really. But travelers this far south were few, and he saw only a flurry of horse tracks heading toward Lothering. By the time dusk fell and a storm began releasing torrents of ice-cold rain, Loghain was truly worried.

It wasn't until he ventured down a hazardous path not far from the town that he finally spotted someone. The route was most often used by smugglers, allowing them to avoid the more patrolled roads in the north on their way toward the western mountains and the dwarves there who cared little for human laws. There were many such paths in the hinterlands, and few who used them had any legitimate reason to be there.

A lone horseman appeared, hood pulled up and his steed stepping carefully in the slippery mud. By the quality of his cloak Loghain would have guessed him a messenger for one of the city guilds, only he didn't appear to be in any kind of hurry.

Loghain approached from well down the road, in full view. It was a friendly gesture, though the rider was wary enough to keep a hand on his sword hilt as he paused and waited. Lightning flared in the gray sky and the rain intensified, but Loghain's leathers were already as drenched as they could possibly get. When he got within twenty feet, the rider backed his horse away and half drew his blade. The message was clear: *You've come close enough*.

"Greetings!" Loghain called out. When the rider did not respond immediately, he reached over his back and removed his bow, slowly putting it down on the ground in front of him.

This seemed to reassure the rider somewhat, though the horse whinnied nervously and pranced about on the spot. "What do you want?" he finally called back.

"I'm looking for friends!" Loghain shouted. "Men dressed like me. One of them might have come down this way, I'm hoping."

"I haven't seen anyone," the rider responded. "But Lothering is filled with so many people they're sleeping in the streets. It's insanity. Your friends are probably there, if anywhere."

Loghain sheltered his eyes from the rain with a hand, trying to make out the rider's face under the hood. He couldn't. "Lothering is filled with people?"

"You haven't heard?" The rider seemed genuinely surprised. "With all the soldiers passing through, I would have thought half the Kingdom had heard already."

"No, nothing."

"The Rebel Queen is dead." The rider sighed sadly, adjusting his hood as the rain splattered down. "Bastards finally caught her in the forest last night, they say. I tried to see the body before I left, but there were too many mourners." The rider shrugged. "They say the young Prince might be dead, too. If you'll pardon my saying so, let's hope that isn't true."

Loghain's blood went cold. "The Prince," he repeated numbly.

"With any luck, he's still out there somewhere. Considering all the soldiers I saw, he'd better be running for his life." As the rain continued to pour, the rider nodded politely and gave Loghain a wide berth as he passed by.

Loghain remained where he was, his mind racing. Lightning flashed high overhead.

Maric picked listlessly at the soup they'd brought him, idly curious about the exact kind of animal that had provided the gamey meat swimming in the broth. Finally, Sister Ailis took the bowl away from him and returned to her sewing. She spent her time patching blankets and clothing, humming softly to herself all the while. He caught pieces of the Chant of Light, if he wasn't mistaken, though the exact verses eluded him. Truthfully, he had other things on his mind.

Such as getting out of the hut. He could hear activity going on outside, like they were packing the entire camp up. The sister denied it. Maric had asked three times if the men Gareth was waiting for had returned before the burly guard outside the door promised he would tell the sister immediately should the situation change, and it had not. Maric sat on the bed, fidgeting. He toyed again with the idea of confessing everything, but where would that get him? What would Gareth do, suddenly saddled with a fugitive who was far more dangerous than he had imagined? Better to get out, get away from these poor people, and find his own way back to the rebel army. Yet the closed door and a single guard proved to be an incredibly effective deterrent to this plan.

An excellent start to your reign, King Maric, he chided himself. *This is the kind of first-class problem-solving that will serve you well when you take charge of the rebellion.*

"You're very hard on yourself," Sister Ailis commented, glancing up from her sewing. She was wear-

ing a set of delicate dwarven spectacles that reminded
Maric of his grandfather King Brandel . . . "Brandel
the Defeated," as everyone else remembered him.
Maric himself remembered the man as being both
very sad and very proud. His grandfather possessed a
pair of golden spectacles that he would immediately
hide whenever he was caught wearing them, lest
someone think him going blind. As a child, Maric
used to think it was a fun game to steal them and
then race around the castle halls wearing them. At
least it was fun until he was finally caught, usually by
his mother. Mind you, even she had to stifle her gig-
gles at the sight of Maric in those things, and repri-
manded him mostly for his grandfather's benefit.
Afterwards in private she would laugh and kiss his
nose, pleading with him halfheartedly not to do it
again. Pleas he ignored, of course.

It was odd to remember that now. He hadn't
thought of his grandfather in many years. He looked
away from the sister and then remembered she was
waiting for a response. "I'm sorry, what?"

"I said you're very hard on yourself. You're frightened, anyone can see that." Her smile was knowing.
"Have you considered that perhaps the reason
you're here, young man, is because the Maker led
you here?"

Maric wanted it to be true. He stared at the floor
until the sister returned to her sewing and left him
be. Maric didn't want these people to be hurt on his
account, and more and more it looked like his best
option was simply to dash out the door the next
time it opened. If they killed him before he got out
of the camp, then so be it. At least he would no longer be putting them in danger.

He kept his stare on the floor for some time, listening to the beat of the rain against the hut and the frenetic activity of the people outside. Men were yelling, things were being covered, children were giggling and being hustled into tents. The smell of fresh rain filled the hut, a scent that Maric had reveled in when he was young because it meant Mother might be forced indoors. But now it only made him anxious. He felt like he was waiting, waiting for Loghain to finally come and kill him, Gareth to command his release, another round of questions, waiting for something to *happen*. In time he slept, though only restlessly and without dreams.

When the door to the hut finally slammed open, Maric was unsure how much time had passed. The rain had barely slackened, the air now thick and damp from it, and at some point the elderly sister had also fallen asleep in her chair beside the bed. She started awake, gasping in surprise, and clutched at the heavy amulet around her neck. Gareth was at the door, soaked to the bone, but those icy blue eyes shone with intensity.

"Maker's breath, Gareth!" Sister Ailis exclaimed. "What's wrong?"

"Men. Soldiers. Coming through the forest." His mouth was pressed into a thin scowl, rivulets of water running down his armor and splattering on the floor. In two strides he was at Maric and hauled him up off the bed by the scruff of his shirt. Gareth slammed him hard against the log wall, seeming ready to explode with rage. "What did you do?"

Maric should have felt frightened for his life, but he didn't. Somehow, he was calm. It was a bizarre reaction, he knew, since Gareth seemed willing to kill him and probably had every reason to. "I told you," Maric said evenly. "They're coming for me. I think if you just give me to them, they might not even bother with you."

"Why?" Gareth bellowed. The wind slammed the door loudly against the wall, and rain blew in with a cold howl. Already, panicked shouts could be heard from throughout the camp. "Who are you!" Gareth shouted, slamming Maric against the wall again hard enough to knock the wind out of him.

"Gareth, stop!" Sister Ailis cried, clutching at his free arm.

He shook her off without looking at her. "Tell me who you are!"

"I can tell you who he is," came a shout from the door. Loghain was standing there, pale and soaking wet and with murder in his eyes. His knife was out, and with two steps he had it against Maric's throat. "Maker damn him, he's the Prince! He's the bloody Prince!"

Gareth grabbed Loghain's wrist with his free hand, and for a moment they fought over control of the knife. It wavered dangerously at Maric's throat and made a shallow cut once into the skin. Loghain snarled with rage, but when he looked at his father, he seemed shocked at the aghast expression on his father's face.

"What do you mean?" Gareth demanded, his tone steel cold.

The battle for the knife paused. Loghain did not relent, but he seemed disturbed by his father's sudden change. "They killed the Rebel Queen in the forest, the news is everywhere. That's the mother he told us about, Father. He just left out the *most important part*, didn't he?"

Gareth's expression was unreadable as he digested this. He stared off into space, beads of water running down his forehead.

Outside, the chaotic shouts continued. Bewildered, Sister Ailis gathered her robe around her and rushed to close the door.

The sound of the wind hissing around the door seemed to stir Gareth from his reverie. He turned his head slowly and stared at Maric as if he had suddenly transformed into something terrifying. "Is this true?"

"I . . . I'm sorry," was all Maric could say in return.

There was a pause. Gareth violently shoved Loghain away, the knife clattering down to the floor as Loghain fell against the far wall of the room.

Then in one smooth motion, Gareth dropped to one knee and bowed his head. "Your Highness . . ." Gareth's voice trailed off into a quiet croak.

Maric looked around the room, completely at a loss in the sudden stillness. The way they stared at him, it was like they expected him to do something but he had no idea what. Pull out a crown, perhaps. Burst into flames. *That might be helpful, actually*, he thought to himself. The storm pelted the hut with renewed force, the only sound in the room. The moment seemed to stretch on forever.

"You bow to him?" Loghain finally asked in an incredulous voice, staring at his father. Then his tone became harsher, angrier: "You're *protecting* him? He *lied* to us!"

"He is the Prince," Gareth said, as if this was explanation enough.

"He's not my prince. He's going to get us all killed!" Loghain jumped to his feet and strode over to Gareth with purpose. "Father, they aren't just coming through the forest! They're coming through the valley as well! We're surrounded, and all because they want him!"

"Look"—Maric tried his best to sound reasonable—"I don't want anyone to be hurt on my account. Just hand me over. I'll go willingly."

"Maker preserve us." Sister Ailis stared at Maric in dawning horror.

Gareth stiffly stood up and walked over to the door, opening it. He stood there, looking out into the storm while they listened to the sounds of the people scrambling in the dark. *His* people. Off in the distance, terrified screaming could be heard, coupled with the deep-voiced shouting of strangers.

"They're here already?" the sister asked in a tremulous voice. Gareth merely nodded. "Then what are we to do?"

Loghain snatched up his blade from the ground. "We give him to them," he argued. "Father, he said it himself. We need to make a deal."

"No."

In a fury, Loghain leaped forward and grabbed his father's shoulder, spinning him around. "Father—" The word was stated with unmistakeable emphasis. It said *listen to me*. "—we don't . . . owe him . . . *anything*."

Gareth's expression became sad, and with a gentle gesture he reached up and removed Loghain's hand from his shoulder. Loghain did not resist, and the fury seemed to drain out of him as realization grew in his face. A witness to the moment that passed between father and son, Maric didn't immediately understand it.

"Can you get him away?" Gareth asked.

Loghain looked numb, but he nodded.

"Wait," Maric protested feebly, raising a hand. "What?"

Gareth sighed. "We need to get you to safety, Your Highness. Loghain knows the forest. You can depend on him." With a swift motion, he drew his sword. "I will buy you time. I and everyone I can gather."

"You could come with us," Loghain said to his father, his voice hopeless.

"They would just give chase. No, that won't do." He glanced over at Sister Ailis, who was watching with tears streaming down her cheeks. "I'm sorry, Ailis. I had hoped for . . . something else."

She shook her head emphatically. Her eyes glowed fiercely despite the tears. "You have no need to apologize to me, Gareth Mac Tir."

Maric's sense of calm was rapidly draining away. Could they actually be proposing what he was hearing? Listening to the distant screams, it was all becoming real far too quickly for his liking. "Stop!" he cried. "What are you talking about? This is madness!"

Loghain stared at him like it was Maric who had gone mad, but Gareth stepped up to him and put a strong hand on his shoulder. "I served your grandfather, once." Gareth's voice was firm and steady, and Maric stared up at him with wide eyes. "The Orlesians don't belong on that throne, and if your mother is truly dead, then it is up to you now to remove them." He paused, setting his jaw, and when he continued, his voice cracked with emotion. "If I can help you do that, then I will give anything, even my life."

"Father . . ." Loghain's protest died on his lips as Gareth turned toward him. Maric could tell that Gareth was resolute, and perhaps Loghain saw the same. Still, Loghain bristled with rebellion, furious at his father . . . perhaps for giving so much to someone they barely knew, the very person who had put them in danger. Maric could hardly fault him for that.

"Loghain, I want your word that you will protect the Prince."

"I can't just leave you here," Loghain insisted. "Don't ask me to just leave you, I won't do it. . . ."

"That's exactly what you will do. Your word, Loghain."

Loghain looked stricken, and for a moment it seemed he teetered on the point of refusal. He shot a deadly look at Maric, no doubt blaming him for all of it, but Gareth awaited his answer. Reluctantly he nodded.

Gareth turned back toward Maric. "Then you need to go, Your Highness. Quickly."

He was completely serious. Maric didn't doubt that for a second, and he believed that Loghain would keep his word despite how reluctant and torn he looked. Still, Maric was stunned. If only he had known, he clearly could have trusted this man as soon as he arrived. He tried to think of something he could say in return, and a thousand inadequate apologies came to mind, along with something his mother had once told him.

What they will give us freely, she had said, *is never free for them. Remembering that is the only way we will be worthy of it.*

"Were . . . were you a knight, Gareth?" he asked.

The question seemed to take the man by surprise. "I . . . No, Your Highness. I was a sergeant-at-arms once."

"Then kneel." It was Maric's best imitation of his mother's tone, and it seemed to work.

Face blank with shock, Gareth knelt.

"Sister Ailis, I will need you to bear witness."

She stepped forward. "I will, Your Highness."

Maric put his hand on Gareth's head, hoping fervently that his memory was not so faulty as he feared. "In the name of Calenhad the Great, here in the sight of the Maker, I declare you a Knight of Ferelden. Rise and serve your land, Ser Gareth."

The man stood stiffly, his eyes glinting beneath furrowed brows. "Thank you, Your Highness."

"For what it's worth," Maric apologized. There was nothing more to be said.

Loghain stepped forward, interrupting the moment. His face was stony as he gestured to Maric. "We need to go. Now."

Maric nodded. Before he could move, the sister put up a hand and rushed over to the pile of clothes she had been mending in the corner. She pulled out a large woolen coat and without a word began helping Maric to put it on.

As they did so, Gareth turned quietly to his son. "Loghain . . ."

"Don't." Loghain cut him off, his voice harsh and bitter. He refused to meet his father's gaze. The two of them stood awkwardly as the shouting outside drew nearer to the hut.

Finally, Gareth nodded. "Do your best."

"Of course," came the curt response.

Maric was now wearing the coat and ready. The sister hesitated and reached into her robe, taking out a dagger so wicked-looking, Maric's eyes widened with surprise. Before he could say anything, she placed the blade in his hand and closed his fingers over it. The sister's eyes looked into his then, and they said, *May the Maker forgive us all*. He nodded his thanks, feeling chilled.

Gareth readied his sword and stepped to the door, all business. "Give me one minute. Then run."

Sister Ailis stood beside him. "I will go with you," she said quietly. Gareth looked as if he would have preferred to argue with her, but decided against it. With a quick nod, both of them rushed out the door into the storm.

Loghain put an arm out, stopping Maric from following them, not that he had been about to. Loghain stared at the vacant door. His face was passive, but his eyes were intense, and Maric decided it was best to say nothing. Instead they waited in the dim light and listened. First they heard Gareth bellowing, his voice carrying even over the thunder and rain as he rallied the panicked outlaws to his side. There was more shouting, and Sister Ailis cried out for someone to stop, in the name of the Maker. The sound of battle erupted, coupled with cries of agony and the ring of steel on steel.

Loghain ran out the door, not saying a word, pulling Maric with him. Maric almost stumbled, but kept his footing while dashing headlong into a sheet of freezing rain. Recognizing nothing in the rain and darkness disoriented him. Something large was burning nearby, and the sound of fighting surrounded him on all sides. He then felt a pull at his coat.

"Pay attention!" Loghain snapped.

Maric barely heard him over the commotion. Though the rain obscured much, he could make out the fight at the other end of the camp. He spotted Gareth, the big man swinging his sword in wide arcs and cutting a swath through soldiers that had undoubtedly expected nothing like this kind of resistance. But the soldiers were armored, and they outnumbered the handful of men Gareth had managed to rally. It was not going to be much of a battle.

Others fled the camp in all directions, some gathering what little they could and others scrambling just to get away as they realized the extent of the assault. Several bodies lay on the ground in Maric and Loghain's path, one of them a young woman. Maric almost tripped on her, causing Loghain to hiss in fury again.

They were running away from the main fight, but Maric could hear other soldiers ahead of them in the darkness. Out of nowhere a man appeared, dressed in chain mail and wearing an undecipherable emblem on his blue tunic. His eyes widened in surprise and he was about to shout for help, but Loghain was too quick for him and ran the man through without slowing down. Loghain pushed the soldier off his sword with his boot, the man collapsing in a gurgling heap.

"Don't just stand there!" Loghain snapped, and Maric realized that was exactly what he was doing. He started to run forward but felt someone grab his arm from behind. Without thinking, he spun around and sank the dagger given to him by Sister Ailis into the neck of a black-bearded soldier. The man roared in surprise and pain, losing his grip, and when Maric yanked the blade out, a fountain of blood followed it. The soldier clutched uselessly at the wound, careening away, and before Maric could stab at his foe a second time, he felt himself being dragged away.

"Go! Now!" Loghain roared. The pair of them sprinted, running past several tents and directly into a clump of trees at the edge of the camp. Loghain led Maric through thick bushes, the branches slapping wetly at their faces, and as they came out into another part of the camp, they veered sharply. Avoiding an obscured scuffle not far away, they ran past two soldiers fighting to drag a screaming woman out of her tent. The soldiers did not even notice them pass, and when Maric slowed out of concern for the woman, he felt himself yanked forward again. Reluctantly, he did as he was bidden.

Two more soldiers sprang up in their path but were dispatched by Loghain with savage precision. The camp was little more than chaos and confusion. Maric heard the bloodcurdling cries behind him and the sounds of people fleeing in every direction. He heard a child wailing and men begging for help, soldiers shouting orders and giving chase. It was all he could do to avoid keeping his foot on the mud and grass, Loghain pulling him forward whenever he began to fall behind. It came as a shock when he realized that they had reached the edge of the camp. The hillside sloped down steeply into the forested valley below—and into the Korcari Wilds, the southern wilderness uninhabited by all but the savages and the most dangerous of creatures. No sane man went there.

"Why are we stopping?" Maric asked, turning back to Loghain. He shivered with cold, the merciless rain pounding down. Loghain ignored him, and Maric followed his gaze to where Gareth was fighting in the distance. He was far away, but the fire had spread enough that he could still be spotted even through the deluge. Heavily wounded and covered with blood, he had dozens of enemy soldiers surrounding him. His swings were becoming desperate. Maric knew they should continue running and not waste any opportunity, but Loghain remained still, transfixed by his father's battle.

Then, though their vision was obscured by smoke and the rushing soldiers, they made out a defiant shout that ended abruptly: Gareth's final cry.

Maric turned to Loghain to say something, but wasn't sure what that might be. He said nothing. Loghain's face was stone cold, his eyes glinting. Almost instantly, Loghain sprang to action. He grabbed Maric's coat once again, practically pulling him off his feet as they bolted down the hill.

Loghain's voice was icy and low. "Stay close, or I swear I'll leave you behind."

Maric stayed close.

3

Maric had no idea how long they continued running. Panic transformed much of their flight into a blur, and even when the sharp edge of fear had worn off, he found it difficult to get his bearings in the rain and darkness. They were deep in the Korcari Wilds now, he knew. The forest's dangerous reputation had yet to prove itself, but it certainly looked unlike anything he had ever seen before. The giant trees twisted like they were frozen in the throes of agony, and a perpetual cold mist clung to the ground. It gave the forest an ominous feel, one that deepened the farther they ran. One of Maric's tutors had explained the reason for the mist, something relating to one of the region's old legends, but he couldn't recall any of the particulars. Especially now, when it took everything he had to keep pace with the seemingly tireless Loghain. Hours of panicked running through the thick and uneven foliage had turned into exhausted trudging, and finally become a limping crawl.

Maric collapsed in a natural alcove formed by the roots at the foot of a fallen tree. It was an elder poplar, papery white and ten times as wide as himself, and some unknown force had ripped it out of the ground. Massive exposed roots snaked around the alcove like giant tentacles, and a bed of thick moss and delicate white flowers grew in the shade.

Dim light filtered down from overhead, and he could just barely make out the overcast sky through patches in the tree canopy. Had they been running the entire night? It seemed impossible that he had survived a second consecutive night fleeing through the wilderness. At least the storm had petered out a few hours before. As Maric lay there inhaling the scent of moss, sweating and gasping for air, he felt the mist settle coolly on his skin and was grateful for it.

"All spent, are you?" Loghain said with annoyance, returning from a short distance ahead. Maric suspected the man was almost as exhausted as he was. He, too, was pale and had rivulets of sweat running down his face and over his stained leather armor. Despite his heavier burden, however, he didn't seem inclined to slow his pace. Maric was beyond caring.

"I think we lost them," he gasped, still trying to catch his breath.

"Are you sure?" Loghain drew his belt knife and hacked viciously at one of the low-hanging root tendrils that hovered near his head. "You're a prince, aren't you? You're an important person. You might have the entire Fereldan army after you. They may have unleashed a small horde of mabari hounds into the forest to sniff you down. They might even have mages scrying after you." He strode over to where Maric lay and stared at him with fury in those cold eyes. "Just how safe do you feel, *Your Highness*?"

"Err . . . at the moment? Not very."

Loghain snorted in disgust and walked away several steps. He stood there, staring into the mist and bristling. "The truth," he stated, "is they're not going to come into the Wilds. This is savage country, and dangerous. They'd be stupid to follow us. About as stupid as we were desperate to flee this way."

"That . . . makes me feel so much better."

"Good." Loghain's calm tone was icy. "Because you're on your own from this point."

"You're just going to leave me out here."

"I got you out safely, didn't I? You're here, you're alive."

A chill ran down Maric's spine and settled uncomfortably in his gut. "You think that's what your father intended?"

Loghain's eyes went wide. With two quick steps, he was on top of Maric, hauling him up off the moss and throwing him against the fungus-covered tree. Maric gasped, the wind knocked out of him, as Loghain lifted a threatening fist. It hovered, as if he wasn't willing to actually punch Maric, but judging by the furious expression on his face, he wanted to. "You shut up about him," Loghain hissed. "You're the one who got him killed! You don't get to tell me what to do. You can't knight *me* to make me throw my life away for *you*."

Maric coughed, trying to regain his breath. "You think I meant for any of this to happen? I didn't want your father to die. I'm so sorry. . . ."

Loghain went rigid. "Oh, you're sorry? You're sorry!"

Maric saw the punch coming and closed his eyes. His chin exploded into a ball of white pain and he bit down hard on his tongue. Metallic-tasting blood filled his mouth as he collapsed on the moss below, too exhausted to put up any resistance.

"How wonderful that you're sorry!" Loghain raged, towering over him. "I watched my father die, along with everyone he promised to protect, but how much better it is now that I know you're *sorry*!" Tearing himself away, he stalked several feet off and stood there with his back turned, fists clenched at his sides.

Maric gasped and spat out blood and saliva, much of it dribbling down his chin. His jaw throbbed like it was about to fall off. Gritting his teeth and sucking back the blood welling out of his tongue, he forced himself to sit up. "I watched my mother murdered, right in front of me. And I couldn't do a thing to stop it."

Loghain made no sign he was even listening.

Feeling shaky and weak, Maric continued to speak. "I was running from her killers when I met you in the woods. I had no idea that you weren't going to just throw me to the wolves once you found out who I was. I was going to go my own way, but you convinced me to follow you." Maric held out his hands in supplication. "Why did you do that? You knew I was being chased. You knew there was danger."

Loghain didn't answer. He remained with his back turned, and for several minutes all he did was cut at low-hanging roots with his knife and toss them aside. Maric couldn't tell if Loghain was ignoring him or just thinking.

Eventually Maric wiped his mouth gingerly with the back of his hand. The flow of blood had lessened, though his jaw still hurt and his ears were ringing. With effort, he pulled himself back to his feet.

"I wish I'd known earlier, about your father," Maric continued. "He was willing to give up his life to save me. And why? Same reason he led all those poor people, I'll bet, when where he belonged was with the rebel army. He was a great man, even I could see that. That's why I knighted him." Tears welled up in his eyes, and his voice became hoarse. "My mother was great, too. Let me tell you, if I . . . If I'd had the chance to say good-bye to her, I wouldn't have wasted it."

Loghain did not move, or even look at him.

It was obvious nothing Maric said was going to get through to him. Maric wiped the tears from his eyes and nodded. "But I get it. I don't expect you to stay and help me, I really don't. You need to go back to the camp, see if . . . anyone survived. If I were you, I'd want to get back to my people. How could I not understand that?" He wiped the last smears of blood from his chin. "So . . . thank you for saving me."

With that, he straightened the torn and wet coat and left. The boots were still his good ones, he figured. He had the dagger the sister had given him, and was not completely helpless. With a bit of luck, he could find a route back out of the forest. Maybe he would run into some passing merchant caravan. The dwarves came this far south on the way to Gwaren, didn't they? It was a long shot, but it was better than nothing. At this point, he had little choice but to try.

Maric trudged across the treacherous terrain, leaving Loghain well behind him. The mist made traveling difficult; he couldn't see where he was step-ping most of the time, and his boots got caught be-tween gnarled roots or in small depressions in the mud. Eventually he cut down one of the low tree branches, making himself a stick to help him find firmer ground in the mist. The forest around him seemed to be getting thicker and darker, if possible, when he realized that he really had no idea even which direction he was going. He couldn't tell where the sun was, as he could barely see the sky. For all he knew, he could be heading farther south into the Wilds.

As he stood there, scratching his head in confu-sion, he heard steps behind him. He turned to find Loghain approaching. Maric had to admit that he had never felt quite so relieved to see anyone, espe-cially Loghain in his formidable leather armor, step-ping as easily in the mist as he might have on even ground. The man certainly didn't look happy. Those icy blue eyes glared at Maric as if to say, *I'm going to regret this.*

Maric waited for Loghain to get near. Loghain didn't say anything right away, but grimaced and unslung his bow, then adjusted the half-full quiver on his back. When he looked up again, he held up a single finger. "One, you have a way with words."

"Really? You'd be the first to say that."

Loghain ignored him, holding up a second finger. "Two, I don't imagine my father meant for you to get away just to die like an idiot in the Wilds. Which is exactly what would happen if I didn't help you."

"No, I'm fine. You don't owe me anything—"

Loghain grunted noncommittally. With a quick motion, he pulled an arrow from his quiver and fired it right past Maric's head. Maric was so startled, he didn't know what to think. He stepped back, and then jumped as he noticed something writhing on the tree behind him. He jumped even farther when he realized it was a shiny black snake at least as large as his arm. The arrow pierced it about a foot behind its head, staking it to the tree, where it frantically writhed.

Loghain stepped up to it, drawing his belt knife and cutting off its head with some difficulty. Angry red blood gushed from its neck, and its convulsions slowed. Yanking out the arrow, Loghain pulled the snake corpse down from the branches and turned back to Maric. "We sometimes saw these outside the Wilds. Silent Crawlers. Poisonous . . . but tasty enough if you can ignore the smell."

"Oh," Maric said, nonplussed.

"So I'm going to see you out of the Wilds and get you back to the rebels." He looked at Maric sternly. "Once that's done, we're through. Do you understand?"

"Yes."

"Then no thanking me. I don't want any reward."

"Right."

"And I'm not calling you 'Your Highness.'"

"Please don't."

Loghain's scowl deepened, like he had been half hoping for an argument. Since there was none forthcoming, he waved vaguely in the direction Maric had been heading. "At least you were walking in the right direction. Accidentally, I bet. Are you hungry?"

Maric eyed the long, shiny snake corpse dangling from Loghain's hand dubiously, but his stomach growled before he could answer.

"Then let's find something else besides a snake to eat. And a place to light a damned fire." He brushed by Maric and headed off, not waiting to see if Maric followed.

For the next three days, the pair of them traveled the deep forests of the Korcari Wilds. It was slow going, considering that Loghain didn't want to backtrack and was instead leading Maric west. Despite what he'd told Maric, Loghain wasn't convinced the men after them wouldn't follow them into the dense forest. At the very least, their pursuers might leave men stationed just outside the Wilds, hoping that he and Maric had hidden within the less dangerous fringe area and might be forced to come out soon.

Of course, that assumed they were even aware the two of them had fled into the Wilds. People had escaped the camp in all directions, and no soldier who had seen them face-to-face survived to tell of it. Still, Loghain believed in assuming the worst. Despite difficult travelling through rough terrain, he thought it best to get as far from the hills as they possibly could.

Shelter proved to be their most immediate issue. Thankfully, the Wilds were full of fallen, ancient trees, sometimes toppled in large groups that made Loghain wonder just what sort of force could do this. His mind turned to tales of dragons, but there had not been actual dragons seen south of the Waking Sea since they had been hunted to near extinction, long ago. Not that there couldn't be other giant creatures lurking in the Wilds. Maric had heard tales of things like great savage bears as large as a house and the blue-skinned ogres with horns as long as a man's arm.

He supposed they should be just as thankful that *those* weren't anywhere in evidence at the moment, either.

The fallen trees offered cover for the night, and for the first two nights, there was no rain. Loghain kept the fire going as long as he dared while Maric shivered in his sleep nearby. The fire wasn't enough to keep the persistent mist at bay, which meant it clung to the clothes and the skin and left one feeling constantly damp and chilled. Each morning Maric had been more and more difficult to awaken, his skin pale and teeth chattering. Luckily, that was their biggest challenge—there was plenty of game to be found, and Loghain was able to detect the larger predators quickly enough to give them a wide berth.

Maric, for his part, was proving difficult to hate. He kept pace and had yet to complain, not about being hungry or exhausted or anything else. He also did as he was told and had saved himself more than once from blundering into danger by responding instantly to Loghain's barked orders. If he had one flaw, it was the talking. The man chattered constantly and amiably about almost anything. If it wasn't his amazement at the size of the trees, it was his assessment of the size of the Wilds or his recollection of the lore on the Chasind people that were supposed to live in the forest. Loghain listened quietly to the constant prattle, wishing nothing more than for him to shut up. After the second night, Maric became quieter and Loghain was disgusted to discover he actually missed the sound.

It must have been easy for the man to make friends, Loghain surmised. Even exhausted and half covered in filth, Maric had a natural, easy charm. As Maric was the favored son of a Queen whom Loghain's father had all but worshipped from afar, Loghain truly wanted to despise him. He had every reason to despise him. But the truth was, he just couldn't maintain the cold fury he had felt before, and that was almost worse than anything else.

On the third night, it rained. Freezing without a fire, Loghain and Maric huddled under an outcropping of rock, their breath coming out in plumes through chattering teeth. That night, the wolves made their appearance. Tentatively the beasts hovered nearby, gathering their courage before making any sort of attack. Several times, Loghain sent them running with a shot from his bow, only to have them edge back into sight later on. Loghain had only so many arrows and no way of making more, so he conserved what he had and used them only when there was no other choice.

By the time morning came, the wolves had decided there was less vigilant prey to be found elsewhere. Loghain was weary, chilled to the bone, and became more than a little concerned when he found Maric shivering and unable to wake up. So pale, he was almost white, Maric could at best be roused to a strange state where he uttered delirious nonsense through his chattering teeth.

Loghain built a fire, no mean feat considering that mist and rain had drenched almost everything. He dug for dead wood, searching for dry moss and twigs hidden away out of sight. And then came frustrating hours of smoke and embers, and him nearly nodding off while trying to maintain focus. When the flame finally caught, he could have jumped for joy and would have given much to listen to Maric ask twenty different questions about how he managed it.

He settled for finessing the fire into a sizable blaze. More damp wood was added, and more moss, and more sticks . . . and after those dried and caught fire, he repeated the process. Eventually he had what he needed: a crackling pyre that gave off more heat than smoke. He pulled Maric as close to the flames as he dared and sat nearby, trying to keep an eye out for the wolf pack's return. After a time, the warm glow made his lids heavy and he fell asleep.

Loghain woke up hours later, discovering that Maric was not only already awake but also tending the fire. He was pale and shaky, but mobile. Maric nodded to Loghain, silently acknowledging his thanks with a slightly embarrassed grin, but Loghain only frowned back. "Do you have any idea how much trouble you've put me through?" he demanded.

Maric rubbed his arms, shivering. "I'm, uh, very happy not to be dead. And that you didn't leave me here. To freeze."

"The wolves would have eaten you long before you froze."

"Well, that's something."

Loghain turned to leave. "I'm going to hunt, while I can. I'd appreciate it if you managed to not freeze while I'm gone. Do you think you could do that?" He didn't wait for a response and felt pleased by Maric's slightly injured expression.

On the fourth day, Loghain realized they were being followed.

The wolves had not returned, which was odd.

After a time of having the strange sensation of being watched, he heard something out in the bushes. Whoever was out there—and he did think it was a *who*, since he doubted a predator would have spent so long stalking them—was skilled. Try as Loghain might, he could not spot anyone in the shadows.

He held up a hand, quieting Maric. "Don't look now," he muttered, "but I don't think we're alone any longer."

To Maric's credit, he didn't look. "Are you sure?"

"Well, it is difficult to hear much with you blathering on like you do."

"I'm not blathering!"

"Really? It's no wonder you nearly froze to death the way you spend all your energy moving your mouth." Their eyes glanced around nervously, without making it obvious what they were doing.

Maric made a subtle motion to his left. Loghain followed it, not quite believing that Maric could be capable of spotting something first. Then, he saw it. Just ahead, in the deep shadows between two of the taller trees, two points of light glinted at them, like a cat's eyes as it watched you in the dark.

Like elf eyes.

"Blast!" Loghain swore, his panic catching him off guard. In a single motion, he shoved Maric to the ground and unslung the bow from his shoulder. As he dove for cover he heard an arrow whistling toward him. It sank into his shoulder with considerable force, sending him stumbling backwards with a grunt of pain.

"Loghain!" Maric shouted. He leaped up and ran to where Loghain was sprawled, gasping when he

saw the arrow had passed almost completely through
Loghain's shoulder. Bright blood stained the tall grass.
Looking around, his eyes wide with fear, Maric pulled
out his dagger.

"Run!" Loghain rasped at him, trying to clutch at
the arrow shaft and get up at the same time. But it
was too late. Elves materialized out of the shadows
around them, running toward them with barely a
sound. They were dressed in hunting leathers, their
foreheads tattooed in vivid colored patterns repre-
senting their pagan gods. The expressions in their
bright alien eyes said murder. Some held bows trained
while others held amber-colored ironwood blades in
hand.

Maric raised his dagger, but even as he did, a thick
net landed over them both. The elves were on them,
grabbing at arms and legs and shouting angrily in
their strange language. Loghain struggled, hissing
in pain as the weight of the net forced the arrow
farther through his shoulder, but it was futile. Maric
thrashed in the net next to him until there was a
loud thumping sound and Maric slumped to the
ground. A moment later, held down by many strong
hands, Logain felt something hard slam his head and
he, too, slipped into darkness.

Loghain awoke to the sharp tingle of pain in his
skull and a bath of heat on his face. He could hear a
roaring fire nearby, a large one, and before his eyes
opened, he could tell he was seated against some kind
of pole with his arms tied together behind it. Was he
going to be cooked, then? Roasted on a skewer over a

roaring fire? Was that something elves did? It seemed unlikely, considering the arrow wound in his shoulder was now treated and bandaged. At least he was finally warm.

He opened his eyes and the light hurt.

Sure enough, he was set up before a bonfire with Maric slumped next to him. Beyond the fire was a group of long, oddly shaped covered wagons, circled in the forest clearing. Each of the wagons had a mast with one triangular sail attached to both it and an elegantly shaped piece of wood off the back, which could have passed for a rudder. Though Loghain had never encountered a landship before, he'd heard enough stories to know one when he saw it.

It was certain, then. These were Dalish elves, wanderers who had remained together in tightly knit clans ever since the destruction of the elven homeland long ago at human hands. Many elves had submitted to human rule and lived in the cities as second-class citizens, but the Dalish had refused. They had fled, and today remained aloof and hostile toward all outsiders. They worshipped strange gods and kept to the most remote lands, passing through forests that parted before them like waves on the sea, and beware the hapless traveler who encountered them unawares.

Travelers like Loghain and Maric. Loghain had no idea how much of the tales was true, as he had never so much as seen a Dalish up close before, but their ambush led credence to the rumors.

The heat from the bonfire was almost blistering this close, so Loghain twisted to try to pull away from it as much as he could. His face felt raw, and a trickle of thickness down his cheek told him his head was still bleeding from the earlier blow. A cloying smell not unlike jasmine lurked in the air along with the aroma of cooked meat. Beyond the smoke, he could see several elves seated on the other side of the fire. They were dressed in simple colorful robes—reds and blues and golds, mostly—and were eating from wooden bowls, their pale eyes flickering occasionally toward him.

Maric stirred and started groaning painfully. Loghain watched him until he finally cracked open an eye, recoiling instantly from the bonfire just as Loghain had. "Maker's breath!" he croaked, then began coughing hoarsely.

"Careful," Loghain cautioned.

"I could really do without being hit on the head anymore."

"Complain to the Dalish. Perhaps they take requests."

Maric sat up, squinting past the fire. "Is that who they are? I was wondering about all the markings on their faces."

"You don't know about the Dalish?"

"Well, you know"—he shrugged—"I had other things I was supposed to learn."

"Such as?"

"How to be taken prisoner by outlaws, apparently."

Loghain smirked. "Here I thought you were just a quick study." The Dalish were listening to them, and several more had come out of the shadows to stand next to their landships and stare. They seemed unfriendly and suspicious, if not outright hostile. What, then, did they have planned? Loghain felt almost on display, an exotic beast that was too frightening to be approached closely.

Maric sniffed, then shivered in disgust. "What's that smell? Jasmine?"

"Maybe."

"What do they do? Roll it up and smoke it?" He sniffed again and gagged at the stench until Loghain elbowed him. This wasn't the time to aggravate their captors by possibly mocking some elven custom. Dalish weren't fond of humans as it was.

Loghain struggled in his bonds, testing the ropes, until he noticed that even more of the Dalish had gathered to stare. This time it was hunters, dressed much like the ones who had captured them, in the same dark leathers and with the same ironbark blades. He had seen a blade like that before. Potter had arrived at the camp carrying one, in fact, claiming that he had traded for it with a pair of Dalish hunters years before. Stolen, more likely. Eventually Potter had pawned it, and for good coin. The Dalish were the only ones who knew how to mold the ironbark as they did: the blades were practically harder than steel and a fraction of the weight.

"Hello?" Maric suddenly called out to them, looking around. "Will any of you speak to us? Hello?"

"Quiet!" Loghain snapped.

"What? I'm just asking."

"Don't be a fool."

Just then, a new figure emerged from the gathered watchers. This was a male elf, young with long brown hair and distinctly slanted eyes. His robe was covered in more complex designs than the others', and unlike his companions, he wore a heavy leather cloak gathered around his shoulders. Loghain noticed, too, an ironbark amulet hanging around his neck. It was polished to a shine and carved with intricate runes that seemed to dance just beneath the surface. Magic. The thought made Loghain's skin crawl.

The young elf approached, and noticing Loghain's gaze, he smiled. He crouched down directly before Loghain and Maric, a gesture that was almost friendly and casual in its nature. "The amulet was a gift from our Keeper," he said, his unaccented voice smooth.

"You speak the King's tongue?" Loghain asked. He distinctly ignored the *I told you so* look that Maric shot his way.

"Most of us do, though only those who go out to trade with the outsiders get to use it often." The elf's manner was gentle, and his eyes seemed filled with compassion, unlike the expressions of the others around them. "Here in the clan, we try to keep our own tongue alive, just as we do our gods." He tilted his head curiously. "Why are you here?"

"Because you attacked us, remember?" Maric answered, incredulous.

"You are outsiders. You approached our camp."

"We had no idea you were even here," Loghain said carefully.

"Ah." The elf nodded, but seemed disappointed. "Then you are with the others who fled here from beyond the woods?"

"Others?" Loghain spoke more quickly than he thought wise. "There are . . . others who have come before us? Recently?"

The elf's purple eyes watched Loghain dispassionately for a moment before answering. "There was one, a man that our hunters caught far away from here."

"Where is he now?"

"I will need to bring you to him," the elf sighed unhappily. He stood up, turning to some of the others who stood nearby. Polite-sounding orders were given in their language, along with gestures that indicated Loghain and Maric and some place beyond the encampment. The other elves looked at each other, clearly uneasy about whatever they had been asked to do. They approached and began untying Loghain and Maric's ropes.

"I am sorry," the elf said, "but if you are indeed from the same place as the other man, we will need to take you as we did him. Please do not struggle." From his tone, he seemed to think they actually might.

Maric looked around, seeming confused. As his ropes loosened, he brought his hands forward and rubbed his wrists gingerly. "Where are you taking us, exactly?"

"To the *asha'belannar*. The Woman of Many Years," the elf explained. "The humans that live in this forest call her the Witch of the Wilds."

Loghain's skin went cold. A witch? Sometimes mages escaped from the clutches of the Chantry, refusing to be herded into one of their towers along with everyone else who showed even a hint of magical promise. They were branded apostates, and the Chantry would send their mighty templars to hunt them down and either return them to the tower or kill them. Most, he understood, were killed, and runaway mages lived in mortal fear of being found. One apostate had come to the outlaw camp, a thin man whom Sister Ailis had seen through immediately. Father sent him away, not wanting trouble with the templars, and the mage had reluctantly gone. He could just as easily have turned his spells on them in anger, Loghain thought.

So was this witch an apostate, hiding out in the Korcari Wilds, someone so desperate to keep her secret that she killed anyone who arrived from outside the forest? It was possible, yet something else tickled at the back of his mind. There was a legend, an old tale about this forest that he couldn't quite summon to his memory. The idea, however, that she might be something else, possibly something worse, was unsettling.

Maric seemed full of questions, but a forceful look from the elf quieted even him. The Dalish were frightened of this "Woman of Many Years," and that disturbed Loghain more than anything else.

The elves lined up to watch them leave, rows of them staring with baleful curiosity, murmuring among themselves in their strange tongue. Several elves spat at the ground as they walked by, and terrified children were herded away and out of sight. Loghain felt like a condemned man. Perhaps he was.

Several hours passed as they marched through the Wilds, and the elves accompanying them stayed grim and quiet, refusing to answer even the simplest questions. The one in the bright robes had yet to introduce himself, though he glanced back at Maric and Loghain with irritation whenever they fell behind. Loghain would have reminded the elf that neither he nor Maric had been fed or allowed to rest, but it seemed none of the Dalish had any interest beyond getting to where they were going.

Deep in the thick of the forest, where the white

mist turned into an obscuring fog and the sun barely reached, there stood a simple weathered hut with a roof of brown moss and old branches. It lay at the end of a short path, and thick, dark ivy crept up the walls on all sides. More significant were the ropes of skulls hanging along the path: rat and wolf and some Loghain couldn't even identify, all tied together with feathers and sticks and mud. They dangled ominously, a sign staking claim to this land. Maybe there was magic here, too, for Loghain felt a strange sensation running up his arms and into the back of his neck. The air bristled with power, and the way the mist flowed seemed to beckon them in farther.

The young elf in the colorful robes stopped then, and so did the hunters. He pointed toward the hut. "There, that is where you need to go."

"What's going to happen to us?" Maric asked.

"I cannot say."

Loghain paused, unease growing as he noticed what were surely human skulls hanging in the ropes. Looking back at the elf, he nodded respectfully. The elf did the same.

"*Dareth shiral*. I wish you and your friend well."

Unfortunately, he didn't sound as if he expected that to be the case. The elf and his two companions turned and walked away, leaving Loghain and Maric standing in the shadows. The smell of the woods was fresh and clean after the recent rains, the sound of excited birds clear far up in the trees.

"Do we leave?" Maric asked hesitantly.

Loghain didn't see what good that would do. If this was indeed an apostate, she could no doubt bring them to her whether they wished to go or not. "Let's see who this Witch of the Wilds is," he muttered, gesturing toward the hut. Maric looked at him as if he must be mad, but said nothing.

As they walked down the path, the shadows seemed to deepen. The trees towered more ominously overhead, and the mist twisted and danced around them. A trick of the light? In front of the hut sat a small rickety rocking chair as well as an old fire pit that had not seen use for many days. Small moldy bones surrounded the pit in neat piles.

"Is that . . . ?" Maric's voice trailed off in horror, and Loghain followed his gaze up into the trees. There hung a corpse, a human man with clammy white skin like a fish. He was strung up by his neck and arms, dangling like a broken marionette, with flies and the smell of turning meat hovering in the air. There was no sign of injury, but he had been dead long enough to discolor, the skin glistening slightly as if sweating. The doughy, swollen face and bulging eyes were not enough to hide this corpse's identity. Loghain knew exactly who he was.

"Dannon?" Maric whispered.

Loghain nodded. There were other bodies hanging farther in, just a few that he could see, hidden in the mist and shadows. Most of them were skeletons with nothing more than tattered cloth and scraps of wispy hair clinging to them.

"I see you're already acquainted with my newest trophy," came a new voice. A decrepit woman hobbled into view from among the trees. She was the very picture of a witch, wild white hair and a robe formed mostly of thick black furs and dark leather. Hanging down her back was a heavy cloak trimmed in fox fur, quite striking and delicately stitched. She carried a basket filled with large acorns and other items wrapped in red cloth, and she waved it absently in Dannon's direction. "He never did introduce himself, foolish lad. I warned him after he started with the bellowing." She stopped and appraised Loghain and Maric carefully, both of whom stared at her agape. "Thankfully, it doesn't seem like either of you has the same problem. Good! That will make this easier."

Her voice was cackling with easy amusement, which made the situation all the more surreal. Loghain wished the elves had left him with at least his blade. The old woman walked toward the hut without waiting for them and sat herself down in the rocking chair with a belabored sigh.

"Well, come on, then," she grumped at them, putting down her basket.

Loghain approached grudgingly, Maric a step behind him.

"You killed Dannon?" Maric asked incredulously.

"Did I say that?" she chuckled. "I don't believe I did, in fact. If you wish to know the truth, the lad killed himself."

"Magic," Loghain swore.

The woman cackled with renewed amusement but said nothing more.

"Who are you?" Maric asked.

"I don't care who she is," Loghain asserted. "I don't like being played with." He stepped threateningly toward her. She responded by narrowing her small eyes, but nothing else. "I demand that you let us go."

"You demand?" She seemed impressed by the notion.

"Err . . . Loghain," Maric cautioned.

Loghain held up a hand, warning Maric back. He stepped closer to the witch, looming over her as she remained seated in her chair. "Yes, I demand," he repeated slowly. "Casting spells does not impress me. You need time to cast, and I can break your neck before you lift a finger."

She smiled at him, a broad grin full of teeth. "Now, who said that I would be the one to do anything?"

Loghain heard Maric's sharp intake of breath behind him but turned only in time to see one of the giant trees reaching toward him with lightning speed. Great branches wrapped around him like giant hands, pulling him up into the air. Leaves fluttered all around while flies buzzed angrily through the air. He struggled and shouted, but it was useless. The tree stepped back into line with its brothers, and Loghain became another dangling trophy only a few feet away from Dannon's bloated corpse. Panicking, he tried to shout to Maric, only to have smaller branches wrap around his mouth and hold his head still.

Maric crouched, eyes wide and heart pounding as he watched Loghain get snatched. It happened so quickly—how could a giant tree have moved so fast? Frightened, he glanced back at the witch, but she only rocked quietly in her chair, regarding him with vague annoyance.

"Are you to be next, then?" she asked.

"I'm . . . hoping not."

"An excellent choice."

Sweat trickling down his brow, Maric cleared his throat and carefully lowered himself to one knee. "I beg your pardon on behalf of my companion, good lady." His voice was quiet, but the old woman appeared to be listening, fascinated. "We have been running for days now, and after the Dalish attacked us . . . we expected more of the same, despite the fact that you have offered no provocation. I apologize." He bowed his head, trying his best to remember the courtly manners so painstakingly taught to him over the years by his mother. To think he had rolled his eyes at those lessons, assuming that he would never have an actual use for them.

The witch laughed shrilly. "Manners? My, but that is unexpected." When Maric looked up, she grinned at him. "But the truth is that you don't know what I intend for you and your friend, young man. I might intend to give you both to the sylvans, just as I did your friend, isn't that so?"

"Yes, it is."

"Yes," she repeated slowly, "it is." She waved a withered hand toward the tree holding Loghain, causing its branches to unwind. He was dumped to the ground, where he immediately jumped up and turned to face the old woman, enraged. Maric held up a hand warning him to stay back, and Loghain snorted as if to tell Maric he was angry, not *stupid*.

"So you are he," the witch said, nodding with approval as she studied Maric. "I knew you would come, and the manner in which you would come, but not the when." She let out a sharp guffaw and slapped her knees. "Isn't it marvelous how very capricious magic can be with its information? It's like asking a cat for directions—consider yourself lucky if it only tells you where to go!" She howled with laughter at her own joke.

Both Maric and Loghain stared at her blankly.

Her laughter slowly quieted into a sigh. "Well, what did you think?" she asked. "That the King of Ferelden could pass through the Korcari Wilds and it would go completely without notice?"

Maric licked his lips nervously. "I'm assuming you mean the *rightful* King of Ferelden."

"Right you are! If the Orlesian who sits on your throne were to run through this part of the forest all by himself, I would happily scoop him up instead of you! Failing that, I suppose you will have to do. Wouldn't you agree?"

"Err . . . good point."

The witch reached down into the basket by her feet and drew out a large, shiny apple. It was a dark red, perfectly plump and ripe. She bit into it with gusto. "Now—" She spoke through her loud chewing. "—I have to apologize if the elves seemed overzealous. They were the only way I could cast out my net far enough to catch you as you passed." She licked the apple juices off her lips. "But one does what one can."

Maric thought carefully. "The elves . . . didn't just happen to find us, then?"

"Now there's a smart lad."

"Who *are* you?" Maric asked breathlessly.

"She's an apostate, a mage in hiding from the Chantry's hunters," Loghain insisted. "Why else would she be out in the middle of the Wilds?"

The witch rolled her eyes and chuckled again. "Your friend isn't entirely incorrect. There are things hidden in the shadows of your kingdom, young man, which you couldn't begin to guess." She looked directly at Loghain, her eyes suddenly sharp. "Yet I was here long before your Chantry came to this part of the world."

"It isn't *my* Chantry," he snapped.

"As for your question"—she looked back at Maric—"the Dalish surely told you my name? I have many, and theirs is as good as any."

"Then what do you want with me?"

She bit into her apple with a loud crunch and chewed it thoughtfully as she sat back in her rocking chair. "Why does anyone desire an audience with their sovereign?"

"You . . . want something from me?" He shrugged helplessly. "You probably would have been better off with my mother, if that's the case. I don't have much of anything."

"Fortunes change." The witch's gaze shifted to far off in the distance. "One minute you're in love, so much in love that you can't imagine anything wrong ever happening. And the next you're betrayed. Your love has been ripped from you like your own leg, and you swear you'd do anything—*anything*—to make those responsible pay." Her eyes focused on Maric, and her voice became soft, caressing. "Sometimes vengeance changes the world. What will yours do, young man?"

He said nothing, staring at her uncertainly.

Loghain stepped forward angrily. "Leave him alone."

The witch turned to regard him, her eyes delighted. "And what of yours? You've rage enough inside you, tempered into a blade of fine steel. Into whose heart will you plunge that one day, I wonder?"

"Maric and I are not friends," he growled, "but I don't want him dead."

Her chuckle was mirthless. "Oh, you know what I speak of."

Loghain paled, but regained his composure almost immediately. "That . . . doesn't matter any longer," he stated evenly.

"Doesn't it? Have you forgiven them already, then? You no longer remember her cries as they held her down? The laughter of the soldiers as they held you back and made you watch? Your father when he—"

"Stop!" Loghain shouted, his voice filled with as much terror as fury. Maric watched in shock as Loghain launched toward the witch as if to strangle her. He lurched to a halt before he reached her, hands clenched tightly into fists as he struggled against his impulse. The trees around the hut seemed to creak in anticipation, like coiled springs. The witch merely rocked and watched him quietly, unconcerned. "You see too much, old woman," he muttered.

"In fact," her tone was dry, "I see just barely enough."

"Please." Maric stepped forward. "Tell me what you want."

She studied him for a moment, and after taking a final bite from her apple and chewing on it in the quiet, she tossed it over her shoulder. It fell with a dull thud in the rotted leaves and moss. An instant later, something long and white slithered out from the shadows and snatched up the core. It was buried under the leaves, almost out of sight, but still Maric got the impression that it wasn't a snake at all.

"You should thank me, young man," the witch purred. "Fleeing into the Wilds as you did, what do you suppose would have happened to you? Taken by Chasind wild folk, slain by the Dalish, eaten by any one of the many creatures that lurk within its crevasses. Do you truly think this one outlaw alone could have seen you through it all?"

"I don't know. Maybe."

She arched a brow at Loghain. "He has quite the estimation of your capabilities, doesn't he?" When he said nothing, she turned to gaze intensely at Maric. "Keep him close, and he will betray you. Each time worse than the last."

Maric was unmoved. "So you brought me here to speak riddles at me, then?"

"No, no." She waved a hand absently. "I brought you here to save you."

Maric stared at her in disbelief. He wasn't quite sure she could have said anything else that would have been less surprising. Well, perhaps a confession that she was actually made of cheese. But this ranked a close second.

"I've snatched you up from the brink of the proverbial pit," she continued, "and I'm going to send you back out into the world. Safe and sound." The witch reclined in her chair then, looking very much pleased with herself.

"And what do you want in exchange for this . . . help?" Loghain demanded.

"A promise." She smiled. "Made by the King to me in private, and then never spoken of again to anyone."

Maric blinked in surprise, but Loghain stepped in front of him. "And if he refuses?" he demanded.

She gestured toward the forest outside. "Then you are free to go."

Loghain turned to Maric, and his opinion was evident in his expression. Mages were not to be trusted, and this old woman less than most. Perhaps Loghain thought the witch might let them leave even if Maric refused and they could take their chances. Perhaps they could even get their weapons back from the Dalish. The one who had brought them hadn't seemed completely unreasonable, after all. . . . If they could make some kind of trade, they might even get a blanket or cloaks or . . . who knows what else.

The wind whistled in the trees far overhead. Maric wondered for a moment if they danced, for it almost seemed as if they did. Restless trees dancing to the music of the wind as they stood there in the shadows and silence. He looked at Loghain searchingly, asking for help, but there was no response. They were cold, battered, and exhausted, and in the middle of the Wilds. What choice did they have?

"I accept," Maric said.

4

They spent the night outside the witch's hut, next to a fire that had roared into life with a single tap of her foot. It stayed lit all night, even though Loghain couldn't tell what was being burned inside it. Magic, he assumed, and decided it was best not to think about it too closely. There were a great many things about the hut and the objects around it that he didn't want to think about too closely—the feeling that the marionette corpses hanging in the trees were watching them, for one. The way the trees seemed to change configuration around them, for another. Indeed, in the morning, the path they'd arrived on led away in a completely different direction.

Loghain also didn't want to think about what sort of promise the witch had elicited from Maric. He had gone into her hut and had remained there for hours, long enough that Loghain grew concerned.

He had been trying to peer in through its one filthy, grit-covered window when Maric walked out the door, alone. The man seemed shaken and quiet and was resistant to even the most casual efforts Loghain made to inquire about what had gone on. So it was to remain a secret, after all.

The witch did not reappear, so the two of them slept on the leaves by the fire. Or, rather, Maric slept. Loghain lay awake, watching the shadows and staring at the darkness where he knew Dannon's body swung. He wondered when Dannon had fled the outlaw camp: before the attack or during? Eventually he approached the tree and looked up at Dannon's sagging, swollen face. With effort, he pulled the body down, freeing it from the branches that clutched it. He struggled at first, but suddenly the body came all at once, as if released. The moist thud as it hit the ground was followed by a sickening belch of foulness. Working with his hands, Loghain collected masses of leaves and moss and small stones and buried Dannon's body with them. It wasn't a proper grave. He had no idea why he did it, but he felt it was right.

Sleep took him later by the fire, a fitful slumber filled with frightening wisps of images but no dreams. When he thought he heard footsteps, he woke and saw it was morning. Thin streams of sunlight came through the trees above, and the fire pit was black once again. Both of them were healed of all wounds, and piled neatly next to them were provisions: a pair of cloaks, their weapons, a bag filled with what looked like small loaves of bread and berries and strips of dry jerky, and one shiny red apple.

The hut was empty of everything but dust and rot,

as if nobody had lived there for years. They searched about, but there was no sign of the witch. There was also, he noticed, no sign of Dannon's body or his makeshift grave. It seemed they were free to go.

It took them four days' travel to leave the Wilds. Supposedly, the witch had told Maric they would see the way out once they left her hut, and sure enough, not an hour away a bluebird appeared in the trees before them. It was so out of place, and sang so sweetly, that both Loghain and Maric took instant notice. As they approached, it flitted to the next tree and to the next until Loghain realized it was leading them. So they followed. When it reappeared the next morning, there could be no doubt.

The weather cooperated for the most part, raining only the first night, then remaining chilly and dry the nights after. Having the thick cloaks made all the difference in the world, and it wasn't long before Maric was restored to his usual chatty self. Loghain threatened to take away Maric's cloak so the man would freeze again and perhaps be quiet for a while, but the annoying truth was that Loghain found himself not minding it quite so much anymore. Pretending not to care, he listened quietly while Maric talked about almost everything.

The only thing Maric didn't talk about was the witch.

Loghain was fairly certain they were passing through areas controlled by the Dalish. Several times he could have sworn that he felt eyes on him, but saw nothing in the trees. Elves were good at keeping themselves hidden when they wanted to, or *these* elves were. All the elves Loghain had ever known were like Potter, and had lived among humans so

long that the ways of the Dalish were just as foreign
to them as to everyone else.

There were no more unexpected encounters,
though on the third night they found the remains of
an overgrown ruin. It was a sight to behold, tall
stone pillars jutting into the sky like rib bones, presumably having once held up a great ceiling. Part of
the foundation remained, along with a set of long
stairs, all of it cracked and almost reduced to rubble
by the encroaching greenery. Maric seemed awed by
the structure and poked around it at length. He
found the remains of an altar that held a great carving of what might once have been a dragon's head. It
was faded now, though Maric seemed to see where
the eyes and teeth might have been and traced them
out. Excitedly, he told Loghain that this was probably a temple of the ancient Imperium, from back in
the times when they had encroached this far south
and warred with the barbarian tribes. To him, the
fact that the temple had lasted as long as it had was
impressive. All Loghain knew of the Imperium was
that it had once been ruled by mages, and he refused
to have anything more to do with magic. The idea of
taking refuge in the bones of a pagan temple made
him agitated, and while Maric teased him for being
superstitious, he didn't object when Loghain insisted
they leave.

It wasn't long after leaving the ruins that they encountered wolves again. For the first time, Loghain
was truly beginning to believe that the old witch had
called on greater magic to aid them than just summoning a bluebird guide. Loghain stood with his bow
at the ready, eyeing the wolves warily, while Maric
remained breathless beside him. The entire pack,

however, maintained its distance and watched, but did not threaten. Loghain and Maric moved cautiously through the trees, with perhaps twenty large wolves sitting and staring at them silently with their feral yellow eyes. Still, nothing happened. As soon as they were out of sight, Loghain let out a long breath. He swore that he never wanted to encounter magic again as long as he lived, and Maric murmured agreement.

On the afternoon of the fourth day, the forest had thinned enough that Loghain declared them out of the Wilds. He couldn't be sure, but he believed the bluebird had led them west, just as he had originally planned, before veering north. This placed them a long way from Lothering, in the hills of the western Hinterlands. Sure enough, the terrain became rockier as they traveled, and off in the distance the magnificent vista of the Frostback Mountains could be seen. Loghain was pleased to see the return of the horizon. Too long spent in that wilderness with its cold and mist could drive a man mad.

When the sun went down that day, the bluebird vanished.

"Do you think it's going to come back?" Maric asked.

"How should I know?"

"Because you're the expert on all things magical and arcane?"

Loghain snorted. "It brought us out of the Wilds. Its job is done." He looked at Maric impatiently. "Just how hard will it be to find this army of yours? It can't be that well-hidden, can it?"

"We've managed to keep ahead of the usurper all these years, so I don't know." Maric hopped onto a nearby boulder and looked out over the hills. Dusk was providing a spectacular show of orange and crimson in the sky, but darkness was coming fast. "I think they actually may be nearby. If you had asked me earlier where we had been camping, I would have said west of Lothering. So . . . here?"

"Wonderful."

Loghain selected a small clearing to make their camp and sent Maric to collect wood. Now that they were away from the eternal mist, it was far easier to build a decent blaze, but he knew being out of the dense woods also meant that the fire could be seen, especially in the hills. Maric's hunters could still be searching for him, even out here. For all Loghain knew, what he'd said to Maric about mages looking for him could be true. They might be watching for people coming out of the forest, and what then?

Loghain already had the beginnings of a fire going. They would take the risk until it was proved otherwise, he thought. If he tried to account for magic, he would end up chasing his tail.

"I saw some more wolves," Maric announced when he returned with wood.

"And? Were they hostile?"

"Well, they didn't attack, if that's what you mean. But they were planning to."

"They told you that?"

"Yes, in fact. They sent a rabbit with a note to inform me of their intentions." He dumped the wood unceremoniously next to the fire. "Rather gentlemanly of them, I thought." Loghain ignored him, and he sat down on the grass, watching the darkening sky overhead. "I wonder if they were werewolves? Is there a way to tell?"

Here we go again, Loghain thought to himself. He didn't look up from his task of slowly adding wood to the fire. "Do I even want to know?"

"I remembered the story one of my tutors taught me, about how the mist ended up in the Korcari Wilds. It has to do with the werewolves."

"That's nice."

As usual, Maric seemed to miss Loghain's uninterested tone. "It was back before King Calenhad united the Clayne tribes. There was a curse that spread among the wolves, and they became possessed by powerful demons. They turned into monsters that preyed on the farmholds and villages in these parts, and when they were chased into the Wilds, they would turn into wolves again and hide."

"Superstition," Loghain muttered.

"No, it really happened! That's why everyone still keeps hounds. Back then, a hound could smell a werewolf approaching and warn you, maybe even attack and give you a chance to run away. It was an epidemic."

Loghain paused and regarded Maric with a weary expression. "And what does that have to do with the mist?"

"The story says that a great arl finally created an army of hounds and hunters and went into the Wilds. For years they slaughtered every wolf they could find, possessed or no. The last werewolf swore vengeance, stabbing himself in the heart with the very blade that had slain his mate. As his blood touched the forest floor, a mist rose from that spot.

"The mist spread and spread, until finally the Arl's army became lost in the forest. They never returned home, and eventually the arling was abandoned. My tutor claimed that the old ruins there are haunted by the ghosts of their wives, forever waiting for their husbands."

"That's ridiculous," Loghain sighed. "There's no such thing as ghosts. And there's not nearly enough mist in the Wilds to make someone lose their way. It's just a nuisance."

"Maybe it was different a long time ago?" Maric shrugged. "Anyhow, they say that some of the were-wolves survived. That they hide in these parts, taking vengeance when they can find a man alone."

"*They* say a lot of things."

"My tutor was a very learned man."

"Especially them." Loghain stood up, brushing himself off, and turned toward the reclining Maric just as an arrow flew by his ear.

Maric sat up, confused. "Was that—?"

"Get down!" Loghain sank to a crouch and drew his sword. Maric dropped to his knees, but also turned curiously to see where the arrow had come from. Unwilling to discuss the matter, Loghain grabbed him by the hood of his cloak and pushed him down to his belly. Already the sound of several riders could be heard approaching the clearing, and Loghain cursed himself for a fool. He had underestimated just how badly they wanted Maric if they were on top of them already.

"We have to get out of here!" Maric shouted. He had drawn his own knife, but Loghain was already watching two horsemen entering the camp at full trot. The men were soldiers, wearing mail hauberks and full helmets, and already had their flails out and swinging.

As the first horseman raced past, Loghain ducked

under the swing of his flail. The spiked ball passed over his head with an alarming whoosh. The second horseman was shortly behind the first, and Loghain sprinted forward, jabbing up with his sword before that soldier could begin his swing. Loghain felt the point of the blade jab into the rider's armpit, and the man shouted in pain and tried to weakly bring the flail down on him. He pulled out his sword just in time to catch the flail's chain, causing the heavy ball to spin around the blade. Girding himself, he pulled hard, and the rider was flung off his mount, crying out in surprise.

The soldier hit the ground awkwardly, rolling away with the flail. This time it was Loghain's blade that was wrenched from him. The first rider had doubled back and was bearing down on him, leaving him with no time to do anything but watch the flail head swinging toward him. It slammed into his chest hard, several ribs cracking as the spikes dug painfully into his chest. He was lifted off his feet and thrown back several paces.

"Loghain!" Maric shouted, rushing into the melee with his dagger. He plunged the wicked blade into the leg of the mounted soldier. The man's horse reared back and whinnied as the rider screamed in pain, unintentionally pulling on the reins. The other fallen soldier was groaning and trying to crawl away, and Maric jumped over him and ran to where Loghain had fallen.

Loghain gritted his teeth against the massive pain in his chest and tried to sit up. He was about to tell Maric to run, but it was too late. Four other horsemen had already arrived, one of them a knight in intricate plate armor. Clearly the leader, this one rode a great black horse and wore a full helmet with a green plume.

Suddenly, the knight motioned for the riders behind him to stop—and they did, several of the horses rearing up and prancing on the spot. The wounded soldier with the dagger in his leg awkwardly pulled his mount back as he hissed and swore under his breath.

Loghain coughed painfully, but slowly got to his feet as he and Maric stared at the riders. Why they didn't attack he had no idea. Perhaps they intended to force them to surrender? In that case, he would send at least one or two of them to the Maker. He stepped in front of Maric and raised his sword, wincing at the spasm this sent through his cracked ribs.

"The first one that comes for us," he vowed, "is losing an arm. That I guarantee."

A couple of the riders backed up a step, glancing questioningly toward the green-plumed knight. He stayed where he was, silently watching Maric and Loghain.

"Maric?" the knight spoke, the voice strange coming from within the helmet.

Maric gasped in astonishment. Loghain, sword still raised, glanced back at him. "You know each other?"

The knight sheathed his sword. Reaching up to his helmet, he pulled it off, and Loghain realized the man's voice had sounded strange because it wasn't a man at all. Masses of thick brown curls were plastered against the woman's sweaty pale skin, yet Loghain found it didn't mar her striking appearance. She had high cheekbones and a strong chin that a sculptor would have ached for, yet carried herself

with a confidence that told him the armor was no
affectation. She was as much a soldier as the men she
led, and while it was not unheard of in Ferelden for
a woman to be skilled in the art of war, it was un-
common enough to be surprising.

She paid no attention at all to Loghain and instead stared with shock at Maric. He looked fairly
shocked himself. "Rowan?" he asked.

The brown-haired woman slid off her black horse,
holding her helmet tucked under one arm and not
taking her eyes off him. Passing the reins silently to
one of the other horsemen, she strode forward to
stand before Maric. Loghain let her, backing out of
the way without dropping his blade. She said nothing, staring with her dark eyes as if she expected
Maric to respond somehow.

He looked distinctly discomfited. "Err . . . hello,"
he finally said. "It's good to see you."

She remained silent, her mouth thinning into an
angry frown.

"Aren't you happy to see me at all?" he asked.

She punched him. Her gauntleted fist slamming
into Maric's jaw sent him sprawling on his back. Lifting a curious brow, Loghain watched Maric lie there,
groaning and clutching his face, and then turned back
to regard the female knight. She was furious now, her
look daring him to go ahead and defend Maric.

He sheathed his sword. "Yes, you definitely know
him."

Maric was glad to see Rowan. Overjoyed, in fact. Or
had been, until she punched him in the face. As far
as he was concerned, there had been entirely too

much punching in the face lately. After he picked himself up off the ground, hasty explanations were made—and none too soon. Rowan had stirred herself into a fury. He had always had a knack for provoking her temper. When he was a child he often blithely enraged Rowan and then ran to his mother for protection. She would simply smile down at him in amusement and leave him to Rowan's tender mercies. By the time he got older, he'd learned to see the warning signs for himself . . . though apparently that skill had become a tad rusty.

Rowan and her men had seen their fire from a distance and assumed Loghain was Maric's captor. In fact, she had seen Maric reclining and believed him unconscious or dead. Upon discovering that he not only didn't run away when he had the chance but actually defended Loghain, she had then assumed they were conspirators and Maric had . . . what? Run away, he supposed, though she stopped short of saying just that. It took a considerable amount of convincing before Rowan grudgingly believed that they had been on their way to the rebel camp and that Loghain was, in fact, responsible for Maric's survival to date.

"Oh," Rowan said, finally looking at Loghain. She didn't seem all that impressed. "I suppose I owe you an apology, then, ser." Her overt suspicion didn't make it sound much like an apology, but Loghain seemed more amused than offended.

"It seems that you do," he said, offering his hand. "Loghain Mac Tir, at your service."

"Rowan Guerein." Her look remained dubious, probably since most men would have bowed and perhaps taken her fingers in the usual courtly fashion,

even if Maric knew she didn't care for it. She took
Loghain's hand, and he gave it a firm shake. She removed her hand from the contact a bit too eagerly,
as if Loghain had some unsightly and possibly infec-
tious skin condition that she was much too polite to
comment on. "And I doubt I'll be needing your service, ser."

"It's a figure of speech, not a proposal."

"It's *Lady* Rowan," Maric interjected helpfully.
"She's the daughter of the Arl of Redcliffe . . . who is
probably still with the army, I hope?"

"Yes . . ." Rowan's gaze lingered uncertainly on
Loghain a moment longer before she turned her attention back to Maric. She frowned at him with
concern. "We searched everywhere for you, Maric.
Father's all but given you up for dead. He's wanted to
move the army for days, now, but I begged him to let
me keep looking." She softened, touching his cheek
with uncharacteristic tenderness. "Maker's breath,
Maric! When we heard what they had done to the
queen, we were so afraid they'd killed you, too! Or
worse, put you in one of the usurper's dungeons . . ."
She hugged him tightly against her breastplate. "But
you're alive! You are!"

Maric allowed himself to be crushed, sending
Loghain a pleading look that said, *For the love of the
Maker, help me!* Loghain merely stood by, appearing
vaguely entertained. When Rowan released Maric,
she paused and stared at him as if uncertain how to
proceed.

"Your mother . . ."

"They killed her in front of me." He nodded miserably.

"The usurper had her body sent to Denerim. He's

declared a holiday, had her paraded—" She stopped herself short, her voice raw. "You don't want to know this."

"No. Probably not." He'd heard about the usurper's fondness for putting his enemies on display, and no doubt the Rebel Queen was a great prize for him. His mind shied away from the unbidden images that conjured. None of them were pleasant.

Loghain leaned forward, clearing his throat with exaggerated politeness. "Not to interrupt, Your Ladyship—"

"Rowan will do," she interrupted.

Loghain glanced questioningly at Maric, who spread his hands as if helpless. "Not to interrupt, *Rowan*," he repeated, "but perhaps we should get under way. You might not be the only one who saw our fire."

She stepped back from Maric, all business once again. Studying the horizon with concern, she nodded. "Good point." She turned back to the horsemen watching politely from nearby. "Leave two of the horses here. The rest of you can double up. I want you to ride back and inform my father that I've found the Prince."

The men looked uncertain, perhaps reluctant to leave her unguarded. "Go," she repeated more forcefully. "We will be right behind you." And they went, exchanging their places on the horses without comment—the one soldier whom Loghain had dragged from his steed limping and needing assistance—before riding off in a cloud.

"Father's had some odd reports," Rowan commented to Maric as they left. "There's been a lot of men sighted in the Hinterlands. The usurper's men, looking for you—or so we thought." She sighed heavily. "We may have stayed here too long."

"And you sent away your guards?"

"As distractions," Loghain said with a hint of approval.

Rowan remounted her horse. "If we did run into the enemy, a few more men wouldn't make much difference." She glanced at Maric and smiled mischievously. "Besides, as I recall, you're a fine rider. We'll just outrun them if need be."

Maric ignored her and mounted his own horse. It was a shaky business, requiring several bounces as the startled animal proceeded to pace forward and drag him along before he was actually on top. Once perched precariously on the saddle, he did his best to try to stay there. His discomfort was pronounced enough to make the horse nicker nervously. "I fall off horses," he explained to Loghain with a sickly grin. "It's this thing I do."

"Let's not run into anyone, then." Loghain seemed to have no trouble riding, and as if to prove it, he trotted around Maric and brought his horse to stand beside Rowan's. Maric watched him with a grimace and thought, *Well, of course he's a good rider, too. Why wouldn't he be?*

Rowan seemed to be thinking the same thing, glancing curiously at him. "You have experience riding? That's unusual for a—" She paused, searching for a tactful word.

"A commoner?" he finished for her. He snorted derisively. "That's an interesting worldview coming from someone who lives in the wilderness and probably has to beg her meals from cowards."

Rowan's jaw set and her eyes flashed with anger.

Maric decided against warning Loghain about her temper; he was a grown man, after all. The sort who could ride and everything. "I meant," she said curtly, "that it's not everyone who has access to horses."

"My father raised them on our farmhold. He taught me."

"Did he teach you your manners, too?"

"No, that was my mother," he replied coldly. "Or at least she tried to before she was raped and killed by the Orlesians."

Rowan's eyes were wide as Loghain turned and rode away.

Maric steered his horse over toward hers with difficulty. "So," he announced, "that was a bit awkward."

She stared at him as if he had suddenly sprouted two extra heads.

"Just to change the subject—" He cleared his throat. "—are we planning on following those other men you sent off? Because if we are, they're getting out of sight really quickly. Really quickly. In fact . . . Well, there they go."

"No," Rowan said firmly. "We're taking a slightly different route."

"Shouldn't we get under way, then?"

"Yes." She put her helmet back on and rode ahead without another word, the green plume trailing behind her.

Watching her, Maric wondered how it might have been for Rowan in a normal world. Fereldans were a rugged and practical people, and women who could hold their own in combat were respected as much as the men, but it was different among the nobility. Had it not been for the rebellion, the Arl would have had his daughter wearing fine dresses and learning the latest dances from the Orlesian court rather than helping to lead his army.

Rowan's family had made many sacrifices for the rebellion. Arl Rendorn had given up his beloved Redcliffe to the usurper. His wife, the Arlessa, had died from fever on the road, and he had sent his two younger sons, Eamon and Teagan, away to live with cousins in the far north. Who knew if the Arl's sons would even recognize him if they returned now?

They had given up a great deal to help Maric's mother. And now she was gone. This wasn't a normal world at all.

They rode into the hills, taking a route that Rowan was noticeably familiar with. Maric wondered just how often she had passed over this territory looking for him, and why she had bothered. He was his mother's heir, without question, but it must have seemed quite hopeless that anyone would chance across him out in the open after the first few days. They should have moved on without him.

The rocky terrain was difficult to ride through, and Maric was pleased that he managed to stay on his horse. They stopped only once when he realized that Loghain was still bleeding from the wounds in his chest left by the flail. Maric flagged down Rowan, and then practically had to wrestle Loghain off his horse so they could bandage him properly. Loghain, naturally, seemed more irritated than anything by the delay, causing Maric to wonder if *he* could take a flail to the chest delivered from horseback and still walk away to be stubborn about it. Probably not.

Eventually they started to see evidence of the rebel army's presence. They rode past several sentries who saluted Rowan before they recognized Maric and stared, mouths agape. Evidently the word had not quite gotten out.

It wasn't long before they got among the tents and into the heart of the camp, situated mostly in a small valley that almost completely hid it from sight. Maric's mother had loved the Hinterlands because it had so many valleys just like this one, so many spots for the army to take refuge in. They could access most of the northern lowlands quickly while still being able to retreat quickly. His mother had slowly built the army here from nothing to a force that had been the vexation of the Orlesians for more than a decade now.

Loghain looked around at the many tents they passed with some degree of surprise. It looked much like the outlaw camp had, to tell the truth, but on a larger scale. The tents were worn and dirty, as were most of the soldiers, and generally it was all that anyone could do to keep so many hundreds of men fed from day to day. The rebels were the product of years of recruitment from among the ranks of angry noblemen, men who had decided it was worth abandoning their own lands and taking what loyal followers and supplies they could to join an uncertain cause without much hope of compensation. Those who couldn't join sometimes offered food and shelter when they had it to spare, which wasn't often. Maric's mother had been reduced to begging more than once— Loghain had been right on that point, too.

As soon as the first cry of "It's the Prince!" went up, men and women started spilling out of the tents and surrounding their horses. Only a few at first, but after a short time they were mobbed. The soldiers surrounded them, joy showing on their filthy faces as many hands reached out toward Maric.

"The Prince!"

"He's alive! It's the Prince!"

A general cheer welled up from the crowd, a sound of relief and excitement. Some of the older men were actually crying—*crying*—and some of them were hugging and pounding their fists in the air. Rowan removed her helmet, and he saw there were tears in her eyes, as well. She reached over from her horse and raised Maric's hand, and the cheer escalated to a roar of approval.

They had loved his mother this much. It must have been devastating to lose the very reason most of them were here. Deeply moved, Maric realized that having him back among them was a victory, of sorts, like having a piece of Queen Moira back. He choked up at the thought of her.

Rowan squeezed his hand. She understood.

Loghain remained slightly behind them, looking pained and out of place. Maric turned and urged him forward. If anything, he was the main reason Maric had made it back to the army at all. Loghain shook his head, however, and remained where he was.

Thunderous footsteps resounded as a ten-foot-tall creature made of stone slowly lumbered toward the crowd from deeper in the camp. The cheering dimmed as some of the men respectfully got out of the creature's way, but most just accepted the creature for the common sight it was here.

Loghain stared at it in shock. "What is *that*?"

Maric chuckled, wiping his eyes. "Oh, that? That's just the golem, nothing to get excited about." He would have laughed at Loghain's incredulous look had the golem's owner not appeared and pushed through the crowd of soldiers. He was tall, but thin enough to appear gaunt and spindly as opposed to intimidating. If men scrambled to get out of his way, it was because of the bright robes marking him as a ranking Enchanter of the Circle of Magi.

"Prince Maric!" he called out, frowning with familiar impatience. The mage had served the Arl as a retainer and advisor for years now and had been on good terms with Maric's mother. He had always treated Maric himself as a recalcitrant student sorely in need of discipline, however, though this was not unusual. The mage was perpetually displeased, always frowning and looking down past his hawkish nose at others. Still, he was loyal and trustworthy. So Maric swallowed his distaste and nodded to the man as he approached.

"I found him, Wilhelm!" Rowan laughed.

"I can see that, my lady," the mage grumped. The cheering continued, but Wilhelm ignored it and turned to regard Maric with open suspicion. "Rather convenient timing, Prince Maric."

"Why do you say that?"

"First, let's see if you are who you claim." Wilhelm made subtle gestures with his hands, his intense gaze seeming to burrow into Maric's skull. Glowing embers swirled around him, brightening until the magic was evident to the entire crowd. The cheering skidded to a halt, and most of the men immediately near the spell backed up so quickly, many of them actually fell.

"Wilhelm!" From her horse, Rowan grabbed his wrist. "This is not necessary!"

"It is!" he snapped, wrenching his hand free. He finished casting, the words uttered just barely audibly under his breath, and Maric felt the magic wash over him. It was a tickle of pinpricks dancing upon his skin and behind his eyes. Loghain watched nervously from nearby but only worked to keep his horse calm.

Wilhelm then stood back, apparently satisfied by whatever his magic had discovered. "My apologies, Your Highness. I had to be sure."

"I think I would know Maric if I saw him, don't you?" Rowan said crisply.

"No, I'm not sure that you would." Wilhelm turned to face the quiet masses of soldiers that were now staring at him. "Men!" he called out. "You must prepare for battle! Your prince has returned to you! Now ready to defend him!" As if to punctuate his shouts, the stone golem fell into place directly behind him, scanning the crowd with its fearsome, baleful eyes.

The soldiers immediately burst into life, several commanders among them bellowing orders. Maric stared at the mage with growing alarm. "Why? What's going on?"

"Come, I'll let the Arl explain." The mage turned and briskly walked deeper into the camp, the golem lumbering after him.

Maric and Rowan exchanged a look and dismounted. A man ran up and took their horses. Loghain remained mounted, however, and looked down at Maric awkwardly. "Perhaps this is a good time for me to leave," he said.

"And go where, exactly?" Maric frowned up at Loghain, but Rowan took him by the arm and led him after the mage before he could receive an answer. He allowed himself to be taken away, but looked back as they walked. Loghain seemed vastly out of place sitting there as the man waited expectantly to take his horse. Maric almost felt sorry for him. Eventually Loghain sighed and dismounted, surrendering his horse before running to catch up.

The activity among the soldiers grew more intense as they went farther into the valley. Something was definitely amiss. Soldiers were falling into formation, tents were being torn down rapidly, everyone seemed to be running and shouting all at once. . . . It seemed to Maric to be controlled chaos, something he was not unused to. There was an edge of panic to it all that he didn't like, however. He had seen his mother's army scramble many times to flee before an attack by the usurper's forces—this had that feeling to it.

At the center of all the activity he saw Arl Rendorn, Rowan's father. He was hard to miss in his silverite plate mail, a gift from Maric's mother to her most trusted friend and general many years before. Silver-haired and distinguished, the Arl was the very picture of nobility, and Maric found himself feeling more than a little relieved to see him. The man was giving orders to the soldiers around him with quick, efficient precision. The orders never needed repeating, and were obeyed without question.

Wilhelm waved to the Arl, though it was hardly necessary, as the stone giant behind him drew notice from almost everyone. The Arl turned, and upon seeing Maric he strode forward through several ranks of men to greet him with a wide and happy grin.

"Maric!" he shouted, clapping Maric on the shoulder. "It is you!"

"That's what everyone keeps telling me." Maric grinned.

"Maker be praised!" His eyes grew sad for a moment. "Your mother would be proud to see that you survived. Well done, lad."

"I told you I would find him, Father," Rowan said.

The Arl regarded his daughter with a look that was both impressed and eternally frustrated. "So you did, so you did. I should never have doubted you, pup." He turned then and barked several sharp orders to his immediate lieutenants, who were staring at Maric dumbly. Now, they snapped to attention and took over whatever preparations had been under way.

"Come," the Arl said, "let us move inside. Whatever tale you have will need to wait. You've come at an awkward moment, truth be told, and not a minute too soon." He stepped to the large red tent immediately behind him and held open the flap. Wilhelm brushed inside imperiously, as if the honor should have been his to begin with. Truly, Maric had never understood why Rendorn put up with such behavior from a man who was technically a retainer, hired from the Circle of Magi. The Arl, however, appeared to be more amused than offended by Wilhelm's antics.

That amusement disappeared instantly, however, when he saw Loghain approach. He put up a hand to stop Loghain from entering the tent. "Hold now, who's this?"

Loghain paused, regarding the Arl's hand with a raised brow. "It's Loghain," he said. "Loghain Mac Tir."

"He came with me," Maric offered helpfully.

The Arl narrowed his eyes suspiciously. "I've never heard of you. Or your family."

"There's no reason you should." The two men locked eyes, bristling. Maric stepped forward between the two, putting up his hands to halt any imminent escalation.

"Loghain helped me," Maric told Rendorn, keeping his tone restrained. "He's the reason I'm here, Your Grace. If it hadn't been for him and his father, I . . . well, I probably wouldn't have made it at all."

Arl Rendorn paused, digesting this before nodding to Loghain. "If that's true, then it's greatly appreciated. You've done a great service, and I'll see to it you're rewarded."

"I'm not interested in any reward."

"As you wish." With a frown, the Arl turned to Maric. "I need to speak with you, lad, and it's not a discussion to be held in front of any commoners—especially men we don't know." He bowed politely to Loghain. "No offense, ser."

"None taken," Loghain growled.

Rendorn turned to enter the tent, considering the matter closed, but Maric interposed himself in front of him. "He's *not* a commoner!"

The Arl looked startled by Maric's vehemence. So did Rowan, who quietly raised her eyebrows from a step away. Even Loghain looked at Maric as if he might have been slightly mad. "He's the son of a knight," Maric insisted. "A man who died in my service. He's also saved my life more than once, and I will see him treated accordingly."

Rowan's father glowered at Maric, the moment thick with tension. He turned an appraising eye toward Loghain, who looked like he felt compelled to speak but wasn't sure quite what to say. Instead, he met the Arl's stare with a simple shrug and the slightest hint of an insolent grin.

"Fine," Rendorn snapped. "I've no time to argue." He held the flap open and let Loghain and the others through, then followed them inside. The golem stood silent guard beside the entrance.

The tent's interior was dominated by the worn table around which Maric's mother had gathered the Arl and her other commanders. Significantly, the large chair she had occupied for as long as Maric could remember stood vacant. He tried not to stare at it.

"The usurper's men are marching on us as we speak," Arl Rendorn announced as soon as the tent flap was closed. They did not sit down. "Our situation is desperate. They know where we are and managed to almost surround us before we became aware of their approach."

"Magic." Wilhelm's hawklike face twisted into a disapproving scowl. "The usurper has gone to great lengths to plan this attack."

"Plan?" Rowan frowned. "But how could he have known we would still be here? You would already have left if I hadn't insisted we look for Maric."

The Arl shrugged. "Perhaps they expected us to do just that. Or perhaps someone told them we intended to remain where we were."

"There's no shortage of Fereldans willing to sell us out," Maric sighed. "That's what got my mother killed, after all."

"There is a plan," the Arl stated. "Now that you're here, lad, we have hope. All is not lost. They haven't surrounded us completely. If we leave now, take only a small number of men with us, and use Wilhelm's magic to our advantage, we can slip out of this noose before it tightens."

"And what of the army?" Maric asked.

Rowan nodded gravely, already in agreement with her father. "It's lost." She put her hand on Maric's shoulder. "It's already lost. It's you we need to get out, Maric. The royal line rests with you."

"No! We can't abandon the army! That's madness!"

"We can rebuild the army again, just as your mother did," the Arl sighed heavily. "The fact that Rowan found you just in time is a sign from the Maker. We need to take you away from here before it is too late."

"No!" Maric paced angrily, staring at Rowan and her father in outrage. "I can't believe what I'm hearing! I didn't come here just to lose my mother's entire army! We have to do something!"

"There's nothing to be done, lad," the Arl said gently. "We've got two groups bearing down on us, one from the north and a larger force coming through the forest in the east. They've got us cornered. If we try to withdraw, they'll be on our flank. There's no way."

"No," Maric repeated. "We fight!"

"That is the fool's path," Wilhelm sneered.

Rowan walked gingerly toward Maric, shaking her head sadly. "Maric, there's no point in fighting. You would just die!"

"Then I die." His voice was firm.

The Arl waved his hand dismissively. "No. I understand that you're trying to be brave, lad. But this is the time for discretion."

Maric set his jaw. "And I understand what you're getting at, Your Grace, but that's not your decision."

Arl Rendorn turned now, regarding Maric with growing rage. "Not my decision? I lead this army!"

"My army," Maric insisted. "Or don't you follow your king?"

"I don't see a king here." The Arl seethed. "I see a boy who's trying to be brave! Queen Moira would have understood. She would have left these men, if she had to, for the rebellion to live on!"

"She's dead!" Maric slammed his fist down on the table, hard. "And I would rather die beside these men than abandon them to save my own skin! I won't do it!"

"Don't be stubborn! There's no point in fighting just to lose!"

"Then win," Loghain suddenly blurted out.

His interruption was unexpected enough that even Arl Rendorn stared in surprise. Rowan arched a brow curiously as Loghain came forward, his expression annoyed. "Don't stay and lose," he repeated. "Stay and win."

Rowan held out her hands helplessly. "We can't. It isn't that simple!"

"Why?" Loghain frowned at her. "Because he told you so?"

The Arl stiffened. "I know what I'm talking about."

"I don't doubt it." Loghain crossed his arms, watching the Arl. "But my father stayed one step ahead of people like you for years by doing the unexpected."

"And I understand your father is dead."

"Our camp was surrounded, just like your army. If we'd had half the warning you have, had half the equipment, had any of the magic, my father would have seen us through it!" His tone was iron-hard. "I know it."

The Arl shook his head. "No, you're wrong."

"You have advantages you don't even know about. Trust me, you can win."

Maric took a step toward Loghain, hope creeping across his face. "Do you have an idea?"

Loghain paused, his eyes darting uncertainly among Arl Rendorn, Rowan, and Maric, as if he'd just realized they all were, in fact, paying attention to him. For a moment it seemed he might back down, but then Maric saw it in those icy blue eyes: resolve.

"Yes." Loghain nodded. "I do."

5

Loghain glanced uncomfortably at the knights who had been assigned to his command, once again wondering just how he had allowed himself to end up here. Thirty mounted men in heavy plate armor, each with more combat experience in the last year than he had in his life, and he was supposed to lead them?

It served him right for suggesting a plan in the first place. If he had been smart, he would have kept his fool mouth shut after that and been on his way. But the more Loghain had listened to Arl Rendorn and Maric argue about who would play the most important role in the plan, the more irritated he had become. Finally he'd thrown his hands up in disgust and volunteered to play the role himself, if only to get the two of them to stop arguing.

Maric thought the idea a brilliant one. That really

should have told Loghain right then that the whole enterprise was doomed to failure.

Even so, there he was, ready to play his part. Loghain wore a fine linen shirt, shining boots, and a helmet to hide his black hair. His heavy purple cloak had once belonged to the Rebel Queen, a signature garment he felt awkward wearing. The leathers he wore were lined with black velvet and almost too tight to wear, but they were the only trousers Maric owned that would fit. He had never worn such expensive, impractical clothing in his life, but it was necessary.

Loghain and the knights kept their horses calm, staying in the middle of a shallow stream as they waited for the enemy to arrive. The scouts Arl Rendorn had sent out reported the bulk of the force approaching from the east would come this way, and that they would see the enemy coming out of the trees along the stream's bank. Loghain planned to make them believe they saw Prince Maric fleeing his army escorted by a small unit of his fastest and most heavily armed knights. To pass as Maric, Loghain figured he just needed to look important from a distance. With any luck, the enemy would see the purple cloak and his finery and assume that Arl Rendorn was doing exactly what he had intended to do: send Maric to safety.

So, Loghain's job was to draw the eastern part of the attacking army away. Then the bulk of the rebel army would be able to deal with the northern attackers without also getting attacked from behind.

And after that? Well, Loghain hoped they would be in a position to come to his rescue. Because he would need one, without question. And that was assuming everything went according to plan, which, as his father had always said, was unheard of in any battle. *How did I end up here?* he asked himself. The truth was that he had no good answer.

It was quiet except for the gentle burbling of the stream as it flowed past and the occasional nervous nickering of one of the horses. A breeze rustled the nearby trees gently, and Loghain breathed deeply, taking in the smell of pine and fresh water. He felt oddly at peace. The imminent battle seemed very far away indeed.

Some of the knights kept glancing his way, their uncertainty about him noticeable despite their efforts to keep it hidden. They had to wonder who he was, Loghain thought. There had been little time for introductions, barely any chance to explain what was in store. The Arl had called for volunteers from among his most experienced men, and here they were. Volunteers, they were told, because the chances that none of them might make it back were quite high.

Why did he think this was a good plan, exactly?

One of the knights leaned toward him, an older fellow with a bushy gray mustache showing inside his helmet. "This place we're to ride to," he asked quietly, "do you know of it, Ser Loghain?"

"No need for the title. It's just Loghain."

The knight seemed surprised. "But . . . His Grace said that your father—"

"I suppose he was. I, however, am not." Loghain looked at the man curiously. "Does that bother you? Being led by a commoner?"

The knight glanced at several of his fellows who

had been listening to their exchange. He looked back at Loghain, shaking his head firmly. "If this plan will truly see Prince Maric safe," he stated, "then I would gladly follow my own enemy into battle. I will give my life, if need be."

"As would I," said another, much younger knight. Others nodded their assent.

Loghain looked around at them, marveling at their determination. Perhaps their chances were not so bad, after all. "I have been through this area once before," he told them. "Down this stream to the south, across the ridge and a plain, there is a bluff—a cliff with a broad and sharp face. It has a single narrow path leading up its side."

"I know of it," one of the men called out.

"When we get there, we ride up that path as fast as possible. There is a flat area up there that is defensible. If we can defend the path, we can hold it."

"But," the same man said uncertainly, "the rocks behind it are too steep. There's no way out of there."

Loghain nodded. "No, there isn't."

He let that sink in. Loghain was guessing the enemy would want what they thought was the Prince badly enough that they wouldn't just give up and ride back to attack the rest of the rebel force. So he and the Arl's volunteers had to make this look good. Gradually, the murmuring among the men quieted and they returned to waiting for the enemy to show their faces. There was nothing else they could do, after all.

Fortunately, it didn't take long.

When the first soldier poked his face out of the trees, Loghain unleashed an arrow. He hit the man in the shoulder when he could just as easily have taken him in the throat, since he wanted the man to run and panic—and he did.

More soldiers followed within moments. Many of the knights around Loghain were armed as he was, and the twang of bowstrings was followed by men shouting in pain and falling. The horses stomped nervously in the water, backing away from the bank.

Now the counterattack began as the enemy realized what was awaiting them. Rather than charging blindly out of the trees onto the bank, they began assembling just inside cover. The din of many feet and shouts resounded through the forest like an approaching storm. As arrows drilled through the air toward them, the knights raised their shields against the angry torrent.

"Your Highness," one of the knights bellowed loudly toward Loghain, "we need to get you to safety!"

"Protect the Prince!" another shouted.

"South!" Loghain raised his sword up high. "Follow me!" With that he turned and sped his horse to the south, splashing water loudly as the other knights followed suit. Even above it all, however, Loghain heard cries from the enemy of "It's the Prince!" and louder cries of "After them!"

More arrows streaked by, a hornet's swarm of angry projectiles that began to come faster and faster as Loghain and the knights raced down the stream. The purple cloak billowed in his wake. One of the men directly behind him shouted out in pain and fell from his horse, splashing awkwardly into the stream. Racing for their lives, the other knights could do nothing but leap over him or go around.

The water was just high enough to slow them. They didn't want to go too fast—they *wanted* the enemy to see them and pursue, after all—but the arrows were coming in too great a volume. The sound of the mass of men behind them was growing too quickly. What if the scouts' estimates had been wrong? "Faster!" Loghain cried.

Another man fell, screaming, as they reached the ridge. Here the stream turned and a steep embankment had formed. Loghain raced up the side, urging his horse to greater exertions as an arrow sang by his ear. For a moment his mount struggled and slowed jarringly on the way up the ridge, and then almost painfully reached the top and leaped forward.

"Follow me!" Loghain shouted to the men behind him.

Like a wave crashing against a wall, they surged up the side of the ridge. The water churned under their hooves as the horses struggled, and not far behind them the enemy spilled out of the forest and into the stream in hot pursuit. They had no riders of their own, thankfully, but they were hardly slow. Now that they were in the open, they could move more rapidly.

Whipping his horse almost until it bled, Loghain led the charge across the open plain. The bluff was in sight, a long cliff along the edge of the rockier hills that marked the southern tip of the valley. He saw the path they needed, as well, and at the same time spotted a group of enemy soldiers coming out of the trees ahead. They were scouts, he assumed, or were part of the enemy's broader lines. They were in heavy leathers and moderately armed, and spun about to face the approaching line.

Well, Loghain thought, *if they truly intend to stand in the way of charging horses, best give them what they deserve.* He let out a cry of attack, raising his blade once again, and sped directly toward the enemy. The knights responded to his cry and followed.

There was a thunder of hooves and war cries as they landed with full force upon the soldiers. For a moment it seemed to Loghain as if time moved at a crawl. He watched the horror dawning on their faces, saw how some of them in the back scrambled too late to get back into the trees. He saw his own horse crush one of them underfoot, an unfortunate man who went down without a single word. A sword slash opened the throat of a soldier to his right, before the man could swing his own blade, and blood fountained out.

And then everything was moving fast again. Men screamed in pain, bones crunched, and steel rang on steel. Loghain struck at several men with his blade, but all too quickly, he was past and riding onward to the path. The rest of his men were busy overriding the enemy behind him; he didn't even need to look to know it was so.

It felt good, though it didn't negate the fact that the army hot on their tails was a great deal larger than anyone could have expected.

Within moments they were on the path, racing up the side of the cliff. At several points the path was wide enough for only two horses galloping side by side. Any more, and they risked someone sliding off and falling to the rocks below.

"Come on!" he urged.

More arrows shot by him as they reached the top of the bluff. He spun his horse around, and for the first time saw exactly what was behind them. The remainder of his thirty men was hot on his heels, and not far behind them were well over two hundred soldiers, charging madly across the field. They filled his field of vision, making his heart race with fear. Off their horses, cornered here on the bluff, they were massively outnumbered and could be pegged off by the archers at a distance.

"Get under cover!" he shouted, quickly sliding off his horse. There were large rocks up on the ridge, which they fell behind.

The flights of arrows halted as the commanders below ordered the archers to stop. There was no point while the knights were out of sight. Loghain couldn't hear what their next commands were, but he could guess. They were preparing to rush the path up to the bluff, using their arrows to keep the knights under cover as long as they could. They would suffer losses, certainly, but eventually they would break through. They had the numbers.

The knight nearest to Loghain looked over at him, breathing heavily with exertion. There was fear in the man's eyes. "Are they going to come up here?" he shouted.

Loghain nodded. "We have what they want. Or they think we do."

"Then what do we do now?"

He tightened the grip on his sword. "We fight."

Inwardly he hoped that whatever the rest of Maric's army did, they came quickly. That was the plan, after all, and so far it had worked. Which made

Loghain all the more nervous as he heard the first cries ring out from below and readied himself for their charge.

When the smaller enemy force entered the valley from the north, its commanders—Fereldan noblemen who were serving their king, Orlesian though he might be—they had expected to find a rebel force in disarray, possibly in the midst of a full rout.

Instead, they found themselves under assault by the bulk of the rebel force. Magical balls of fire landed in their midst, the explosions sending them scattering. Immediately afterwards, a giant stone golem was the first to reach their line, great fists swinging and sending men flying into the air. Rebel infantry followed immediately thereafter, shouting their war cry and charging into the line.

Maric was with that infantry, but well enough behind the front line that he wasn't face-to-face with the enemy. Rowan watched him from farther up the hill, her own mounted troops pawing impatiently to enter the fight. Her father had told her to wait, hidden in the trees, until Maric's force was well and truly engaged before she rode in to attack from the flank. Their only chance was to hit the enemy fast and hard, and hopefully to scatter them in time to reach Loghain. If they could catch the enemy at the bluff, they could smash them against the cliffs—they would be caught, unable to rout.

It was a long shot. The worry that had lined her father's face as he agreed to the plan told her that much. But if the plan had been impossible, he would sooner have clubbed Maric over the head and dragged him off personally than agreed to it.

She could see Maric shouting orders to the men, urging them forward. He was trying to push through to the front, attempting to join the fight. The men immediately around him pressed close, however, forming a circle. Father would have told them to do that, she assumed. Even though Maric was wearing a helmet, she could tell he was becoming frustrated as he realized what the soldiers were doing.

More magic crackled in the air as a blizzard formed around a large part of the enemy forces. They were beginning to retreat back out of the valley and re-group, their commanders becoming frantic, but the ice that was magically forming on the ground beneath their feet was making that difficult.

One of the enemy commanders started shouting loudly and pointing at Wilhelm, who was standing on a rock not far beyond Maric's men. The mage's yellow robes unfortunately made him stand out, as did his exposed position. He needed to see his targets, however, and his range was limited. As arrows began to fly in his direction, he was forced to jump off his rock, his angry swearing so loud, even Rowan could hear it from where she stood. A wave of Wilhelm's hand sent the stone golem ponderously charging toward the archers, its fists swinging. That would definitely keep them distracted.

It would be close. Rowan couldn't see just how many men there were here, but she figured it likely they had at least as many as the rebels did. As soon as they dug in and began to fight back, their offense would be ground to a standstill.

Her warhorse whinnied nervously and she patted its head, shushing it gently.

One of the riders nearby looked to her, apprehensive. "When do we charge, my lady? If they back out of the valley, we'll never flank them."

"They won't back out completely," she assured him. "But we have to wait."

Still, she shared the anxiety. Already she could see signs of the enemy reorganizing and struggling to outflank Maric's men by racing into the valley proper. Many of them were urged on, in fact, by their desperation to get away from the rage of the golem's fists. It was going much as her father had forecast, but there were more men than the scouts had reported. That meant this would take longer. Even if they were able to defeat this part of the usurper's forces, what would become of Loghain?

Picking up the reins, she rode over to where her own lieutenant was waiting. A stout woman by the name of Branwen, the lieutenant was one of the few other women who served with the rebels as a soldier. Rowan knew that many of the men who didn't know either of them well believed she had promoted Branwen for that reason only, but it wasn't so. The lieutenant was strong and determined, perhaps because she had more to prove. Rowan knew exactly what that was like.

"Lieutenant," she called, "I need to speak to the Arl."

Branwen nodded solemnly. "Any orders, my lady?"

"If I'm not back within twenty minutes, charge the flank as planned." Rowan smiled grimly. "I'll trust your judgment on everything else."

Branwen blinked with surprise and her lips thinned,

but she otherwise took the unusual order without comment. "Understood, my lady."

Rowan spun her horse about and raced out of the trees and down into the valley. She tried to pay little attention to the battle that was still going on, though she did notice that Maric had at last gotten his wish: the circle of men around him had been spread out by the melee, meaning Maric could engage. Rowan worried about that, but not as much as her father would have. He had wanted to keep Maric out of the fight completely. Rowan knew that Maric was well-armored and a much better swordsman than he would ever admit to. One of the reasons she had worked so hard, after all, was to gain his respect.

Her father's men were waiting on the opposite side of the valley, and it took several minutes of hard riding to reach him. She splashed across the wide but shallow part of the stream, and when she came up the other bank, her father's men were already running out to intercept her. Her father was brought out a moment later, riding on his own dark stallion, and looking more than a little concerned by the interruption.

"What is it?" he asked. "You should be with the horsemen."

"There's more men here than we thought, Father. That means that there might have been more coming from the east, as well. We need to help Loghain."

Her father grimaced. Sunlight glinted brightly off his silverite armor as he turned back to the soldiers standing just a few feet away. "Go"—he waved to them—"I wish to be alone for a moment."

His men hesitated momentarily, confused, but did not question the order. They left.

He slowly turned back to her, white brows furrowed with concern. Rowan couldn't tell exactly what he was going to say, but she already understood what he was thinking. She felt her fury rising. "I can see the same things you do," he began. "And I agree. It will be difficult enough to defeat the usurper's men here in the north."

"But . . . ?"

He held up a hand. "Maric's friend has done his job. We've yet to see any of the eastern force coming through the valley. He's drawn them all off, and that gives us time to do what we must."

"Which is?" she snapped.

"Which is," he stated with force, "saving Maric as well as this army." The Arl stepped closer to Rowan and put his hand on her shoulder. His expression was grim. "Rowan . . . the moment we drive these men into any kind of retreat, we need to flee the valley with whatever we have left. It is our only chance."

"Loghain is expecting us to reinforce him."

"He is expendable." The Arl said the word with unease, but said it even so.

Rowan stepped away from her father, frowning deeply. What he said wasn't entirely a surprise, and yet still she felt disappointed. "We gave our word," she protested. "He gave us the plan that is giving you your chance, and you're going to abandon him?"

"The part he is playing in his own plan," her father sighed, "is that of the sacrificial lamb. Perhaps he didn't realize it, but there it is." He took hold of her gauntleted hand firmly, looking her straight in the eyes. "It's a good plan. We must not waste it, for Ferelden's sake."

She pulled her hand away and turned from her father, but didn't leave. He patted her on the shoulder again. "There are things we must do, things that must be done. To survive. Queen Moira did them, and so shall her son. This Loghain is doing a service, as are the men with him."

She nodded slowly, grimacing. The Arl's hand lingered on her shoulder a moment longer, but whatever else was on his mind he kept it to himself. "Go, then," he finally said. "There isn't much time."

She didn't look back.

When Rowan rejoined her own forces on the other side of the valley, she saw they were already preparing to ride. Her lieutenant rode toward her, flagging her down. "We were just about to charge," Branwen informed her. "Did you want us to hold off, my lady?"

"What's the situation?"

"The Prince seems to be doing well enough so far. He stopped the enemy from encircling him. The wizard is almost an army unto himself." Her attention was then drawn as the sound of horns signaled from down in the valley. Two of the watchmen nearby waved to her, and she nodded an acknowledgment to them. "The Arl is engaging now, my lady."

Rowan did not answer right away. The green plume on her helm fluttered in the breeze as she stared hard at the ground from atop her horse. The sounds of many men shouting and screaming could be faintly heard in the distance. Any of them could be Maric, she thought.

"My lady?" her lieutenant asked hesitantly.

"No," Rowan stated. She looked up and spun her

horse about. "We are reinforcing the bluff now, before it's too late."

"But my lady! What about the Prince?"

Rowan began to ride forward, her expression firm. "The Maker will watch over him," she muttered solemnly. Then, louder to address the startled riders assembled behind her: "All of you! Follow me! We ride south!" Without waiting for a response, she kicked her warhorse into a gallop and began to head into the valley.

The enemy was on their third charge up the path.

Loghain was soaked in sweat and blood both, a burning, fiery pain in his chest from where a blade had successfully stabbed earlier. He ignored it and fought on. Seven were left of the thirty knights that had ridden up the path with him, and they stood their ground at the top of the bluff as wave after wave of the enemy soldiers tried to break through. These were Fereldan soldiers they were fighting, urged on by Orlesian commanders who remained safely below. *Sending their dogs to do their dirty work*, he thought angrily.

The enemy had brought halberds this time, wicked axe blades attached to long poles that gave them the advantage of reach. He had lost almost ten men immediately to the first rush of the halberdiers as they reached the top of the path and had nearly overtaken them. One man lost his arm as it was hacked off, blood spurting as the man stared at it, aghast.

"Push them back!" Loghain shouted.

An enemy soldier leaped on him, half to attack

and half because he had been shoved forward from behind. Startled, Loghain was pushed back for a moment. The soldier, a short man with a weasel-like face, looked excited at the thought he might have struck a blow at the mighty prince and moved to strike again.

Loghain grabbed the man by the throat and threw him back. The short soldier stumbled, and his flailing hands caught onto the royal purple cloak—which by now had been stained a sticky black by blood and filth. He fell to the side, tugging hard on the cloak, and Loghain slashed with his sword to cut the fabric. Released, the soldier stumbled back even farther and went careening over the cliff edge, screaming shrilly.

Another man was on top of Loghain before he could recover, a large man with a robust red beard. And then a second charged him, axe held high overhead. Loghain ducked down low and spun around, swinging a wide arc with his sword. It took the axe-wielder across the abdomen, slicing him open. As the man stumbled, Loghain struck out with his elbow and took the red-bearded soldier in the throat. It didn't stop him from stabbing Loghain in the shoulder, but Loghain merely hissed in pain and jumped back, forcing the blade to be pulled out of him

He struck out with his sword again, and the red-bearded man barely parried as he gasped and coughed. They traded several blows, Loghain gaining greater strength and position with each one until finally he ran the man through.

The few knights with him were barely holding on, and yet still the enemy pressed forward. Loghain almost couldn't see with the sweat stinging his eyes, and the gore covering the ground at the lip of the path made getting one's footing on the rocks difficult.

Where is the damned reinforcement? he thought, striking out at new enemies as they pressed forward. Even as he asked the question he knew the answer. They weren't coming. It didn't make sense for them to come. In fact, if he was in the Arl's shoes right now, he wouldn't come, either.

He grunted angrily and slashed even harder, trying to keep the enemy from getting past their line. Another man rushed him and he got his boot up onto the man's midsection and then kicked out, sending the man flying back and over the cliff edge with a horrified cry.

And then a horn sounded.

Loghain wiped his eyes and looked down the cliff, then began laughing out loud in sheer surprise. The thundering of hooves heralded the charge of the rest of the rebel's force of horsemen as they struck the larger enemy force from behind. The armored figure leading the charge could only be Rowan, the green plume atop her helmet trailing.

The effect on the enemy was dramatic. The Orlesians were pushed back toward the cliff, their shouts turning to confusion and surprise. Almost immediately their organization broke. Panic overtook the foot soldiers, and they began to scramble and run, even as the commanders screamed ineffectually for them to hold.

Loghain had no more time to watch as the enemies still on the path became desperate. Caught between the crush of men trying to run up behind them to escape the cavalry charge and Loghain's remaining men, their fearful cries became deafening.

"Now! Do it! Push them back!" he shouted. Six knights stood next to him, their armor smeared with gore and all of them heavily wounded, but they gritted their teeth and did as he commanded. They pressed their advantage and began swinging hard to drive the enemy back.

There was a long moment of frenzied resistance as steel met steel, and then the enemy line broke. With a victorious shout, Loghain moved forward and stabbed his blade into two men who scrabbled backwards while screaming for mercy. The knights beside him did the same, and as the enemy fell back, they ran out of ground and forced a whole group of their own soldiers off the cliff.

There was mass panic below. The enemy was racing to get out of the way of the horsemen, dashing into the forest at the edges of the valley. Some even dropped their weapons in their rush. One of the Orlesian commanders screamed at his men with indignation, attempting to lead a rally, but Rowan put a quick end to that. A pair of hooves cut the pompous fellow off in midshout, sending his body flying against the rocks and galvanizing the nearest enemy soldiers into even quicker retreat.

Calling to several of her men to follow her, Rowan turned and raced up the path toward Loghain.

Encouraged by the sight, Loghain urged his knights to continue pushing—and they did. They were shoving forward now, sweeping the line of enemy soldiers before them off the edge of the path like so much debris off the front steps. The bloodcurdling screams as those men were sent falling to their deaths were difficult to bear.

And then they stood at the edge, Loghain and his

six men. They stared down at the carnage below, the many men lying broken at the bottom of a hundred-foot drop. Like dolls scattered by an angry child, Loghain thought grimly.

The few soldiers left on the path were now leaping off the side to get out of the way of Rowan and the several horsemen charging with her up the path. Those that stood their ground were cut down mercilessly. One of them was a lone, quaking halberdier who leveled his weapon toward the horse racing at him. Rowan pulled her horse to one side at the last moment and efficiently sliced her blade deep into the man's neck as she rode past. He went down without so much as a blink.

When Rowan reached the top of the path, she slid off her horse in one smooth motion and ran toward Loghain, lifting up her helmet. Brown hair spilled around her face as she took in the sight of the small number of wounded, haggard men standing there with him. They all stared back at her dumbly, numb with exhaustion and the fading remnants of adrenaline.

"Are you . . . all right?" she asked uncertainly, her expression concerned.

Loghain walked toward her and held out his hand. Rowan hesitated, staring at him as if she wasn't sure what it meant before she relaxed and shook it.

"That was quite the charge," he congratulated her. Their eyes met, lingering a moment longer than was necessary. Rowan quickly disengaged her hand and glanced away.

"I can't believe you lasted this long. I wish I'd come sooner." She nodded officiously to the other men behind Loghain, several of whom had dropped to their knees. "Well done, all of you."

"It's not over yet," he sighed. Already he could see the enemy recovering below. The charge had spooked them and taken a toll on their forces, but it wouldn't be long before the Orlesians would recover from the shock. They still had the superior numbers, after all, and if they realized it quickly enough, they could race back into the clearing and surround Rowan's men. They needed to get out—now.

Rowan was nodding, understanding the situation exactly as he did, he realized. Loghain found himself hardly surprised. "Maric will need us. Let's go while we still can."

Maric panted at the edge of the battle during a few rare seconds he could even breathe in the chaos, ears ringing with the sound of steel on steel. His sword arm ached so badly, he thought it might just fall off. He also suddenly noticed an arrow sticking out of his shoulder, the shaft having penetrated between the grooves of his fine armor. *Well, that would explain the jabbing pain I felt earlier*, he thought to himself.

The ebb and flow of the melee seemed to go on forever. He had lost the ability to judge what was actually going on with the overall battle once Arl Rendorn had charged the line. It had become his only concern just to survive, facing an endless array of opponents that charged at him from every direction.

So far, he remained alive despite it all. The heavy dwarven armor he wore had repelled dozens of strikes without so much as a dent. Far too many rebels had been killed before Maric's eyes, trying to buy their prince a few more moments of life. Even with all this protection, his sword dripped with the blood of men who would surely have killed him, if Maric hadn't been a second faster than they. And then, of course, there was the blind luck.

At one point he had been barrelled over by a giant of a man in chain armor, and when Maric had rolled over, he'd seen a great axe ready to come down right on top of his head. None of his protectors had been near enough to help. All that had saved him was an errant gauntlet flung from some unknown soldier nearby, probably by accident, which struck the giant in the back of the head and knocked him off balance. The axe came down just shy of Maric's ear. His breath had steamed on the metal of the axe-head buried in the ground not an inch away from the tip of his nose.

The giant soldier yanked the axe back up, but this time Wilhelm had intervened. An arc of lightning streaked across the battlefield and left a gaping, smoking hole in the fellow's chest. Maric had at least enough sense to roll out of the way before the man toppled over like a falling building.

Evidently, Maric's time on Thedas was not quite up yet.

He gritted his teeth against the pain in his shoulder and cast an eye over the battlefield. The first thing he wondered was what had happened to Rowan. He couldn't see the green of her helmet, either racing across the field or lying on it. Nor were there any horsemen in the battle. How long had they been fighting? Was the bulk of the enemy force about to fall on them from the south?

He found himself worrying about Loghain most of all and the possibility that he might have asked the man to commit himself to a useless sacrifice. If Gareth's son died trying to keep him alive, as well . . .

And then the horn sounded. Belatedly, to be sure, but it still had the desired effect. In the distance he could see Rowan's horsemen charging into the enemy line, scattering them in every direction.

It proved to be enough. Over the next ten minutes, desperation surged among the soldiers on both sides. Maric could hear the Arl shouting to the men, urging them to press toward the hill, and Maric began to do the same. Blood was spilling rapidly as casualties mounted, but as the horsemen took their toll, the enemy began to pull back. The enemy commanders ordered a retreat, shouting for their men to regroup outside the valley.

Maric was almost tempted to give chase as he watched the enemy soldiers scrambling to get away, but Arl Rendorn's arrival prevented him. "Let them go! We must make a run for it!" he shouted. The man was clutching his chest and bleeding heavily as he was supported by two others. Seeing this, Maric merely nodded and began calling for the men to fall back.

It was not a victory.

In the end, after hours of confusion and running as the rebel army retreated out of the valley, they managed to regroup at the edge of a small river several miles to the north. The men arrived in dribs and drabs, exhausted and wounded and sometimes carrying each other. Men on horses were sent out to look for others who had fled in different directions, but in the end it looked as if they had lost at least half their numbers. On top of this, much of their supplies and equipment had been left in the valley out of necessity.

But it felt like a victory to Maric. Instead of losing everything that his mother had built, they had survived. They had evaded the usurper's trap and even dealt him a bloody nose on the way out. As sore as their condition was, the usurper's forces would not be so quick to be on their trail. Not tonight, and that was all the rebels needed.

When Rowan finally brought a bruised and bloodied Loghain to the fire at their new tent, still wearing fancy leathers and the soiled, tattered remains of the Queen's purple cloak, Maric cried out with glee and ran forward to sweep up the startled Loghain in a great bear hug. Loghain winced in pain but tolerated the display, staring down at Maric as if he had gone mad.

"It worked!" Maric cried. "Your plan bloody well worked!"

"Enough," Loghain griped, shoving Maric away so that he was quickly dropped.

"Have a care, Maric," Rowan chided him with amusement. "Loghain's taken several wounds to his chest."

"Bah! He's invulnerable!" Maric laughed, and then danced away exuberantly. He circled the fire like some kind of barbarian shaman performing a strange victory ritual, all the while laughing maniacally.

Loghain watched him, mystified, and then looked incredulously toward Rowan. "He does this often?"

"I'm thinking he may have taken a blow to the head."

Arl Rendorn walked up then, now out of his armor and sporting thick bandages around his midsection, the cloth already darkening with bloodstains. One of his eyes was likewise bandaged, and he limped heavily. His expression was angry enough to draw notice, and when Rowan went to offer him support, he waved her off with a glower. "Apparently," he stated with muted rage, "you have decided that my orders do not need to be followed."

Maric detected the tension and stopped his wild careening, turning to address the Arl. "Your Grace? Is something amiss?"

"Plenty. As she well knows."

Rowan nodded soberly, accepting the recrimination. "I know you are angry, Father—" She held up a hand to stave off any further outburst from him. "—but I did what needed to be done. Had I not routed them, at least for a time, they might have marched north once Loghain was slain."

"She also killed one of the Orlesian commanders," Loghain pointed out. "Quite spectacularly."

"We might have been away by then," the Arl snapped. Then he looked at Loghain and softened somewhat. "But . . . it is good that you live, lad. And your plan did succeed." From Loghain, he turned toward Maric, frowning. "I would be happier, however, if our condition were not so poor. We have lost a great number of men and much equipment. Moving forward will be difficult."

Maric walked over to Rendorn and put a comforting hand on the Arl's shoulder, grin remaining even if his enthusiasm was diminished. "I agree, but still I think there is much to celebrate. The rebellion drew blood, and lives on."

Arl Rendorn attempted a wan smile. "Your mother," he began, voice thick with emotion, "would have been very proud to see you today, my boy."

Maric was startled at both the display of emotion and the tears he fought in his own eyes as he and Arl Rendorn hugged roughly. Backs were clapped fondly, and when Maric stepped away, he could only nod awkwardly to the Arl in the silence.

Maric turned then to Loghain, who had taken a seat by the fire. He held out a hand, and Loghain slowly shook it. "Thank you for everything you did today, Loghain. I do hope you'll consider staying with us."

"You should have seen him up on that bluff," Rowan said. "He was magnificent. The knights that fought with him are already talking about it."

Loghain smiled, a bit shyly. Maric wondered if it was, in fact, the first time he had actually seen the man smile. "It was a difficult situation, and we did what we had to." He then looked up at Maric almost apologetically, holding up what remained of the purple cloak. "I, ah, also ruined your mother's cloak."

Maric laughed, and Rowan joined in. "You're being modest," she teased.

"Indeed." The Arl limped up to Loghain and shook his hand as well. "I misjudged you. You clearly have excellent instincts, and we could use your assistance."

Loghain's blue eyes shifted among the Arl and Maric and Rowan, and for a moment Maric thought he looked almost trapped. He glanced down at the fire and stared at it for a time before reluctantly nodding. "I . . . very well. I'll stay. For now."

Pleased, Maric turned at last to Rowan. Even

bruised and battered, she looked radiant: it was just her way. She brightened as he took her hands in his. "When you hadn't charged, I thought perhaps we'd lost you," he said seriously. "Don't scare me like that again."

Her eyes teared, though she grinned and laughed. "You don't get out of it that easily, Maric."

"Funny," he answered wryly.

Loghain looked up from the fire, nonplussed. "Get out of what?" he asked the Arl.

"Maric and Rowan are betrothed." Arl Rendorn smiled. "She was promised to him when she was born."

"Ah," Loghain said simply, and returned his gaze to the fire.

Not much later, Maric slipped away from the fire and walked alone under the night sky. The moon shone down, and glowing moths fluttered in a great swarm nearby. It was strangely peaceful, he thought. The campfires that dotted the riverbank were far too few, and the faint groans of wounded men were the only sounds that punctuated the silence.

He walked nearer to one of those fires, wincing as he saw the huddle of bandaged and exhausted soldiers around it. Some tents had been hastily erected, but there were a great number of soldiers who were sleeping on the ground, some without even blankets. The men around the fire stared into it blankly, trying very hard not to hear the anguished cries of those who would not survive the night coming from farther upriver.

Maric watched, hovering just out of sight and yet

feeling strangely drawn. He tried to tell himself they might all be dead now had he not insisted on the battle.

"Your Highness?" he heard from nearby.

Maric started and turned toward the sound. A soldier was there in the shadows, lying against a tree. As Maric approached, he noticed that the man was older, probably too old to still be fighting. Then he saw that the man's right leg stopped at the knee, a mass of bloody bandages showing a recent amputation. The fellow was pale and shaking, drinking liberally from a wineskin.

"I'm . . . so sorry about your leg," Maric offered, feeling inadequate.

The man grinned, glancing at his new stump and patting it almost affectionately. "It doesn't hurt so much now," he chuckled. "The mage even said he might come by and do what he could."

Maric didn't know what to say. He stood there a moment until the man offered up his wineskin as a toast. "I saw you on the field today, Your Highness. Fought not twenty feet from you at one point."

"You did?"

"I'm going to tell my grandchildren one day: I fought beside the Prince," he said proudly. "You were quite the sight, my lord. I watched you take down three men in a row, like it was nothing."

"I'm sure you were distracted." Maric grinned. "I was scared."

"I knew we were going to win," the soldier insisted. He looked at Maric with shining eyes. "When you came back to us this morning, we all knew it. The Maker sent you to us. To protect you."

"Maybe He did."

The man grinned at him and drank deeply from the wineskin. "To the Queen!" he toasted drunkenly to the moon. "You rest in peace now, Your Majesty. You did your part."

Maric felt tears well up in his eyes but ignored them. Quietly he took the skin and drank deeply from it. "To the Queen," he toasted to the moon.

And suddenly it all didn't seem quite as daunting as before.

6

_____

"To the King!"

Severan heard the toasts to the King even before he entered the throne room. The chamber would be near bursting by now, filled with nobles from throughout Fereldn who had arrived to honor the day of His Majesty's birth.

Honor, of course, might not be quite the word for it. The native Fereldans were terrified the King would strip them of their land as he had done to so many of their fellows in punishment for some crime, real or imagined. The Orlesians, those members of the aristocracy who had chosen to seek out their fortunes away from the Empire and had been given those stripped lands, feared much the same. The King, after all, was a bored and capricious member of an ancient aristocracy, who had been sent to assume the Fereldan throne only after angering the

Emperor—his first cousin and, so the scandalous rumor claimed, onetime lover—and now took out his own displeasure on subjects who had little choice but to bow to his whims.

Severan had tactfully informed the King that the rebels might have been curbed by now if he just took a lighter hand with the locals. Despite his hatred of the rebels and the embarrassment they represented, the King refused to heed the advice. He would do as he wished, and no one could tell him otherwise.

Just as he did with his court, Severan thought, recalling how the King had tried to bring the Orlesian tradition of wearing masks to the Fereldans. He had declared that all members of the nobility would be required to wear as fancy and as beautifully adorned a mask as they could acquire, and that at the end of each court, the wearer of the mask that pleased him the least would be punished. Needless to say, the frantic run on masks and the demand for those who could make them almost resulted in riots in the streets. Finally, when a would-be assassin managed to slip into the palace by wearing such a mask, the commander of the royal guard begged the King to lift the edict for the sake of security. The collective sigh of relief when the King finally did so was almost palpable.

King Meghren was a tyrant, and one did not honor tyrants; one appeased them. So the nobility put on a great show of adoration for their beloved monarch, their smiles a thin veneer covering their terror. The King, meanwhile, knew the nobles were acting. The nobility understood this, but also knew that the charade was required of them, nevertheless.

Such was the sad state of things in Orlesian-occupied Ferelden.

Severan could not have cared less. He was from neither Ferelden nor Orlais, but from across the Waking Sea and far to the north, as his swarthy skin implied. He would have watched his own land be subjugated with no more than a raise of his eyebrow, for mages had no true home at all. His interests were his own, and the King accepted this. Severan's ambition was as reliable as the rising sun, and that was why he remained King Meghren's closest advisor.

"Amaranthine brings to its beloved King a sword of finest silverite, fashioned in the dwarven halls of Orzammar! May it serve him well in the years to come, and offer proof to all of Thedas that his might cannot be denied!"

As Severan entered the throne room, he saw the young Arl was standing amid the rows and rows of nobles seated at their supper tables, giving an overdone speech as several elven servants scampered up to the throne to present a long ornate case to the King. King Meghren, meanwhile, was the very picture of boredom. He was slumped low in the throne, one leg thrown over an arm and propping up his head with a hand. The King was a handsome and virile young man, all dark curls and olive skin to go with that crooked sneer—yet today he looked very much like someone who had overindulged for too many days nonstop. Which was exactly the case.

Meghren sighed heavily and stirred himself enough to sit up as this new gift was presented. The area immediately around the throne was already littered with other gifts, which had been ignored or discarded with little more than a shrug. Mother Bronach stood immediately behind the throne, scrutinizing the proceedings intensely. She was a severe woman, her face lined with the cares of her office as the Grand Cleric of the Holy Chantry in Ferelden, and despite her small frame she loomed as large in the chamber with her resplendent red vestments as the King did. Meghren rubbed his nose in his rumpled velvet doublet and took the sword case from the prostrating elves, who immediately withdrew.

Lifting the brilliant blade out of the case, Meghren gave it a few practice swings and regarded it with interest. "Of the dwarven make, you say?"

The Arl bowed low, sweating despite the presumed pleasure that the King had deigned to take notice of his offering. "Yes, Your Majesty. It was a gift from the King of the dwarves, made to the first of my line long ago."

"Ah, so then it was not made for me." A hush came over the chamber, general dinner conversation halting as the nobility picked up on Meghren's icy tone.

The Arl blanched. "It . . . it is of great value!" he stammered. "Never has a finer blade been made! I thought . . . surely you can see—"

"Emperor Florian, he has given me a blade," the King interrupted. He swung the silverite sword idly to one side of the throne, each swing like a slow pendulum slicing at some invisible head. "Made by the finest crafters in the Val Royeaux, it is a thing of great grace and beauty. Shall I inform him, then, that you consider your blade to be superior?"

The Arl's eyes went wide. "No, I . . ."

"Perhaps it is your opinion I should return to him the gift? After all, there is no point in keeping the inferior blade to collect the dust, is there?"

The entire chamber was silent now. The Arl glanced

about the room, pleading with his eyes for help from the assembled nobles, but everyone was looking elsewhere. He suddenly dropped to one knee, lowering his head. "Forgive me, Your Majesty. It was a presumptuous gift! I apologize!"

Meghren smirked, and looked up as Mother Bronach stepped forward from behind the throne. Severan despised the woman utterly, a feeling that was mutual. "If I may offer a suggestion, Your Majesty?" she asked.

The King waved his assent. "Yes, yes, of course."

"If the blade is as valuable as the Arl suggests, a gift made of it to the Chantry would do much to prove Amaranthine's piety in these dark times. There is much that remains to be done, after all, before the holy braziers of Ferelden shine with the glory that befits a great nation."

"How true," the King cooed. He arched a brow at the Arl. "So how will you have it, Your Grace? Shall you instead give your blade to Mother Bronach?"

The Arl's bow was quick and breathless. "Of course, Your Majesty!"

Mother Bronach snapped her fingers at two palace servants that stood nearby. They rushed forward and gently took the sword from King Meghren, placing it back in the case and running off while the Mother watched. Once they were gone, she bowed low to the King. "The thought is most appreciated, Your Majesty."

He sighed and turned his attention back to the Arl, who remained bowed. "So, what will you do now, Your Grace? Can this mean you have no birthday gift for the King?"

Shocked, the Arl opened his mouth several times as

if to speak, but no sound came forth. The silence in the hall became excruciating, not a single fork or knife touching a single plate. Several Orlesian chevaliers, the elite knights of the Empire easily distinguished by their bright purple tunics and feathered hats, stepped forward with their hands on their sword hilts.

Meghren suddenly laughed, a maniacal sound that cut through the hush in the hall. He continued to laugh until the assembled nobles slowly joined him. They twittered uncertainly at first and then became louder and louder. Meghren clapped his hands as the room roared with amusement. The Arl of Amaranthine remained quiet, sweat pouring down his brow.

"I jest, my friend!" the King declared. "You must forgive me! Such a gift made to the Chantry in my name? What more could I ask?"

The Arl bowed low, his head almost touching the floor. "I am relieved, Your Majesty."

Still chuckling, Meghren clapped his hands loudly to signal that the merriment should continue. "Come, friends! Eat! Drink! Our celebration, it continues and is the sweeter now that the head of the pretender witch sits on a pole outside the gate! Is she not the pretty one?" He roared with laughter again, the nobles joining in too quickly. "And refresh the Arl's goblet! Those robes, they are obviously too hot!"

The feast resumed, and Severan took the opportunity to cross the chamber toward the throne. The stench of wine and sweat hung thickly in the air. A number of the men and women quickly averted their gaze as he passed, becoming entirely interested in the pheasant on their plate or whoever was seated next to them. Severan understood. The Chantry had done its best throughout the ages to ensure that mages were vilified and held responsible for every catastrophe to have befallen mankind. To think that once mages had ruled over all of Thedas, and were now barely tolerated servants monitored by their Chantry watchdogs. A sad plight, to be sure.

King Meghren brightened when he saw his advisor approaching. Mother Bronach did exactly the opposite, her scowl twisting the lines of her face into something entirely unattractive. "Can you not even leave your King to enjoy a single celebration in peace, mage?" she murmured icily. "Must you darken his hall with so many guests about?"

"Now, now," Meghren chuckled. "Do not be so hard on our dear friend the mage. He works very hard for his sovereign, is it not so?"

Severan lowered his head and bowed, the silk of his yellow robes shimmering. With his hair thinning and his features made entirely of sharp angles, he was nowhere near as handsome as the King. The finest compliment Severan had ever received was from a young prostitute who had said he looked clever, that his tiny eyes could seize her, chew her up, and spit her out all with a single gaze. He had liked that so much, he'd waited until morning to have her dragged off to prison. "I have news, Your Majesty," he said.

"Could you not have sent a messenger?" Mother Bronach asked, the chill remaining in her voice.

"When I have news for you, dear woman, I will *always* send a messenger."

Meghren slowly sat up and yawned, rubbing his bloodshot eyes and blinking rapidly. He stood, straightening his rumpled doublet and waving to his servants not to follow. "Then let us be quick." He walked off, Mother Bronach and Severan following quickly and leaving the noise of the throne room behind.

The sitting room was used as a retreat for more private audiences. Meghren had had the sturdy and practical Fereldan furniture replaced by more ornate Orlesian furnishings, all mahogany and bright satins that were works of art on their own. Vivid red paper covered the walls, a practice Severan knew was becoming popular in the Empire.

Meghren threw himself down upon a padded settee, yawning again and rubbing his forehead. "Is this what passes for an evening of entertainment in this backwater? Did you hear the musicians they brought in?"

Severan shook his head. "Before or after you had them sent running from the chamber?"

"Bah! What I would not give for a real orchestra! Or a masquerade! The country lords I am sent from Orlais would not know a proper *basse danse* if it kicked them in the arse!" He snorted with derision and sat up, glaring at Severan. "Do you know what one of those local fools from the Bannorn gave me? Dogs! A pair of filthy dogs!"

"Hounds are valued in Ferelden," Mother Bronach interjected, her voice laden with disapproval. "Those were warhounds, a mating pair. From such a minor bann, it was a gift that showed great respect, Your Majesty."

"Great fear, more like," he sniffed, barely mollified. "I am sure it was some kind of insult, giving me beasts still half covered in dung. All of those backward fools in the Bannorn are alike!"

"It is indeed sad that you must be inflicted with so

much dung on your birthday, Your Majesty," Severan said calmly.

Meghren threw his hands up and sighed. "Tell me, good mage, the news you carry is a response from our Emperor."

Severan hesitated. "I . . . do have a response, yes, but that is not—"

"Nothing is more urgent than a letter from Florian."

Severan straightened his robes, steeling himself. "His Imperial Majesty sends his regrets. He is certain that your duties will continue to hold you in Ferelden, and so there is no place within the Imperial court for you now."

Meghren sank into the cushions. "Ah. Still no forgiveness, then."

Severan almost sighed in relief. Some days a letter from the Emperor could result in a tantrum or far worse. But not today, evidently. "You were expecting a different response than the last fourteen attempts?" he asked reprovingly.

"I am the eternal optimist, good mage."

"The definition of insanity, Your Majesty, is to perform the same action repeatedly and expect different results."

Meghren tittered with amusement. "You are calling me insane?"

"Insanely persistent."

Mother Bronach's lips thinned. "You are still a king, Your Majesty."

"Better to have been made a lowly baron in the provinces," the King complained. "Then I could still keep a house in the Val Royeaux, still visit the Grand Cathedral." He sighed heavily. "Ah, well. I may be the King of a backwater, but at least it is my back-water, yes?"

"Shall I begin another response? Fifteenth time's the charm?" Severan asked.

"Perhaps later. We shall see if we can wear him down, yes?" He then considered for a moment, and his look became serious. "Now, then. This news you carry, it is from the Hinterlands?"

"Indeed."

"Well? Out with it."

Severan took a deep breath. "The information I received was accurate. The rebel army was exactly where it was supposed to be. The attack, however, did not have the result I wished. Many were killed, but the rebels slipped the noose."

Meghren's brows shot up. "Oh?"

"There is more. Prince Maric lives, and is with the rebels. He led a distraction and held out with a handful of men atop a cliff before escaping with the rest of his army." Severan held out a large scrap of cloth. It was tattered and soiled, but the deep purple color could still be seen. "The rebels were inspired, rather than dispirited."

Nettled, the King frowned at Severan as his fingers drummed on the arm of the settee. "Inspired? You told me he would not be there. The boy was supposed to be killed along with the mother."

"He was tracked to a camp of outlaws," Severan answered slowly. "They were slaughtered, but somehow he escaped into the Wilds and survived."

"So am I to understand this correctly?" Meghren continued to drum his fingers, his tone irritable. "The boy, the incompetent prince, managed not only to escape your men in the forest, but trekked through the

Wilds and appeared safe and sound, just in time to lead the spirited defense of the rebel army?"

"I am as incredulous as you, Your Majesty."

Mother Bronach's face was hard with anger. "His spells bring you nothing, King Meghren! Throw him out! He serves his pride and nothing else!"

"And what have you done for the throne except provide a string of platitudes each more useless than the last while you demand tribute for your hungry flames?"

Her eyes went wide with outrage. "The Maker will never allow Ferelden to prosper while it keeps a cancer in its very heart!"

"Your Maker is gone, as is said in your own Chant of Light. He has abandoned His own creation and has no care for anything further. So spare us your useless prattle, woman."

"Blasphemy!" she roared.

"Silence!" Meghren shouted, his face twisted in fury. Mother Bronach calmed reluctantly in response as the King rubbed his face in agitation. "You said that without their beloved Queen, the rebels, they would be done, Severan. You said you could wipe them out with the one blow."

"I . . . Yes, Your Majesty."

"Pride," the priest declared.

Meghren raised a hand to cut off Severan's reply. "Obviously, this boy Maric is more than you assumed."

"Perhaps." Severan was not ready to assume the opposite was true just yet, either. "It is also possible that he found help, somehow. He certainly has the support of the Queen's lieutenants. The daughter of the former Arl of Redcliffe, Lady Rowan, is said to have slain your cousin Felix in the battle, for instance. Rode him down in cold blood."

"Felix?" Meghren shrugged. "I never liked that one."

"Still, the backbone of the rebels proved to be far stiffer than I'd imagined. I do apologize for my mistake, Your Majesty." He bowed his head down low. "I ask for another chance."

Meghren grinned slyly. "You have something in mind?"

"I always have something in mind."

The young king chuckled and glanced over at the Grand Cleric, who stared intently down at her hands folded in her lap. "I suppose your advice is the same as always, my sweet lady?"

"Marry a daughter of Ferelden," she said wearily, as if she had said this many times before, "and produce a child. You cannot rule this country until you are truly its King."

All humor vanished from the King. He glared at Mother Bronach, who paled but did not flinch. "I rule this country," he snapped, "and I *am* its King. You would do well to remember this."

"I speak from the perspective of your people, Your Majesty. They are good, simple folk who could accept you—"

"They are ignorant fools," he snapped, "and they will accept me because they have no choice. So long as the chevaliers remain, so do I." He calmed, rubbing his chin thoughtfully. Then he turned back to Severan. "You have another chance, good mage. We will do things your way once more, but only because I have no wish to marry some dog-faced local. That is clear?"

Severan bowed again. "I will not fail you, Your Majesty."

Severan returned to his quarters deep within the palace, greatly relieved Meghren had not sent him back to the Circle of Magi. Within the Circle, under the watchful gaze of the Chantry's templars, his every spell would be scrutinized and monitored. At least in King Meghren's employ he had power, even if he had to use it carefully. Men like Meghren were permitted by the Circle to have one of their mages as an advisor under the condition that the mage was watched by the Chantry. Meghren could defy Mother Bronach's wishes only to a point.

He cursed whatever luck had allowed Prince Maric to ruin his plan. It had been an excellent one: the Theirin bloodline and the rebellion both wiped out. The King would have been allowed to return to the Imperial court, and Severan, the hero of the day, might even have been left as governor.

But now? Now he had to try again.

Severan's quarters were dark, as befitted his mood. With a wave of his hand, the lantern hanging by the door flared brightly. As the room was bathed in firelight, he noticed a figure leaning against one of the posts of his great bed.

"Greetings, my lord mage." It was an elven woman, beautiful in the way that only her kind could be, with porcelain skin and slanted eyes an impossible green. This one was dressed in leathers that accentuated her curves, and her golden honey curls cascaded around her shoulders artfully. She was a spy, of course. The fact that he could see the dagger sheathed at her waist meant she was not here to kill him, or so he assumed. If he was wrong on that point she was certainly welcome to try.

"Do you always enjoy standing in dark rooms?" Walking into his quarters, he brushed by her and quickly gathered up the many papers that were spread over his desk.

She chuckled, watching him with keen interest. "If my purpose here was to read your precious letters, do you not think I would already have done so, my lord?"

"Perhaps you did. If so, then I should have you executed, no?"

"I am here at your invitation."

He put down the papers slowly, nodding. "You are the bard, then."

"I am." She bowed politely. "Our mutual friend in Val Chevans sends his regards, just as he sends me."

Severan stepped toward her, taking her delicate chin in his hand and turning her face from side to side to scrutinize her more closely. She did not bat an eyelash. "He sent me an elf, did he? You seem very tarted up for one of your station."

"I can be less so, my lord."

"Of that I have no doubt." Bards in Orlais had a notorious reputation. They masqueraded as minstrels or actors, traveling from court to court in the Empire ostensibly to entertain their noble patrons while plying their true trade in secret. Politics in the Empire were a devious business, and thus bards were never in short supply. One would think the nobility would simply stop receiving entertainers altogether, but the truth was that the possibility of any traveling minstrel being a dangerous spy added an exotic allure. That a nobleman might be important enough to be spied upon, and courageous enough to take in a possible spy, made the temptation too much for any self-respecting aristocrat to bear.

"If my lord believes an elf cannot do as he needs . . . ," she began.

"No." He released her chin. "Simply remember your place. I have a contract with your master, and that means you are now mine." His gaze was steel, and he was pleased to see that she did not flinch. He wondered if there was a single elf in Ferelden who could manage the same. "Succeed in your task and you will be rewarded. Fail and you will end up begging for scraps in the alienage along with your fellows, wishing you had stayed in Orlais. Is that sufficiently clear?"

She went silent for a moment, her face assuming a calm veneer. Stiffly she bowed to him again. "I understand," she said smoothly. "I am told the contract is for a single task, yes?" Stepping away from him, she perched on the edge of the bed and regarded him with an artful come-hither look. "Is it to be something of a . . . personal nature?"

"No need to exert yourself for my benefit." He waved her off contemptuously. "Do you know who Prince Maric is?"

The elven woman paused, thinking. "Yes, I think I do," she said, her tone now all business. "The son of the proper Queen of Ferelden, out hiding with her in the wilderness somewhere? Is that not so?"

"The Rebel Queen is dead. You might have seen her head outside the gates."

"Is that what that was? It was looking a little

green and putrid. *Queen* wasn't the first word that came to mind."

"Nevertheless, the boy is her heir. And he is alive. I need you to get close to him."

The elf considered the idea, twirling one of her locks between her fingers thoughtfully. "That will take time."

"Time we have."

"And are we to negotiate my reward, then?"

"Complete your task first," he said dismissively. "Afterwards, King Meghren can and will provide whatever reward you desire."

She stood from the bed and then bowed again, this time low and servile. "Then it seems you have a bard at your disposal, my lord."

Severan nodded, pleased. One more chance, then, to destroy the rebellion.

In the distance he heard the muffled sounds of forced laughter in the throne room. The laughter was punctuated by someone screaming in pain, probably for Meghren's amusement. It was the only reason the King delighted in such gatherings. Someone always had to suffer before the night was through.

Someone always suffered.

7

In the months that followed their retreat from the valley, things were as difficult for the rebel army as Arl Rendorn had predicted. Pressing farther into the western hills made it too dangerous for the usurper's forces to follow, but left them in harsh territory with little food or supplies. They fished in the mountain streams and hunted in the thin forests, but still the men hovered just short of starvation. With few proper tents, few blankets, and fewer ways to stay occupied and entertained, they were scattered, restless, and short of nearly everything.

Nor were they left alone for those months. Small groups of the King's soldiers made occasional forays into the hills to probe the rebel defenses, a threat that kept the rebels vigilant. Stretched to the point of exhaustion, they found it more and more difficult to maintain a watchful eye. When a small group of enemy soldiers made it right to the command tent and were taken down by guards not twenty feet from where Maric ate his scant dinner, Arl Rendorn determined that they could no longer afford to just stay hidden within the hills.

It was Loghain who led the first small groups of archers out under cover of darkness. Elves naturally saw better in darkness than men, so he recruited those few that marched with the rebels as runners and camp followers to join his group. Though surprised by their sudden elevation, they quickly stepped up to the challenge. Within weeks they had racked up an impressive body count, enough so the enemy began to fear the appearance of the "night elves" in their camps. It was a name Loghain took for his group as a badge of courage.

The enemy could not react effectively to these constant strikes, spread out as they were in their struggle to keep the rebels enclosed in the hills and starving. More attacks followed as Rowan led her horsemen in raids during the day. Should the enemy dare to try to follow her men back into the hills, Maric and the Arl would ambush them in the narrow passes.

The rebels were taking losses, but they were exacting a toll from the enemy in far greater numbers. As they were stretched to the breaking point, it came as a great relief when their scouts finally reported that the enemy was pulling back from the hills to a safer distance.

Within days the Arl gave the order to march, and the army was split into four groups that slipped through the northern passes under a full moon. It was a tense night, the march made slow by the lack of torchlight, but in the end they were successful. The outlying enemy camps did not detect their movement, and by dawn the army was almost to the southern shores of great Lake Calenhad.

Here there were numerous friendly farmholds that were willing to barter and even provide a little secret assistance. Riders were sent out to several of the local villages, and even as far as Redcliffe, to quietly gather supplies.

The celebration when the first of those supplies started arriving to the camp was as spontaneous as it was jubilant. The mere appearance of soap was enough to send Rowan and Maric into a mad display of joy. Biting into a fresh apple seemed heavenly. Fresh linens appeared, along with new tents and medicine. That evening there was music and laughter and dancing around the campfires, and for a single night the war was forgotten.

Arl Rendorn awarded Loghain the rank of lieutenant and commissioned the Night Elves as an actual company. Reluctant to accept the honor, Loghain did so only after being cajoled by his fellow archers and teased by Rowan. Maric presented the red cloak of his rank to him in a brief ceremony in front of the collected army. Loghain looked distinctly uncomfortable throughout, disparaging the need for such a display, but the resulting cheer from the men was so vigorous, not even he could deny the positive effect it had on morale.

Reasons to celebrate were, after all, few and far between.

The rebel army had lost a great number of its men, and it became apparent that much of Ferelden assumed the rebellion had died with its queen. It was a notion that the usurper worked hard to spread.

Still there were those who knew better and were willing to offer help, no matter how surreptitious. After months spent traveling along the mountains and then eastward across the hilly coastlands, the army found shelter in the gentle forests near the coastal port of Amaranthine. Whatever his reasons, Arl Byron of Amaranthine ignored their presence and quietly let it be known that they could remain for now. It was not the first time the rebels had needed to rely on someone looking the other way, so Maric accepted Arl Byron's generosity—for now.

To Maric, their primary was task to regain their lost momentum. This meant splitting up so they could cover more ground spreading the word, at least for a time, and though Arl Rendorn seemed grave at the risk it represented, he agreed that the effort was necessary.

Rowan and Loghain rode out first, though their pairing naturally didn't come without argument. Neither of them was inclined to leave Maric's side, nor did they particularly relish the idea of traveling together, but in the end Maric's insistence won out. They reluctantly left the camp, taking with them a handful of men who were familiar with the Bannorn, the fertile heartlands of central Ferelden. For months they traveled together, camping where possible while Rowan and Loghain made short trips into nearby villages to spread what word they could. Occasionally they would make a visit to one of the local banns who they felt might be receptive to overtures.

Rowan found herself impressed by Loghain's

ability to quickly assess whether a bann was legitimately interested or just eager to gain favor with the King by trying to trap them. Once she had become infuriated with Loghain as he pulled her away from a dinner table without explanation, only to belatedly realize that guards had been quietly maneuvering in the shadows. He had seen it coming, not her. Blades were bared and the two of them were forced to fight back to back in order to escape capture.

In such situations, Loghain never once treated her as if she required saving or any sort of special protection. He expected her sword arm to be as strong as his own, and she made sure it was.

Once they had been in an area for too long, they usually moved on quickly, often chased by agents of one nobleman or another. There seemed to be no shortage of those who were willing to sell out their rightful ruler, especially when it seemed the usurper had all but won.

Occasionally, Rowan's heartfelt pleas would find a ready audience among banns whose fortunes had dwindled and who remembered better days. The Orlesians had taken a harsh toll on the Bannorn, their taxes plundering the countryside as surely as any army. Fear, however, made many hesitant to consider helping the rebels, especially when they might be a lost cause. Too many graphic examples had been made by the usurper; rotting carcasses hung in cages at nearly every fork in the road, glaring examples of Imperial justice.

Still, the will of the Fereldan people was not completely broken, and Rowan and Loghain saw evidence of their stubbornness and independence during those months of traveling the heartland. Men with little more than rags on their backs and skin on their bones would listen as Loghain told them of Prince Maric's survival, and their eyes would shine with a fierce determination, a hope that perhaps not all was lost. Old men would spit angrily into tavern fireplaces and speak of the days when Maric's grandfather still ruled, of the great war with Orlais and the bitter defeat that followed. Those listening in the flickering shadows would nod their heads grimly, and one or two would quietly approach Rowan and Loghain afterwards.

The belligerence Rowan remembered from first meeting Loghain gradually vanished, though she was not quite certain why, and was replaced by something that varied between gentlemanly courtesy and indifference. Loghain was quiet to begin with, but just as Rowan believed he was warming toward her, he would promptly cool.

In fact, the only time Loghain said anything to her of real significance came on an evening in the middle of winter. They were camping in the woods to avoid a pair of bounty hunters that Rowan was certain had been hired by Bann Ceorlic, both of them huddled on opposite sides of the tiny campfire, shivering in their woolen blankets. Their breath came out in white plumes and Rowan considered once again asking for the fire to be built up. Undoubtedly Loghain's response would be a stern frown. It would give away their position, she knew that. But freezing to death simply didn't seem like a helpful alternative.

Rowan glanced across the fire then and realized that Loghain was staring at her. He said nothing, and the intensity in those icy blue eyes made her heart skip. She looked away quickly, wrapping the blanket around her more tightly as she shuddered. How long had he been staring at her so quietly?

"I haven't thanked you," he stated.

She looked up, confused. "Thanked me?"

"Back at the battle, you rode to my rescue." He smiled grimly. "Quite literally, in fact."

"There's no need to—"

"There is," he cut her off. She watched with fascination as he took a deep breath and then stared straight into her eyes, as if he wanted to be certain she understood his sincerity. "I know what you did, and I'm grateful. I should have told you so before."

The cold went away.

Loghain nodded curtly, having made his peace, and quietly turned his attention back to the fire. He went back to warming himself like nothing had happened, and she had no idea what to say in response. So she had said nothing.

In the end it made little difference, for they had much to do during the months they were on the road. Often they struggled just to stay alive. Rowan preferred traveling companions who were more personable, perhaps, but she could not deny that Loghain's competence saved her from real trouble many times over. If he had ever owed her anything for her defying her father, he repaid it with interest. She could see why Maric was so keen on him.

Maric, meanwhile, was also spending months on the road. Throughout the winter he traveled secretly with the mage, Wilhelm, and a small honor guard to visit nobles who had been friendly to the rebels previously. He went to remind them that the rebellion was not over, and to urge them to consider throwing their lot in with the army.

The lesson of his mother's death was still fresh in his mind, of course. He never trusted his safety to any of these men and women, despite their past associations. Times were desperate, and if the Queen could be fooled into thinking men like Bann Ceorlic were genuine, then so could he. Every meeting was a carefully arranged affair, the ill-tempered mage fretting right up until it took place. On the few occasions that one of the nobles tried to ambush him, the sudden appearance of Wilhelm's stone golem made short work of the attackers.

The main thing that helped Maric during those long months was the usurper's unpopularity. By ruling through fear, Meghren made no secret of his antipathy toward his own subjects. This meant most of those Maric sought out were at least willing to listen and offer sympathy even if they were skeptical of actually joining the rebel cause. Joining the cause, after all, meant abandoning one's home. It meant having one's ancestral lands handed over to an Orlesian lord who would bleed them dry, and many of the nobles were reluctant to subject their people to such treatment.

No, only the truly desperate and those without options joined the rebels. What made Maric optimistic, as well as sad, was that as the months passed, it became apparent that more and more nobles were being pushed to that extreme. Already Maric had heard of banns that had been forced off their estates and took what men they could muster and made for the rebel army. King Meghren might have gained an Orlesian ally in whatever lord he handed their land to, but Maric gained a loyal and determined rebel as a result.

Real trouble came in the spring, once rumor had begun to circulate of a small group of strange travelers with a conspicuous golem moving through the Hinterland roads. When the usurper's men descended upon them, Maric was forced to flee for his life. Wilhelm insisted they return to the army, but instead Maric veered north and made the journey to Kinloch Hold, the ancient tower that was the home of the Circle of Magi. The spire rose impossibly out of Lake Calenhad, the impressive remnants of the old Imperial Highway still leading out to it even though boats were required to actually reach the tower today.

The mages were ostensibly neutral in any political conflict, and the First Enchanter received Maric nervously at the tower entrance. He was a tiny man, almost wizened in his advanced age, and he informed Maric in a tremulous voice that the Grand Cleric was in attendance at the same time. The implication was clear: the Chantry didn't yet know about Maric's arrival and the mages would be more than happy if he simply moved on, nobody the wiser.

Their concern was understandable enough. The Chantry watched the Circle of Magi closely and offered them no trust whatsoever. If there was even the suspicion of involvement by the mages with the rebellion, the Chantry's templars would be unleashed upon them. Very likely even Wilhelm's presence was cause for alarm.

Still, Maric had never met Mother Bronach previously. He knew her only by reputation. When else was he ever going to have a chance to meet the woman when she wouldn't be flanked by an army of templars?

The First Enchanter blanched when Maric explained his intention. Maric almost felt sorry for the man. After a great deal of fuss and many terse messages sent back and forth to the Grand Cleric's entourage, Maric was finally ushered alone into the vaulted assembly chamber at the heart of the tower.

It was an impressive room, great columns reaching up to a ceiling a hundred feet up while small glass bulbs dangled and glowed with dim magic to form a starlike array overhead. Normally it served as a forum of debate for the senior mages, but today it would serve as neutral ground. The Grand Cleric sat stiffly by herself, wrapped in her glittering red robes, and rhythmically tapped her withered fingers on her chair. As he approached, she eyed him accusingly but did not deign to acknowledge him otherwise.

He was sweating profusely. How very large the chamber was, for just the two of them. He felt dwarfed and somehow insignificant.

"Prince Maric," she said with forced politeness as he reached her.

He fell to one knee and lowered his head in a show of respect. "Mother Bronach."

A tense silence ensued, after which Maric rose to his feet again. The priest regarded him with interest, not entirely displeased by his display. "You are fortunate," she began crisply, "that I am not here with a proper honor guard. I would have taken you prisoner immediately. Surely you understand that."

"We wouldn't be talking, if that were the case."

"Indeed." She tapped her fingers on the chair again, and Maric got the feeling that she was studying him. Looking for a weakness, perhaps? Trying to see if he matched his no doubt lacking reputation? He wasn't sure. "Are you an Andrastian, boy? A believer in the Maker and His Chantry?"

He nodded. "My mother taught me the Chant of Light."

"Then submit to the proper ruler of Ferelden. End this nonsense."

"It's not nonsense," he snapped. "How can the Chantry support putting an Orlesian on Ferelden's throne?"

Her eyebrows shot up. Mother Bronach was not accustomed to contradiction, he surmised. "It is the Maker's will," she said with belabored patience.

"He is a tyrant!"

She paused, pursing her lips as she watched him. "How many innocent lives had your mother wasted in this hopeless struggle? How many will you? Do your people not deserve peace?"

Maric felt rage bubbling up from within him and threatening to explode. How dare she? He closed the distance between them, marching up to her chair and stopping directly in front of her, fists clenched at his sides. It was all he could do to stop himself from throttling her. She still deserved respect, despite her arrogance. He had to remind himself of that.

He breathed out slowly, forcing himself to calm. Mother Bronach watched him, seemingly undaunted by his proximity and his unspoken threat. He could tell that she was nervous, however. He could see the bead of sweat on her forehead, watch as her eyes flicked toward the nearby doors. "Is it true," he asked icily, "that he put my mother's head on a spear outside the Denerim palace? My mother, your rightful queen?"

A long minute passed as they locked gazes. Finally, Mother Bronach rose imperiously out of her chair. "I can see there is nothing for us to discuss," she said with just the slightest quaver in her voice. "You are an impertinent boy. I suggest you take your men and leave while you can, and pray to the Maker that when your end comes you receive more mercy than your mother did." With that, she turned and strode out of the room. Maric's knees turned to jelly as she left.

Maric's brief meeting with the First Enchanter that followed fared little better. The Circle of Magi were unwilling to abandon their neutrality. At best they were willing to tacitly overlook the fact that one of their own was helping the rebels. Maric supposed he couldn't expect more than that. The entire trip to the tower had done little for the rebel cause.

Still, meeting the Grand Cleric face-to-face must have been worth something, he thought. Even if she thought him rude and unready, at least he had looked her in the eye, one of the closest advisors to the usurper, and not buckled. She had left Kinloch Hold in a hurry, no doubt headed at full speed back to the palace. Maric was gone from the shining tower long before she could send anyone back to capture him.

The reunion in the forests near Amaranthine was a glad one. Arl Rendorn greeted Maric as he returned, as well as Rowan and Loghain. All of them were exhausted but pleased the others had returned safely. Rowan ran forward to embrace Maric happily and tease him about the beard he had grown over the winter, and if Loghain looked on silently, neither of them noticed. Maric was eager to hear the stories of the months spent in the Bannorn, and that first evening back at the camp he stayed up until the small hours, drinking and extracting one reluctant tale after another out of Loghain.

It proved to be the only reprieve they would have for some time. Arl Rendorn had already been warned that the army's position was becoming too well known; they had remained in one place far longer than they ever had previously. Small bands of recruits had been making their way to the forest over the months, and word had spread, and when a secret messenger arrived from the Arl of Amaranthine to tell them the usurper's forces were on their way, they started packing up quickly.

Maric told Arl Rendorn that he had only one thing to do first. He took Loghain with him and paid a visit to Arl Byron. Loghain suggested that he was foolish to do so, but Maric didn't care.

The young Arl came out of his estate at Amaranthine as they approached, flanked by his guards. He waved amiably to Maric. "Your Highness," he greeted them, "I have to admit I am a bit surprised to still see you here. Did you not receive my message?"

Maric nodded. "I did, Your Grace. I wanted to thank you for sending it."

The man nodded, his expression unreadable. "It was . . . the least I could do."

"The very least," Loghain growled emphatically.

Maric shot an angry look at Loghain, who scowled but otherwise remained unrepentant. "My point," he stated, looking back at Arl Byron, "was that we are grateful for the months you have provided us safe harbor. I hope nothing ill comes to you as a result." He bowed deeply to the Arl, who appeared nonplussed and did little beyond muttering polite niceties as Maric and Loghain withdrew.

Certainly Maric never expected much from it. If anything, the Arl's confused response forced Maric to grudgingly agree with Loghain's assessment that they might have simply been better off not making the attempt. So when the rebel army began its march the next morning, Maric was shocked to encounter a force of soldiers wearing Amaranthine heraldry just as they left the forest bounds.

The soldiers had not come to attack, however. Arl Byron rode to the front of his men and quietly, in front of them all, bent knee to Maric.

"The usurper can take my land," he said, his voice thick with emotion. "I've sent my wife and children to the north, and brought with me what loyal men I have and all the supplies I could gather." As he looked up at Maric, tears welled in his eyes. "If . . . if my lord Prince will have me, I would gladly offer my service to the rebellion, and I beg your forgiveness for not having the courage to offer it sooner."

Maric was rendered speechless, and it wasn't until both the Arl's men and his own began cheering that he remembered to accept.

Battles followed, first as the rebel army sought to evade the usurper's men as they headed back west into the hills, and then as Arl Rendorn decided that they needed to take the offensive. A series of small battles fought mostly in the spring rains sent the usurper's unprepared forces into a hasty retreat. A larger force that the enraged Meghren had hastily assembled arrived weeks later, but by then the rebel army had already moved on.

In the lean two years that followed, that was how the rebel army stayed alive.

True battles were few and far between, however, and life with the rebels primarily consisted of waiting. Weeks were spent camping in the rain or snowed in during the winter, waiting for the enemy to find them or waiting for the opportunity to attack. When they weren't waiting, they were marching, trudging through the most remote parts of Ferelden to flee a larger enemy force or to find a new place to hide and wait.

Only once did the usurper gain a serious advantage over them. A lightly armed caravan bringing supplies from Orlais in the early winter proved too tempting a target, and only too late did Arl Rendorn realize it was a trap. Before the rebels knew it, hundreds of Orlesian chevaliers rode out from the hills, hidden amid the rocks, their silvery armor and lances glittering against the snow. They would have flanked the bulk of the rebel force and pinned it there until more forces arrived had Loghain and the Night Elves not acted quickly.

Loghain and the elves ran into the hills in order to intercept the chevalier charge. Peppering the knights with arrows forced them to stop and deal with the archers instead of finishing their flanking maneuver. Lightly armored elves were no match for chevaliers, however, and more than half of them were slaughtered as the Orlesians overran their position. Loghain himself was gored by a lance.

The sacrifice gave Maric time to call off the attack

on the caravan, and the rebels pulled back to safety. Insisting on going to Loghain's rescue, Maric brought the rebel forces around to clash directly with the chevaliers in the hills. The casualties were high, but both the wounded Loghain and the surviving Night Elves were saved before Arl Rendorn finally called for the retreat. The chevaliers gave chase, but eventually desisted before the rebels turned the tables. The trap had not succeeded.

Other battles were chosen more carefully. Arl Rendorn was the one who did the choosing most times, and when he and Maric would differ in opinion it ended up as an argument. In the end, the Arl's long experience would always win out.

These lost arguments were not things that Maric took in stride. For days afterwards he would stay out of sight, spending his time brooding and bristling at the idea that he was not being taken seriously. He complained of being treated like a figurehead, though the Arl repeatedly told him this wasn't so. Once, Maric walked in on a meeting of the Arl and both Rowan and Loghain, and belatedly realized that he had not been invited. He spent almost a week drunk and miserable, avoiding everyone until finally Loghain tracked him down and told him he was being an idiot and physically dragged him back to the camp. For whatever reason this seemed to mollify Maric considerably.

After that, Maric made an effort to ensure his presence was felt in other ways. Adamant that he would share the danger with his men, he insisted on fighting on the front lines in every battle. The soldiers watched him ride along the front, purple cloak

billowing and dwarven armor shining brilliantly, and
they worshipped him; he gave no indication if he
knew just how much.

Rowan got truly upset on those occasions when
Maric was carried in from the field, bleeding profusely from a horrible sword gash. Wilhelm would
immediately come running and use his healing magic,
even as Rowan shouted furiously. Maric would grin
through the pain and tell her she was making far too
much of it.

Then Loghain invariably arrived from the battle,
still armored and covered in blood and sweat. He
would take one look at Maric, frown thoughtfully,
and declare that since Maric came out of the fight
alive, all was well. Rowan would storm off, ranting
about their idiocy, while Maric and Loghain shared a
private grin at her expense.

The three of them slowly became closer over the
two years. They fought together in battle, and Arl
Rendorn included Loghain in planning discussions
more and more. Indeed, the Arl increasingly praised
Loghain's abilities and once suggested that if
Loghain's father had been the one to train Loghain, it
was a tragedy he had ever left the service of the
throne. Things might have been different, the Arl said,
and he would have liked to have met the man.

Loghain accepted the compliment with his usual
stoic silence, his thoughts unknown to anyone but
himself.

With the long weeks spent camped, Loghain de-
voted a great deal of time training Maric on the finer
points of swordsmanship and archery. He claimed
Maric was a poor student, but the truth was their
training sessions became an excuse to spend time in

each other's company. Maric found Loghain endlessly fascinating, repeatedly trying to pry a story out of the tight-lipped man regarding his days as an outlaw, asking and insisting until he relented out of pure exasperation. Maric's endless supply of charm was apparently capable of wearing down almost anyone, and it wasn't long before Maric and Loghain were a constant sight together on the practice field.

Rowan often watched the training sessions, amused by the constant bickering and banter between Maric and Loghain. Outside of the Night Elves, Loghain was regarded as a taciturn and even unfriendly man. Maric had a way of drawing him out, she noted, which she had been unable to do during their months traveling the Bannorn. Often she laughingly criticized Loghain's sword techniques, primarily because it nettled Loghain and thus vastly amused Maric. Loghain became so incensed by Rowan's comments that, seething with anger, he challenged her to a duel to prove which of them knew more of swordsmanship. Grinning, she accepted.

Maric was incredibly excited by the entire idea, and immediately ran about the rebel camp announcing that the duel was about to occur. Within an hour, Loghain and Rowan had an audience of hundreds of cheering men.

Leery of the size of their audience, Loghain turned to Rowan. "Do you truly wish to pursue this?" he asked her, his expression solemn.

"I believe it was you who challenged me."

"Then I withdraw the challenge," he said instantly. "And I apologize for losing my temper. It will not happen again."

Amid the boos and sounds of disappointment

made by the soldiers nearby who had heard him, Rowan appeared nettled instead. "I do *not* accept your withdrawal," she replied, "provided you fight me to the best of your ability. You want to see which of us knows how to use our sword better? So do I."

Loghain stared at her appraisingly, wondering if she was, in fact, serious. She said nothing, instead drawing her blade and returning his stare defiantly. After a long minute he finally nodded his assent, cheers going up from the crowd.

Loghain was the stronger of the two, but Rowan was the quicker—and perhaps the more determined. Their initial feints drew loud cheers from the audience, and then they settled into a series of back-and-forth blows to test the other's defenses. Rowan soon realized that Loghain was holding back, however, and angrily dived in with a blindingly fast slash, cutting him across the leg. He waved off aid, staring sternly at Rowan for a moment before nodding. If this was how she wanted it, this was how it would be.

The following battle lasted almost an hour and was the talk of the camp for months afterwards. Loghain and Rowan fought savagely, each giving as good as they got, and both of them were bloodied before long. A slash across Rowan's forehead sent blood dripping into her eyes and gave Loghain the opportunity to go for the final blow—which he took. Only at the last second did she roll out of the way, then tipped her sword toward him respectfully. With both exhausted and sweating, a worried Maric tried to end the duel by calling a draw. Not looking away from Loghain, Rowan waved him off.

Minutes later it was over when Loghain came in

low and unexpectedly thrust upward with his blade, disarming Rowan. The audience murmured excitedly as her blade skittered far out of her reach. Instead of giving up or going for her weapon, Rowan dropped down and kicked out with her leg, tripping Loghain, and leaped to grab his sword. The two of them fought for control of the blade, rolling around on the ground, their sweat and blood intermingling. Finally Loghain kicked Rowan off, the audience cheering as he rolled after her and sprang to his feet, sword pointed at Rowan's throat.

She glanced at the sword, her breathing ragged and blood still running down into her eyes. Loghain was similarly panting, pale and favoring his wounded leg. He held out a hand to Rowan and reluctantly she took it, allowing him to pull her to her feet. The audience went wild, cheering with approval.

They got even louder when Rowan shook Loghain's hand, congratulating him. She then wavered weakly and stumbled, and Maric scrambled to catch her. She chuckled as he called for Wilhelm, telling him that perhaps Loghain was a good enough tutor for him after all.

Later, as Maric stood outside the tent where Wilhelm was busy healing Rowan, Loghain limped up, freshly bandaged, and stiffly apologized. He had let his pride get the better of him, he said, and very nearly hurt the future queen. Maric listened, wide-eyed, and then laughed heartily. From where he stood, he said, it seemed like the opposite had very nearly been true. Loghain merely nodded gravely, and that was where the matter was left.

As spring melted the snowdrifts left by a hard winter, Maric remarked to himself that it had been almost three years since his mother was murdered and he returned to the rebel army for that fateful battle. As slow as their progress had been since then, the rebel army managed to survive and continued to frustrate the usurper's efforts to corner and eliminate them. If anything, their numbers had increased. Meghren was a merciless ruler, and the more he taxed and the more he punished, the more the ranks of the rebel army swelled. They had reached a size where they couldn't even afford to be in the same region all at the same time. Even with the support of many farmholders, it was becoming difficult for the army to feed itself. So, too, had the risk of taking in informants become too high. The speed with which the usurper's forces found out where the rebels were camped increased with each passing month.

The time had come to act.

The town of Gwaren was a remote place on the southeast corner of Ferelden past the great tracts of the Brecilian Forest. A rough town full of loggers and fishermen, it was accessible to the rest of the country only by boat or along the narrow trail leading through the miles of forestland to the west. It was a defensible place, but Arl Rendorn had ascertained that the majority of its forces were off in the north—levies supplied by the ruling Teyrn of Gwaren to the usurper to help hunt the rebels. This meant the town was ripe for the taking.

Weeks earlier, the Arl of Amaranthine and his men had split off from the main force. He had gone westward to engage in raiding and draw the attention of the King's forces in the region toward him. Maric assumed he had been successful, as they encountered no pursuit when moving through the forest toward Gwaren. By the time they reached the town, it was apparent the defenders had become aware of their approach, but had little time to do more than rouse their militia. A number of the locals had fled on fishing boats, but most were trapped.

The assault began immediately. The town was spread along the rocky shore, a veritable maze of cobbled streets and plaster-covered brick. It had no wall, but it did have a stone manor atop the hill that overlooked the town, and that was where the majority of the Teyrn's men had withdrawn.

Maric and Rowan charged down from the forest and into the town itself, meeting the line of poorly trained militia that tried to keep them out. Very quickly things had fallen to chaos. The militia fell back almost immediately, withdrawing into the alleyways and the buildings and forcing the rebels to search for them, building to building.

Despite Maric's insistence on not causing more destruction and hardship for the townsfolk, several fires began to spread. He could see the smoke rising, and the panic of the populace made the search difficult. People were running in the streets, fleeing from the rebels and militia both. They carried the few valuables they could manage and ran for the forest, hoping that the rebel army would ignore them. The streets were a mass of people, all smoke and screams everywhere, and after turning a corner, Maric realized he was separated from his own men.

His warhorse stamped in agitation, and he fought to bring it under control as a group of people came through the smoke toward him. They halted, terrified.

Dressed in simple clothes, many were carrying belongings wrapped in cloth, and several had children hiding behind them. Not more militiamen. He moved his horse aside and waved them by. Tentatively, they went. One of the children burst into frightened tears.

More smoke billowed through the streets, and he heard the sound of fighting ahead. The port was not far away, and he was certain that some of his soldiers would be there, but as he turned his horse about, he found he had no idea which direction that might be. *Just follow the smell of salt and fish*, he told himself. But all he could smell was smoke and blood.

Three more men came out of the smoke toward him, this time running and shouting. Maric spun his mount around to face them, and saw that they belonged to the militia. They were armored in dark leather and carried small wooden shields and cheap swords. That they charged at a mounted man in full armor probably meant they recognized the cloak and thought they might drag him from his horse and overwhelm him.

Come to think of it, they just might, he thought.

He dismounted smoothly and drew his sword, getting the weapon up just in time to knock aside the first man's thrust but not in time to prevent the man from slamming into him. Thrown back into a brick wall, Maric had the air knocked from him even though his dwarven armor took most of the impact. Maric's horse backed off but did not run, neighing anxiously.

"Get on him! Get on him!" the man shouted excitedly, spittle flying from his mouth. A fat and balding fellow whose leathers barely covered his belly slammed his sword down on Maric's shoulder, though it merely bounced off.

Maric gritted his teeth and kicked out at the first man, sending him stumbling away, and then turned and punched the fat man in the face before he could bring his sword down again. Maric's gauntlet took him right in the nose, and he screamed as blood sprayed out. The third man rushed him, blade ready, but Maric parried and spun around, then ran him through.

The fat man reeled and ran away, covering his face while he squealed in agony. The first man scrambled to his feet and lifted his blade as Maric turned to face him. For a moment the two of them stared at each other, their swords at the ready. Maric was calm, but the man licked his lips nervously and clearly wanted to run. More smoke poured into the street as a nearby roof collapsed and flames licked the sky.

"Still willing to try?" Maric asked.

Behind the man, four new militia soldiers ran into view. Some were bloodied, and all of them halted as they spotted the confrontation occurring before them. Seeing his comrades, the man in front of Maric suddenly grinned at him.

"I think I just might," he snickered.

Then Maric heard a new sound: hooves pounding on the cobblestone. The four soldiers realized they were being chased and began shouting in fear and running forward again, only not quickly enough. Several horses with armored riders overran them, blades slashing down and dispatching them instantly. One of the riders was Rowan, her green plume fluttering behind her.

She rushed ahead of the others, her sword held high. The soldier in front of Maric stared at her dumbly, mouth hanging open, and only belatedly did he think to try to run. It was too late. Rowan ran him down, slicing him deftly across the throat.

Maric grimly watched the man stumble and then slow, his dark blood gushing over the cobblestones. It was unnecessary, he thought to himself. These soldiers were his people, too, were they not? But there was nothing he could do about it. Not yet.

The horses clattered to a stop as Rowan pulled up beside Maric. She removed her helmet, her face covered in soot and sweat. "Fall off your horse again?" she asked with just a hint of a mocking grin.

"It's what I do," he agreed with a belabored sigh. He hadn't actually fallen off his horse for several years, now—except for that one time the previous winter when he'd ended up buried in a snowbank. It had saved his life, hiding him from the enemy until Loghain reached him and pulled him out. Loghain had called him absurdly lucky, and Maric had agreed through chattering teeth. Loghain and Rowan both continued to tease him about it mercilessly.

Maric turned and walked back to where his horse had retreated, taking its reins and calming it before finally leaping back into the saddle. Rowan watched him appreciatively before she glanced back at the horsemen waiting behind her. With a gesture, they rode off to continue their sweep.

"We've still got part of the town to search," she said. "It will probably take the rest of the night to find them. I was hoping they would start coming out and surrendering—" She nodded to the various fires around them. "—but it looks like they would rather burn half of Gwaren down around our ears first."

"So it seems." Maric wiped the sweat off his brow. He wiped his bloody sword clean using a hay bundle that stood nearby. "Last I saw, the fighting was going well up at the manor. Loghain broke through the wall, I think."

Rowan looked annoyed, as she tended to whenever he mentioned Loghain. She had denied doing so when challenged, so now he just ignored it. "So Gwaren is ours, then?" she asked crisply.

"Soon enough it will be."

Rowan waved to her men to continue on without her, and they rode off, leaving Maric and Rowan to survey the town together. The area they were in had quieted considerably. Several blazes were going, but most of those who had decided to flee were long gone, and most of the enemy in this area had already been found. Maric felt helpless, watching the buildings burn, knowing that the fire would spread unchecked for some time yet. He could see the faces cowering behind the windows, watching Rowan and him as they rode past, but he could hardly expect them to come out now. Later, perhaps, but for now, he was the invader, the one responsible for the bloodshed and fires. Perhaps some even believed him to be the villain that King Meghren claimed. Most were no doubt justifiably terrified.

The streets were strewn with litter, as well as the occasional corpse. Many doors were hanging open or outright demolished, and surprisingly there seemed to be chickens everywhere. Where had they come from? Had someone let them loose? The birds were furious, strutting about the streets as if they were the true owners of Gwaren now.

Thunder rumbled in the sky and Rowan studied the swatch of gray clouds. "We can hope for rain," she said. "That should help with the fires."

There was another sound, however, that drew Maric's attention. From somewhere nearby, he could hear the muffled sounds of a woman shouting for help. "Do you hear that?" he asked Rowan, but she looked at him quizzically. Without waiting for her, he spun his horse about and charged toward the shouting.

Maric heard Rowan's shout of alarm behind him, but he didn't care. Urging his steed forward, he raced down a street cluttered with empty crates. When he turned the corner at what appeared to be an ale-house, he saw the source of the shouts. A beautiful elven woman with long honey-colored curls and dressed in simple white traveling clothes was struggling wildly as three men held her down. Her shirt was half ripped from her body, and only her wild twisting kept the men from completing their task.

"For the love of the Maker, help me! I beg you!" she screamed, spotting Maric.

One of the burly men slapped a meaty hand over her mouth as the other two turned to face Maric. These weren't his men, and he couldn't imagine them being ordinary townsfolk. Convicts, perhaps? They were certainly filthy enough and had a dangerous look that left no question as to what they intended.

One of them drew a knife. Maric didn't hesitate—he kicked his warhorse so it charged the men. The knife-wielding man lunged toward Maric. His mistake. Maric turned the warhorse and it kicked the man

right in the head and sent him flying, dead before he
hit the ground.

"You will leave her be!" Maric roared. He dismounted, drawing his blade to confront the remaining pair as his steed ran off. "In the name of the
crown, I command it!"

The burly man tightened his grip on the elf as she
struggled, screaming into his hand. The other man
bared his teeth and ran at Maric, shouting in rage.
Maric did not step out of the way, instead stepping
forward and letting the man run into the pommel of
his sword. He gasped and fell back, and Maric swung
the blade around to bash the man in the head with
the pommel again. He collapsed like a sack.

Rowan rode in, leaping off her mount and drawing
her sword. The burly man looked at Maric, and then
at her, and deciding that discretion was the better option, he abandoned the elf and ran for it. Rowan gave
chase, her silent glare toward Maric saying everything
of what she thought of the situation.

Maric went immediately to the elven woman's
aid. She lay in the street, trying to hold the tatters of
her shirt together and crying pitifully. Her clothing
was filthy and bloodstained, but Maric didn't think
the blood was hers. Other than some ugly-looking
bruises on her arms and legs, she seemed unhurt.

"Are you all right, err . . . my lady?" Maric realized belatedly that he wasn't sure what one called an
elven woman. They had elves in the rebel army, of
course, but one spoke to them as soldiers. He'd never
had servants, though he'd seen them in some of the
castles Mother had brought him to. Still, even then
he'd never spoken to them.

The elf looked up at him, tears streaming down

from eyes so incredibly green, he couldn't look away. "My name is Katriel," she said quietly. "You are too kind, Your Highness. Thank you." With his help, she retrieved a cloth package from where it had fallen nearby. As she stood up, she attempted to keep her tattered shirt together. It was hardly possible. Maric removed his purple cloak and put it around her shoulders.

She stared at him with horror and tried to get away from his cloak. "Oh, no! No, my lord, I couldn't!"

"Of course you can. It's just a cloak."

Reluctantly she allowed him to close it around her, blushing and looking away. Maric found himself staring at her neck, at how it gracefully flowed down into ample cleavage only barely concealed by the cloak. She seemed like such a delicate creature. He had heard that elven women held a certain fascination for men, the kind that made them popular in the brothels of Denerim. He had never been to the capital city, however, and had never understood what the appeal could be—until now.

He started as Rowan walked back into view, an annoyed look on her face. He stepped away from the elf almost too quickly, and Rowan's expression darkened into a scowl.

"This is Katriel," Maric offered lamely. Then he belatedly looked back at the elf. "And this is Lady Rowan. My, ah . . . She is my betrothed."

Katriel turned to Rowan and curtsied. "I am grateful to you as well, my lady. I had asked them for help. It seems I should have been more careful."

"I'll say," Rowan muttered. "Just what were you doing out here at all?"

"I had no other choice." The elf turned to Maric,

self-consciously clutching the cloak tighter around her. "I have been looking for you, my lord. The horse I was given died not far from here. I ran the rest of the way, but there was so much chaos. . . ."

Maric was confused. "You were looking for me?"

From underneath the purple cloak, Katriel produced the package she carried. It appeared to be several scrolls bound in leather casings. "I came as quickly as I could. I am a messenger sent by the Arl of Amaranthine."

Rowan's eyes went wide with alarm. "A messenger!"

Katriel's green eyes lowered nervously. "His Grace has been defeated. I did not see it with my own eyes, but he said he would hold the attackers as long as he could. He said it was vital that I reach you, my lord." She held out the scrolls again, and Maric reluctantly took them. She seemed relieved, her charge fulfilled.

"Defeated!" Rowan strode toward the elf in outrage. "What are you talking about? When did this happen?"

"Four days ago," Katriel replied. "I sped here on the horse I was given, and it died from exhaustion. But I had no choice. The same men that attacked His Grace were not far behind me in the forest." She looked at Maric pleadingly. "I had to reach you before they arrived, my lord. His Grace said that was more important than anything!"

Maric took a step back, stunned. He opened one of the scrolls and read it, his eyes scanning the content even as it confirmed what his sinking gut was telling him.

"What?" Rowan demanded. "What does it say, for the love of the Maker?"

Face paled, he looked up at her. "We sent Byron to

draw their attention, and he got it. A full legion of chevaliers, with mages. The King had to have planned it."

"And they're coming here?"

"They're perhaps a day behind me, my lord," said Katriel. "I wish I knew for certain."

Maric and Rowan stared at each other, unmoving. Overhead, the faint sound of thunder could be heard in the gray skies. Rain would prevent the spread of the fires in Gwaren, though much damage had already been done. Fighting still raged inside the manor, and the town was in complete chaos. It would take more than a day to get the situation under control, and even if they did, the only routes out of Gwaren were out on the sea or back through the forest, toward the approaching army.

They were trapped.

8

Loghain frowned. The shop he was crowded into smelled faintly of fish, and it contrasted sharply with the nervous fear of the elven archers who crouched next to him. The group of them were hiding in the shadows, waiting quietly for the enemy to appear.

From his vantage point by the window, Loghain could see most of Gwaren's town square. It was the kind of place where merchants would have gathered regularly to sell their wares. Normally it would have been full of bright colors and barrels and crates and people, but in the early morning light filtering down from the clouds, all he could currently see was smoke and debris left over from the previous day's battle. The rain had prevented the fires from gutting the town completely, but still many of the buildings around the square were ruins, smoke smoldering up from their blackened bones. Pieces of wood and belongings no doubt dropped by people fleeing into the forest littered the cobblestones right next to the bodies of the fallen, which they had not had time to collect.

The attack on the manor had barely been finished when Maric and Rowan madly rode up the hill to inform them of the approaching army. Arl Rendorn, who had been wounded by a stray arrow, promptly broke into an uncharacteristic string of expletives, but Loghain tried to think it through. The messenger sent by Arl Byron brought useful information: the composition of the usurper's forces, no doubt gathered by Byron's scouts prior to the enemy's attack.

Loghain wondered why the Arl hadn't come himself. If an elven girl had ridden hard enough to escape from the usurper's attack, then so could he. Surely one of his commanders could have led his men if he truly wanted to delay the enemy. But it seemed there was no shortage of men who were willing to sacrifice themselves for others in the world. He had to wonder if he would do similarly, given the chance. He still wasn't quite sure how he had ended up staying with the rebels when he said he would leave once he did what his father had asked him to do, yet here he was. There were times when Loghain looked in a mirror and didn't recognize the man who was staring back out at him. A lieutenant in the rebel army, confidant to the prince whom fate had deposited in his lap so long ago—was it only three years?

It felt like an eternity.

Loghain's notion had been a simple one: Gather

the army together as quickly as possible and hide them in Gwaren. Let it look like the rebel army had sacked the town and fled by sea. He had suggested executing all the prisoners they had taken to prevent them from complicating the plan, but Maric had summarily refused. Arl Rendorn hadn't been keen on the idea, either. Not that Loghain had expected them to do any differently. Most of the prisoners were locked away up at the manor without even anyone to watch them, and that was just how it had to be.

So the entire night had been spent scrambling to restore order and ready the men for yet another fight with barely a rest in between. Injuries were hastily bandaged, with the worst off being treated up at the manor by a handful of locals and camp followers. The locals had been fairly compliant once they realized the dreaded Prince Maric had no intention of having them all executed and raped.

Rowan had organized men to go around and find as many of the huddled townsfolk as they could and assure them that they would not be harmed, nor would their belongings be stolen. Many were herded up to the manor, but most elected to remain hidden. Those in dire need were provided supplies and told to remain where they were until the coming battle was over. They were suspicious—Rowan had told Loghain she could see it in their eyes. Many refused even to show themselves when her men passed. Even more chances for his plan to go wrong, Loghain thought to himself.

Not everyone had been unhappy to see them, of course. As the night wore on and they scrambled to get ready, a trickle of people appeared and approached the command post Maric had set up outside the manor. Arl Rendorn had been concerned at first, assuming that any of them could turn out to be assassins, but the expressions of relief and adoration on their faces were genuine. Loghain would never forget the mixed look of horror and helplessness on Maric's face as those people surrounded him, pawing him, and some of them even crying tears of joy.

Loghain knew who they were. These were the people who had been treated like dogs by the Orlesians. Stripped of all but their dignity, they had been left to pray in the darkness that one day the true ruler of Ferelden would return to save them. And he had come, hadn't he? Loghain had grimly watched them, knowing very well that Gwaren's liberation might be short-lived. The rebel army could be smashed here and forced to retreat in tatters through the thickest parts of the Brecilian Forest, something they would never survive.

Arl Rendorn had naturally procured a single ship for Maric to flee on if it came to that, a small sloop that might hold a handful of them. Loghain knew the Arl needn't have bothered, of course. Maric would have to be knocked out and dragged onto the boat. Rowan would go only if she were the one to drag him.

All the other buildings around the square held rebels within, as well, even if Loghain couldn't see them. Maric was holed up in an abandoned bakery across the way, and he imagined he could see Maric's blond hair through one of the windows. They had all finally assumed their hiding places not two hours before, and yet none of the elves with Loghain had slept. Despite their exhaustion, nervous energy kept them watchful. If the enemy didn't show up soon, he thought it might become unbearably tense.

Fortunately the enemy was in no mood to disappoint.

A misty rain began as the first chevaliers advanced into Gwaren. They were easy to distinguish from the rank-and-file soldiers with them, mounted knights in heavy armor with their distinctive purple tunics. Loghain could even make out the Imperial crest from this distance, the golden blazing half-sun. His fist clenched tightly on the shaft of his bow as he saw them appear.

Not yet, he told himself. *But soon.*

They were cautious, wary of attack from the shadows, but Loghain felt reassured. So far they had not begun to search the buildings. They expected to be attacked openly, or at the very least to encounter resistance in the streets. The fact that no one was in sight was keeping them alert and on their horses for now, but he knew that would not last very long. That was all right. It didn't have to. They just needed to get as much of the usurper's army into the town as possible.

More of the mounted knights moved slowly into the square, and now Loghain saw a new figure: a dark-skinned old man in yellow robes. He had a long white beard and a bearing that said he was used to power. A mage, then. The chevaliers beside him were adorned with golden cloaks and fancy plumes and surrounded by the thickest array of the riders. They were concerned. Where were the rebels? He could see them asking each other. It was time for the next part of the plan to begin.

Several figures moved out of some of the buildings

and began to run furtively toward the chevaliers. The horsemen wheeled on them immediately, drawing their swords and preparing for an immediate counterattack. The new figures shrieked in fear, however, and cowered before the blades. They were commoners in dirty rags, some of them splattered in blood. The chevaliers realized this quickly and relaxed their weapons, though not completely. Shouts went up along the enemy line, and the commoners were grabbed and brought before the mage and his commanders in the middle of the square.

Three women and one old man, and Loghain recognized only one of them. The young woman with the curly chestnut locks, her face covered with smudges of soot, was Rowan. She had volunteered to play what Loghain considered a risky role. Her father had nearly forbidden it, but Rowan had insisted— Loghain wasn't the only one who should have to risk his life in these plans, she had said, glancing toward him when she said it. He had kept his eyes strictly on the ground. In the end, the Arl had relented. Maric had commented that he couldn't remember the last time he had seen Rowan in a dress, filthy and tattered though it was.

And now she was on her knees before the dark-skinned mage as he studied her and the others who had run out with her. They were locals, fishwives and an old carpenter, who had begged Maric to let them help. Loghain had argued that only Rowan should go. What if one of these fools were to betray them? All they needed to do was blurt out that the rebels were hiding in the buildings, or collapse under the pressure. But Maric's belief was unshakable. *Let them help*, he had said. *It will make Rowan more believable.* The Arl had agreed, and Loghain watched nervously now, wondering if they would be proved fools after all.

So far, so good. The fishwives and the old man were suitably terrified and prostrating themselves before the mage. Loghain could clearly hear them babbling about the rebels attacking and then fleeing, but they gave away nothing of the plan. Indeed, they sounded like they were trying desperately to tell the mage anything and everything they possibly could. Rowan was bowing her head, but saying nothing.

"Silence!" the mage shouted angrily, the commoners immediately quieting and prostrating themselves again. The dark-skinned mage glared back at the commanders, who were now removing their helmets and looking far more peevish than concerned. If the cowardly rebels had actually fled, they were not going to have a battle after all. "Now, one of you— only one! Tell me how it is that the rebels fled!"

Rowan looked up now, seemingly nervous but calm. "They left on the ships, ser."

"What ships? What are you talking about, woman?"

"There were ships, many of them. They came and took them away."

"Lies!" he roared, slapping her across the face. Loghain almost leaped out of his hiding spot right then, but controlled himself. Rowan was no wilting flower—she put on a good show, cringing from the mage in fear and holding her cheek, but Loghain knew her far better than that. "The ships all left here days ago!"

"I . . . I don't know what to tell you, Ser Mage."
She sounded desperate. "There were ships! I don't
know who they belonged to!"

The mage seethed in rage and raised his hand to
strike her again. One of the commander knights distracted him, however, stepping forward to whisper
in his ear. After the two conferred for a moment,
the mage seemed displeased but no longer furious.
When the commander left the mage's side, he shouted
orders to the chevaliers that were still slowly riding
into the town. They were in Orlesian, but Loghain
understood the intent well enough and smiled. It was
too easy for them to believe, after all, that the lowly
rebel prince would rather run than fight.

The old mage turned back to regard Rowan once
again. "Stand up," he commanded her. Reluctantly
she did so, covering her tattered dress and keeping
her eyes averted.

"Describe these ships," he snapped.

"They were large," she stammered. "They had a
picture on their sails, like some sort of golden beast.
I . . . didn't get a very close look."

"A golden beast? Was it a drake?"

"I think so, Ser Mage." Rowan dropped her head
low. "They were not here long."

The mage stroked his chin thoughtfully. Loghain
could almost see the calculations running through
the man's head. Golden drakes were the symbol of
Calabria, a nation far to the north. The idea of an
alliance between Calabria and the rebels was unlikely,
but enough to give even him pause.

The Orlesian commanders were conferring among
themselves, and after a long minute, they turned and
spoke quietly to the mage. He nodded reluctantly, and

more orders were shouted. These, too, Loghain could understand in spirit. *Stand down your guard. Search the town for supplies. Send someone up to the manor.* They were the orders he would have given in their stead, had he been as eager as they to walk blindly into the town to begin with. The chevaliers were already visibly relaxing, chatting in their foreign tongue as they started to spread out. Many began moving farther into the square, calling for the supply wagons to set up tents.

It wouldn't be long now.

Satisfied, the mage turned back to Rowan. He smiled lasciviously and held out his hand before him. Raw power coalesced around him, the air crackling with energy, causing the other commoners to scramble away from him in terror. Rowan looked up, standing her ground, and the energy surged toward her. It curled around her like tendrils, lifting her up off the ground while holding her still. She did not struggle, but instead kept her face stony and calm.

The mage stepped close, brushing some dirt off her dress just above her breasts. Rowan recoiled from his touch, eliciting a delighted leer from him. "My," he said admiringly, "rather pretty for a common little mutt, no? It is sad that the rebels did not take you with them when they left."

His hand stroked across one of Rowan's breasts, and she violently spat in his face. The mage paused, nonplussed, and wiped the spittle from his cheek. The tendrils of energy tightened around Rowan. She hissed in fury but still did not struggle against the mage's spell.

"Brave," he said, his tone a mixture of amusement and contempt. "And fiery, too. I cannot say that I mind this at all." Almost casually he struck her with a backhand slap, hard across her face. "But you must learn your manners." He chuckled.

The mage turned away from Rowan, rubbing his hand, when suddenly he stared with shock at his chest. An arrow had sprouted there, the dark stain of blood already spreading on his yellow robes. He turned to look helplessly at an Orlesian chevalier who stood nearby, and as the two stared at each other in quiet horror, another two arrows flew toward the mage. One narrowly missed him, and another lodged in his throat. He went down gurgling, clutching at the arrow uselessly.

"Now! Attack now!" It was Maric shouting, leaping out of the bakery window with his sword held high. The archers beside him were already firing into the chevalier lines, and more men were running after him. The rest of the rebels suddenly sprang into action, spilling out of their hiding places throughout the square.

This wasn't the plan. It was too soon! *Damn you, Maric!* Loghain swore. With a sharp wave of his hand, he called the Night Elves beside him to action. They began firing into the gathered crowd, trying to protect Maric as he charged madly toward Rowan. One armored knight turned to skewer Maric as he passed, only to fall as Loghain placed an arrow neatly into the flesh near the base of his helmet.

In the erupting chaos, a great roar of noise could be heard outside the square. Loghain was sure Arl Rendorn was charging the rear flank, closing off those within the square from reinforcement. There was no way the enemy would have committed their entire force to walking into Gwaren, so they'd planned to lure as many enemy soldiers inside as possible before bisecting their line and blocking the narrow main street that led to the square.

Had they waited long enough? Loghain watched Maric carefully as the man finally reached Rowan in the great melee. She had been released from the spell and was crouched low, and when Maric drew near, he tossed her a blade. The first thing she did was use it to stab the gasping mage on the ground, sinking the point deep in his chest. She even put her weight into it, causing blood to gush from the mage's mouth as he groaned in agony. Maric stared at Rowan in momentary shock, but was forced to deal with two knights who suddenly rushed at him from behind.

"Cover the Prince and Lady Rowan!" Loghain called to his men. More arrows flew. Rowan leaped to strike at one of the knights who had attacked Maric, but he was having trouble with the other. The chevalier was skilled, parrying Maric's blade easily. One or two arrows struck home, but not enough to slow the chevalier down. With a sudden rush, he closed in on Maric and thrust his sword deep into the Prince's flank. Maric struggled to push his attacker off, and then weakly collapsed.

"Maric!" Rowan screamed in terror.

With a kick, she pushed away the knight she was battling and launched herself at the one who had wounded Maric. Her sword banged uselessly against the knight's armor, and when he turned to face her, she spun around and slashed her blade across the man's neck. Blood sprayed from him as he stumbled back.

The other chevalier rushed at Rowan's back, and she turned too late to face him . . . only to watch him hit by several arrows at once. One of them hit him in the side of the head, and he was knocked aside before he ever reached her.

She didn't pause, turning instantly and racing to Maric's side as he lay bleeding heavily on the ground. Rowan tried to rouse Maric, but he didn't move, and when she tried to adjust his armor to see the extent of his injury, her hands came away coated with thick blood. Her eyes went wide with horror, and she looked about helplessly. All she saw, however, was the intense battle around her as more of the rebels poured into the square.

Loghain grimaced and tossed aside his bow, drawing his sword. "Cover me," he ordered the Night Elves as he leaped over the window's ledge and sprinted into the street.

The battle continued for several hours afterwards, though of course Maric had been aware of none of it. By the time he finally awakened in his tent, it was already dark out. Wilhelm's magic had healed the worst of his wounds, but the mage still commented sharply that Maric had very nearly bled to death. If Loghain and Rowan had not dragged him from the middle of the battle and staunched the gaping wound in his side, he almost surely would have perished.

"So Rowan is all right, then?" Maric asked.

Wilhelm regarded him with a puzzled expression. "Alive, last I checked. I shall do so again, with your leave?" At a nod of assent from the Arl, the mage bowed and withdrew.

They had not trapped as many of the chevaliers inside the town square as they had hoped, due in no small part to Maric's early attack—or so Arl Rendorn sternly reminded him. Still, the Arl could hardly fault Maric for protecting his daughter. And in the end, the chaos had proved sufficient. Two other mages had been slain, and the chevaliers in the square had been routed. Arl Rendorn had chosen to open the main road and let them flee rather than wait for the larger force outside Gwaren to press the attack. The few commanders who got away were more interested in regrouping as far away as possible. The Arl let them go, sending as many archers to harry them as the rebels could afford.

"They will be back," the Arl informed Maric solemnly, "but we have time to prepare. We have options, for once."

"What kind of options?"

The Arl considered carefully. "The forest path forms a narrow approach," he said. "We can guard it quite easily. By the time the usurper assembles a force large enough to chance a crossing, we might be able to acquire enough ships that we could move the army up the coast."

Maric blinked, surprised. "Ships? Where would we get ships?"

"We could hire them . . . or build them, if necessary. If there is anything that Gwaren is not short of, it is lumber and fishing boats."

Maric mulled the information over. "So . . . the town is ours, then?"

The Arl nodded. "It is. For now."

Despite the caution in the Arl's voice, Maric lay back on his pillows and smiled. They had freed a town, clawed back a chunk of Ferelden away from the Orlesians for the first time in many years. He wondered what King Meghren would say now, how he would explain this embarrassment to the Emperor. For all Maric knew, he might send the King another dozen legions of chevaliers to crush Gwaren into dust, another show of how mighty the Empire was.

It was a disheartening thought.

"Despite our hope that one of the mages killed might be the King's right hand, Severan," the Arl frowned, "it seems we have no such luck. None of the three dead mages match the description our informants gave us. These were all men freshly sent from the Circle of Magi in Orlais."

"At least that means the Fereldan Circle has kept to their word," Maric offered.

Arl Rendorn nodded. "There is that."

Maric suddenly brightened. "And Loghain? Is he well?"

"Injured, but not seriously." The Arl sighed. "He was so furious at you, he swore that he would wring your neck. He did not leave your side until Wilhelm arrived, however. And even then, we could not pry Rowan away until she was certain you would live."

"I have good friends, what can I say?"

The Arl studied Maric for a moment, frowning. He seemed as if he was about to say something but then thought better of it. He smiled faintly. "Who knows what that mage might have done to Rowan had you not acted? You might have saved her life, Maric. I think she knows this."

"She would have done the same for me." Maric shrugged.

"Of course." The Arl abandoned the effort. He reminded Maric of numerous sundries, some reports of looting in Gwaren, and the need to restore order to the populace as soon as possible. He also mentioned the idea of sending out messengers to other Fereldan nobles to announce Gwaren's liberation, but by then, the details were swimming in a haze of fatigue. Maric's injured side was throbbing, and before he knew it, he was drifting in and out of consciousness.

Finally Arl Rendorn chuckled and told Maric he would handle the remainder of the details himself. He told Maric to rest, and then left the tent.

Maric listened for a time to the sound of the men putting up other tents in the manor's courtyard next to his own. It amused him to eavesdrop on their banter, their earthy jokes and easy laughter. Eventually they realized they were outside the Prince's tent and started shushing each other in increasingly loud measures before finally finishing their task and leaving to raid the cellar of an abandoned tavern they had spotted down by the docks. Part of Maric wanted to go with them, but chances were he wouldn't even have successfully crawled out of his bed. It was for the best, he supposed. Chances were he would just have made the men nervous, anyhow.

With silence came sleep. He had no idea how much time passed before he stirred again. The shadows were deep in the large tent, and his wounded side throbbed far less than it once had. A figure was quietly entering through the flap, a flickering lantern in its hand casting the shadows that had stirred him.

Maric blinked his bleary eyes, and for a moment he thought he saw the silhouette of a shapely woman behind the light. "Rowan?" he asked uncertainly.

But as the figure entered, he saw quite clearly that it was not her at all. Katriel, the elven messenger, stood at the entrance, clean and changed into fresh garments. Maric thought the glow of the lantern made her seem almost unearthly amid the shadows, her golden locks falling around her shoulders like a beautiful, ethereal spirit that had come to visit him in the night.

"I . . . I am sorry if I am disturbing you, my lord," she said hesitantly. Her green eyes fluttered away from Maric, and he realized that aside from his bandages, he was covered only by the thick furs on his bed. "I should leave you be." She covered the lantern with her hand and made as if to retreat.

"No, wait," Maric said quietly, sitting up. He could not get up, of course, and pulled the furs to keep himself covered. He blushed, but at the same time was grateful the elven woman hesitated.

She looked back at him, biting her lower lip nervously. He found himself admiring the curve of her simple white dress. "I see someone found something for you to wear?" he asked. "Those men did not hurt you, did they?"

"No, my lord. You came just in time, in shining armor just as in the tales." She smiled at him, and their gazes touched, and bashfully she looked away. She then noticed the bandages around his midsection as if for the first time. "Oh, no! It's true! They said you had been injured badly, but I had no idea!" Almost unwillingly she stepped forward and touched his bandage with her delicate hands.

She was full of nothing but concern, but still Maric's back stiffened at her touch. His blush deepened as she jumped back.

"Oh, I apologize, my lord, I should not have—"

"No, no," he said quickly. "No need to apologize. If you hadn't arrived when you did, there's no way we would have had time to prepare. We are in your debt." Then he paused, perplexed. "But . . . I have to admit I'm not sure why you're here. In my tent."

She stood there awkwardly, staring back at him, and then slowly smiled. He thought her smile looked very warm and genuine. "I . . . I had to see it for myself, my lord. I prayed that the man who so bravely saved my life would not perish, but I had to know for certain. . . ."

"I'm fine, Katriel. Really I am."

Her eyes twinkled with sudden delight. "You . . . remember my name?"

Maric was taken aback by the statement. "Is there a reason I shouldn't?"

"I am just an elf, my lord. Your people . . . Most of them do not see us. They look, but they do not see. My mother was maid to a human man her entire life. He never once called her by her name." She then realized whom she was talking to and looked horrified, curtsying low. "Oh, my . . . I am forgetting myself. I should not—"

He chuckled, holding up a hand to cut her off. "It's fine. And of course I remember you. How could I not? You're beautiful."

She paused, tilting her head slightly as she regarded him. Her elven eyes shone bewitchingly in the firelight. "You . . . think I am beautiful, my lord?"

Maric wasn't sure how to respond, even though he knew he didn't want to take it back. He was suddenly very aware of his lack of clothing, and awkwardness threatened to overtake him. Katriel stepped forward slowly, her eyes holding his in the silence. She put the lantern on top of a chest by his bed and then sat down on the edge.

Their faces were only inches apart. Maric was breathing heavily, but still couldn't bring himself to look away from her. Even her smell was intoxicating, like a rare flower that bloomed only in the darkest gardens. Enticing and sweet without being cloying.

She reached out, and silently she ran a slender finger from his bandages up along his chest. His skin shuddered where she touched, and he gulped. It was the only sound in the hushed darkness.

"I would stay with you, my lord," she whispered. "If you would have me."

He blinked and looked down at the furs, blushing again. "I . . . I wouldn't want you to feel obligated," he stammered. "I mean, I wouldn't want it to seem like . . . I wouldn't want to take advantage. . . ."

Katriel touched her finger to his lips, quieting him. He looked up at her, and found her gazing at him from under heavy lids. "You are not, my lord," she said seriously, her voice husky.

"Please . . . don't call me that."

"You are not," she repeated.

The distance between them closed as if they were drawn together, and Maric kissed her. Her skin was as soft as he'd imagined, and she melted under his every touch.

Outside the tent, Rowan watched in stony silence as the lantern light within was extinguished. She wore a red dress of silk, a Calabrian garment that bared her shoulders. The sharp-faced woman who sold it to her had pointed out that Rowan was too muscled to wear such a dress, that her shoulders were too broad. The silk felt luxurious against her skin, however, so much different from the leather and metal she was used to. So she had bought it despite the woman, though she had never once had the occasion to wear it since.

She regretted wearing it now, and regretted coming, yet as she stood there in the darkness, she found she could not will herself to move.

The guard slumped nearby, fast asleep and snoring lightly. Rowan shook her head in exasperation, tempted to kick the man awake. What if it had been an assassin come to visit Maric instead of the elven woman? But they were all exhausted from the long battles, and no doubt the guard was assigned to his post while nearly asleep on his feet. She could forgive the nameless guard his lapse in judgment, but only his.

When she heard the first faint moan coming from inside, finally she stepped away. Perhaps it was only her imagination, but either way, she decided she could not stay where she was. *I do not want to hear this*, she told herself, coldness clutching at her heart.

Her steps were stealthy as she maneuvered among the tents. Many bodies were slumbering on the ground, some even on top of each other. The smell of ale was everywhere. The celebration had been lengthy after the Orlesians had taken to the forest in disarray. Even though looting was discouraged, they couldn't help but look the other way as the men scoured the town's taverns for ale barrels and wine. They deserved a celebration after two such fine victories.

Rowan had watched them drink, but did not partake. All she could think about was thrusting her sword into the mage, the fury she had felt blinding her reason. Making him suffer was all that had mattered to her. Was there to be nothing more to her life than blood? She had gone to Maric thinking . . . thinking . . .

You weren't thinking at all, she scolded herself. *This was a terrible idea.*

She came out of the tents into the unoccupied portion of the manor's courtyard. On clear ground, Rowan slowed to a stop. She breathed the night air deeply, standing stiffly under the glare of the moon. She felt ill, and part of her wanted nothing more than to rip the dress away from her skin, tear it into shreds. She wanted to keep walking, to leave the manor grounds and become lost within the restless shadows of the forest.

"Rowan?"

She turned sharply toward the sound and saw Loghain approaching. He was bandaged and wearing a simple longshirt and leather trousers, and he seemed more than a little confused to see her. Finally he stopped, staring at her with those unsettling eyes. They made her shudder, as they always did.

"It *is* you," he said, his tone guarded.

"I couldn't sleep."

"So you . . . decided to put on a fine dress and go for a walk?"

She said nothing in response, folding her arms around herself and staring at the ground. Instead of leaving, however, Loghain remained where he was.

She could feel those eyes fixed on her even if she didn't see them. The forest shadows beckoned, but she ignored their maddening call.

"You look beautiful," he told her.

Rowan held up a hand to stop him, taking a painful breath before speaking. "Don't do this," she protested weakly.

Loghain nodded somberly, and for a long moment he said nothing. The wind whistled through the stones of the manor walls, and the moon shone high overhead. It was easy to pretend there was no army camped around them, no sleeping soldiers and men in their tents a stone's throw away. They were alone in the darkness, a gaping chasm between them.

"I am not a fool," he said quietly. "I see how you look at him."

"You do?" Her tone was bitter.

"I know you are promised to him. I know you are to become his Queen." He stepped toward her, taking her cold hands in his. She looked away from him, grimacing, and it only made him look at her sadly. "I have known these things since I first met you. For three years, I have tried to accept that this is how it must be, and yet . . . still I can't stop thinking of you."

"*Stop!*" she hissed, pulling her hands away. Loghain stared at her, his eyes tortured, but she couldn't care, couldn't. Angry tears streamed down her cheeks as she backed away from him. "For the love of the Maker, don't do this," she begged.

Loghain's stricken look twisted up her insides all the more. She clamped down on her anguish and turned away. "Just leave me alone. Whatever you thought . . . Whatever you wanted from me—" She wiped at her eyes, and found herself wishing again that she was in her armor instead of that flimsy, useless dress. "—I cannot . . . I will not be that woman." Her tone was brusque and final.

Rowan fled, her back stiff and the train of her red dress trailing behind her. She didn't look back.

9

Dawn had come and gone in Gwaren, and the town was already bustling with activity. Those residents who had spent the previous two days in hiding were now slowly coming out into the streets, eyes blinking in disbelief at the devastation surrounding them. The morose skies blew in salty spray from the ocean, disguising the stench of decaying corpses that was already beginning to permeate the air. The town was almost too still, a gloom cast on the wreckage like a shroud that was only just now being disturbed.

Arl Rendorn was quick to realize that order was needed. After waking a number of officers who were still half drunk from the previous night's exertions, he got much of the rebel army up and moving. Men were sent to patrol the streets and spread the message: The people of Gwaren would be safe under Prince Maric. The grain stores were opened and matters of shelter seen to for those who had spent the night huddling in the burned-out husks of their homes. Most important of all, the soldiers started collecting the dead.

It was not long before plumes of black sickly smoke rose from the pyres, quickly snatched up by the breeze and scattered. The stench of burning flesh was everywhere, and a dark grease settled over every surface. Those who ventured outside did so with handkerchiefs covering their mouths. Even so, laundry was still hung on the lines, and a smattering of fishing boats still sailed out into the waves. Life had to go on, no matter who ruled.

Atop the hill overlooking the town, the manor was largely peaceful. Those who had not been wakened to assist with the activity in town slept on, though here and there signs of activity could be seen. A few of the Teyrn's servants had tentatively returned, uncertain of their status but unwilling to abandon the only home they had ever known. Likewise, the camp followers that kept the army in food and clean linens were already tiptoeing about the manor's halls, taking stock of its food supplies and sweeping up the worst of the debris.

The manor's stables were still quiet, the majority of its new occupants either sleeping on their feet or munching away quietly on hay. One of the larger warhorses had been brought out of its pen, and patiently soaked in the dusty morning sunlight as Loghain saddled him. There were several saddlebags waiting to be tied on, as well, though none of them were particularly heavy. One did not load a warhorse down with giant packs like a mule.

It was fortunate, then, that Loghain had little to take. He had found his old studded leathers in one of the supply wagons during the night after an hour's search by torchlight. It felt good to be wearing them again, like a pair of familiar boots long ago worn in. After a bit of hesitation, he had decided to keep his lieutenant's cloak as well. He had earned it, after all. Then he had acquired a tent and some camping gear with the help of a very startled young maid. All of this had been done quietly, with the hope that he would be gone and on his way before the rest of the manor awoke.

Sadly, that was not to be. Loghain heard angry steps approaching and identified them as belonging to Maric even before he stormed into the stable.

The Prince was sweating and pale, blond hair askew. The fact that he had arrived in a rush was painfully apparent, as he was wearing neither shoes nor shirt—only a pair of baggy trousers no doubt donned in haste. The heavy bandages around his chest were already spotted with dark bloodstains from the exertion. Maric leaned heavily on a wooden staff he was using as a crutch and stood panting in the doorway, glowering at Loghain indignantly.

"Where do you think you're going?" Maric demanded, gasping for breath.

Loghain ignored him, keeping his attention focused on tying up the saddle.

Maric frowned and hobbled inside, scattering the loose hay that covered the floor. A fat tabby, which had been cleaning itself contentedly nearby, decided that enough was enough and trotted out the door he had left open, tail jutted indignantly up in the air.

Maric marched over to Loghain and stopped an arm's length away, almost stumbling and cursing the staff as he tried to maintain his balance.

"I know you're not due to ride anywhere," he said warily. "And I already know that you've been sneaking around, collecting your things."

Loghain didn't look up. "I'm not sneaking."

"So what do you call it? Saddling up before dawn, not bothering to say anything to anyone? Where are you going? Are you coming back?"

Loghain finished tying the saddle with an exasperated tug and then spun on Maric, his teeth clenched in fury. He paused, sighing inwardly as he saw Maric's confusion growing. With a grimace, he looked Maric straight in the eyes. "I should have left a long time ago. I said I was going to bring you back to your army, and I did. But now it's time for me to go."

"I knew it!" Maric stormed a step away and then spun back about, clearly frustrated that his injury prevented him from properly pacing. "As soon as they told me what you were up to, I knew that's what you were doing!" He shook his head in disbelief. "Maker's breath, Loghain, why now? What brought this on, all of a sudden?"

Loghain's face was stone. He turned back to his horse, picking up one of the sacks. "It's simply time. You're fine, Maric." His tone sounded hollow, even to himself. "You don't need me."

"Don't be an idiot!" Maric scoffed. Then he stopped, regarding Loghain curiously. "Are you angry at me about the charge yesterday? I had no idea what that mage was going to do to Rowan, I just thought that—"

"No, that's not it."

"Then what?"

"I need to go back," Loghain stated firmly. The emphasis was such that Maric didn't need to ask where he meant. "I need to find . . . what's left of my father. I need to bury him. I need to know what happened to everyone else, if they got away or not. What happened to Sister Ailis?" He looked at Maric seriously. "These are people he cared about. He wouldn't want me to abandon them. I've done my part, here. I need to go and . . . I have a duty. And not just here."

"So why does it feel like you're running away?"

Loghain sighed. This was the man who had stumbled into Loghain's life and brought all his troubles with him. Because of him, Loghain's father was dead and Loghain had been swept up into a war he never even wanted to become part of. Yet somehow over the last three years, Maric had become his friend. How had that happened? He still wasn't sure.

Outside, the sounds of the manor stirring to life could already be heard, men shouting and boots running. No doubt Maric had roused the entire army before coming. He wasn't about to make this easy, was he? How very like him.

Loghain chuckled wearily, scratching his head. "I'm not used to talking this much," he admitted.

"Nonsense. You talk to me all the time. Rowan always says I'm the only one who can make you string more than three words together at once." Maric grinned, and then his face became very serious. He reached out and put a hand on Loghain's shoulder, the hand of a concerned friend. "So talk to me. Do you really have to do this now?"

"If not now, then when? It's been three years."
Loghain turned back to the task of tying the saddlebags. "I'm not one of your rebels, Maric, not really.
Nor am I one of your knights. There's no place for
me here."

"I could knight you." It sounded almost like a
threat.

Loghain locked stares with Maric, and the challenge hung there in the air for a long moment. Then
Maric relented, reluctantly. Nothing more needed to
be said on the matter.

Maric leaned on his crutch and watched Loghain
prepare his bags and gather his quiver. He remained
silent, though it was evident that he desperately
wanted to continue objecting.

The sounds of activity increased outside until
Loghain heard new footsteps arriving. Armored footsteps. He stiffened and sighed inwardly, purposely
not looking as Rowan walked in a moment later, her
heavy plate newly scrubbed and gleaming. Her brown
locks were still wet from washing, the damp curls
plastered against her pale skin. She was still lovely, he
thought, even if her expression was icy and stiff.

"What is going on?" she demanded.

Maric was about to answer but hesitated as Rowan
shot a pointed look in his direction, frowning. He
seemed taken aback, and clearly uncertain what he
had done to deserve such a hostile greeting.

"I'm leaving," Loghain announced, interrupting
the confrontation.

Rowan's head snapped back to Loghain, her expression softening into confusion. "You're leaving?
For good?"

"Yes. For good."

"I've been trying to convince him to stay," Maric chimed in, sighing with exasperation.

Rowan stood in the doorway, shifting in her armor uncomfortably. She opened her mouth several times as if to speak but said nothing, and Loghain did his best not to notice. If Maric was aware of the tension, he made no indication of it. He turned and hobbled toward one of the horse pens, leaning against it with a wince. Finally Rowan found her voice. "Don't go," she pleaded. "Not like this."

"There's no reason for me to stay," Loghain said gruffly.

"What about the Orlesians?" Maric asked. "I know how you feel about them. We're finally making headway against Meghren. Don't you want to see him defeated? If you were going to do anything for your father, why not do that?"

Loghain snorted scornfully. "You don't need me for that."

"You're wrong! We do!"

Rowan stepped forward. "Maric is right. You told my father once that he is not flexible enough. All the best plans have been yours, Loghain. Without you, we would not be here."

"I think you are giving me too much credit," he snorted. "The Night Elves were my doing. Everything else you could have done on your own. I am only a lieutenant, if you'll recall."

"There's nothing wrong with our memories." Rowan's cool expression returned. "If you truly wish to leave now, with so much left to be done, then we cannot stop you." Her eyes became hard. "But I had assumed you a better man."

Maric's eyes widened with shock. Loghain went

still. He clenched and unclenched his fists in fury while Rowan stood her ground, unflinching. "I have done everything that was asked of me," he said in even, angry tones, "and you would demand even more?"

"Yes, that's right." She nodded. "We do not have the same luxury you do, Loghain, to come and go as it pleases us. We either defeat the Orlesians and drive them from Ferelden or we die. But if there are more important things to concern yourself with, then by all means . . . leave."

"Rowan," Maric cautioned uncertainly.

She ignored Maric and walked up to Loghain, placing her face an inch away from his own. He did not flinch away. "Are you not a Fereldan?" she demanded. "Is this not your future King? Do you not owe him your loyalty? From what Maric has told me, your father understood that."

"Rowan, don't," Maric said more forcefully.

She gestured toward Maric. "Is this or is this not your friend? Have the three of us not shed blood together for years now? Is that not a bond that is more important than *anything*?" The plea in her gray eyes betrayed her harsh words. Loghain found it hard to hold on to his fury.

So he said nothing.

There was silence for a time, and then Rowan backed off reluctantly. Loghain sighed heavily and turned away. He couldn't face those eyes.

"Loghain," Maric began slowly, "I know you never promised you would stay. I know I was dumped in your lap and all of this should never have happened." He grinned sadly and shrugged. "But it did. You're here and I've come to rely on you. We all have, even the Arl. Please don't walk away from this."

Loghain winced. "Maric . . ."

Holding tightly on to the staff, Maric got down on his knees. Alarmed, Rowan ran over to support him, to try to pull him back up, but he refused. The staff quivered, and he grunted with effort as he dropped down fully and then looked up at Loghain. "Please, I'm begging you. You and Rowan are the only friends I have."

Rowan stopped short, her hand flinching away from Maric as if he were red hot. She stiffly backed away from him, her face a mask of stone.

Loghain stared down at Maric, horrified by the grandiose gesture. Worse, he felt his resolve crumbling. This had felt so much clearer in the night. Now he felt like a coward. "You are opening your wound," he complained at Maric.

Maric winced, holding his bandaged side gingerly. "Umm . . . probably, yes."

"Must be from all the exertion," Rowan commented dryly.

Loghain shook his head in disbelief. "Maker's breath, man, aren't you supposed to have some dignity? Somewhere?"

"Me? Dignity?"

"Being the supposed future King and such."

"I think Rowan took my dignity."

She snorted derisively, folding her arms. "There was nothing else worth having."

Maric chuckled and then looked up at Loghain again, serious. "So does this mean you're staying, then? I practically ran here in my smallclothes, you know."

"If you had, that would certainly make this quite the picture, wouldn't it?"

"I'm serious." Loghain could see that he was, serious beyond a doubt. "I don't think we can do this without you."

Apparently he should have sneaked off while it was still dark, leaving his leathers and everything else behind. Because there was no other way he was going to escape, was there? He sighed irritably at Maric. "Well, if you intend to come running after me every time I try to leave—"

"Not *every* time."

"Very well. I'll stay."

Maric grinned broadly and struggled to stand back up, but did so far too quickly. He cried out in pain and almost fell, but Rowan rushed forward and caught him first. Her armor scratched against his bare chest, and he flinched in her arms, laughing at the same time. "Ow! Careful with those!"

"How very manly you are, my prince," she sighed.

They laughed and smiled at each other, a moment that quickly faded as Rowan's smile faltered. After she helped Maric to his feet, she moved away. He glanced after her, baffled, before the quickly spreading bloodstain on his bandages drew his attention. "Ahhh," he breathed, "Wilhelm will frown at me for certain now!"

Loghain regarded his warhorse, standing there all saddled up and ready to go. With a silent shake of his head, he began untying the bags. Rowan turned to go, but Maric held up his hands to stop her. "Wait!" he shouted. Then he grabbed the staff and quickly hobbled out the door, a man on a mission.

She stared after him, frowning. "What has he planned now?"

Loghain shrugged. "With him, it could be anything."

The two of them stood there in the dust and hay listening to the faint sounds of commotion outside and the occasional nickering of the horses. Loghain thought he should speak, but as the tension built, it seemed to become an insurmountable obstacle. He returned his attention to the saddle, feeling Rowan's eyes on his back.

After what seemed like forever, she spoke, her voice pained and hesitant. "Were you leaving because of me?"

He stopped. "I was leaving because I was the lesser man. According to you."

She flinched. "I . . . shouldn't be the only reason you stay."

"You're not." He turned toward her, his gaze hard. "He is."

She nodded slowly, her eyes brimming with tears she didn't shed. He didn't have to say anything else. They stood where they were, the distance between them filling the entire room, neither of them speaking. The moment stretched into agony.

Loghain wondered if he would have to remember this moment, if he would have to memorize the curve of her jaw, the gray eyes that blinked at him from under those brown curls, the strength behind her desperately unhappy frown. He wondered if he would need this memory as a shield, if he was indeed going to stay. Surely he was mad.

Eventually Maric hobbled back through the door, Arl Rendorn and several other soldiers in tow. Rowan and Loghain looked away in different directions, their moment abruptly ended. The Arl appeared non-plussed and quizzically looked at Maric, who seemed rather pleased with himself.

"I think we need to do what we were discussing a few days ago, Your Grace," Maric announced, breathing heavily and sweating from all the running about.

The Arl looked dubiously at Maric. "You mean now?" Then he noticed the warhorse and the packs, and frowned. "Going somewhere?" he asked Loghain directly.

Loghain shrugged. "Not anymore."

"Yes, I think we should do it right now," Maric insisted.

Arl Rendorn chewed on that thought for a moment as the other soldiers looked at him questioningly. Then he nodded. "As you wish. Perhaps it is for the best." He turned to face Loghain. "Loghain Mac Tir, you have served your prince well in these past years. You have proved yourself to be an able leader of men, and there is—"

"Wait," Loghain interrupted. "I said I would stay, I don't need—"

"Let me finish." The Arl smiled. "There is not a day that has passed where Maric and I have not commented on how we value your presence. Your current rank is no indication of your importance to our cause. Thus, despite your lack of knighthood, we feel it is fitting that you be given the rank of commander."

Loghain had been about to interrupt again, sensing some kind of reward forthcoming—but he stopped short. He'd no idea that Maric intended this. The protest caught in his throat, and he stared at the Arl, flabbergasted. Maric grinned in delight.

"This places you immediately beneath me in the chain of command, Loghain," the Arl continued. "My orders to the other officers will be relayed through you, and I would expect you to take on more logistical duties. This is provided, of course, that you are willing to accept the promotion?" The corner of the Arl's mouth twitched ever so slightly with amusement. "You have proved yourself to be . . . unpredictable over such matters in the past, after all."

Loghain stared, his mouth agape.

"It's not a bribe," Maric mentioned. "I just wanted you to know that I was—"

"I'll do it." The words tumbled out of Loghain's mouth almost before he realized he was saying them. He looked up and saw the Arl's hand offered to him and shook it numbly.

"Well done." The Arl grinned.

Loghain retrieved his hand and turned toward Maric, who was grinning and offering his own hand. Loghain stood there silently and stared at it as if he had no idea what it signified.

After a moment, Maric awkwardly lowered his hand. "Err . . . is something wrong?"

"No." Loghain stared hard at the ground, grimacing.

Then he awkwardly lowered himself to one knee before Maric. His face felt hot and flushed, and he knew he must have looked quite the fool. The shocked soldiers behind the Arl looked at each other incredulously.

Maric looked down at him with abject horror. "What are you doing?"

Loghain frowned thoughtfully, but then nodded. He knew this was what he needed to do. "I may be no knight," he said firmly, "but I'm certain it wouldn't do to have a commander in your army who hadn't sworn an oath of some kind."

Now it was Maric's turn to be flabbergasted. His mouth dropped open, and he looked helplessly from Arl Rendorn to Rowan and back to Loghain. "No! No, no, I don't need any kind of oath from you!"

"Maric—"

"You misunderstand, I would never . . . I mean I know how you feel, your father was a completely—"

"Maric," Loghain interrupted. "Shut up."

Maric's mouth snapped shut with an audible click.

Behind them, Rowan slowly retreated to the doorway. No one noticed as she silently turned and left.

"If you really want me to stay," Loghain began, looking up at Maric, "then I will. And if you are going to trust me with your army, if you're going to trust me that much, then I'm honored. I may not be highborn, and I have no idea how much my word is worth to you . . . but you have it. You are my friend and my prince and I swear to serve you well."

Maric swallowed hard. "Your word means a great deal to me, Loghain," he said simply. He seemed deeply touched.

Slowly Loghain stood back up. Arl Rendorn nodded at him silently, pride in the old man's eyes. The soldiers behind the Arl saluted. He stood there dumbly in front of them, not sure what to say.

Maric grinned like a fool. "Commander Loghain," he said aloud, as if testing out the title.

Loghain chuckled ruefully. "That does sound strange."

"I'm willing to bet there's still a wine bottle or two to be found from last night."

Loghain snorted. "Full of swill, perhaps."

"And what better way to celebrate your promotion?"

"Will you put on a shirt, at least?"

"Fine, fine. If you insist." Maric chuckled, shouldering his staff and hobbling out the door.

Loghain waited a moment, shaking his head in quiet disbelief. *I am a fool*, he thought.

Then he followed Maric out.

10

The main hall of Gwaren's manor was crowded, as it was never intended to be used as a royal court. Not even a court presided over by an exiled prince, attended by nobility already part of the rebel cause and a smattering of those who had dared the journey despite the threat of the usurper's wrath. Even so, Loghain saw that many more had come than he had assumed might. Certainly many more were present than Maric had dared to hope. Loghain had to suppress a grin as he watched Maric sitting on the ornate chair at the head of the hall and becoming more and more nervous, watching his guests crowding among the tables.

The usurper had not made it easy for them over the past several weeks. Fortunately it seemed that there was little King Meghren could do. The Brecilian Passage through the great forest was easily defended, and though the King's forces had attempted to reach Gwaren several times, they had been forced to turn back long before nearing the town each time. The tactics the rebels had learned in holding the southern hills benefited them here, and Loghain was proud of the role his Night Elves had played in harassing the enemy lines from within the forest. Their reputation among the enemy as brutal killers had only increased, and it was said that many men within the King's army were refusing to take the night watch for fear it would mean a silent arrow in the throat.

This meant the overland route to Gwaren was closed, but fortunately it was not a route that the town relied on. The port had remained open, and after an initial period of uncertainty, it had resumed a bustling business. Maric had met with the local mayor, a portly fellow who had scraped the floor in abject terror when the men brought him in. The mayor was a decent man, Ferelden-born and ill-treated by the Orlesians who had assumed rule over the land. Naturally he had no reason to believe that the invaders were any different, and was shocked when Maric put him back in charge of the town and gave him discretion in using the rebel army to restore law and order.

After a few nervous tests of his authority, each decision backed by Maric with little question, the mayor performed his duties with vigor. The man's relief was almost palpable, and by convincing him of Maric's honest intentions, so, too, were most of the local Fereldans convinced. The acceptance of Maric as the true prince became commonplace, with lines at the manor by the well-to-do who were now only too willing to pledge their allegiance. Efforts accelerated to rebuild and provide shelter to those displaced by the fighting, and there were even reports of some who had fled Gwaren returning to their homes.

Of course, the few local Orlesians who had been unable to flee the terrifying prospect of rebel control were the least pleased by their situation. They were less fortunate folk, servants to the wealthy gentry as well as guardsmen and a handful of merchants and entertainers. Poor or not, Loghain was not about to risk them proving their loyalty to King Meghren by assassinating Maric. The guards had been rounded up and imprisoned in the manor's dungeon while the rest were being carefully watched.

They weren't the only potential problems, Loghain was certain. The smiles of the locals would fade quickly if the wind changed direction, without a doubt. Maric scoffed at the idea, but even Rowan agreed that security needed to be tightened around the manor. Taking over a town was one thing; controlling it was quite something else.

In time, the usurper would rouse a sufficient force that they would push through the Brecilian Passage and attack, and Arl Rendorn worried about exactly when that was going to happen. Gwaren was defensible but difficult to retreat from, after all. Their saving grace was that the sea lanes remained unhindered. Ferelden had never been a seafaring culture, and thus the usurper had been forced to resort to offering exorbitant bounties for those willing to raid ships bound for Gwaren. Much to his frustration, there were few takers. Those nobles who had arrived by ship had reported little in the way of obstruction. If the rumors were to be credited, Meghren was fit to be tied over the ability of the rebels to seemingly come and go as they pleased and already had a new set of heads adorning the palace gates.

Arl Rendorn worried that eventually the Emperor would send the usurper a fleet to patrol the coast, but it had not happened yet. For the moment they were safe. Gwaren's occupation was a black eye to the Orlesians, showing that Maric was strong enough to hold his own court, the first since his grandfather's time. So the curious had come.

At least half the room, Loghain surmised, consisted of men and women who had never marched with the rebels. On the surface, these were all loyalists, the old and the dispossessed who all were affecting relief and loyalty at the rebels' progress. The wine was flowing freely, and all the ruddy faces were smiling broadly, but Loghain wondered at the end of the day how many of them would offer more than encouragement? Very few, he imagined, and even then only if the usurper didn't find out about it.

Rowan insisted that even their presence was a risk, a level of defiance against the King that they would not have dared before Gwaren was taken. After all, how certain could anyone be that news would not reach Denerim? Some of these men had to be spies. The King was not known for giving anyone the benefit of the doubt, so Rowan was certain that either hope or desperation had brought some of these men here.

Remembering the time they had spent in the Bannorn, Loghain was inclined to agree. Still, diplomacy was Maric's job.

The hall had reached a fever pitch of chattering voices and clinking wine goblets when Maric finally stood from his seat. Loghain thought he looked small in his black robe, an ermine-lined garment that they had appropriated from the former owner of the manor. He did look regal, however, and would have looked more so were it not for the nervous sweat dripping from his face.

The noise in the hall hushed, and many of the nobles took their seats at the tables. Loghain remained standing, as did the Arl and Rowan and many of the other rebel guards who watched from the walls. A soldier stepped out from behind Maric's chair carrying a large staff and a scroll. The staff he ceremoniously stamped on the stone floor three times, the thumping sound ringing throughout the hall and causing the last whispers and fidgets to cease. The soldier presented the scroll and read:

"On this, the ninety-ninth year of the Blessed Age, thou art welcomed to the court of Prince Maric Theirin, son to she who was Queen Moira Theirin and heir to the blood of Calenhad, First King of Ferelden. Bare not thy blade, and respect shall be shown to thee in turn."

The soldier stamped the staff again, once, and Loghain quietly joined the entire room in chanting a low and solemn, "Our blades are yours, my lord." If only it were truth and not a formality.

The soldier put away the scroll and bowed low to Maric before withdrawing. Maric continued to stand there, gauging the crowd. Some of the nobles began whispering to each other, but most watched closely.

He's going to disregard everything the Arl told him, isn't he? Loghain thought to himself. Rendorn had spent many hours coaching Maric on exactly what he should say, the formalities observed in a true court. But Loghain saw in Maric's eyes that he had different plans.

You cheeky bastard, Loghain thought.

"I know what you're thinking," Maric began. His voice carried easily throughout the quiet hall. "Many of you have been asking me about it tonight. I know some of you were at Redcliffe when Arl Rendorn declared my mother the rightful Queen, but I didn't ask you here to witness a coronation."

A stir of surprised voices erupted, but Maric held up a hand. "When I am coronated"—he raised his voice over the din—"I intend for it to be while seated on Calenhad's throne and with the crown that currently sits on the usurper's head!"

Shouts and cheers greeted Maric's cry, many of the nobles standing and clapping their hands vigorously. Some were quiet and perhaps even shocked, Arl Rendorn among them. Loghain watched the poor man pale, seeing his careful coaching go awry. Maric looked out at the hall intensely, fire in his eyes. Loghain approved.

"So why are you here?" Maric began again, before the shouting subsided. He walked forward into the hall, moving slowly among the tables. The noise in the room quickly quieted. "Part of it is to recognize that we have made the first step in reclaiming our homeland. If only Teyrn Voric were still alive. He was a friend of my mother's, and I would have been very happy to see him sitting back on this chair that belonged to him. But we know what happened to him, don't we?"

The room grew somber, and the few whispers that

continued stopped as other nobles looked up at Maric. They knew only too well. "Teyrn Voric was accused of giving us safe harbor, so Meghren had his entire family hanged. He let them dangle in Denerim Square until they rotted, and then he gave Gwaren to one of his own cousins."

The room was silent. Many eyes dropped, some in remembrance and some in shame. There was no one present who was not painfully aware of the price the Orlesians had exacted after their victory, or of the sacrifices that had been made by those Fereldans who had chosen to remain with their holdings and their families rather than join the rebellion.

"Meghren's power is in the chevaliers, those men sent to him by the Emperor. Without them, the Fereldan people would have risen up long ago. I hear your question: 'What can we do against the chevaliers? They defeated us once during the invasion, and even if we defeat them now, the Emperor will just keep sending more!'

"We have gained new information, information that gives us a rare opportunity to strike back against the chevaliers themselves." He paused to let that news sink in, and the level of surprised whispering increased. "We suffered a great loss to learn this. Arl Byron is dead, but because of him we now know that the pay for the chevaliers is being sent from Orlais and will arrive at the fortress of West Hill on the northern coast. Well over five thousand sovereigns—their pay for the entire year."

The whispering had dropped to a hush, and for a moment the entire room stared at Maric with wide, startled eyes. "Without that coin, Meghren will be forced to either outrage the Fereldan people with new taxes or he must go to his Emperor with cup in hand to ask for more." He grinned mischievously. "We intend to take it from him."

The hall erupted into exclamations of shock and angry questions. Loghain saw that many of these men were worried, and leaned to shout questions into each other's ears. He could imagine what they were. They didn't know Maric as he did. They knew his mother, and perhaps Arl Rendorn. Of Maric, all they knew was that he was either bold or foolhardy enough to capture Gwaren, a town he might not hold for very long.

Two of the younger banns, small landholders from the north who had been hovering unenthusiastically near the back even before Maric revealed his plan, now quietly made their exit. Loghain caught Rowan's eyes across the room, and she nodded almost imperceptibly in response. She and three other soldiers inconspicuously followed after the banns.

Maric would not approve, Loghain was certain. But Maric didn't have to know.

The shouting went on for a full minute as Maric listened, seemingly unconcerned as he returned to the chair at the head of the hall. One of the elder banns, a well-known and respected man Loghain remembered from his time in the Bannorn, stood and held up a hand for attention. As eyes turned toward him, the volume in the room diminished greatly.

"Bann Tremaine, isn't it?" Maric asked him, loudly enough to be heard.

The Bann bowed respectfully, his heavy blue robes threatening to topple his weathered bones to the floor. His skin was like pale parchment, and when he spoke, his voice was a quiet rasp that the rest of the room had to strain to hear. "My prince," the Bann began, "I do not understand. How will you reach West Hill? The usurper is said to have his army camped on the Brecilian Passage. Must you not do battle even to reach the north?"

Maric nodded. "Ships. The usurper does not control the seas yet, so we have contracted several Antivan galleys to ferry our men to the northern coast." He grinned slightly. "I'm not going to say exactly where, if you'll forgive me."

There were a few knowing chuckles among the crowd, but concerned glances as well. The elder Bann Tremaine appeared confused and asked what most others were likely thinking. "But . . . does this mean you will be abandoning Gwaren?"

Maric listened to the shouts of approval that accompanied the Bann's question. "We need to strike at the usurper's support," he stated firmly. "If we do not, we will not be able to hold Gwaren no matter what we do."

Several shouts of "But what will happen here?" went up from the crowd. Loghain noticed the portly mayor of the town seated at one of the tables, his face pale as a bedsheet. It would be very easy, Loghain imagined, for some to construe the mayor as having supported the rebel's presence. No doubt the mayor was thinking about how the usurper might view those who had done so, should Meghren regain control.

Maric held up a hand, but the concerned chatter barely stilled. "We have no choice!" he shouted. "We shall leave a garrison, and hope to draw the usurper away to the north! But if he comes, we cannot stop him!"

General upset arose again, with numerous men

jumping up from their chairs and shouting angrily at Maric. The idea of abandoning the first town the rebels had liberated did not sit well with them. Loghain knew Gwaren was not defensible enough to last against a full assault from the usurper, and with nowhere to retreat to, it was foolish to try and hold the town with a small force. But most of these men knew nothing of the sort.

Maric looked nervous now, sweating more profusely as he watched the room fall out of his control. Bann Tremaine sat down, shaking his head in sad disbelief, and many of the other nobles seemed to take that as a sign of condemnation. Loghain watched the men who were already part of the rebel cause and saw that they remained quiet in their chairs, their lips pursed.

Why the approval of any of these men was required, Loghain wasn't certain. But Maric wanted it, hoping that approval might mean additional support and even more recognition from the Landsmeet that he was still the rightful ruler of Ferelden. It was risky, in Loghain's mind. What if they refused him? Even if they approved, would that equate to more soldiers? The rebellion stood to lose more than it gained with this court. Loghain had argued as much and had been overridden.

"What does Arl Rendorn think of this?" The shout came from a gray-haired noblewoman, and was repeated as several others leaped on the idea. Others began to turn to the Arl, who glowered uncomfortably from near Maric's chair. He said nothing as the cries increased in volume, until finally Maric grimaced and nodded.

Looking ill at ease in his formal coat, the Arl

stepped forward, and the room quickly hushed. "I will not lie," he announced gruffly. "I do have my misgivings about this plan." His words were met by an immediate uproar of disapproval, which he had to bellow to be heard over. "But! But it is not without merit, my friends!"

Many of the nobles in the room were now on their feet, some looking ready to walk out. Arl Rendorn stepped forward, his brow knotted in consternation. "What Prince Maric says is not untrue—remaining here is not an option! It is true that we are spending all that we have on these ships, and it is a risky plan, but imagine what will happen if it works!" The sound of chatter hushed even further. "Have you all lived so long under the Orlesian thumb that you do not remember what it was like to strike a real blow against them!" Some cheers greeted his words, with several men pounding on their tables. "My misgivings are those of an old man . . . all the successes that your prince has enjoyed so far have been due to such risks!"

The Arl stepped back as a smattering of applause rang through the hall. Maric smiled at him in gratitude. Loghain knew it could have been much worse. Arl Rendorn's objections in private had been strenuous. He did not trust the sea, like any good Fereldan, and the idea that the rebels should spend all the silver they had plundered in Gwaren on ships left him cold. All the more reason to do so, as far as Loghain was concerned.

Still, the Arl's endorsement was hardly ringing. Skepticism reigned, and the babble of argument among those gathered increased. Maric stood, and it took several tries for his shouts to be heard over the din.

"The reason I am bringing this before you," Maric yelled, "is that we need your help! If those who wish Ferelden to be free do not rise up now, they will never have the chance to! We cannot shoulder this burden alone!"

More negative cries rang out, and Loghain watched Maric's heart sink. His words were being ignored. They didn't believe him, didn't think the plan had real merit, or they were frightened. The notion of Mad Meghren's vengeance had kept most of them from joining the rebels to this point. Arl Byron had been the most powerful man to abandon his lands for Maric, and what had happened to him? Old men shook their heads, and many were getting ready to leave.

Loghain was done listening. He strode forward, elbowing past several others to enter the middle of the hall. *"It can be taken!"* he roared. He drew his sword, and the metallic sound combined with the appearance of a weapon jarred the room. Those who had been about to leave stood still, while others stared openly in shock.

"You doubt our ability to take West Hill," he shouted, turning to glare defiantly at the faces in the crowd, "and yet how many of you would have thought we could be standing here tonight? How many of you did I meet with that said you were certain that the death of the Rebel Queen meant that the rebellion was over? Yet here we are!"

Silence greeted his words. He turned and looked into the crowd until he spotted the blond elven woman who had brought them Arl Byron's information. She stood against the far wall, now garbed in an elegant green dress but staying almost hidden in the shadows. Loghain had initially assumed her to be little more than a messenger, but after considerable interrogation he had grudgingly revised that opinion—indeed, it seemed likely that the elf had been instrumental in acquiring the information on West Hill in the first place. They were unable to ask Arl Byron now about her history as his agent, but her skills alone made her valuable. They were fortunate that she had made it to Gwaren in one piece.

He pointed his sword toward her. "You there! Katriel! Step forward!"

Katriel's green eyes flicked to Maric, and he nodded reassuringly. She collected herself and moved forward into the light until she could be seen by all the noblemen. Shyly, she curtsied while keeping her head low.

"This is the woman," Loghain gestured towards her, "who brought us our information. We know the names of those within West Hill who provided this information, men and elves like her friendly to the rebellion. They will provide us the chance to have our own people sneak in as servants, to open the fortress gates from within."

He paused to let that fact sink in. "In fact, she has even volunteered to be one of those servants." He rounded on the nobles, staring at them coldly. "She, an elf, has proved herself braver and more eager to aid her Prince than an entire room full of the pride of Ferelden."

The angry retorts began again, with many men

leaping up defensively and shaking their fists at Loghain. He stood his ground.

Some of the noblemen were outraged, and one in particular shoved to the front of several of his fellows. He was a fat man with curly red hair named Bann Donall, if Loghain remembered right. Loghain and Rowan had met briefly with him during their travels in the Bannorn, and had been summarily dismissed by him without so much as a discussion or even an offer of hospitality.

"You *dare* compare us to a knife-ear?" he hollered, his cheeks flushed with fury. "What do we care if some elven slattern offers her worthless life for her betters? What chance do you think *she* has of opening the fortress gates!"

Loghain saw the elven woman's eyes go blank, and her face turned red—though whether from embarrassment or anger, he couldn't say. Before he could respond, however, Maric dashed into the middle of the hall. His eyes were wide with a rage that Loghain had never seen in him before.

"If anyone has a chance, she does," Maric snapped. He stared challengingly at the red-haired bann, and for a moment he seemed all of ten feet tall. "And her life isn't worthless. If you want a reason why we're standing here at all, look no further than her. I value her life greatly, and the fact that she is willing to risk it even for ignorant men such as you makes me value it all the more."

He turned and coolly regarded the rest of the nobles, all of whom watched him in silence. Katriel's eyes were wide with astonishment, but she continued to stare at the floor where she stood.

"You think me capricious?" Maric snarled. No one answered him. "You think me ready to throw our fortunes away on foolish plans? I tell you that we can strike at the usurper only through the chevaliers, and in order to do that, I will use whoever I believe can get the job done!"

He marched up to Bann Donall, staring him in the face, and the fat man retreated a step. "You think we can pick and choose who that is, my lord? Do you think we are holding a court to decide at our leisure just how the usurper will be defeated? We must act because we can, and we must act *now*!"

Maric spun around and marched back toward Katriel. He held out a hand to her, and though she stared at him in horror, she took his hand and he brought her closer, smiling gently. "I believe that the Maker brought this woman to me for a reason," he announced, "and furthermore I believe she and those we send with her are meant to succeed." He turned to frown at Bann Donall. "I believe it enough that I promise this: If the gates of West Hill are not opened, we will not attack. I will not throw lives away on a hopeless endeavor."

Maric turned to look at Katriel again, reaching out with his free hand to lift her chin. He grinned, staring into her eyes. "But they will be open. I believe it," he said firmly.

Katriel blinked rapidly, clearly disconcerted and moved and uncertain how to respond. "I . . . I will do my best," she finally stuttered. A blush rose up her cheeks, and she looked away.

The babble began again, voices clashing against each other in argument. Some applauded, and many bowed their heads in thought, while others shook them in dismay. The anger had drained out of the room, however, and when Maric turned to regard the line of tables before him, he seemed very much the ruler he was supposed to be. Some of the men and women nearest him began to kneel.

Bann Donall stepped forward again. "Are you all mad?" he shouted, looking around at the gathering. He was so beside himself, he was shaking, his meaty fists pumping furiously at the air. "Are you actually going to listen to this child and his fantasies!"

The room fell silent again. Maric stared at the man coldly but said nothing.

"The only reason he has gotten this far is because of the Arl! You all know this!" The Bann spun about, looking for support from the room. Many refused to meet his gaze, but others appeared indecisive. "We must face reality!" he screamed, gesticulating wildly. "King Meghren is going nowhere! We would be better off locking this pup in a cage and giving him up before the King finds out we were even here!"

An uncomfortable silence greeted the red-haired man's words, and before he could continue, Loghain leaped across the room and put his blade through the man's chest. The Bann stared down with naked disbelief at the sword protruding from his chest, and as he did so, bright blood gushed from his mouth. He made a wet, sucking noise of dismay, and Loghain pulled the blade out of him.

The fat man slid to the ground and landed with a dull thud. A gasp of horror rippled through the crowd, and the sound of many chairs scraping along the stone floor echoed as the nobles retreated from the sight. They stared at Loghain with trepidation, uncertain whether he was about to turn on them next. Even Maric watched Loghain with a questioning look, still protectively holding the elven woman's hands.

As the room fell into an uneasy quiet, Loghain calmly wiped his sword on the Bann's expensive robe. He noticed that some of the nobles were still backing away as if repelled by the murder, and some were even about to make surreptitious exits. He didn't need to look up to know that Rowan would have returned by now, and that she would be sending men to block the doorways that led out of the hall.

"You forget yourselves," Loghain snapped. The room was absolutely still, and he had everyone's complete attention. "This is not some beggar asking you for a handout, but your rightful King. We are at war with the Orlesians, the very ones who conquered our land and have been slowly taking it from you."

With a grimace, he kicked Bann Donall's body and it rolled several feet away from him. It stopped faceup, revealing the Bann's horrified expression and lifeless eyes. A dark, wet stain was slowly spreading across the front of his robe, and blood was pooling around him. Many stared at the body, but nobody moved. "You all can get busy trying to think of how many ways you can commit treason in order to kiss the usurper's feet," Loghain continued, "or you can act like Fereldans and stop waiting for us to do all the work on our own. The choice is yours."

Loghain stopped, wiped his mouth, and sheathed his blade. Not a single word was spoken in the hall, but he could see many faces nodding grimly. With any luck, he hadn't sunk Maric's chances completely.

He turned to Maric, who was still standing in front

of the elven woman. She regarded Loghain warily, but hardly seemed frightened for all of Maric's protectiveness. "I'm sorry," he told Maric with a shrug. "It had to be said."

Maric seemed caught somewhere between horror and amusement. "No, no," he said. "That seemed . . . appropriate?"

"I certainly thought so."

In the end, they got what they had been seeking.

If anything, the death of Bann Donall had served to shock many into remembering why they had been asked to come. It was not to argue over whether or not they approved of Maric's actions or thought his tactics sound, but to be reminded that there was still someone who was waging the war with the Orlesians. And a chance existed now to strike back that had not come up once in the entire reign of the Rebel Queen.

Many of those men and women had left the hall without promising anything. Their faces uncertain, they seemed half-convinced they were about to meet the same fate as Donall—though of course, they did not. They had stayed and listened, and Maric was determined to let them leave his court unmolested. They would not be leaving Gwaren even so, not until there was no chance they could affect the battle at West Hill that was to come.

Loghain doubted they had much to fear. Those who had declined to offer their support to Maric had done so with heavy hearts. He had seen the fear in their eyes. Deep down, they just couldn't bring themselves to hope that Maric might do better than his grandfather had back during the invasion. They feared the repercussions that would follow a loss by the rebels, and to tell the truth, Loghain could hardly blame them. Not a one had offered argument when they were informed they would be Maric's guests for the next several weeks. No doubt the idea that it could potentially be argued to King Meghren that they were Maric's prisoners crossed their minds.

Of those who did offer their support, it came with one major requirement: that Maric be kept out of the battle at West Hill and out of danger. The idea took Maric rather by surprise, but when it was brought up by an earnest female bann, it was quickly championed by others until finally Maric had no choice but to agree.

Their concern was a simple one: a dangerous assault made by the rebel army was acceptable, but the last Theirin could not be risked in such a battle. If he was lost, so was Calenhad's bloodline.

It was Calenhad's memory, and the memory of Maric's mother, that truly made them offer their support in the end. To these men and women, that tradition was Ferelden, and for Ferelden they would offer the rebels whatever support they could afford. Food, equipment, even soldiers. Some of them even knelt before Maric and pledged themselves just as Arl Byron had, tears in their eyes and hands on their hearts.

If Ferelden called, they said, then they would answer.

The size of the rebel army would be increased almost by half again, once all their men were added to their ranks. It was strength they would need if they were going to take West Hill, whether the gates opened or not. Loghain was pleased, as it very easily could have gone in a different direction.

Loghain also noticed that none of the nobles would look him in the eye. Maric they adored, but to them he was nothing but a killer. It didn't bother him.

Severan walked briskly down the dark hallway, ignoring the luxuries he passed. The paintings of ancient battles on the walls, the plush carpet of delicate geometric patterns, the vase of red crystal forgotten and dusty in its cubby hole . . . all these things had been brought from Orlais to decorate the palace, and yet none of it seemed to please Meghren. How could one appreciate such beauty, he cried, when all one could smell was dog dung and cabbage?

The mage snorted derisively at the memory. His yellow robes swished behind him as he approached the great double doors that led to the King's private chambers. The doors were wooden and extremely old, carved with a delightfully detailed relief map of Ferelden itself . . . as well as the two hounds rampant that served as the nation's symbol. For that reason alone, Meghren swore daily that he would have the doors removed, chopped into kindling, and burned in the Chantry's brazier. Thankfully he had not done so yet, as it would be a shame to waste such artistry.

Severan used one of the knockers to pound on the doors, and without waiting, he shoved against one to push it open. The room within was adorned with the finest furniture from Orlesian woodcrafters, blue silk draperies, an enormous four-poster bed made of mahogany, and a gilded mirror gifted to Meghren by the Marquis of Salmont himself, yet none of these furnishings could disguise the fact that the room was oppressive and dark, the windows small, and the wooden beams loomed large overhead. It suited the Ferelden character for everything to be sturdy and large and preferably made from wood, as if they were still barbarians living in their great forests. Naturally it didn't suit the King.

At the moment, however, Meghren hardly cared about his surroundings. He had acquired a bout of fever after his latest escapade; a night spent frolicking in the gardens with barely two stitches of clothing on during one of his parties. Severan had warned him that it was too cold this time of year to be running about so, but had the King listened? He had told Meghren his fever was proving resistant to magical cure. Perhaps a few days spent miserable and sneezing in bed would remind him that Severan was a voice to be heeded.

At the moment, Meghren was surrounded by bedsheets that looked as if they had suffered through a windstorm. They covered the mattress in great disarray, no doubt the product of some fever-induced rage, while the King lay sweating in his nightgown and looking very much like an overgrown and forlorn child.

Two footmen stood by the wall, alert and ready for their king's slightest command. Mother Bronach, meanwhile, sat on a stool by the King's bedside, the red robes of her office neatly spread about her. She closed a book as Severan entered, placing it on her lap and looking as if she had swallowed something distinctly unpleasant. He noticed that the book was a transcription of one of the longer verses of the Chant of Light. It seemed he wasn't the only one interested in torturing the King today.

"Tell me you have news!" Meghren shouted in exasperation, wiping the sweat from his brow with an embroidered towel. He lay back on his pillows with a great sigh.

Severan removed a rolled-up piece of parchment from his robe. "I do indeed, Your Majesty. This arrived not an hour ago." He offered it to Meghren, but the man waved it aside weakly and continued to nurse his forehead.

"Oh, just tell me what it says! I am dying! The terrible diseases that swirl about in this land, it cannot be borne!"

Mother Bronach pursed her lips. "Perhaps His Majesty might consider the possibility that his illness is a lesson sent to him by the Maker."

Meghren groaned loudly and looked to Severan for support. "This is what I put up with now. This from a traitor who actually spoke to that rebel dog!"

She frowned deeply. "I did not arrange the matter, Your Majesty. Perhaps it is the mages you should be eyeing more closely." She stared suspiciously at Severan, a look he pointedly ignored.

"You spoke to him!" Meghren suddenly shouted, sitting up in bed and looking rather wild-eyed. "Exchanged words! And here you sit and lecture *me*!"

"I bring the word of Andraste and the Maker, Your Majesty. Nothing else."

"Bah!" He collapsed back onto his pillows, defeated.

Severan unrolled the parchment and glanced at it, though he didn't really need to see what it said. "Our agent says that the plan is a success. They intend to attack West Hill, and have gathered up all the other Fereldans still willing to defy you. They have even agreed to use her as an integral part of the attack."

Meghren chuckled, taking a rumpled napkin from a small pile of equally rumpled and soiled napkins and blowing his nose into it. "So she does well, then?"

"Oh, yes. Our rebel prince is quite enamored of our agent, it appears."

"For this we sacrificed so many chevaliers?" Meghren snorted. "We should have crushed them in Gwaren when we had the chance. Burned it down, all of it. Shoved it into the sea."

"Now we can get all of them," Severan assured him calmly. "We can eliminate the rebellion for good. Prince Maric will be delivered to you before the month is out; that I guarantee."

King Meghren thought on this for a moment, playing idly with the soiled napkin in his hand. He wiped his nose with it again and then chanced a look over at Mother Bronach. The woman glared at him unrelentingly, and he sighed. "No," he finally said, "I have changed my mind. I want him killed."

Severan frowned. "But you said—"

"And now I say this!"

Mother Bronach nodded approvingly. "The King has given his order, mage."

"I hear him," Severan snapped at her. He rolled up the parchment irritably. "I do not understand, Your Majesty. Had you wanted Prince Maric dead, we could easily have—"

"I have changed my mind!" Meghren shouted, and then collapsed into a fit of coughing. When he was done, he looked miserably up at Severan. "There will be no trial, no gift to the Emperor. I . . . wish him to vanish! To disappear!" He waved a hand about dismissively. "He dies in the battle; the rest will go as you planned."

"Is this your desire, Your Majesty? Or the preference of the Chantry?"

Mother Bronach stiffened her back in her chair, her lips thinning into a single line. "It benefits no one to have the last son of Calenhad paraded in front of his people," she snapped. "I have reminded His Majesty of his duty in this matter. It will be better this way. Final."

Meghren did not look thrilled by the notion, but waved his assent absently at the Mother's words. He snatched up a large pewter goblet from his nightstand and gulped down the water greedily before belching.

Severan glanced between the two and frowned. He had hoped to get his own hands on the rebel prince, once he had been delivered to the palace alive. They had expected losses at Gwaren, but he had been quite embarrassed to report just how many chevaliers had been killed. Worse, they had lost three mages sent by the Circle in Val Cheveaux. Severan had been humiliated in front of his colleagues, and now neither they nor the Fereldan Circle were being cooperative. He would have twisted Maric's spleen in his own fist, given the chance. Now he would have to be satisfied with another.

Slowly Severan bowed. "The rebellion will be destroyed at West Hill, and Maric will die. Quietly. It shall be as you say, Your Majesty."

"And do not forget, good mage," Meghren muttered between miserable sniffles, "you will not fail me again, yes?"

Severan walked out without comment. It seemed the King's fever would prove resistant to a cure for several days longer than he had initially thought. Pity.

11

West Hill was a drafty, poorly maintained place. Sitting high in the rocky hills overlooking the Waking Sea, the stone fortress had once existed to watch the waters for signs of Marcher corsairs raiding the coast. The decline of the corsairs had brought a decline of the fortress along with it, and today the tall watchtowers stood mostly empty. The fortress was useful mainly for its position along the coastal roads bringing sparse traffic from Orlais.

Still, it felt forgotten. Soldiers were stationed here, with a handful of freeholders and servants to attend to them, but once the fortress had held many more. Thousands, whereas now it held hundreds. Many of the upper floors were closed off, as well as most of the underground chambers that weren't still used for storage. Some doors hadn't been opened in decades. It was very easy to make a wrong turn in West Hill and end up in a dark hallway full of crumbling furniture covered with drapes and layers of dust. There were many old ghosts here, or so it was said, and the locals spoke only in whispers as if fearful of stirring their wrath.

Katriel waited quietly in the shadows, listening to the wind whistling through the dark rafters overhead. She didn't like this place. Too often business required one to pass through the lonely hallways where the only sounds were the echoing of your own footsteps.

It had been one week since she and the other rebel agents had arrived, sneaked in one by one to take their places among the servants. Katriel had been brought in with the washerwomen, a replacement for an older woman who had taken ill and been forced to move back to her home village. The guards hadn't given her a second glance, and why would they? Katriel had been here before.

Prior to finding her way into the Prince's company, she'd spent almost a year insinuating herself among the rebel sympathizers, slowly making herself indispensable to them. She had seduced a guardsman into introducing her to Arl Byron as a trusted contact, and that had been all she needed. The guardsman disappeared easily enough afterwards.

Now she had returned. After a week of quietly leaving notes in prearranged locations, she noticed that the other rebel agents had disappeared. So too had the sympathizers, those simple folk she had worked with for so many months. She quickly quashed the pang of regret she felt in their behalf.

She could take no chances. In the courts of the Empire, there were no innocents—there were only fools and those who took advantage of fools, as the saying went. Those who had any power were forced to play the same game as the rest of the aristocracy. Whether one was a bored provincial magistrate's wife or a fashionable count living in a glorious manse in the capital city, one used others to get ahead. Others must be made to look worse so you looked better, gossip and intrigue being the weapons of choice to carve out your niche. It was a blood sport, and all who partook enjoyed it as such or quickly got left behind.

In all her years there, she had never met a player who did not deserve their fate. Smiles hid daggers and even the poorest servants connived to attach themselves to the fastest and strongest horse.

Yet this was not Orlais, was it? Here it was quite different. Here the people knew little more than hardship, but they looked each other in the eye. It had taken a long time for her to become used to that.

And then there was Maric. Katriel found herself smiling as she thought of her blond, grinning fool of a prince. He would not have lasted five minutes in the courts of Val Royeaux. If she had known it was going to be so simple to draw him into her confidence, she needn't have tried so hard. How very earnest he was!

And yet how very much like his country he was, as well. Completely without artifice. She had kept expecting to find some vile secret hidden within him, some taint floating just beneath that gleaming surface, and yet there was nothing. She told herself it was that he lacked depth, but when he had looked into her eyes that first night, even she had found it

difficult to maintain her composure. The Master who
had trained her all those years as a bard would have
been ashamed.

Still, it would be a shame to see the man dragged
off to a dungeon. His smiles would vanish into those
dark depths and never return, and that was because
men like Meghren knew that the game existed
everywhere—even here in Ferelden.

The wind howled in the rafters once more, and a
pigeon was startled into sudden flight. Its flapping
wings high overhead almost masked the distant
sounds of footsteps on the stone.

Katriel turned and watched the hooded figure approach, fingering the dagger hidden inside her surcoat. A young lordling had once mocked the small
blade when she drew it on him—he had stopped
laughing when its razor-sharp edge had opened his
throat before he'd a chance to lay another finger on
her. She had little doubt that this was the mysterious
contact she had been feeding information to since
her arrival, but there was always reason to be cautious.

The hooded figure stopped a few feet away, bowing slightly from the waist as a sign of respect. She
nodded to him but said nothing. His robes were
filthy, and she couldn't judge if they covered armor
or not. He reached up and pulled back his hood, revealing a swarthy-skinned Rivaini face with sharp
features, one Katriel had not seen among the fortress
denizens. A hidden agent, then? Certainly there were
many places to hide in West Hill.

"You are Katriel," he stated, his accent clipped
and foreign.

"And you are Severan's man."

He glowered at her. "You should not mention our benefactor's name so casually, elf."

"And you should remember who it is that has delivered this fortress to you." She arched a curious brow. "I'm assuming that you've dealt with all my fellow agents by now?"

He nodded curtly. "We waited until last night, as per your instructions."

"I wanted to wait until we received the last message from the army." She reached into her surcoat and pulled out a rolled-up parchment. Though she held it out to the Rivaini, he did not move to take it. "They have been marching in small groups in the hills and will be in place by this morning. They will attack as soon as the gates are opened, as I promised."

"They are opening now." He smiled coldly. "There is a great force hiding beyond the western ridge, ready to strike. They will be crushed. Severan will be pleased, and sends word you shall be rewarded as he promised."

"There is one problem." She tapped the parchment thoughtfully against her forehead. "Prince Maric is not riding with the army. There is a camp to the south of West Hill where he will be staying during the battle, an arrangement he made to—"

"We know this," the Rivaini interrupted, his voice sharp and impatient. "It is being taken care of."

Katriel paused, frowning. "Taken care of? What do you mean? I was hired to deliver the Prince to King Meghren personally. I can hardly do that if—"

"It is taken care of," the man snapped irritably. "The rebel prince is no longer your concern. He must perish, and so he shall die as the battle begins."

"What?" She took an angry step toward him. His

black eyes followed her warily, but he did not flinch or retreat. "This is preposterous! I could have easily accomplished that my very first night with the Prince. What is the meaning of this?"

He shrugged. "What does it matter? The fool would have been executed eventually, surely. It is faster for him to die this way, no?" He sneered at her, his eyes knowing. "They say he is handsome. But you have done what you came to do. Now it is done."

"I came here to deliver him," she insisted. "Not to kill him."

"You have delivered him, and his army. To us." One of his hands slipped gently into his robe, reaching for whatever weapon he had stored there. She made no indication that she was aware of it, however, and continued to meet his steely eyes. "I came here to give you your new orders, elf. It would be a shame if I were to send word to the mage that his little spy met an accident during the battle instead."

She paused, very aware of the distance between them. The tension was punctuated only by the shrill howls of wind overhead. "I am not Severan's servant," she said clearly.

"No? Are you not in his employ?"

"I was brought here at great expense to perform a specific task. Once that task is done, he and I are through."

He chuckled, low and menacing. "Then I suppose you are through."

The Rivaini made to draw his blade and lunge at Katriel, but she was too fast for him. Her dagger was out and flying through the air before he had taken half a step toward her, and his eyes went wide with shock as he realized a blade was stuck up to its hilt in his throat. Stumbling to a stop, he let out a muted gasp and reached up with a hand to pull the dagger out. His eyes widened still at the resulting fountain of blood gushing from his neck and running down his robe.

He looked at her helplessly, and she shrugged. "Perhaps Severan did not tell you. I am far more than just a spy. Or just an elf." Her tone was icy, and when the Rivaini lunged at her with his short sword, she adeptly stepped aside and let him stumble to his knees.

The gurgled gasping continued as Katriel watched him dispassionately. Then she stepped near and reached down, pulling her blood-coated dagger from his hand. He let go with little struggle and collapsed. The blood pooling around him on the floor was bright and angry, a sharp contrast to the dull color of the old stones. Whatever ghosts roamed this place had no doubt gathered to greet the newest addition to their number.

And there will be many more yet to come, she thought grimly.

She stared down at the body of Severan's agent thoughtfully and considered her options. Technically this was self-defense. Part of her was enraged that Severan would change the terms of their arrangement, and if he actually instructed his agent to slay her then he was more the fool than she would have guessed.

Even so, it was done. The Orlesians were obviously dealing with Maric on their own. She could leave now and say whatever she wished about the Rivaini, one more body amid the pile would make no difference. If Severan truly was trying to betray her, she could deal with that then. The smart thing to do would be to get out now before the fighting began.

So why wasn't she moving?

It's not done yet, she reminded herself. *Not yet.*

It was an impossible thought that ran through her, and yet she could not dismiss it. Even if she were to somehow help Maric now, he would not thank her for it. She had already delivered him up like a calf for the slaughter; what would be the point? As the Rivaini had said, if Maric did not die now he would certainly die later.

The thought of his face crossed her mind. Those innocent eyes, so trusting. And when he had touched her that night in the tent, he had been gentle. Far more gentle than she had expected, certainly.

Looking down at her own hands, Katriel found herself troubled by the amount of blood she found there. Removing a kerchief, she began to wipe her hands and her blade, and tried to remind herself what it meant to be what she was. *A bard must know history so she does not repeat it. She tells the tales but is never part of them. She watches but remains above what she sees. She inspires passions in others and rules her own.*

But it was pointless. She stopped wiping, as the kerchief was already soaked through with blood and she was no cleaner.

In the distance, a great muted clanging sound began to ring. It was the sound of the fortress gates opening.

Katriel dropped the kerchief and began to run.

———

"Commander Loghain, the gates are opening!"

Loghain nodded and continued to watch the fortress off in the distance. So far, everything was going according to plan, and that was beginning to disturb him. They had met no other ships during the stormy passage into the Waking Sea, pirates or Orlesian frigates or otherwise. There had been no troops waiting for them at the sandy cove where they disembarked in leaky longboats, and no surprise ambushes as they spread out into the rocky hills. Not a single lieutenant had reported meeting resistance, and other than a few late-season merchant wagons trying to avoid the main roads, they really hadn't met much of anyone at all.

He had been camped directly east of the fortress, an old and ominous-looking stone sentinel that stood high in the hills and looked down on the vast sea sprawled beneath it. Its high towers made him nervous, despite the assurances from Katriel and the other agents inside that said those towers were rarely manned—indeed, if anyone actually tried to ascend the stairs to the old watch stations, they were more like to end up falling through the boards to their death. Chances were good that no one could see Loghain's forces, or Arl Rendorn's forces on the other side of the fortress to the west.

Still, it bothered him that everything was going so smoothly. He had hoped for a surprise attack on Gwaren before they left, an ambush, an alarm raised at the fortress, *something* to put his mind at ease. He had over four hundred men in his command, and the Arl was in charge of an even larger force, easily the greatest army they had assembled to date, with many strangers provided by the nobles who had joined them at Gwaren. Any one of them could be a traitor. They had been careful, but for it all to go exactly as planned made his skin itch.

Maric was pleased, naturally, and taunted Loghain for deliberately looking for trouble. Loghain was tempted to punch him in the mouth to wipe that smile off his face, but that probably wouldn't look good in front of the men.

"We stand for now," he informed the lieutenant. "The Arl attacks first."

The soldier saluted and marched off to deliver his orders. Nearby, several of the Night Elves fingered their bows anxiously as they perched on higher rocks to watch the battle. He waved to one of them. "Any sign of movement, yet?"

The elf looked off into the distance, shielding his eyes from the sun. "I think . . . Arl Rendorn is here, now."

It was true. Loghain watched as a large force of men marched into view at the base of the hill and began ascending the rocky path up to the open gateway. There were signs of frantic activity in the fortress, but no resistance had appeared yet. He half expected the gates to swing shut, but they remained open. Katriel had said in her last response that it would not be difficult to sabotage the crank, which meant the gates could be closed only with difficulty. So far, she seemed as good as her word.

Surely it couldn't be this easy, could it? If the Arl's forces got inside the fortress, they could overwhelm the defenders within the hour. Loghain's men might never even have to march. Had they caught the usurper completely unawares? Was that possible?

Almost as if on cue, he heard the distant sounds of a horse riding hard toward them, and several men nearby shouted. He turned in his saddle and was startled to see Rowan approaching, fully armored but missing her helmet. She was sweating profusely as she rode full-bore toward him.

Worse was the look on her face: terror.

I knew it, he swore to himself. Without hesitating, he kicked his warhorse into a gallop and raced down the hillside to intercept Rowan. Many of his men were stirring now, uneasy as they sensed something was amiss.

"Loghain!" Rowan pulled her horse to a halt as Loghain reached her. "They've attacked the camp! Maric is in danger!"

"What! Who? Who has attacked the camp?"

Rowan gasped for air and tried to collect her breath. Her horse pranced nervously beneath her, and she had trouble keeping him under control. "Some of my scouts didn't come back . . . we thought maybe they were delayed or . . . or deserted, but—" She shook her head in disbelief. "—I rode out with some men to look. There's a whole army approaching." She looked at Loghain with wide, horrified eyes. "The usurper . . . he's here, they're all *here*!"

His blood went cold. They knew, then. They had been waiting.

"I sent my men to try to warn Father," she continued numbly, "and then I rode back to the camp to tell Maric. But . . . the camp is gone. It was attacked. I didn't even see Maric. I didn't . . . I don't . . ." She stopped herself, unable to continue, and looked at Loghain as if he might be able to right everything.

Loghain considered. His horse nickered irritably,

and he patted its head absently. Then he looked at Rowan and nodded curtly. "Let's go. We need to find him."

"Find him? Find him how?"

"There's going to be tracks. Let's find them, and quickly."

She nodded, relieved, and spun her horse about. The men in the area were talking, a ripple of fear moving through the ranks, the sounds of concern getting louder and louder. "Commander Loghain!" One of his lieutenants ran up anxiously, with several others behind him. "What is happening? You aren't leaving?"

Loghain looked at the man sharply. "I am. You're in charge."

The lieutenant's face turned ashen. "Wh-what?"

"Do it," he ordered. "Take the men and charge, get to the fortress and help the Arl. The King's army is coming."

The ripple of fear became even stronger. The lieutenant looked at him in stark terror. "Take the men? . . . But . . ."

"Maric . . ." Rowan sounded uneasy.

Loghain frowned at her. "Maric needs us. Do you want to stay?"

Rowan stared off in the direction of her father's forces and a look of guilt crossed her eyes. Then she reluctantly shook her head. Loghain kicked his warhorse, and the two of them rode off, leaving the panicked lieutenant and the rest of the rebel force behind. Loghain felt an unaccustomed coldness inside him. It was about to fall apart, all of it. He could feel it slipping through his fingers.

But it didn't matter. If they won this battle and

Maric died, it was all for nothing. Even if it meant abandoning their charge either they were going to find Maric and save him, or they would avenge his death. He owed his friend that much. He exchanged glances with Rowan as they rode swiftly into the hills, and he saw that she felt the same way. She knew he would help; that was why she'd come looking for him.

The Arl was on his own.

Pain lanced through Maric's leg as he rode hard through the forest. His horse was struggling and whinnying in pain, but fear kept it running. He was certain that it had been struck with an arrow or two at the same time his leg had, but it was impossible to stop and look. He clutched the horse's neck, shutting his eyes as low-hanging branches slapped at him. He wasn't even sure where he was or where he was headed, or how far his pursuers were behind him.

At some point, the horse had raced off the path into the lightly forested hills, and he thought he could try to lose them among the trees. The forest was proving to be more of an annoyance, however. With each leap of the horse over a log or an exposed root, the arrow in his leg was jarred. He was bleeding heavily, he knew, and fighting against a weakness that threatened to drag him off the horse's back. He had no saddle, or his armor, though luckily he did have his sword.

It had happened so quickly. One second he was watching the army march off and complaining about how he had to remain behind, and the next, his handful of guards were being slaughtered outside the tent.

Maric barely had enough time to cut through the fabric and leap onto a nearby horse. His bodyguards had bought him a few seconds, but that was all.

Thoughts ran frantically through his head. Was he headed toward the battle or away from it? How had the enemy known where their camp was? How had they known he was going to be left behind?

The afternoon sunlight filtered down through the trees in patches, leaving shadows deep enough that he had no idea where to turn. Sometimes it seemed like a path was forming only to have it disappear just as quickly. As a wave of light-headedness washed over Maric, he realized he was letting the horse find its own way more often than not. For all he knew, it could have turned around and headed back toward his attackers.

Maric felt a sudden jolt and was thrown from the horse as its leg caught between some roots. The horse whinnied in pain as its leg snapped with a sickening crack. For a single moment he flew, twisting in the air, and then slammed hard against an oak tree, the wind knocked out of him all at once.

He slid upside down, cracking his head hard on the uneven ground. Everything went white and numb. He barely heard the horse as it collapsed and thrashed on the ground, screaming madly. That sound seemed very far away and not quite connected to him. He hardly felt the searing pain in his leg as well, though he finally did spot the broken haft of the arrow in his thigh now. That pain also seemed very far away.

As he lay there on the ground, he looked up into the bright sky and the tops of the trees around him lightly swaying in the wind. It was chilly. The breeze touched his face, and there was a tickling on top of his head where blood flowed. He was reminded of the night his mother was killed, of his flight through the forest. The memory wasn't laced with fear, however, but seemed quiet and almost pleasant, as if he might easily float away at any moment.

The sound of shouting nearby brought Maric jarringly back to earth. The horse was squealing in agony, thrashing about in the leaves and bush. The sound made his head throb. He was covered in mud, and his back felt twisted and battered, yet somehow he still forced himself up to his knees.

For a moment, all Maric could see were trees and bright light as the world danced around him. As it swayed dangerously, he stuck out his hands to maintain his balance—only to fall over anyway. His forehead banged against the tree roots, covered in cold mud, and he hissed as pain blinded him once again.

"I see him!" The muted shout was not a friendly one.

Steeling himself, Maric shakily got to his feet. His wounded leg spasmed and threatened to give out from underneath him. He gritted his teeth against the pain and wiped his eyes, backing up warily as he saw the silhouettes of many men approaching. Eight men in total, perhaps, soldiers in brigandine who wore the colors of the usurper. They leaped off their horses and started moving toward him as a group.

He backed into the oak tree, leaning against it for support as he fished his sword out of its scabbard. It almost dropped from his numb fingers. *Wonderful*, he thought. *Is this how I die, then? Cut down while floundering about like a dazed calf?*

The advancing soldiers looked confident. Their quarry was dangerous; a wolf who could snap back if treated without caution, but caught without a doubt. Maric's horse whinnied piteously nearby and tried to stand itself back up, only to collapse again in a pathetic heap.

"What do you think you're going to do with that?" one of the soldiers shouted mockingly. He was handsome, with a dark mustache and beard and a thick Orlesian accent. Their commander, Maric suspected. "Come now, put down your sword, you foolish boy. It looks like you can barely hold it!"

The others with him chuckled and came closer. Maric tightened his grip on the blade and forced himself to stand straight, ignoring the pain in his leg. His lips curled into a snarl as he pointed the sword at each of the men in turn. "You think so?" he said in a low and deadly tone. "Which of you wants to be the first one to see how wrong you are?"

It wasn't a very good bluff. The dark-haired commander chuckled. "It would be better for you if we made this quick. Even now King Meghren crushes your pathetic army. We have been waiting for you all this time."

Maric almost stumbled. "You . . . you're lying." It couldn't be true. But it explained a great deal. It explained how they had known about him, for one. Could the whole thing have been a trap? But how?

The commander smiled even more broadly. "Enough." He waved his hand impatiently, turning to the other soldiers around him. "Finish this," he ordered.

The soldiers hovered, none of them wanting to be the first one to meet Maric's blade.

"I said do it!" the commander shouted.

Maric braced himself as two soldiers rushed him

together. They slashed down hard with their swords, but their strikes were clumsy. Maric ducked aside the first and raised his own sword to deflect the second. His body cried out with pain, but he ignored it and heaved against the second soldier's blade. He stumbled back, and as the first soldier recovered his footing, Maric slashed at him quickly. The attack was lucky and cut across the man's face, causing him to reel away, covering his face with his gauntlets.

The others backed off a step, their eyes flickering nervously to their wounded comrade, who fell to the ground nearby, screaming in agony. Their expressions held doubt; perhaps their prey wasn't so helpless as he had seemed?

"I said finish it!" the commander behind them snapped. "Together!"

They raised their blades, setting their jaws and ignoring the screaming. They were preparing to do as their commander bade, and Maric saw that this time they would act together.

Rage welled up inside him. The thought of his head decorating some pole outside of the royal palace in Denerim, right next to his mother's, passed through his mind. The thought of Meghren smugly laughing to see him up there. This was how it ended? After everything he had accomplished? His friends dead, the rebellion defeated? It was all for nothing?

Maric raised his blade high over his head and let out a cry of fury. It rang through the trees and startled a flock of birds into sudden flight. Let them come. Let them try. He would take as many of them with him as he could; they would respect the Theirin name.

The soldiers appeared unnerved. They readied their blades . . . and paused.

A new sound grew behind them, the sound of hoofbeats approaching. Maric glanced up, sweat dripping into his eyes, and saw two horses racing through the shadowy trees. More of their fellows, perhaps? Did they really need more? It seemed like they had plenty.

The handsome commander turned irritably toward the noise, raising a hand as if to wave the new arrivals away—and then an arrow sped out of the shadows and struck him dead in the chest. He stared down at the protruding shaft in confusion, as if its presence were unthinkable.

The horses slid to a halt in the mud and leaves while their riders leaped from their saddles. Maric strained to see through the shadows. One was in heavy armor, a female figure that began dashing toward the soldiers. The second was in leathers, carrying a longbow, and let another arrow fly as soon as he hit the ground. It streaked through the air and struck the Orlesian commander in the eye. The commander was knocked backwards by the force of the strike, dead even as he hit the ground.

Relief washed through Maric. There was no question who they were.

"Maric! Are you all right?" Loghain shouted, loosing another arrow that just barely missed one of the other soldiers. Rowan burst toward them, swinging her sword in a wide arc that one soldier just barely parried, the force of her blow knocking him off balance. The enemy broke apart in confusion.

"Do I look all right?" Maric shouted back. "What are you doing here? Where's the army!" The enemy split up their efforts, and the chaos was more than Maric could follow. He found himself fighting two soldiers at once, their initial rush almost overwhelming him immediately. They were trying hard to strike him down as quickly as they could, their blows clanging against Maric's blade and numbing his arm.

"We're saving you, you dolt!" came Rowan's shout from nearby. Maric was peripherally aware of her fighting several men at once but he couldn't actually see what she was doing. Winning, from the sounds of it, though he wondered how long she would be able to keep that up. Longer than he could, he feared.

A blade stabbing into his collarbone snapped him back to reality. Maric cried out in pain and knocked the sword aside, but both the men on him pressed their advantage.

"Maric!" came Loghain's concerned shout. Another arrow flew through the air, and one of Maric's attackers screamed in pain, clutching at something impaled in his back. He fell to the ground, squirming. The other attacker stared in shock at his comrade, and Maric used the opening to run him through. It took all Maric's strength and several heaves as bright blood gushed in waves from the soldier's mouth.

He fell backwards to the ground, taking Maric's sword with him. Maric stumbled, almost falling on top of him, but managing to land on one knee. His wounded leg threatened to buckle completely.

Maric looked up, his hands shaking with exhaustion, and saw Rowan and Loghain battling furiously against four soldiers nearby. Loghain had dropped his bow and come to Rowan's aid, but these last few opponents were fighting for their lives. Blade clashed loudly against blade. Maric wanted desperately to help them, but it was all he could do to stop himself from passing out.

Maric looked up as he heard more men approaching. His hopes fell as he saw several soldiers in the usurper's colors coming into the forest, pointing and shouting angrily, drawing their swords as they realized what was happening.

"Maric!" Rowan shouted, fear creeping into her voice. "Run while you can! We can't hold them back!"

Gathering his strength, he limped over toward the soldier he had run through and yanked his sword out with great effort. He could barely hold the blade up, however, and almost fell backwards as it finally came free from the corpse. He had almost no strength left. But he was not going to run away and leave his friends behind. Not while he had a breath left in him.

Rowan finally bypassed the defenses of one of her opponents, slicing open his neck with a swing of her sword. Blood sprayed out as he stumbled to the side, gagging, and she turned to another. Loghain was gritting his teeth and holding his own, but it was inevitable that the three soldiers running their way would quickly overwhelm them both.

"Maric! Go!" Loghain shouted urgently.

"No!" Maric cried. He pushed himself to his feet with pure effort, his legs shaking. He heard the sound of another horse approaching and looked up, expecting fully to see another Orlesian arriving. However, the cloaked and hooded rider didn't dismount and join others. Instead, the horse rode directly at them without slowing down. The three soldiers realized belatedly that this new arrival was not one of their own, turning in surprise just as the rearmost man was trampled. He went down screaming.

The second soldier tried to leap to the side, but

there was nowhere to go except into the nearby trees. He dived down only to be trampled by the horse as well. His horrid screams were quickly cut off.

The third soldier successfully scrambled out of the horse's path. The horse stopped and reared up, neighing loudly as the cloaked rider slid off its back. Maric realized it was a woman, wearing a blue hood and black leathers, and when she pulled a long dagger from a scabbard and leaped on top of the third soldier, the hood fell back and revealed pointed ears and a mass of curly blond hair.

It was Katriel.

Maric watched in shock as Katriel quickly stabbed the soldier beneath her. The man desperately tried to fend her off, but his efforts became feebler as each strike hit home. Raising the blade high, she sank it into the soldier's neck and cut open his throat. Blood splattered across her cloak and ran down her hand from the dagger. The look on her face was intense and vicious.

As the last three men fighting Rowan and Loghain realized their reinforcements had been run down, they began to panic. Rowan intensified her efforts and disarmed one, sending his sword flying as she spun about and cut off his arm. Loghain turned and kicked his opponent toward her, and she obliged by letting the man impale himself on her blade.

The last soldier turned and ran deeper into the forest, screaming in panic. Loghain grimaced and tossed his bloody sword aside. He casually unslung his longbow and notched an arrow, tracking the man as he fled. The shot sped past the trees, cleanly lodging deep into the soldier's back. He grunted and fell, sliding through the mud and leaves before coming to a stop and not rising again.

And then everything was eerily quiet again.

Rowan wiped her sweaty brow, her breathing heavy and ragged. Loghain turned toward her, putting a hand on her shoulder as he looked to see if she was uninjured. She only nodded and gestured toward Maric. "Never mind me," she gasped.

Maric was stunned. Katriel was still seated on top of the man she had slain, jagged knife still in her hand. She looked around warily, as if searching for more attackers to spring out of the shadows. Overhead, a flock of birds startled into flight from the treetops. Dead bodies were everywhere, the smell of fresh blood thick in the air.

"Katriel?" Maric asked out loud, his voice shaky.

"Your Highness." She nodded carefully, staring at him with her green eyes. She replaced the dagger in the sheath at her waist and stood up slowly, collecting her blue cloak around her.

"Didn't I say . . . not to call me that? . . ." Maric grinned madly, feeling light-headed. The sense of numbness and distance had returned, and it felt as if Loghain and Rowan and Katriel were all staring at him from an absurdly long ways away. His strength drained from him, as if someone had opened up the spigot and let it flow.

He fainted.

"Maric!" Rowan shouted, running toward him as he went limp and fell to the mud. He was heavily wounded and pale, the broken arrow jutting out of his thigh looking particularly grave. When Rowan reached him, she realized quickly he was still breathing. He was shaking and had lost a lot of blood, but he was alive.

"Is he . . . ?" Loghain asked, almost fearing to go closer.

Rowan shook her head. "No. Not yet."

Katriel stepped away from the soldier she had slain and approached Rowan. She unslung a small pack from her shoulder and offered it up. "I have bandages, and some salves," she said quietly. "They may be of help."

Rowan looked at her suspiciously but took the pack. "Thank you," she said reluctantly. She tugged off her gauntlets and began rummaging.

Loghain stared at Katriel curiously as he went to retrieve his sword. She seemed to feel his gaze and regarded him in return, her eyes betraying nothing of her thoughts. "Did you have a question, my lord?"

"I'm wondering how you got here."

She gestured toward the many horses that remained among the trees, some of which were already wandering away nervously. "Did you not see me arrive?"

"I simply find your arrival . . . convenient."

She appeared unfazed by the question. "I did not arrive here by chance, my lord. I overheard these men talking about their attack on the Prince, but it was too late for me to send a message. I followed them out after the gate opened." She glanced to where Maric lay, her concern evident. "I must confess I wasn't certain what I would do. His Highness is most fortunate that you were here to defend him."

Rowan stood up and interrupted. "Maric will recover, but Loghain, we need to get back. Who knows what could be happening?"

Loghain looked at Katriel. "Did you see anything on your way here?"

"Only that the battle had begun."

"Damn. Then we will need to move quickly."

Maric was slung over the back of Loghain's warhorse, and the three of them raced back toward West Hill. It was not difficult to see which direction it lay in: already a great cloud of black smoke could be seen rising into the sky. It seemed as if an entire forest was burning, or perhaps it was the fortress itself. Magical fire was the likely culprit, though whether it was Wilhelm's doing or more of the usurper's mages' was impossible to tell.

Twice as they drew closer they were forced to change course as they encountered the enemy. The first time was immediately before leaving the forest, when they found hundreds of soldiers marching in formation along the road. The enemy gave the hue and cry, but the three of them were able to evade them and avoid a chase. They rode carefully through the treacherous forest only to spot a field of soldiers in purple marching northward.

Loghain turned them about and circled around to the east. When they finally came out of the brush, the sight that greeted them was horrifying. A battlefield of the dead, bodies strewn about grotesquely. The thick smell of blood lingered over the field, and the low sound of anguished moans indicated that some of these men still lived. The battle had proceeded elsewhere into the hills, and indeed the clashing of arms could be heard. The battle was still going on.

It didn't escape their notice that most of the men in the field belonged to the rebels. Rowan stared out at the scene, her face stone. Loghain thought it was probably best that Maric was unconscious for this.

Attempts to locate the fighting were thwarted. A change in the wind blew smoke across their path, confusing their sense of direction and making it difficult to breathe. They saw vague shapes that looked like groups of men running through the smoke, but Loghain avoided them for now. He needed to find the Arl—where was the main body of the rebel force? Had they holed up inside the fortress? Had they fled?

The sounds of battle and shouting became louder as they headed farther into the thick of the smoke, and it wasn't long before they encountered a large group of chevaliers. The soldiers challenged them, and when they turned around and fled, the chevaliers gave chase.

It was a desperate, terrifying ride. Several times Loghain was afraid that Maric would slide off—it would be just like him to fall off a horse *now*, Loghain grumbled to himself—but thankfully he remained where he was. The smoke worked in their favor, and eventually the chevaliers gave up. Either that or they were distracted. Certainly there seemed to be men everywhere; it was mass confusion.

When they finally came out of the smoke, Loghain realized they were out of the hills and heading south. Numbly, they sat there on their horses, staring at a brilliant sunset in the distance. The peace of that moment was unsettling. It seemed a crime somehow that the rest of Ferelden did not recognize what had happened. It seemed as if the earth itself should be buckling and heaving.

Loghain traded a look with Rowan, both of them covered in smoke and splattered with blood, and he knew she understood.

The rebel army had been routed. Their plan had been an utter failure.

Katriel watched with them in silence, and then quietly suggested that they should find shelter before dark. Maric would need to be properly tended to. Rowan nodded absently, and they began to ride down the rocky hillside. Loghain thought to cover their tracks—if the rebel force had been routed, it was possible that the usurper could be trying to chase the men down to finish them off. They could be coming this way.

They traveled until the sun set and the shadows arrived to swallow them up.

12

The dwarf eyed Rowan suspiciously from his seat on top of the wagon. His long, proud beard was full of intricate braids, and he had a rectangular tattoo just under his right eye. The tattoo meant that back in Orzammar he had been one of the casteless, the lowest of the low. Even the casteless were considered better than those dwarves who chose to come to the surface, however. Despite the vital role to dwarven society the surface dwarves had as farmers and traders, they carried a stigma with them and could never return to Orzammar again.

As Rowan understood it, some dwarves who came to the surface were political refugees, but far more were desperate criminals. Only those few born on the surface, without the tattoo, were marginally more trustworthy. Some of the formerly casteless even went to the mages to try to have their tattoos removed, or so the rumor went. The fact that this dwarf didn't bother made her wary. He could be a smuggler. . . . In fact, his covered wagon full of goods hidden away from sight and the three human brutes lazily hanging off the sides as "guards" made that idea likely.

"How is it that a human woman like you hasn't heard these things, already?" the dwarf asked in his deep, gravelly voice. "There been talk of nothing else. It's difficult enough to get you cloudheads to shut up long enough to actually do business."

"My friends and I have been traveling," Rowan explained, pulling her shawl more tightly around her front. She didn't like the way his beady eyes lingered on her breasts. She hated the tattered dress Loghain had bartered out of a group of traveling pilgrims a week earlier, but she had no choice but to wear it. A woman parading around the countryside in a full suit of armor was the sort of thing that drew notice. "We haven't had a chance to stop in at any villages recently."

"That so?" He smiled, showing teeth stained a brackish brown. "Which friends are these?"

"They are at a camp not far from here."

"Why don't we go and see them, then? Maybe I'll even spare a few extra supplies if you and your friends are nice and accommodating." His emphasis on the word and the slight darting of his tongue over his lips made it clear exactly what kind of accommodations he preferred.

She stared back at him, letting the revulsion show on her face. "I don't think my friends are all that eager to share their fire tonight."

"And what about you, hmm? Lots of room in the

wagon." One of the thugs hanging off the wagon perked up, apparently liking the turn the conversation was taking.

"Perhaps you missed the part where I am wearing a sword, one that I know how to use." She placed her hand on the hilt of the blade hanging off her belt, not that the dwarf could have missed it earlier.

Her comment hung there in the air as the dwarf chewed on his lip thoughtfully, his beady eyes leaving her weapon only to flick unconsciously toward her breasts. No doubt he was wondering just how well she could actually handle herself, and whether it was worth the trouble. His eventual, exasperated sigh said probably not. "Have it your way, then," he grumbled. "Only being hospitable."

"I'm sure." She smiled. "Before I go, have you seen anyone else on the road in these parts? Or maybe heard of them from others?"

"On the road? Such as?"

"I don't know. Soldiers, perhaps? We saw a pack of soldiers marching through the other day, and I've no wish to run into them again."

He grunted in agreement. "Only soldiers coming through these parts are them Orlesians, and they're all heading southward to chase after your rebel folk." The notion seemed to amuse him greatly. "You cloudheads are a forgiving people, I'll give you that. If any of the castes tried to rise up back home, the Assembly would crush them inside of a day."

"It sounds like a very orderly place."

He nodded, becoming melancholy as his eyes stared off into the distance. "Sometimes it is, yes."

———

The merchant seemed less interested in talking after that and far more eager to return to his travels, so she was able to get little else out of him. In return, she told him which roads she thought were clear back in the direction they had come from, and warned him about the trail washed out by the previous night's rains. With a curt nod he was off, one of the hired guards hanging off the cart looking longingly at her as he was carried away. She kept her hand on her sword hilt where he could see it, and he sheepishly averted his gaze.

Money well spent there, obviously.

She took a circuitous route back to the camp, just in case he changed his mind, and found it where she had left it, just off the main road. Katriel was alone by the fire, warming her hands, while Maric slept nearby in a lean-to tent they had set up by a tree. The canvas had been given by the pilgrims, and it offered some protection. But mostly they were filthy and the worse for wear. They'd spent most of the last nine days avoiding patrols and putting as much distance between them and West Hill as they possibly could.

Rowan had lost count of the number of times they had needed to elude patrols that became too curious for their own good. It helped a little when Maric had woken on the third day and was able to ride, but even then his wounds left him tired and dizzy. Katriel voiced her opinion that Maric had suffered a concussion when he had been thrown from his horse back in the woods, and Rowan didn't disagree. The best they could do was use the herbs the elf had brought with her and wait for Maric to heal. Healing supplies, at least, they had plenty of.

Rowan hesitated at the edge of the camp. She disliked being left alone with Katriel, which happened frequently, as Loghain needed to hunt. Despite the fact that the elven woman had come to their rescue, Rowan still had to bite her tongue when she watched her dote on Maric. And whenever Rowan tried to speak to her, all she would do was stare with those strange green eyes. It was difficult to tell what elves were thinking, like they were always hiding something. But Rowan felt guilty for thinking such things, even if the thoughts the elves reserved for humans were no doubt equally uncharitable, so she kept her feelings to herself.

Perhaps unsurprisingly, that left little to discuss.

Katriel finally noticed Rowan. She blinked in surprise and stood up. "I found dry wood, my lady," she said awkwardly.

"I see that." Rowan walked toward the lean-to, feeling those eyes following her every move. Maric was moaning irritably, but still asleep. His bandages had recently been changed; Katriel's doing, no doubt.

She stood there by the tent, uncertain if she should discuss the dwarf's news now or not. Maric and Loghain would just want to hear it again, and she was hardly in the mood to repeat herself. So she waited as Katriel watched, and the minutes passed with excruciating slowness.

Had Maric and Katriel continued to see each other after that night? She wanted desperately to ask but couldn't bear to. She had avoided Maric back in Gwaren, and he had been too busy to notice. Once they were at sea, they were on different ships, but this made it harder to dodge the thoughts running rampant in her head.

This was so unlike him. All the years she had known him, she had never seen him chase after anyone. Some men did, even after they were married. She had been raised by a father clueless in such matters ever since her mother died long ago, but she knew that much. But what would the proper ladies of the court think of this? Rowan was a soldier, and no stranger to the lusts that men possessed—especially those of her fellow soldiers, men who could die tomorrow fighting what sometimes seemed a hopeless cause. Should she even be concerned? She was no lady of the court, and it seemed that to Maric she was more *friend* than betrothed, was that not so?

Part of her had held out hope that Maric might come to her of his own accord. If this was more than a single night's desire, if this was . . . something else . . . then she deserved to know.

Katriel pointed to the small pot lying by the fire. "I can boil some more water if you like, my lady. I boiled some earlier, but I needed to change His Highness's dressings."

"No, that's not necessary." Rowan said. "And there's no need to keep calling me that, not out here."

The elf frowned and lowered her gaze, busying herself by picking up a shirt she had been mending. Maric's, Rowan assumed. She seemed too nettled to sew, however, and eventually put the shirt down in her lap with an exasperated sigh. "You all do exactly the same thing," she said. "Even the commander, Loghain. It is as if you believe you are doing me a favor by pretending that we are equals." Her tone was crisp and disapproving. "But we are not. I am not your servant, but I will always be an elf. To pretend otherwise is insulting."

Startled, Rowan had to bite her tongue to keep from saying something far less kind than would be helpful. "You're not from Ferelden, then," she finally managed.

"Not originally. I was ... brought here from Orlais."

"I would have thought you might have learned by now. Orlesians might believe in the righteousness of their empire and that the Maker Himself put their rulers on their thrones, but it is not like that here. Here all men are proved by their deeds, even kings."

Katriel snorted derisively. "Do you truly believe that?"

"Don't you?" Rowan asked, annoyed. "What are you doing here, if you don't believe that? Why would you help the rebellion in the first place?"

Katriel stiffened, and her eyes became hard, making Rowan regret her words. Many of the men who had been driven to the rebellion had done so out of desperation. They had difficult lives, and she could only imagine how bad it could get for an elf like Katriel. Rowan was hardly wealthy, living as she did, but even so, she knew little of true hardship. "I'm sorry," Rowan sighed. "I don't have any right to—"

"Of course you do," Katriel cut her off. "Don't be foolish. You don't know anything about me."

"I only meant—"

"I know what you meant." The elf stared into the fire, her eyes picking up the flickering of the flames. The harsh lines of her frown deepened. "I am not here for any love of Ferelden, or out of any hatred of Orlais. There was a time I would never have dreamed that I might do what I have, but I have discovered that even I have limits. Some things are worth protecting."

She's here for Maric, Rowan thought as she watched. She could be mistaken; Katriel's tone was so sad and even . . . regretful? Perhaps she wasn't talking about Maric at all.

Even so, there was something about Katriel's demeanor that rankled. What kind of servant was she that she spoke so? That she rode horses and knew how to use a dagger? She had never claimed to be a milkmaid, Rowan reminded herself, but there was certainly more to her than met the eye. There was far, far more than the timid, frightened elven maid that she and Maric had discovered being assaulted in Gwaren. She had been exhausted then, and unarmed, but still something did not sit right.

Perhaps it was jealousy. The way Maric had looked at Katriel, like she was an exotic and intoxicating flower, was a way he had never looked at Rowan.

She realized that Katriel was staring at her again and hurried to explain. "I never meant to insult you. I was merely trying to be friendly."

"Oh? Is that what you call it?"

Rowan frowned. "Yes. It is."

"Are we to be friendly then, my lady? Is that what you are suggesting?"

"It would be easier," Rowan snapped. "If you'd prefer we be something else, then by all means, let me know." The two of them locked gazes, and Rowan did not flinch. Neither did Katriel. In the cold silence that ensued, Rowan decided she had given this woman her last apology.

"What's going on?" The groggy voice came from the lean-to. Bleary-eyed, rumpled, and with his head bandaged, Maric looked more than a little worn for the days he had spent sleeping. For a moment, the challenge between Rowan and Katriel lingered, and neither of them responded to Maric's query. Then Katriel turned, harshness melting into a warm smile. Without responding, she went over to help Maric stand up unsteadily and led him to sit by the camp-fire. Shirtless, he rubbed his arms vigorously and complained about the chilly breeze.

Rowan watched quietly as Katriel presented him the mostly mended shirt, which he accepted grate-fully and slipped on. There was an awkward famil-iarity between them. His words hitched, and the elf seemed to find excuses to touch his arms with her delicate, slender fingers.

She felt like an unwanted outsider.

Her face clouded with grief, and it took effort for her to push it back down. It was best just to get this over with, wasn't it? "Maric," she said grimly, "I . . . have bad news."

Maric belatedly realized that she had spoken and he grinned crookedly. "About my shirt? Looks pretty good now," he joked. Gingerly he began to test the bandage around his head.

Rowan pressed her lips together in annoyance. "No. This isn't about the damned shirt."

Maric looked confused by her tone. Katriel stared into the fire, pretending not to notice. "Shouldn't we wait for Loghain?" he asked.

"Wait for me to do what?" Loghain said as he casually walked into the camp, a pair of rabbit car-casses tossed over one shoulder. Infuriatingly he was the only one with any skill at hunting. She had tried her hand at it, but it was pointless. She couldn't even fish. So they needed to rely on him to survive now, which was maddening.

Upon noticing Rowan's anger, Loghain paused, frowning at Maric. "What did you do now?"

Maric blinked in surprise. "Me? I didn't do anything."

"We should talk," Rowan snapped. "Now."

Katriel gracefully stood, walking to Loghain to relieve him of the rabbits. He looked at her curiously. "There's no need. I can skin these myself."

"There is a need," she insisted. "I wish to feel useful."

That was enough to give him pause. Katriel succeeded in taking the carcasses and quietly leaving the camp to go down to the nearby stream. Loghain watched her go, his look curious. Rowan saw that Maric watched her go as well, his look something else completely. *He can't even be bothered to hide it*, she thought angrily, restraining the urge to choke him. In his condition, it would hardly be a challenge.

Finally Loghain shrugged, walking over to the fire and crouching to warm his hands. He removed his bow and laid it down beside him. Rowan noticed that there were only a few arrows left in his quiver. "So let's hear it," he sighed.

"It's not going to be good." Maric grimaced.

She slowly sat down on the log beside him, letting the warmth of the blaze wash over her. "No, it's not," she agreed, rubbing her hand over her face in exhaustion. "First things first. At least some of the army still lives. They were routed at West Hill, but not all of them were killed."

Maric brightened. "Well, that's not so bad, is it?"

Rowan steeled herself, watching only the dance of the flames on the wood. "My father is dead." It was strange how easily the words came out. When the dwarf had told her, she thought all the breath had rushed out of her right there in the road. The fact of it had become this . . . *weight* on her chest that she couldn't remove.

Maric stared at her, stunned. "No . . . oh, Rowan! What about your family?"

Rowan thought of her two younger brothers, Eamon and Teagan, still with cousins in the Free Marches. She hadn't even considered how they might be handling the news. Eamon would be fifteen now, Teagan only eight. They were still just boys. "I don't even know if they've heard the news," she admitted grimly.

Loghain frowned thoughtfully. "Are we certain? That it's true?" he asked.

"His head is outside the palace, right next to—" She cut herself off, clearing the catch in her throat. "But, no. I'm not sure. The usurper has announced victory, and says that Maric is dead as well."

Maric looked up from his hands, his eyes hollow. "What?"

"That's the claim. The Arl and the Prince, both killed at West Hill." She glanced at Maric, crooking one corner of her mouth in grim amusement. "Apparently your body was not distinguishable from those of regular Fereldan men and thus couldn't be found, according to the usurper."

"Well that's just rude."

She sighed. "Be that as it may, some of our army managed to flee. According to the merchant, the word is they've run to rejoin those we left behind in Gwaren."

"Then we need to get there, and soon."

"Not so fast." She held up her hand. "The usurper

is chasing them. Even if we thought we could reach Gwaren before the usurper's army does, they'll be blocking the Brecilian Passage. They're between us and Gwaren."

"What about hiring a ship?" Maric asked.

She shrugged. "We've no money. The merchant says that the roads to the east are all blocked, crawling with soldiers. It's why he left."

"Smuggler?" Loghain's eyebrow shot up.

"That's what I thought." She nodded. "We could go back to the northern coast, try to find a—"

"No," Maric interrupted. "Not north."

"Then we get off the roads, try to get to the Brecilian Forest? Go through it to Gwaren without using the passage?"

Loghain rubbed his chin thoughtfully. "Difficult. I'd need to find a path through the mountains, and I don't know that area. If we try to stay closer to the passage, it's bound to be crawling with the usurper's men."

None of them spoke. The fire crackled somberly as new gusts of cold wind blew across the camp. Each of them searched for an answer that wasn't forthcoming, and none of them wanted to admit it. The truth hovered in the air before them like a black, unwelcome cloud.

"So that's it?" Maric's voice was cracked with emotion, and he stood up angrily. He looked from Loghain to Rowan and back. "That's it? If Arl Rendorn is dead and we're here, that means that nobody's there to lead the army!"

"There is still the chain of command," Loghain grunted. He looked troubled, however, and stared into the fire. "The Arl was not a fool, and neither were his lieutenants. There are men who will do what must be done."

"You know what I mean," Maric snapped. He looked like he was trying to hold back enraged tears. "Maker's breath! Why did you come after me? Why?"

"Don't be an idiot," Loghain scoffed. "You're the last of the royal blood."

"I don't want to hear that anymore," Maric sighed in exasperation. "This isn't about putting the blood of Calenhad on the throne. This is about getting that Orlesian bastard *off* it. Because if he was a good king for Ferelden, *none* of this would matter."

Rowan shook her head. "I think you—"

"No," he interrupted her. "I know exactly what I'm saying." He stared hard at Loghain. "Loghain, if you hadn't come after me, you might have made a difference in that battle. At the very least, you might have gotten more of them out alive."

Loghain did not meet Maric's stare, instead frowning into his steepled hands. He said nothing.

Maric sighed deeply and shook his head, his anger evaporating. "You both saved me, and while I'm grateful . . . you have to be prepared to let me go. My mother died. I could die. I would *rather* die than have the blood of all those men on my hands."

"You're insane," Rowan snapped. "Their blood is not on your hands."

"If you both had been where you were supposed to be, maybe we might have won. Maybe you could have pulled your men out in time, and you would be in Gwaren right now."

"I suppose we'll never know, will we?" Rowan

stood up and glared at Maric. "Quit being such a damned idealist. We're struggling just to *survive*—have you forgotten?" She walked up to him and pushed his chest, hard. Maric stumbled back into the lean-to and almost knocked it over, barely keeping his feet. He righted himself and stared back at her, more in indignation than in anger.

"I'm sorry you feel guilty that we came after you," she continued, "but you're important. Those men would all have willingly laid their lives down for you, had we told them what was at stake. That's why they were there!"

"I was responsible for them!" he insisted. "Just like you were!"

"We're responsible for you! You're the bloody Prince!"

"And this is my command!" he shouted stubbornly.

They stood there, staring at each other, the fire popping loudly in the wind. She wanted to slap him. She wanted to kiss him. How very noble he could be, yet at the same time, how very stupid he could be as well. Did he really think she could just abandon him when there was anything she could do about it?

Loghain continued to stare into the fire thoughtfully. "Maybe you have a point, Maric, but there's no point in fighting over it now. We're not leading anything at the moment."

Maric looked over at him. "But when we are . . ."

Loghain glanced up at Maric, eyes intense in the firelight. "Next time, I don't come to your rescue. You're on your own." Something significant passed between the two of them. Rowan could see it, but she couldn't understand it. Still, Maric seemed pleased by it.

He turned and looked at her next, apparently expecting her to agree with Loghain. She stood there and let him look at her, feeling nothing but rage building up inside her. "Is this a command, then?" she asked, acid dripping from her voice. "A royal command from Prince Maric to one of his commanders?"

Maric set his jaw. "I'm only asking for a promise."

She slapped him. The crack of the blow sounded in the quiet, his head snapping back. He rubbed his cheek, confusion and hurt in his eyes. Loghain made no comment, only his eyebrows shooting up. "I'd rather the command," she said icily.

"I'm sorry," he mumbled pitifully. He stumbled backwards and turned to sit back down on the log, his shoulders slumping dejectedly. "I just . . . I suppose this must seem very ungrateful of me."

She fought the urge to feel sorry for him, to pat him on the shoulders and tell him it would be all right. "Somewhat, yes," she commented.

Maric looked up at her, his eyes moist. "Your father is dead. You made a huge sacrifice to come and find me. I understand, I just can't help but think of them all. They were there because of me."

Rowan sat down stiffly, saying nothing.

"My father once led the outlaw camp too near a nest of blight wolves," Loghain said softly. "He knew they were there, but took us anyway because the other direction led us to the law. We lost fourteen people, six of them children." He grimaced at the memory. "My father was . . . upset. He wanted everyone to stop looking to him for guidance. Sister Ailis told him that she would rather have a leader who found it difficult to lead than one who found it easy."

He reached across the fire and patted Maric reassuringly on the shoulder, in the awkward manner of one who was completely unfamiliar with such gestures. Maric stared at Loghain in astonishment. "Wow, you're pretty good at that," he chuckled.

"Shut up." Loghain grimaced.

"I agree with Maric." Rowan smiled grimly. "Console me, now."

"You know"—he looked at her with complete seriousness—"the Arl may not be dead. Maric isn't dead. Just because the dwarf told you there's a head in front of the palace doesn't mean it has to be your father's."

She was surprised by his answer and fought to hold back sudden tears. "You *are* good at that," she muttered, her voice thick. "But if the usurper was so prepared to lie, why not just put a second head in front of the palace and say it is Maric's?"

"There might not be any head."

She shrugged. "I hope you're right." She didn't believe it, however.

The three of them sat there in front of the fire, watching it slowly begin to dwindle in strength. Maric huddled in his shirt, shivering. They shared a sense of exhaustion that left them hollow and empty.

"I guess we should decide what to do," Maric finally announced with a deep sigh. "We're bad at this, aren't we?"

"Perhaps the army is better off without us?" Loghain suggested, amused.

"Better off without Maric, maybe," Rowan commented.

"Ow!" Maric chuckled. "I felt that! I'll remind you both that it was your idea to save me. I would have been fine killing those . . . six soldiers? Were there six?"

"Try eight," Rowan said dryly.

"Try eleven," Loghain corrected. "The three Katriel killed."

Rowan rolled her eyes. "Ah, yes. Let's not forget her."

"I thought I was just seeing double." Maric smiled. Then he looked at Rowan queerly. "You slapped me."

"Would you like me to do it again?"

"Why did you slap me?"

Loghain cleared his throat to get their attention. "We were deciding what to do," he reminded them. "I think the only thing we can do is try to find a route through the Brecilian Forest. If we can reach it, that is."

Maric nodded glumly. "Do we have any other choice?"

"Actually you do," came Katriel's quiet voice as she returned to the camp. She carried the rabbits, freshly skinned, as well as a small bundle of wood and sticks under one arm. Maric stood to help relieve her burden, and she immediately crouched down to restore the fire.

Loghain waited patiently, watching her work, until finally he couldn't wait any longer. "We have another choice? You heard us speaking, I take it?"

"Half the countryside could hear the three of you, ser. I was not trying to, but I heard most of it from the stream." She dug around with the new wood, and the flames roared back to life, the moist bark hissing and popping violently as it began to blacken. "And yes, you have another option."

"Don't keep us in suspense," Rowan sighed.

Katriel nodded, frowning. "I know, my lady. I am merely . . . hesitant to mention it." Satisfied with the fire, she took the carcasses from Maric and began skewering them on a pair of branches. "Have you heard of the Deep Roads?"

Loghain nodded slowly. "The underground roads that once belonged to the dwarven kingdoms. But they no longer exist."

"Oh, they exist. The dwarves closed off the Deep Roads when they fell to the darkspawn long ago. The entrance into the Deep Roads from Orzammar is sealed, normally." She looked at Loghain pointedly. "You can, however, enter them from the surface . . . if you know where to look."

Maric blinked. "And you . . . know where to look?"

Katriel nodded. "I do, Your Highness. Or, rather, I believe I do."

"And one of these . . . Deep Roads goes to Gwaren?"

"Believe it or not, Your Highness, Gwaren was built on top of a dwarven outpost. The humans came later, to use the port that the dwarves had built and abandoned. They even took the outpost's name, though they doubtless no longer remember it."

"And just how do you remember it?" Rowan asked. "How do you know this?"

Katriel's smile was enigmatic. "I know many things, my lady. History is full of lessons to be learned if one cares to listen."

Loghain glanced at Rowan, and she saw he shared her suspicions. Maric, however, was more concerned about the idea Katriel proposed. "But aren't these Deep Roads full of darkspawn?" he asked. "I mean, wasn't that the idea behind closing them off?"

The elf nodded slowly. "No one knows how many darkspawn are below now. It has been centuries since they invaded the surface lands and were defeated. The Deep Roads could be teeming with them . . . or empty."

"But . . . we could use the Deep Roads? To travel? Theoretically?"

"Theoretically," she agreed. "If they are clear, Your Highness, we could travel very swiftly indeed."

"Or be slain and eaten as soon as we enter," Rowan snapped.

"Or the path could be blocked." Katriel nodded. "Hence my hesitation."

The thoughts were whirling in Maric's head; Rowan could see them. Her heart sank as she saw his hopes rise. "If we go through the Brecilian Forest, it's guaranteed to take a long time," he said to Loghain, his voice excited.

Loghain seemed dubious. "Several weeks, perhaps, though I can find the way."

"At least with these Deep Roads we have a *chance*." Maric grinned.

"Maric!" Rowan chided him. "Do you even know anything about the darkspawn? They are horrible, tainted creatures! An unthinkable fate could await us down there, assuming that Katriel even knows where the entrance is."

"We passed it, my lady," Katriel said. "A great stone column in the hills. I saw it from afar. It is the reason I thought of this at all." She looked at Maric with concern. "Though . . . there is a seal. I am not sure we could even open it, Your Highness, I would have to see it to be certain."

Maric looked at Loghain. "What do you think?"

"I think it is a lot to rest on this story." He arched a brow at Katriel. "Are you certain? These Deep Roads go straight to Gwaren? And we would be able to navigate down there?"

"I remember the tale," she replied cautiously. "But . . ."

"Then we go," Maric said firmly. "Let us find this seal. If we cannot open it, or we see any hint of creatures below, then we go through the forest instead." He paused as he realized what he was saying, but then nodded again, more certain. "I say we take the risk."

"Or die trying," Loghain said grimly.

"Or die trying," Maric agreed.

Rowan looked at them both incredulously. Finally, she sighed in exasperation. "Or die trying," she said without much enthusiasm. Men were such fools.

"I will do my best to get you back to your people," Katriel swore, looking at Maric as she did so. "I promise you that, Your Highness."

He rolled his eyes mockingly. "You keep calling me that."

"That is what you are."

"You helped save my life and now you're going to lead us into the Deep Roads, and you want to stand on ceremony?" He chuckled lightly. "Besides, you're the only one doing it, now. It's weird."

She shook her head, bewildered. "You are a very strange man."

"Well, don't you start slapping me, too. I've had enough of that for today."

And with that, their decision was set. Rowan and Loghain shared another quiet glance as Katriel and Maric continued their banter. She hoped halfheartedly that the elf wouldn't be able to find the seal, or would not be able to open it, despite the supposed speed it might offer them in reaching Gwaren. Somehow she suspected that Katriel's information would prove to be good.

Katriel's information was always good, evidently.

Thunder finally clamored off in the distance. It appeared their camp was about to get a great deal colder.

13

———————————

It took most of the next day to backtrack to the column Katriel had mentioned, and they found what she called the seal there. It was open. The four of them stood in the rain, staring at what would have easily been mistaken for a cave opening in the rocky hillside from a distance, and yet up close it contained the remains of what had once been an impressive pair of octagonal steel doors.

They were decorated with geometric patterns; thick, solid grooves carved into the steel that might once have formed words or pictures. Now they were too covered in brown lichen and thick piles of rust to be decipherable as anything. One of the doors hung off its great hinges, the elements literally eating away at it. The way inside was clear save for a mound of rocks and dirt at the entrance, look-

ing as if the debris had been spewed from the great
orifice.

It wasn't until they got closer, stepping carefully
among the wet and uneven rocks, that they realized
the mound was mostly made of bones. Old bones,
encrusted in earth and mud and mostly buried.

"Hard to say what they were," Maric observed,
picking among the bone pieces with faint disgust.
"Might be human."

"More important, they're not new," Loghain
pointed out. "That's a good sign."

Katriel poked her head warily into the cave. "I
agree. If any creature other than bats has used this
cave recently, they haven't left a trace. All I see is
guano."

"Charming." Rowan rolled her eyes.

Katriel glanced at Rowan. "There are many legends of travelers going missing in these hills. We
should still be careful, as such legends often have
some truth in them."

"Duly noted," Loghain commented, ushering everyone inside.

They set up camp just inside the cave opening, the
four of them going to work on making as many
torches as they could by tearing up strips of the tent
fabric. Katriel mentioned that she had no idea how
long they would be down there. There would be no
hunting for food, she cautioned, and no way to
know if there was fresh water.

Loghain had them fill up as many bottles and flasks
as they could. He then took stock of their meager
food supplies, laying out dried strips of meat on the
rock as he listened to the rhythm of rain pounding on

the rocks outside. Rowan sat beside him, wearing her full set of gleaming armor again.

"This is a foolish thing you agreed to, you know that," she whispered grimly.

"Perhaps."

"Do you actually believe we should trust her?"

"No." Loghain glanced farther down the cave, where Katriel and Maric were clearing rocks. "But that does not mean she is lying about this." Rowan seemed unconvinced, and Loghain attempted a reassuring smile. "We will go in as far as we can. If it proves unsuitable, then we return."

"And what if we can't? Return, I mean."

He went back to his count, his face grim. "Then we die."

It was not long before they managed to find a way down. Parts of the cavern were nearly blocked, as if there had been an effort long ago to seal it up with rocks. Whether that had been to keep something below from getting out or something above from getting in was impossible to tell. Either way, it was possible to squeeze by most of these piles with only a little effort.

Otherwise the passages were largely regular and flat, having long ago been smoothed by dwarven craftsmen. They might even have been beautiful once, but now they were coated in thick dust, moss, and a great deal of bat guano. There was evidence of graffiti near the beginning, crude drawings left by those who had inhabited the early section of the cave and left a reminder of their presence, but these disappeared as the passage dropped off sharply.

They traveled in silence, the tension growing as the faint light vanished completely to be replaced by a stuffy gloom. Dust floated in the still air, giving a faint corona to their torches, and Loghain expressed concern that air might become limited. Katriel explained that dwarves used ingenious ducts to keep the Deep Roads supplied, but who knew if such things were even working still?

It would certainly explain why no one had seen darkspawn on the surface in so many centuries, if they had all suffocated down there in the still shadows. That idea brought little cheer with it.

After several hours, they reached what might have been some kind of way station or checkpoint built into the passage. Perhaps it was intended as a fort, and certainly the building would have been defensible had its walls still been intact. Katriel pointed out where a gateway might once have closed off the passage entirely to traffic, but whatever had been there had been demolished. Littering the halls were a great number of rusted mining carts, loose sacks near faded away to nothing . . . and ancient bones. Old webs clotted with dust hung from the ceiling and gave them the feeling that they were walking into a graveyard. Nothing moved here. No bats were this deep, and though it seemed as if someone had looted the remains of the way station long ago, there was nobody there now.

"Was there a battle here?" Rowan asked, examining the bones. No one could answer her. Most of the bones were barely distinguishable as belonging to humans or dwarves or even elves. A few of them were very definitely none of those things.

After that came the steps—wide steps that seemed

to lead down forever into darkness. They had to be careful, as many of the steps were cracked and brittle and likely to give way under their weight. . . . Indeed, many had already done so. Occasionally they needed to use the steel rails that lay in the middle of the hall for purchase, rails that once must have been used to carry the metal carts.

The old webs covered everything now. Mostly they were clotted with dust, nearly unrecognizable lumps of gray hanging like sacks from the walls and ceiling, but occasionally Loghain would point out new webs and even little spiders that scuttled away from the torchlight. He was reassured by the sight, he said. Spiders meant insects. They meant life.

By the time they reached the bottom of the steps, they had been traveling for many hours. Rowan expressed nervousness that they seemed mostly to be going down rather than heading in any particular direction. Maric, however, was just glad that they had seen no darkspawn. They cleared away a section of the road in order to make a camp, though Loghain insisted they keep the fire small. There was no telling how much air was down in the tunnels, or what might be attracted to the light if they kept a blaze going for too long.

It was a discomforting thought, and that first night, none of them truly slept. They took turns keeping watch with a single lit torch, staring into the shadows that danced around the camp. In truth, anyone could have crept up on them. With the dust in the air and the dim light, anyone keeping watch couldn't see more than ten feet. But having someone on guard made them feel better, and it let the others close their eyes while trying to pretend that many miles of rock weren't pressing down on them overhead.

If anything, the silence was the worst. It lay heavy, like a shroud, broken only by the sound of labored breathing and the faint scratching sounds of feet moving on stone. When the group stood still, sometimes they could hear the faintest clicking sounds off in the blackness. The clicks came and went, and none of them could identify what the sounds might be. They kept their weapons out after that, but no attack manifested.

For two days, they traveled in this way, heading farther and farther underground. They stopped regularly to rest and get their bearings, and this allowed Katriel the opportunity to attend to Maric's bandages. She worried about infection, particularly with his head wound, but after a time declared that the poultices were working. He was healing nicely. Maric declared that it was about time something good happened.

The fact that they were traveling on a road became more evident. Even with the general sense of decay, they could see the regular stone columns along the walls and statues of grim dwarven figures barely discernible for all the wear. There were deep grooves along the bottom of the walls, which Katriel claimed would once have channeled lava. That same lava would have been collected in pools along the walls for light. Loghain asked where the lava came from, but she didn't know. It might have been magic, though the dwarves didn't use any. Wherever it might have come from, there was none now. There was only the dust and the quiet gloom.

The first intersection of passages they reached had great runes carved into the walls, and after clearing away as much dust and debris as they could, they waited while Katriel studied them closely with torch in hand.

"It's definitely dwarven," she muttered. She tapped on one rune that was repeated several times. "See this one? It has two parts: *gwah* and *ren*. 'Salt' and 'pool.'"

"Gwaren?" Maric leaned forward, his head close over Katriel's shoulder as he studied the rune for himself. She blinked nervously, but he didn't notice. "That must be it, right? The dwarven outpost has the same name."

"I believe it's pointing down the right-hand passage." Katriel looked up at Maric with a frown. "But I can't be certain."

"Better your guess than mine." Maric grinned.

Rowan and Loghain traded leery glances, but they could do little but trust the elven woman's knowledge. Loghain had long ago given up on his sense of direction.

Less than a day later—though their estimate of how much time was passing was becoming increasingly inaccurate the longer they were surrounded by constant darkness—they encountered a thaig, a cavern where the dwarves had built a settlement. There was a large amount of debris and rocks at its entrance, perhaps due to some kind of cave-in, and it required hours of labor to clear a passage. Once through, they stood at the edges of a place no dwarf had likely touched in living memory.

The flickering light of their torches didn't reach very far into the thaig, but what they did see evoked a memory of grand stone buildings rising high up toward the upper reaches of the cavern. The walkways between these buildings had once been lined with giant columns carved with lines upon lines of runes. Now most of these things were collapsed and in ruin, jagged stone skeletons covered in massive webs.

Here the webs were everywhere. They hung from building to wall like gentle gauze, and as the cavern rose, the webs seemed to get thicker and thicker until the torchlight couldn't penetrate them any longer. It was as if the webs kept this place cocooned, suspended out of time in darkness and quiet.

"Careful," Loghain warned softly, moving his torch so as not to light the webs. Such a blaze would have spread quickly into the upper reaches of the thaig, and likely brought all of it raining down upon their heads.

"Do you feel it?" Rowan asked, stepping uncertainly forward amid the uneven debris. She touched her cheek and looked around with concern. The others opened up their eyes wide, feeling the same thing she did: a gentle brush on their cheeks, the slightest sense of movement in the dust-choked air.

"It's air," Maric breathed. "There's air flowing here."

He was right. Air was coming from somewhere high up, and if they looked carefully, they could see the faint glowing webs waving ever so slightly overhead. Perhaps there was a sort of hole leading up to the surface. The dwarves must have had chimneys of some kind, or perhaps these were the ducts that Katriel had mentioned.

There were also sounds. As the four of them stood there, the distant clicking became more prominent.

It started and stopped, but it was definitely there. After hearing little else but their own movement, such alien sounds were very easy to notice.

Katriel blanched, her fear made noticeable by her agitated glances up into the darkness despite her effort to conceal it. "What . . . what are those sounds? Rocks?"

Nobody answered her. Even she didn't really believe it.

"Should we go back?" Rowan whispered.

Maric shook his head. "There's no way around that we saw. It's either forward or it's all the way back."

There was really no discussion to be had. Loghain moved forward, sword held cautiously in front of him as he stared nervously up into the webs above. "If we need to, we'll have to burn them."

Maric stepped closely behind him. "Wouldn't that be worse?"

"I said if we need to."

They proceeded slowly, keeping their backs toward each other and blades out. Each step was carefully placed among the rubble, and they made not a single sound. They barely breathed. Each of them slowly waved their flickering torches in the air before them, trying to discern anything in the dark ruins. But all they saw was ruined archways and stone columns and more rubble. The shadows danced mockingly in the silence.

They crept through what appeared to be a long causeway, cracked and crumbled between the towering walls of gutted buildings. One of the walls still had faded chips of colored paint, turquoise and red and the remnants of what might have been a face.

The eyes were the only part of the face still discernible, eyes that stared out at them in mute surprise.

Loghain stopped, and Maric almost bumped into him from behind. They were at the feet of an enormous statue, a giant warrior that reached up hundreds of feet into the air and could very well have been holding up the ceiling of the cavern. It was tarnished, and the details were lost in the shadows, but it was easily the largest thing he had ever seen in his life. It looked almost as if it had been made from pure marble.

"Maker's breath," Maric breathed, staring up at it.

The others turned, and Katriel walked up to the feet of the statue, her eyes wide. "Don't touch it," Loghain cautioned her, but she ignored him. The statue appeared to rest on a great square column, itself covered in dusty runes.

Katriel held the torch in front of the runes and swept some of the dust off with her hands. "This . . . I think this is a Paragon," she whispered.

"A what?" Maric asked.

"A Paragon. They are dwarves that achieve legendary status among their people. The greatest of their warriors, the founders of the houses." She brushed off more of the dust, enraptured by what she was unveiling. "I think this one was a smith."

"Wonderful, it's a dwarven smith," Rowan muttered. "Can we keep moving?"

The elf shot a glare with her green eyes. "A Paragon isn't just anyone. They were the greatest dwarves that ever lived. The dwarves revere them as gods. This—" She stared up at the expanse of the statue above her. "—is something the dwarves would pay a great deal to know about."

"Then let's tell them about it. Later," Rowan insisted.

Loghain nodded. "We need to see if there's a way through."

Reluctantly Katriel nodded. She stepped back from the statue's base, taking one last sad look and shaking her head as if she couldn't quite believe it. Only Maric saw the single strand of thick, glistening thread that dangled behind her. He was already leaping forward as she was suddenly jerked up into the darkness.

"Katriel!" Maric shouted, grabbing on to the elf's legs as his sword fell to the ground. She screamed in terror, and while Maric's weight pulled her back down, they both dangled above the ground precariously.

Excited clicking sounds suddenly erupted up in the dark webs above, as well as all around them. They echoed and circled, and many shadows began to move just at the very edges of their torchlight.

"Loghain!" Maric shouted again, his legs kicking wildly. "Help me!"

Loghain moved quickly, reaching up and grabbing one of Maric's legs as it swung by his head. He yanked down hard. Katriel screamed again as a loud chittering erupted from high above, and with a wet snap, both she and Maric came crashing down to the ground.

"There!" Rowan shouted as something ran into view. Her eyes went wide as she realized it was a giant spider, easily as large as herself. It was a thing of dark bristles and many wet eyes, a great and swollen abdomen rearing up behind it. Its hairy legs moved with startling speed as it scuttled to one side, nervous of either Rowan's sword or her fiery torch.

Loghain was already leaping back to his feet, spinning about to face more quick shadows that sped past out of sight. Rowan's spider emitted several loud clicks and rushed toward her, two forelegs raised and dripping fangs bared.

"Rowan!" he shouted in warning.

The spider batted her sword aside with one of its forelegs, almost succeeding in tearing it from her gauntlets. It lunged forward with its fangs, hissing, and she succeeded in interposing her arm. The weight of the spider carried her back as its fangs tried repeatedly to pierce the metal of her armor. They didn't, and black venom coursed along its surface, leaving a sizzling, smoking trail.

Rowan grunted with the effort of keeping herself from being toppled, and she pushed back with her arm. The spider chattered in anger and tried to leap off her, but her sword swiftly chopped into the side of its head. White ichor spurted from the wound. The spider squealed, vaulting up into the air and smashing into a far wall. It spun about madly, almost seeming as if it was trying to get away from its injury.

Another giant spider dropped down from above, nearly landing on Loghain. He leaped out of the way, spinning about at the last instant and slicing at the creature's forearm. It deflected the blow, turning its head to stare down at Katriel right next to it with its many pairs of glittering black eyes. She screamed in terror.

Maric plunged his sword into the side of the spider's head, gritting his teeth with the effort. The blade glided past its chitinous armor with a wet, crunching sound. The creature's body shivered, and then it whipped about more quickly than Maric could react, its forelimbs striking him in the shoulder and sending him tumbling back along the ground.

Loghain leaped forward and kicked the giant spider solidly, flipping it over with a horrid squealing sound. Even as it scrambled to right itself, white fluid gushing from its wounded head, Loghain stepped on its thorax to hold it still and thrust his sword down into its body. He twisted the blade around with difficulty as the spider flailed its legs and screeched loudly.

"Maric!" Katriel shouted with concern, scrambling after him. Rowan noticed as well and leaped to the spot where he lay. Even as she did so, another spider raced down the vertical side of a wall toward her. She slashed at it with her sword, causing it to jerk backwards and retreat.

Katriel got to Maric. He shook his head, dazed, and she helped him stand. Then his eyes went wide as he saw something above them. His scream was echoed by hers as a giant spider landed on top of them, its fangs sinking into Katriel's shoulders.

She jerked away from it, spinning around and stabbing at the spider's eyes with her dagger. The spider scrambled away instantly, but not before Rowan rushed it from the side and stabbed her sword into its abdomen. Fluids rushed out as it squealed and spun to face her. She spun at the same time, meeting its head with a great swing of her blade. The creature's head was instantly decapitated, its body spinning and kicking on its own in reaction, ichor splattering everywhere.

"No!" Maric shouted as he saw Katriel collapse, her eyes rolling up into her head. The vicious punctures on her shoulder were already swelling, black tendrils radiating out from it underneath her skin like a dark corruption. Maric scooped her up in his arms before she hit the ground and stared down in horror as she began to spasm uncontrollably. "Loghain! We have to get out of here!"

Gritting his teeth, Loghain yanked his blade out of the dead spider beneath him and leaped off. He snatched up Maric's sword and a torch that lay on the ground, threatening to extinguish completely. The sword he tossed to Maric, who caught it deftly even in the poor light, and the torch he reached up toward the strands of webs that hung down above him.

It took a moment for the flames to begin to catch, but as they did, they began to spread upward rapidly. Very rapidly. "Brace yourselves!" he bellowed.

The echoes of clicking around them seemed to rise even as the *fwoosh!* of the flames became a loud roar. The fire fanned out overhead, instantly lighting up the entire area of the ruins. Maric looked around, blinking in the sudden glare, and saw many spidery shapes skittering on the walls. An alarming number of them. One of the giant spiders scrambled down the wall toward Rowan again, and she sliced upward, hacking off part of a forelimb. Screeching, it retreated again, and Rowan backed up toward Maric.

"There!" he cried, pointing at a nearby building that had been revealed by the light. It had a dome of tarnished gold, one of the few ceilings they had seen that had not collapsed.

Rowan moved to help Maric carry Katriel, and they began to race as fast as they could toward the domed building. Loghain dashed after them, covering his head as great gobs of burning webs began to rain down from above. The giant spiders had halted their attack and were fleeing in every direction, their maddening screeches becoming a cacophony that threatened to drown out even the roar of the flames.

The stench of charred foulness threatened to become overwhelming, and along with it came a sudden suction from above. It was as if the air was being pulled upward, only to be replaced a moment later with a thick oily smoke that belched downward toward them. It spread quickly, blocking their vision and choking them with its thickness. It seemed more dust than smoke, coating their faces and arms and reaching like little hands down their throats and into their lungs.

Maric began to cough hoarsely and heard Rowan doing the same, even though he could barely see her right next to him. It was like stumbling through molasses. Rowan collapsed to the ground, taking the unconscious Katriel with her and pulling Maric along. He swore, forcing the inhalation of more of the smog and then gagging. They couldn't see where they were going anymore.

Something touched Maric's shoulder, and his first instinct was to swing his sword at it. Whatever had touched him apparently counted on that move, and a hand grabbed at Maric's wrist to stop him. It was Loghain.

"Come on!" he shouted, his voice raspy from the effort.

Loghain pulled Maric to his feet, and together they collected Rowan and Katriel and began dragging them in the direction of the dome. All they could see

in the swirling blackness was the bright aurora of fire
that blanketed the cavern roof and the great drop-
pings of flame that rained down. The air continued to
be sucked away.

For a moment, Maric wondered if the entire roof of
the cavern—with all its masses of webs and spiders
along with it—was going to come crashing down on
their heads. The searing heat was unbearable, and he
was breathing it.

And then he passed out.

When Maric woke up, it was still dark and he was
confused. He was lying down on something hard,
and someone was wiping his face with a wet, cool
cloth. He still couldn't see anything. How much later
was it? Were they still down in the Deep Roads? Was
it safe? When he tried to ask a question, all that came
out was a dry rasp, and he began to cough explo-
sively, the pain racking his entire body.

A hand pushed down on him to keep him from
sitting up, and he heard Rowan's calming voice urging him to lie still. "Don't move yet, Maric. I'm going to give you something to drink, but you need to
drink it slowly." A vial was put to his lips, and in it
was blissfully cool water. He wanted to gorge himself as he realized just how much of that inky dust
still coated his throat, but Rowan pulled the vial
away before he could tilt it forcefully. Even so, he
began gagging on the water until finally he turned
over and forcefully expelled a huge amount of vile
blackness from within him.

It came out in waves, leaving him weak and shivering. Rowan sighed and put the vial to his mouth

again, letting him have a real draft this time. "That . . . could have gone better," she muttered. "But at least it's out."

The water felt good going down, and Maric lay back, feeling the coolness reach the deeper parts of him. Then he opened his eyes, alarmed. "Is Katriel—?"

"Stable, but she hasn't woken yet," Rowan answered, annoyance creeping into her voice. "Loghain was able to suck most of the poison out. Lucky that she had wormroot in her pack, or that wouldn't have been enough."

There were clicking sounds in the background, differing from the clicking of the spiders, however. It sounded like rocks being smacked together, and after a moment, Maric realized that was exactly what it was. He saw some sparks in the darkness, followed soon afterwards by a gentle flame spreading.

"Do you think that's wise?" Rowan asked.

"There's been no sign of spiders," Loghain commented from above the tiny flame, "and we're starting to get fresh air again. I think the worst is over."

Loghain was blowing on the flames to urge them to spread, and they did. The near-rotted pieces of wood he had piled crackled and popped as they caught fire, but as the flames got higher, they pushed back the shadows, and Maric could see again at last.

They were inside the building, the dome barely visible high overhead. It was gutted, full of piles of rubble and stone that might have been crumbled walls or furniture that had fallen to dust. He could see long terraced steps that led down into the lower, center part of the chamber directly under the dome. Had this been a forum once? A theater? Maric had heard once that the dwarves held fighting matches called "provings," matches where warriors battled for honor and glory. Perhaps this had been a proving ground? It didn't seem large enough.

Katriel lay nearby, her shoulder bandaged. She was nearly coated with black dust, turning her blond curls oily and dark, though someone had clearly taken pains to wipe her face. They were all coated with the same dust, he noticed, and it seemed to be layered unevenly over any part of the room that was near the gaps in the walls or the windows. Outside it looked far worse, like a sea of blackness with dust hovering in the air like a cloud.

The quiet was near absolute, almost muffled like on the first day after a snowfall. All Maric could hear was the sound of trickling water somewhere nearby. He couldn't place it due to the echo, but it was very clear.

"There is water in here, believe it or not," Loghain commented. He seemed satisfied at the size of the fire and sat back, wiping the smears of soot on his face once again. "There is a large basin in the back," he pointed toward an area on the far side of the room where the wall was more crumbled than else-where, "that seems to generate fresh water on its own. It was turned over, and had made a creek."

"Magic, obviously," Rowan offered. "But it's fresh. Too bad we can't take it with us."

"How long has it been?" Maric croaked, pulling himself up to a seated position. Rowan reached out a hand to steady him, but relented when she realized he was fine. "How did we get here?"

"I was able to drag you in before it really started

coming down." Loghain grunted. "And then I passed out. I don't know for how long. It's impossible to tell time down here."

"Those spiders could come back." Rowan shivered.

"Yes, they could." He turned away from the fire and faced Maric, his expression serious. "We shouldn't stay here too long. If there's a way to get back onto the road to Gwaren, we should find it. Soon. We'll need to carry Katriel if we have to."

"Or we could leave her," Rowan said quietly, looking at no one.

"Rowan!" Maric said, shocked.

She glanced at Loghain, who grimaced and looked distinctly uncomfortable. But he did not turn away. Maric looked from one to the other, saw the way they were sitting together, facing him, a united front. They had been discussing this. While he had been unconscious, they had talked about leaving Katriel.

"Are you actually serious?" he asked, his shock slowly giving way to outrage. "Leave her? Because she's injured?"

"No, it's not that," Rowan said firmly. She held up a hand to stop Loghain from joining in. He frowned but complied. "Maric, we don't think it's wise to trust her."

"What are you saying?"

"We're saying there's a lot of things that don't add up. You can't say that this is the same woman who we found screaming for help in Gwaren."

Loghain nodded. "I was willing to accept her as a messenger, even one of Arl Byron's agents . . . but these skills she's shown, the knowledge she possesses. This is no simple elven servant, Maric."

Maric stiffened, feeling his anger growing. "And even if she isn't, why is this a bad thing?"

"Maric . . . ," Loghain said uneasily.

"She came to my defense," Maric insisted, "when she could just as easily have helped those soldiers kill us. She's offered her knowledge freely, when she could just as easily have led us into the usurper's hands." His eyes narrowed. "What is it, exactly, that you think she's done?"

"I don't know that she's done anything," Loghain said truthfully. "All I know is that she makes me uneasy."

Rowan took a deep breath. "Consider that you may not be very objective about her, Maric," she stated evenly.

Maric paused, taken aback. And then he saw the hurt pride in Rowan's eyes. She was trying to hide it, but it was obvious even to him that she wanted to be anywhere other than here.

She knows, he realized. It made sense now. The day before they had embarked at Gwaren, the way she had looked at him so expectantly, and when he had asked her about it, she had stormed off. The anger. The slap.

"Oh," he muttered, his anger quickly dissolving. He had practiced a hundred times how to tell Rowan about Katriel, and it figured that when it happened, it would be like none of those times. He had wanted to tell her. He had wanted to say that Katriel made him feel capable, he didn't have to prove anything to her. But how would that sound? It wasn't that he felt the need to prove himself to Rowan, exactly. She had known him as a child, she knew his every fault and his every mistake better than he did. He loved Rowan, it was simply . . . different.

Part of him had hoped that Rowan would understand. As teenagers, they had both complained bitterly about their parents' arrangement, had secretly laughed at the idea that they would someday be married. Surely she didn't . . .

But she did, didn't she? As Rowan stared at him, it occurred to him that she had not complained about their betrothal for many years. And he couldn't claim ignorance, not really. If he truly didn't know how she felt, it wouldn't have been so difficult to tell her about Katriel, would it?

"Rowan," he said gravely. "I didn't want to tell you like this."

"I know."

"Tell her what?" Loghain asked, looking as if he had swallowed something sour. He looked from Maric to Rowan and back . . . and then his face became still. Very slowly, he turned and looked at Rowan, his eyes pained. "Ah," was all he said.

"I don't know what to say," Maric pleaded quietly. "I never thought . . . I mean, we never talked about this, not for years. We were always at war, I didn't think—"

"Stop," Rowan said calmly. "This isn't the place to talk about it."

"But . . ."

Her eyes met Maric's. "Just tell me one thing: Did it continue? Past that first night?"

Maric felt helpless. He had never wanted to hurt Rowan, but it had already been done. There was nothing he could say to make it better. "Yes," he said helplessly.

Rowan nodded slowly. Loghain turned and looked at Maric in surprise. "Maker's breath, man! Do you love her?"

Maric flinched. Far better for Loghain to have taken a knife and stabbed it into his back. Rowan stared down at the ground, but Maric knew she was listening intently. He took a deep breath and exhaled raggedly. "Yes," he said, "I think I do."

Even if Rowan had expected the answer, Maric could tell it still hurt her. She avoided looking at him, her face hard as stone. He felt cruel. Loghain stared at him in disbelief.

Maric took a deep breath.

"I'll end it," he said quietly. He looked up at Rowan, his jaw set and his expression firm. "I never wanted to hurt you, Rowan. I should have known better. You are important to me, you have to know that. If this is how you feel, then I'll end it. Katriel and I are through."

There was a long and awkward pause. The silence in the caverns loomed larger, and for a moment Maric wished for the sound of wind, the cries of birds far overhead, even the clicking sounds of the spiders. Anything but the wall of silence.

Finally Rowan looked at him, her expression hard. "No. That's not what I want."

"But—"

"What I want," she insisted icily, "is for you to listen to what we're saying. How do you explain these inconsistencies about Katriel?"

Maric sighed. He stared at Rowan, wanting to talk about anything else, but she was determined. "She's an elf," he stated helplessly, "and she's an extraordinary woman, one with skills that we should be thankful for. She saved all of our lives, if you've forgotten." He stopped and looked at the two of them reproachfully. "And even if I agreed with these suspicions of yours, do you really think I could just leave her down here? Nobody deserves that fate."

Loghain rubbed his chin thoughtfully. "Perhaps we should question her, then, see if she—"

"No. Enough, both of you."

Loghain and Rowan exchanged looks again, reluctantly nodding. They didn't like it, but they clearly hadn't been all that committed to just leaving Katriel behind, either. Maric wasn't certain why they thought he might agree to it. The thought of leaving anyone down in this spider-infested blackness made his skin crawl.

"Rowan," Maric began, "maybe we should talk, go and—"

She stood up quickly, brushing the black soot off her armored legs. "There's no need," she said coldly. "I get it. You love her. I just wish you had told me. I could have released you from any obligation you might have felt."

There was nothing Maric could say to that. She collected the pack, pointedly ignoring him. "I'm going to try to wash up a bit. Excuse me." Without looking back, she marched off to the dark recesses in the back of the chamber.

Loghain shot Maric a look that had "you are an idiot" written all over it. "Take care of the fire. Give us a shout if Katriel wakes up." Then he followed after Rowan.

Maric sighed, leaning back on his elbows and wincing as the uneven rocks behind him jutted into his back. At some point, everything had gone wrong.

His plan had been a failure, he'd gotten most of his army and Rowan's father killed, and he'd betrayed Rowan's trust. Perhaps even Loghain was angry at him now. And he didn't know if any of it was fixable. Even if they managed to get through these tunnels somehow and reached Gwaren in time, would it be just to see the remnants of the rebel army be crushed once and for all? Did he really want to be present for that?

But why were they taking out their anger on Katriel? He just couldn't get it. He could understand Rowan, maybe. He had sensed tension between her and Katriel previously, and now it made sense why it had been there. But Loghain? Loghain was normally a sensible man. Why would he express baseless suspicions? Why would he urge Maric to abandon Katriel here? It made no sense that she was here to harm them. She'd had every opportunity to do so—why would she help them first?

He stared into the flickering campfire, slowly becoming mesmerized by the flames as they consumed the wood. The fire was slowly ebbing, and he knew he should tend to it, add some more fuel, but he found he preferred the shadows as they crept closer. He preferred the chill in the air. The thought that there could be spiders crawling closer seemed unreal, somehow.

"You are right," came a quiet voice nearby.

Maric turned over to see Katriel's eyes opened. She slowly sat up, her green eyes looking distant and sad. For a moment, she looked around at the ruined chamber, at the dome above and the rubble, satisfying whatever curiosity she felt about their location.

"You're awake!" he exclaimed, crawling quickly

over toward her. He took her hand and helped her move by the fire. "How do you feel? Does it hurt?"

She seemed glad to be near the fire, and turned her head awkwardly to study the large bandage on her shoulder. "It's throbbing, a bit." Her tone was unconcerned. She looked back at Maric, her expression nervous. "Did you hear what I said?"

"You said I was right. I don't hear that very often."

"I was listening," she began, staring into the fire glumly. "And you are right. We should not be together."

"No, don't listen to me," he protested.

"You should listen to your friends." Katriel looked at him, the dim fire shrouding her delicate face in shadows. She spoke with sad resignation. "Why do you defend me, Your High— Maric? You know nothing about me. Yet you keep defending me against your friends, against your countrymen. . . . You need to stop." She seemed actually concerned, emphatically placing a soft hand atop his. "You need to stop defending me. Please."

Maric took her hand in his, rubbing it tenderly. He found it amazing how even half covered in soot, she still felt softer than anything he had ever known. He smiled at her ruefully. "I can't do that. Just because you're an elf, they can't say those things about you. I know they're not true."

"It is not because I am an elf."

"A stranger, then. Or a woman. A woman I happen to love."

The word seemed painful to her, and she turned her head away from him, on the verge of tears. "You really are a fool," she muttered. "How can you say such a thing to someone you have known such a short time?"

He reached up and gently took her chin in his hand, turning her head back into the light. Tears were streaming down her cheeks. "Oh, I know you," he whispered to her. "I may not know what you've done or where you've been, but I see who you are. I know that you're a good person, and worthy of love." He reached up with his thumb and wiped away a tear on her cheek. "How is it that you don't know that?"

She cast her eyes down and reached up with a hand to remove his hand from her cheek. For a moment it looked as if sobs would overwhelm her, but she choked back more tears. "I am not who I pretend to be," she confessed.

"Neither am I," he replied.

Katriel looked up at him, her confusion genuine.

Maric chuckled ruefully. "Do you have any idea how long I've been pretending to be a prince? To be this man that everyone looks up to? Someone that they'd be willing to fight for? To put on the throne?" He shook his head in disbelief. "Can you imagine if they succeeded? The joke would've been on them, wouldn't it? Maybe it's better it ended this way."

Her mouth opened and closed several times as if she meant to speak, but no words came out. Finally she sighed in resignation. "It hasn't ended," she said quietly. "There is always something that can be done. Always."

"See?" He smiled. "This is why I like you so much."

She smiled back, but it was melancholy. Her strange elven eyes searched his, looking for . . . what? He couldn't tell. "Maric—" She took a breath. "—you should know—"

"I know," he cut her off, "everything I need to know. I don't care who you were. I care who you are now."

Katriel blinked back new tears, unsure how to respond.

"And I care whether or not you think you could love me."

She nodded, letting the tears finally come with a sad, bitter laugh. "More than I should. You'll be the death of me, my prince, I swear it."

"'My prince'? I like the sound of that much better than 'Your Highness.'" He reached up and took her chin in his hand again and leaned in closer. "At least when you say it," he breathed.

And then he kissed her. And she relented at last.

Rowan sat in the dark, at the far end of the chamber. It was well out of sight of the campfire, though the ambient glow still allowed for the faintest bit of light to reach her. She didn't mind the darkness. She found it comforting, even with the thought that one of the spiders could sneak up on her where she sat. A small part of her welcomed the chance. *Let it come.*

She had removed much of the armor on her upper body, each plate unfastened by the sense of touch alone, and now she was dipping a cloth in the stream and wiping it clean. The water from the urn had slowly carved a channel here over the years, a channel full of fresh flowing water that continued on outside the building. It would be impossible to tell how far it went without bringing a torch to see, but there was little point. A torch might only draw trouble.

She didn't really need to clean her armor, despite the uncomfortable gritty feeling it had now. She had just needed to get away, to be by herself. The tears had been few, but she didn't want Maric to see them. He didn't deserve to see them.

She heard Loghain approach before she saw any hint of him in the ambient light. He was being quiet, tentative. Perhaps he didn't want to disturb her, but intended instead to watch over her and ensure her safety. It would be just like him.

"I hear you," she complained to the shadows, putting down her wet cloth.

"I'm sorry," he responded quietly. "I can leave, if you like."

She thought about it. "No," she said reluctantly. "It's all right."

Loghain came closer, settling beside her on the stream bank. She could just barely make him out in the faint light, enough to see that his expression was grave. He ran his fingers absently through the fresh water, making a slight trickling sound.

"I didn't know," he said.

"I didn't think you did."

They were both quiet for a time, and she picked up her cloth again, dipping it in the cold stream. Slowly she wiped the front of her breastplate as Loghain watched her in the darkness. Even now she could feel his eyes on her. They made her nervous. "It would be easier," she sighed, "if I could simply hate him. After what he's done, I should be able to, shouldn't I?"

"He's a hard man to hate."

"I miss my father," Rowan said suddenly. "And I miss the way Maric used to be. It was easier to pretend, once. I didn't even care about the throne like my father did. Maric's smile made everything worthwhile, and sometimes I could make believe it was just for me." Her throat caught on the end, and she stopped. Then she realized what she was saying. "But you don't need to hear this. I'm sorry."

Loghain ignored her. "You deserve more than pretend, Rowan."

"Do I?" She felt the tears come, unbidden, and chuckled at their ridiculousness. Here she was, a warrior and commander of men, and yet every time she turned around, she was dismayed to discover that she was as brittle and weak as she feared. "I'm not sure that I do. Maybe I really do hate that poor elf just because she ... because she's the one that caught his eye and not me. All those years I thought we were meant to be, and I was just fooling myself."

He hesitated for a moment. "He could still change his mind."

"No," she said quietly, "I don't think he could. And I don't think you do, either." Then she shrugged. "And it shouldn't matter. At least he's happy."

They sat in the silence, and she began to clean her armor once more. Loghain seemed to be considering something, to the point where she could feel him brooding. "Do you blame him?" he reluctantly asked.

"For all this? No."

"What about for your father?"

She had to think about that. "No." Then, with more certainty: "No. We knew what we were doing. I think Father would have approved."

"I blamed him," Loghain said, so quietly he was almost whispering. "For my father's death. For being dumped in our lap, for forcing our hand. I wanted to hate him, too; you're not the only one." He paused, considering. "But we can't hate him. And it's not because we're weak. It's because we're strong. He needs us."

"He needs *you*, not me."

"You're wrong," he whispered gently. A hand reached up to brush a lock of her hair away from her face. "And I hope one day he sees that."

Rowan shivered. She could feel Loghain sitting right next to her, but she couldn't see him. She hoped that he couldn't see her, either. She clutched the breastplate closer to her chest. "Th-there's nothing to see," she insisted.

"That's not true."

She felt the tears come in force, threatening to turn into sobbing, and she turned her face away from him. "It isn't?" Her voice betrayed her emotion, and she cursed herself silently in dismay.

"One day," he said bitterly, "he will see what he had all along. He will see a strong warrior, a beautiful woman, someone who is his equal and worthy of his utter devotion, and he will curse himself for being such a fool." And then his voice became husky. "Trust me."

With that, Loghain started to silently move away. She quickly turned and reached out with her hand, grabbing his forearm. He froze.

"I'm sorry," he whispered, "I didn't mean—"

"Stay."

He didn't move.

"I'm not him," he finally muttered, bitterness in his voice.

She took his hand and brought it slowly up to her face. His fingers cradled her cheek gently, fearfully, almost as if he expected she would vanish into a dream. Then he rushed forward, snatching her up in his arms and kissing her with an urgency that almost overwhelmed her.

He was burning hot in the chill cavern, and when their lips parted, he halted once more, holding her there fearfully, as if they stood on a precipice. Rowan reached up and gently touched his cheek as he had, and was surprised to feel tears there. "I don't want him," she whispered, and realized it was true. "I've been a fool."

And then Loghain leaned in and kissed Rowan again, slower this time. He laid her gingerly down on the rocks by a magical stream in a forgotten ruin with darkness all around them, and it was perfect.

14

Katriel awoke to darkness. There was a moment of terror when she had no idea where she was, and the thought of being strung up in some giant spider's cocoon almost overwhelmed her. It seemed as if there was no air, that she would suffocate wrapped up in spider silk and left to go mad as she felt unseen legs skittering over her flesh. Then she calmed herself as she realized that the only things surrounding her were Maric's arms.

He slept, curled into her as he held her protectively. She could hear his soft breathing against her neck, feel the beating of his heart through his chest. It was a comforting feeling, and Katriel relaxed and let her heart slow. It was seductive, the idea that they might be able to lie there in the shadows forever, that she would never need to tell Maric who she really was. The fact that they weren't actually safe, that the giant spiders were undoubtedly still out there, was somehow easier to ignore when she was in his arms.

The spiders did not appear, but by the time they all began to stir, the faint clicking sounds had returned. Katriel shivered and fumbled about until she was able to light the campfire again, and this drew Loghain from the dark recesses at the back of the chamber where the water was. He emerged, the flickering firelight revealing his bare chest as well as her own lack of covering, Maric stirring beside her. Their eyes met, and then they looked away and began donning their armor.

When Maric awoke, he smiled warmly at Katriel and brushed his hand across her cheek. She clutched at that hand and held it there. All the things that were unsaid seemed like they were now forever beyond saying. It was too late.

None of them said anything, or acknowledged what had happened during the night, if indeed night it was. It was as dark as when they had slept, the gloom around them as oppressive. All of them seemed much more interested in moving quickly than in talking, and quietly they packed up what little they had and left the camp. They needed to move fast if they were going to avoid another encounter.

Torches held aloft, they moved through the narrower paths between the remnants of the old buildings, stepping carefully among the ancient rubble. The shadows flickered around them, and each time they heard the distant clicking sounds, they stopped and warily stared into the darkness, waiting with swords ready for the spiders to rush out at them.

The dwarven ruins were now covered in black

soot, scorched from one end of the cavern to the other. The dust still clung to the air, but most of the webbing that had covered the upper reaches of the thaig was now gone. The faint torchlight did not allow them to see up that far, but there were hints of what the dwarves who had once lived here might have seen: great stone buttresses carved with runes and enormous crumbling statues of dwarven kings staring down from the heights at their people.

The sight of those ancient statues filled Katriel with a sense of sadness. How must they have felt now, to see their people fled, their city fallen to pieces and covered in ash?

"Is it possible to get higher?" she asked. "If we could shine a bit more light on the roof, I could see more of the statues."

Rowan stared at her incredulously. "Those statues are probably covered in the spiders' nests. Do you really want that close a look at them?"

Katriel shuddered at that thought and reluctantly shook her head. Still, she couldn't help but wish there was a way to convey this story to those who had no hint of the ancient lands that lay under their feet. As much as her bard training made her a spy, it also made her a storyteller. These ruins cried out to her, and it broke her heart that they needed to pass by it all so quickly.

The group moved through what might once have been a great promenade of the city. Once a palace had been carved into the face of the rock wall itself, and Katriel pictured beautiful archways and stairs leading from one gentle terrace to the next. She imagined merchants selling goods from their stalls on the colored cobblestones, with great fountains shooting columns of water in the air. Once there had been grandeur, but now there was little more than crumbling ruin and the husks of buildings so fallen apart, they could not even be approached for all the scattered rocks and collapsed floors.

The remnants of the palace now showed only as broken columns and worn holes that no doubt led into a veritable labyrinth of passages within the rock. The home of the spiders, Loghain pointed out. Indeed, as they passed through the promenade, it was easy to see that here the greatest amount of burnt webbing had collapsed from above. Great mounds of charred ash and sticky tendrils clung to everything, some of it several feet thick or worse.

As the webs had burned and collapsed, they had brought down with them the charred remains of spiders, some of them still quivering lifelessly as they lay on their backs with hairy legs splayed. There were many bones, as well, black and burnt. Most were only small shards, while others seemed to be bigger and a few were even whole. Katriel noticed something odd amid the piles and fished it out. It was a skull, vaguely human but clearly monstrous. And large. The entire promenade was all but filled with bones just like it, like a great rat's nest of a graveyard had been spilled over the entire ruin all at once.

"This must be what they eat," Katriel said quietly.

"They eat darkspawn?" Maric asked, looking at the skull uncertainly.

There was no answer to give. None of them had ever seen a darkspawn before, and until they saw the bones, they had never seen anything that might have suggested the tales of the old wars, of times when the darkspawn had spilled onto the surface world in great events called Blights, might actually be true. But there they were.

"Those bones could be anything," Rowan suggested.

Nobody could answer. If those bones didn't belong to darkspawn, then they belonged to something else just as monstrous, something equally unknown.

They trudged through the soot and bones, sometimes wading through piles up to their hips in order to keep going. They then climbed over a large region so choked with piles of rubble, there was no telling what sorts of buildings might once have been there. Not a single wall or column remained upright. It was as if the entire area had been leveled by some great event, or maybe just had not been built as well as the rest of the city to begin with.

"These could be the slums," Katriel remarked as they climbed. "All the thaigs were supposed to have them, areas where the casteless lived. There are stories that when the noble houses pulled out of the Deep Roads, they actually left the casteless behind. Forgot them." She spread her arms to indicate the crumbled stones around them. "One day the casteless came out of their slums only to find everyone else gone. An empty city with no one left to protect them from the darkspawn."

Maric shuddered. "Surely they wouldn't do that."

"Why not?" Katriel asked him sharply. "Every society has its lowest of the low. Do you think it would be so different in human society? Do you think anyone would go out of their way to ensure that the elves in the alienages were safe if a crisis came to the city?"

Maric seemed taken aback. "I would."

The anger dissolved in her immediately, and she chuckled, shaking her head. Well, of course Maric would. And with it coming from him, one could almost believe it was true. She wondered if he would be different once years of power had worn on him, chipped away at his naïveté. Would he still be the same man?

"It's said some of the casteless tried to run," she continued, "tried to reach Orzammar on their own. But they couldn't run fast enough. The rest of them simply . . . waited for the end."

"Really?" Rowan snorted with derision. "And who would have survived to carry that tale, then?"

Katriel shrugged, unfazed. "Not all of them died, perhaps. Some of those who fled must have reached Orzammar. The rest perhaps lie under our feet even now."

"We've heard enough stories," Loghain snapped, though even he looked disturbed. Katriel shot him an annoyed glance but remained silent. She wasn't trying to frighten anyone; these things actually happened here, and there was no point in pretending that they didn't. But she wasn't about to press the idea.

None of them spoke after that. The thought that they were climbing over the bodies of dwarves seemed worse, somehow, than dead spiders and darkspawn. Not fled but left behind to die, their screams still echoing in the caves centuries later.

It seemed like hours before they finally found the way out of the thaig. A great set of metal doors, over forty feet high, led into the rock face. Unlike the doors they had encountered at the cave entrance up on the surface, these had not fallen through age and

rust but had been burst inward by some force powerful enough to buckle metal many feet thick. Mostly
they lay in rusted pieces, having long ago admitted
whatever invader had come to decimate what the
dwarves had left behind.

Beyond it lay only shadows.

"How do we know this is the way to Gwaren?"
Loghain asked.

Maric turned to Katriel. "Is there anything you
can do?" he asked her.

"I can try," she said hesitantly.

Kneeling with her torch and studying the various
runes nearby for over an hour, she declared most of
them scoured beyond reading. Much of the rock surface had been cracked or chipped off through whatever violent event had knocked the fortress doors
inward, and try though she might, Katriel could not
find a single rune that she recognized.

"I don't know where this passage leads," she confessed, "or if there are even directions." She felt frustrated. It was her advice that had led them down
into the Deep Roads, and they were counting on her
to guide them. But it seemed increasingly likely that
they would die down there, perish in the darkness
with so much dirt and rock pressing down over their
heads, and that made it so much worse.

"Wonderful," Rowan swore under her breath.

Maric looked down at the rubble strewn on the
ground, and after a moment's hesitation reached
down to pick something up. The others turned, surprised to see him holding an axe. It was large, with a
wickedly curved blade and a spike on the reverse
end to prove that it had never been meant for any
tree. The more interesting aspect, however, was its

primitive make. This was made by no dwarven smith; it was a rusted piece of black metal, crudely attached to its long handle and heavy enough that Maric needed both hands even to pick it up.

As Maric stared at Loghain grimly, the axe head finally fell off the handle and landed back on the floor with a loud thud. The echoes rang throughout the cavern, and almost seemed to be answered by distant clicking back in the ruins.

"Let's go," Loghain murmured.

Several hours were spent cautiously traveling down this new branch of the Deep Roads. There was still webbing, and some of it was strewn across the passages waiting to ensnare them. These they needed to burn through, but Loghain remarked that there seemed to be far less of it than before.

Instead, it seemed as if the passages were darker, if that were possible. The torches shone less brightly, and the shadows closed in on them as if they resented the presence of travelers. Even the stone of the walls seemed tainted, somehow. There was a feeling of oppression that made it difficult to breathe, and all of them waited in anticipation for what was to come at them next.

And something was coming. They could feel it.

"Perhaps we should turn back," Rowan suggested quietly. Her voice was low and afraid, and she stared off into the distant blackness. It truly felt as if there were eyes out there, watching. Circling.

"Back to the spiders?" Maric rolled his eyes. "No, thanks."

"We've no webs to burn down this time, should

the spiders come again," Loghain said with concern. He, too, stared off into the distance, and seemed less than pleased with the nothing he saw.

Katriel took out her dagger warily. "But there's no other way. We have to continue." The fear crawled into her stomach and settled there. She was not unaccustomed to battle—but her training had been in fighting men. She knew how to cut a throat, and how to plant her dagger in a vulnerable spot such as an armpit. She could take on an opponent far more armored than herself without fear. None of her training had prepared her to fight monsters.

Maric sensed her discomfort and put an arm around her shoulders to comfort her. It was a small gesture, but still Katriel appreciated it.

They had no choice but to press forward. The number of bones strewn about slowly increased, as did general litter and the smell of earthy decay. The walls gradually became wet-looking and sticky, speckled with rot and fungus. Some of the fungus even glowed in the dark, but did so with a strange purplish tinge that unnerved them far more than it actually lit their path.

They passed an area full of old spider corpses. Some of them were easily twice the size of the creatures they had fought, old and desiccated husks that were dusty and brittle to the touch. Most of them were in pieces.

"Something ate these," Loghain pointed out.

"Ate the spiders?" Maric made a disgusted face. "Maybe it was revenge."

"Maybe whatever ate them doesn't care what it eats," Rowan remarked.

"Darkspawn," Katriel said ominously, and then

scowled when the others looked at her reproachfully. "There is no need to avoid the truth. Obviously they hunt each other."

Rowan glanced at the rot on the walls, looking nauseated. "Should we be worried . . . about disease? The darkspawn spread some kind of sickness, don't they?"

"They taint the land around them with their very touch," Katriel spoke in a hushed voice. "We're seeing it now, on the wall and everything else here. We are in their domain."

"Oh, that's nice," Maric said lightly. "All we need is a dragon to come along now, to really top off our day."

Loghain snorted. "You insisted on coming down here."

"So now it's my fault, is it?"

"I know whose fault it *isn't*."

"Great!" Maric shrugged. "Just throw me at the darkspawn, then, whenever they show up. The rest of you can get a head start while they gobble me up."

Loghain hid his amused smile. "Nice of you to offer. You have been getting a little chubby these last months. There's more of you to eat, I'll wager."

"Chubby, he says." Maric laughed lightly, looking toward Katriel. "If they ate him, they'd choke on the bile."

"Hey, now," Loghain complained without heat.

"There is no 'hey, now.' You started it."

Rowan sighed. "You two are like such little boys sometimes, I swear."

"I was just offering up a very reasonable—" His words were cut off as a new sound came from far ahead in the passages, a soft and unnatural rasping sound. Like many things awakening in the darkness, like many things slithering gently over the rocks. They all spun and stared ahead into the shadows, rooted to the spot.

The sound was gone as quickly as it began, and they shuddered.

"On second thought," Maric muttered, "don't throw me to them."

Their weapons out and ready, they edged forward carefully. It was not long before they came to an area where much of the passage walls had collapsed, revealing caves beyond. There were more underground passages than the ones they walked in, it seemed. Everything was coated in black fungus, and the smell grew increasingly more potent, more rancid. Dead maggots littered the floor amid bones and pieces of armor.

The skeleton of a dwarf lay against the wall. He still wore a rusty breastplate and a large helmet that covered most of his skull. It seemed as if he had merely sat down to rest, or to contemplate his death in these roads so far from his home.

"What's that?" Maric said curiously, approaching the skeleton. These were the first bones they had seen so far that actually indicated that anything other than monsters had once moved through these passages. Katriel wondered why the body would have been left undisturbed, if it had died here. There seemed to be no shortage of creatures in these parts willing to feed on corpses. Or that was her assumption.

"Be careful," Katriel warned him. "The Veil is thin in places like this, and it could attack you." Wherever there had been a great deal of death the Veil became thin, allowing spirits and demons to cross over from their realm. They hungrily possessed anything alive, or that had once been alive. This was where tales of walking corpses and skeletons had come from, spirits driven mad to find themselves in a body devoid of the life they craved. She had never seen one herself, but that didn't mean they didn't exist.

Maric slowed his approach and poked the skeleton's helmet carefully, and exhaled in relief as it did nothing. Then, his eyes squinted curiously as he noticed something strange. He moved to look where the dwarf's right hand was covered by several large rocks and gingerly stuck his own hands in between them and tried to pull something out.

"You need help?" Loghain offered.

"No, I think I—" Maric suddenly stumbled back as the rocks gave way. The skeleton toppled over, the helmet falling loose and rattling loudly on the ground, and most of the bones crumpled under the weight of the old armor. Maric fell backwards, his hands coming up with a longsword that he waved about while trying to get his balance.

Loghain darted forward, ducking under Maric's inadvertent swing and catching him. "Careful, there," he said with annoyance.

Maric was about to reply, but when he held up the longsword he had pried from the stones, he became enraptured with it instead. The entire weapon was a pale ivory hue, the hilt wrought with gentle curves and the blade inlaid with brightly glowing runes. It was untouched by rust, and the blue glow from the runes was almost brighter than the light from their torches. Maric swung it about gently, his eyes wide with awe.

"Andraste's blood," he swore under his breath. "It's so light! Like it weighs nothing!"

"Dragonbone," Katriel said without hesitation. She could tell from the hue, as well as from the fact that it contained so many runes. Enchanters claimed that certain metals held the magical runes far better than others, and dragonbone best of all. It was why the Nevarran dragon hunters were said to have hunted dragons nearly to extinction ages ago. The value of such a sword was incalculable.

Rowan's brow furrowed. "And why was it just sitting there? Why wouldn't these darkspawn have found and taken it?"

As if in answer to their question, one of Maric's swings brought the longsword close to the wall. In response, the black foulness that clung there crawled to move away from the blade. He paused and touched the sword to the wall directly, and the rot moved away even more quickly. It made a faint unpleasant keening sound, and after a moment the stone where the sword touched was bare.

"Maybe they couldn't take it," Maric commented, awed.

They stood and stared at the remnants of the crumbled skeleton. How long had he sat there? Had he tried to hide the sword, or had the rocks fallen upon him? Was this some dwarven nobleman, or one of the casteless who had tried to make the dangerous journey to Orzammar? Had he died here alone?

"I guess you got yourself a new sword," Loghain remarked.

"I think it suits a king." Katriel smiled at the thought of Maric having a magical sword, just like in the old tales where it seemed every handsome king and every erstwhile hero possessed such a blade. More often they wrested such weapons from the hands of terrible beasts or found them in the treasure hordes of mighty dragons—but the idea that Maric could be such a king like in those tales pleased her. Those tales always ended well, didn't they? The hero got out of the labyrinth, and the hero always ended up with his true love. Everything turned out well.

Rowan nodded to the skeleton. "He may have been a king as well, for all we know. Let's hope we don't end up with a similar fate."

It was a sobering thought.

The minutes inched by as they moved on, leaving the dwarven skeleton behind. Maric walked at the fore, his new blade bared. The soft glow from its runes offered a small degree of comfort, though it was fleeting. The faint sounds of movement ahead got more frequent, and along with them, they began to hear a strange humming. It was deep and alien, a reverberating sound that they felt in their chests and that made their skin crawl.

"What *is* that?" Rowan asked. She looked at Katriel. "Do you know?"

Katriel shrugged, bewildered. "I've never heard anything like it."

"It's getting louder." Loghain frowned. He wiped the sheen of sweat from his forehead and glanced at Maric. "How many do you think there will be?"

Maric stared ahead, licking his lips nervously. "No idea."

"We may want to find more defensible ground."

"Where?" Rowan seemed ready for an imminent attack, her eyes wide and nervously searching the shadows. "Back to the ruins? Will they come that far?"

"Look there!" Katriel shouted, pointing ahead.

The four of them froze as they saw a humanoid shape slowly shamble toward them out of the darkness. At first it seemed to be a man, but as it drew closer, they saw it clearly was not. It was a hideous mockery of a man, skin puckered and boiled with bulging white eyes and a toothy, malicious grin. It wore a mishmash of metal armor, some rusted and some of it held together with scraps of frayed leather, and in its hands it carried a wicked-looking sword, all points and odd angles.

The creature held its sword in front of it in a menacing manner, but it did not charge them. It moved slowly but incautiously, staring at them hungrily as if they didn't represent a true threat of any kind.

The deep humming was coming from it. The creature was moaning softly, almost chanting, and this moan built upon the sounds of many others behind it in the shadows. They hummed in unison, a hushed and deadly whisper the creatures spoke as one.

Maric took a step backwards, gulping loudly.

More began to appear behind the first. More tall ones, some wearing strange headdresses and blindfolds, others in more impressive armor covered in dangerous spikes. Some wore little armor at all, their black and diseased skin covered in scars. There were shorter ones, as well, ones almost dwarf-sized with pointed ears and wide, demonic grins. All of them walked as calmly as the first, shambling toward them while moaning and hissing softly. The sound was loud now, reverberating around them like a physical force.

"Darkspawn," Katriel announced unnecessarily.

Loghain held his sword up before him warningly, watching the creature at the head of the emerging pack. "Move back," he murmured.

They slowly backed up, warily matching the pace that the darkspawn approached them with. At the back, Rowan turned about and suddenly halted, gasping in fear. "Loghain!"

In the flickering light of Rowan's torch, more of the monsters could be seen drawing near from behind. They were surrounded.

"How did they get behind us?" Maric asked, panic creeping into his voice.

"Careful," Loghain warned. The four of them backed up against the wall of the passage, keeping close. They watched the darkspawn advance, their weapons held at the ready. Even with their prey cornered, the creatures did not accelerate. Their hum became louder, reached a hungry, fever pitch.

"Will your sword keep them back?" Rowan cried at Maric, forced to shout to be heard over the unnerving sound.

Maric tested his glowing blade, waving it threateningly at the nearest darkspawn. The creature flinched and hissed at Maric angrily, baring rows of jagged teeth, but it did not retreat. "It doesn't look like it!" Maric yelled.

The darkspawn continued their slow, inevitable approach. Twenty feet. Then ten. The four of them stood with back pressed against back, sweat pouring as they watched and waited.

As the first of the taller darkspawn got close, it bared its fangs and roared. Maric stepped forward and slashed the dragonbone longsword across its chest in a wide arc. Where the blade touched, the creature's skin sizzled and it reared back in agony, issuing a gurgling scream.

This finally seemed to energize the rest of the horde. They roared in turn and began to push forward. Katriel barely knocked a wicked blade aside with her dagger, just escaping being stabbed. Rowan pushed Katriel behind her, interposing her armor to take the darkspawn blows. Maric swung widely with his longsword, taking advantage of the fact that it repelled whichever darkspawn it touched. Loghain kicked one of the smaller creatures back into its fellows, knocking them down, and then began to stab with precise, clean blows.

The ferocity of their defense worked in their favor, at least for a moment, before the darkspawn surge began to push them against the wall. They could not knock the blades aside fast enough, and though Loghain and Rowan kept pushing the creatures back, the others would heedlessly step over their fallen to strike.

The great moaning sound reached a crescendo, drowning out everything but the ring of steel upon steel. Katriel looked around despairingly. She was no warrior like the others, and felt all but useless. Was it truly all going to end here? After all they had been through?

And then a new sound interrupted the battle: the blowing of a horn, three strident notes that rang out into the passages, silencing the darkspawn completely.

Many of the creatures began to turn and hiss with outrage at something that was descending on them from behind. Blue lights lit the Deep Roads from that direction, and it took only a moment for the first dwarves to appear—dwarves, not some new monster of the deep. Maric glanced in Katriel's direction, shocked, but she felt the same as he did. After journeying all this time, to find someone else down here in this oppressive darkness, to find *anyone*, was beyond belief.

Was this their salvation? Were they rescued? Or were these dwarves here to fight the darkspawn for their own meals?

They were warriors, short but bulky dwarves rippling with muscle and covered with bronzed chain. They wielded ornate swords and longspears, and some of them held lanterns hung from long poles that shone with a glittering sapphire light that seemed to cut through the shadows with ease. More strangely, these dwarves all had their faces painted—images of skulls with fangs, giving them a dread and frightening appearance. In some ways they looked almost as frightening as the darkspawn.

As one the dwarves shouted a guttural war cry and began carving through the darkspawn lines with relative ease. The darkspawn all but abandoned their attacks on Maric and Loghain and the others, realizing that these dwarves were the more immediate threat, and turning to defend against the onslaught. The sheer rage and hatred of the darkspawn as they leaped at the dwarves spoke of the fact that these were true enemies. They knew each other and killed each other gladly.

Loghain did not let up, stabbing his blade deep into the back of a darkspawn that had turned away from him. The creature roared in pain as he kicked it off his sword and then turned to the next. Encouraged, Rowan and Maric did the same and began to fight toward the dwarves. Katriel went with them—

for all they knew, the dwarves could be worse than the darkspawn, but for the moment they were the enemy of their enemy. They were willing to take their chances.

The result was dramatic. A great cry of terror went up from the darkspawn as their ranks began to dissolve. The ones behind Loghain and the others turned and fled, while the ones caught between them and the dwarves began to fight viciously and desperately. Several of the dwarves were hacked down, only to have their darkspawn killers immediately leaped upon by enraged dwarves.

Within minutes it was over. The last of the darkspawn had fled screaming into the tunnels behind them. What remained was a charnel house of gore, darkspawn bodies littering the tunnel with their black blood pooling over the rocky floor. Only a few dwarves had fallen, and now at least fifty stood staring suspiciously at the humans and elf as if wondering if they shouldn't be their next victims.

Loghain held his blade firmly and crouched to attack the first dwarf who charged his way. Rowan stood beside him, equally ready though clearly winded by the fight. Katriel moved behind them, wondering if the battle was not yet over. Were the dwarves going to rob them? Slaughter them? Leave them here?

The silence continued until Maric cautiously stepped toward the dwarves. He had black blood splattered across his surcoat, and his sword was dripping with it. He seemed nervous and perhaps even frightened, yet still he put up his blade before the dwarves to show them that he meant no harm. Very slowly he put it down on the ground, and then raised his hands in front of him again. Empty hands, no threat.

"Do you speak the King's Tongue?" Maric asked, making certain to pronounce each syllable carefully.

One of the larger dwarves, a thick man with a long black beard and a bald head entirely painted to resemble a white skull, sized Maric up. He was dressed in golden plate covered in large spikes, and wielded a warhammer at least as tall as himself, covered in darkspawn blood. "Who do you think taught it to you surfacers?" he growled. The accent was thick, but very understandable. "What sort of fools are you to come down into the Deep Roads? Are you seeking your deaths?"

Maric coughed uncomfortably. "Well . . . your group is here in the Deep Roads, aren't you?"

The dwarf glanced at his fellows, and they exchanged an amused if grim chuckle. He looked back at Maric. "That is because we *are* seeking our deaths, human."

Katriel moved to stand beside Maric, lowering her head respectfully toward the dwarf. "You're . . . all of you, you're the Legion of the Dead, aren't you?" It was only a suspicion, considering what little she knew of the dwarves. But there were only so many of them who would be out in the Deep Roads and away from Orzammar, and these—with their skulls painted onto their faces—brought up something from her memory, a tale she had thought forgotten.

The dwarf seemed impressed. "Aye, you've the right of it."

Loghain shot up a brow, glancing toward Katriel. "And what is that, exactly?"

"I know only a little," she protested.

Sighing with exasperation, the dwarf turned back to the others with him and mulled over an unpleasant decision. After a moment he shrugged. "Collect our fallen," he ordered them, "and bring the surfacers back to the camp with us."

Loghain lifted his sword threateningly, Rowan standing resolute beside him. "I don't remember us offering to go with you," he stated in an even tone.

The dwarf paused and regarded them with amusement. "I'll give you that; I didn't think you surfacers would want to stay here and let the darkspawn swarm back down on top of you the moment we've left . . . but by the Stone, if that's what you truly want, I'll not stop you."

Maric stepped forward and gave the dwarf a pained smile. "We've had a difficult time down here, Ser Dwarf. Please excuse our manners. We'll gladly go to your camp." He then shot Loghain an incredulous look that said, *What are you doing?* Loghain stared back at him, and then at the dwarf, before reluctantly sheathing his blade.

The dwarf shrugged. "So be it." He hefted his warhammer onto his shoulder. "And the name is Nalthur. You'll not fall behind if you know what's good for you."

15

It took several hours for Nalthur and the rest of his Legion of the Dead to lead their guests back to the camp. They carried the bodies of their slain companions reverently, first wrapping them up completely in cloth and then carrying them high overhead. They sang a sad dirge in a guttural, unfamiliar language, their march almost a funereal procession through the underground with their blue lanterns lighting up the passages around them.

The song echoed off the stone walls of the Deep Roads, carrying far into the depths, a challenge to those dark places that here life still existed. Alone in the Deep Roads, these dwarves cared when someone died. Katriel could not understand the words, but she knew it spoke of loss.

She watched Maric as he listened to it, his eyes far away. Did he think of his mother? He reached over

to Rowan and comforted her, and Rowan let him.
Her eyes were far away, too, and Katriel remembered she had lost her father only recently. So, too,
were Loghain's eyes dark as he listened to the funeral dirge. They had all suffered great losses, and
how many of them had had time to properly mourn?

Katriel had added to their losses, as well. She
knew that. She watched Maric's tears, watching him
mourn with Rowan under the sapphire lanterns, and
she felt emptiness in her heart, knowing she could
not join him. She did not deserve to join him. A vast
chasm was opening up between them, and he didn't
even know it, one that she would never be able to
cross.

She wondered if she would cry if Maric died. She
had never cried for anything, since the bardic training she had received had wrung the sympathy out of
her; a necessity for a spy whose loyalties were up for
sale. Sympathy was a weakness, she had learned, and
yet now she wondered. Part of her quailed at the
thought of living without him, but need was not love.
She had no idea if she was as capable of love as she
was of treachery.

She saw the dwarf, Nalthur, studying her carefully. And she watched him turn and study Maric
and Rowan and Loghain in turn, intrigued by their
mourning. Perhaps he thought they cried tears for
his fallen comrades? For all she knew, they did.

As the hours wore on, it was simple to see they
would have been lost. Twice they passed intersec-
tions where the dwarves turned without a second
thought. Katriel craned her neck at those places to
look for signs of markers or anything at all to indicate where the other directions might have led, but

there was nothing but rubble and decay. Whatever corruption the darkspawn spread, it covered everything as they proceeded farther in, like a slick coating of filth and oil.

It was a frightening thought, to her. The farther they went, the more she realized that the chances of finding their way back to where they were diminished. They were now completely dependent on the dwarves for their lives. Maric seemed willing enough to trust their fate to Nalthur and his men, but that was part of the problem. Maric was far from infallible. He trusted her, after all, and thus his instincts were more than a little suspect.

Still, there was nothing else for them to do now but follow.

Eventually they arrived at another outpost not unlike the one they had found when they first entered the Deep Roads, although this was far more intact. The massive gateway that bisected the passageway had been repaired, the heavily armed dwarves standing guard outside snapping to attention as soon as they saw the blue lights approaching. The cavern beyond was small but high, with reinforced walls and a number of smaller caves radiating out from the core.

Dominating the center of the cavern was a great statue of a dwarf, holding up the ceiling as if it were a tremendous burden upon his shoulders. It was not unlike the great statue they had seen back at the ruined thaig, though this was much more majestic. He wore a large helmet with horns as broad as his shoulders, and his armor was a coat of linked octagons covered in glittering runes.

It seemed that the dwarves had done a great deal to clean up the outpost and push back the filth. Even their supplies were neatly stacked, right down to the last cup on a table. Nothing was left astray. Cleanest of all, however, was the statue. It was possible that they had even cleaned it first.

"Is that Endrin Stonehammer?" Katriel asked, staring at it in awe. She had seen a painting once, in a tome that told of the oldest dwarven legends, but it had been a faded depiction, and not a good one. To see a likeness in the flesh, so to speak, rendered in such magnificent detail . . .

"That is *King* Endrin Stonehammer," Nalthur muttered angrily. "And mind how you speak that name, woman. We'll make only so many allowances for surface folk." Without waiting for a response, he turned to the warriors who filed through the gate behind him. All of them halted in unison as he spread his hands high over his head. "We have survived one more night, my brothers and sisters!" he shouted. "One more night to deliver vengeance on the spawn that stole our lands! One more night to spill their blood and hear their cries of terror!"

The dwarves thrust up their weapons as one and roared in approval. "It has been one hundred and twelve nights since our deaths!" he shouted, and they roared again. "And tonight five more of us have found peace."

The shouting died, to be replaced by a somber silence as the wrapped bodies were delivered forth, passed overhead from dwarf to dwarf until the five lay before Nalthur on the floor. "Rest well, my friends. For one hundred and twelve nights you lasted. Now it is time for you to return to the Stone, in the sight of the First Paragon."

Quietly, a large number of the dwarves marched

into the rear of the cavern and returned with picks. Immediately they began pounding away at the ground a distance away from the statue. The noise was incredibly loud, but they appeared to be making quick progress in digging a pit.

Noticing his guests watching with bafflement, Nalthur turned to them. "There is enough room in this cavern to bury most of us. They will dig a tomb and seal the bodies within, so the darkspawn cannot get to them." He shot them a dark look as if this was to prevent something he did not want to discuss with strangers. "Most of us will be returned to the Stone."

"Most of you?" Rowan asked.

The dwarf nodded grimly. "Eventually there will only be a handful of us left. Then the darkspawn will come." His dark eyes became distant. "We will not be returned to the Stone," he said flatly.

The sound of the picks cracking at the stony ground rang throughout the cavern. The dwarven warriors who were not taking part in the digging spread out quietly into the outpost, removing their armor and tending to their injuries. They spoke only in hushed voices. As Nalthur moved around, inspecting his ranks, they glanced respectfully at him and then their eyes moved suspiciously up to the tall humans and the elf who followed behind him.

Eventually they reached an area with several earthen ovens carved into the stone walls. Three male dwarves and a large, pretty female dwarf were sweating profusely as they worked over massive iron pots bubbling with meaty-smelling stew. The female dwarf turned to regard Nalthur with a displeased look, wiping her filthy hands on her smock.

"Still alive, then, are you?" she chuckled.

"So far." Nalthur shrugged.

Her eyes glanced up at Maric and then at the others. "Those don't look like darkspawn. Where did you pick them up?"

"Out in the Deep Roads. Alone, if you can imagine." He turned to look at them. "Are you hungry?"

"No," Loghain said instantly.

"Yes," Maric amended. He looked at Loghain. "We all are, in fact."

"It's not ready just yet," the female dwarf grumped, "but for you I'll make an exception." She dug up several bowls and scooped out the stew into each. When no one was immediately forthcoming, she cleared her throat at Maric until he belatedly rushed forward to take his bowl. The others followed suit, followed by Nalthur.

They followed him out into one of the side caves, ducking their heads to get through the door. It was his quarters, Katriel assumed, though it was also neatly packed with enough barrels and crates and piles of fur and odd weapons that it might have doubled for a storage room. The cot was thick but sturdy, and Nalthur sat down on the edge of it. The others found seats wherever they could and began to eat.

Maric dug into his stew ravenously. Katriel picked at hers gingerly, sipping on some of the broth. The dwarf all but gulped his down greedily, finishing it long before the others were even half done, and then belching loudly. He wiped his beard with the back of his hand.

"Not as hungry as you thought?" he asked, watching their progress.

"No, it's fine," Maric quickly commented. "What is it?"

"Deep stalker." He grinned.

Loghain paused. "Deep what?"

"You would have encountered them before the darkspawn if we hadn't been hunting them around these parts for more than two months, now. We ran out of our perishables a few weeks back. What I wouldn't give for a good nug steak." He eyed them closely. "Don't suppose you'd have one in those packs of yours?"

Rowan looked down at her stew queasily. "Nug steak?"

The dwarf sighed, disappointed. "Thought not." He put his bowl down and watched them eat, and then his eyes drifted over to Maric's longsword. "That's quite a weapon. Mind if I see it?"

Loghain looked like he was about to object, but Maric waved a hand at him. He stood and pulled the stained sword out of his belt, handing it to Nalthur. "It's dwarven, I think."

"You don't know?"

"We found it on a skeleton not long after we left the ruins. Maybe it was one of your men? Even if it wasn't, if it's a dwarven weapon, your people should have it back."

"You went through Ortan thaig?" Nalthur seemed impressed. "That would explain it. We don't go near the thaig on account of all the tainted spiders. So I don't know what you found, but it wasn't one of mine." He studied the blade with interest, running a stubby finger over the glowing runes, before finally handing it back hilt-first. "I've no use for it. It's your blade now, human."

Maric took the sword back slowly, looking confused. "But . . ."

"It won't get back to Orzammar through me," the dwarf explained with a grin. "I'm not going back, or didn't you understand that part?"

"They're dead," Katriel explained hesitantly. "They ... have a ceremony before they enter the Deep Roads, a funeral. They say good-bye to their loved ones, pass on their possessions, and then they go and they don't come back."

Rowan blinked in surprise. "Why would anyone do such a thing?"

Nalthur chuckled ruefully. "To clear our debts. To clear our names. To clear our houses' names." His face went grim. "Orzammar politics are more deadly than the Deep Roads, by far. Best to have left it behind, really."

"I think I know what you mean," Maric sighed.

"That so?"

Loghain frowned. "I don't think you need to explain that, Maric."

"No, it's fine." Maric shook his head. He held out a hand to the dwarf. "My name is Prince Maric Theirin, and these are my companions." He introduced each one of them in turn.

The dwarf stared at Maric quizzically, and then shook his hand in an awkward way as if he had never performed the gesture previously. "Human royalty, eh?"

"Sort of." Maric smiled. "I am fighting to regain my family's throne. That is, in fact, why we're down here."

The tale took surprisingly little time to tell. Nalthur listened to it quietly enough, nodding his head empathetically. "We dwarves do things much the same, when it comes time for the Houses to contest the

throne," he admitted. "Though there's rarely any of
this bystanding business you speak of. No House is
neutral in the Assembly, not ever. In Orzammar,
things are solved quickly and with as much bloodshed as we can stand . . . and then a little bit more."
His grin was sardonic, as if sharing a private joke.
Seeing that none of them got it, he shrugged. "Which
is all well and good, I suppose, but if it's Gwaren
you were headed to, you were going the wrong way."

"What!" Loghain shot up, shocked.

Nalthur put his hands up. "Now, now, big fellow,
no reason to get upset over it. You were headed north.
Didn't you figure that was the wrong direction?"

"We can't tell such things underground," Katriel
explained. She knew that dwarves could, their
vaunted "stone-sense" being as much a part of their
religion as it was a matter of practicality. A dwarf
who didn't have stone-sense was truly blind and considered a figure of pity, rejected by the Stone that had
birthed them.

"Oh." The dwarf seemed surprised, looking askance
at Loghain and Maric as if his opinion of them now
had to be revised to include such a sad handicap.
Then he shrugged. "Well that explains it, dust to dun-
kels. You're actually closer to Gwaren here than you
were, though there's not much there to see. The sea's
gotten into the outpost, last I heard."

"We need to get to the surface, actually," Maric
said.

"Ah! Of course!"

"If you could direct us there . . . ," Loghain suggested.

Nalthur grinned. "We can do better than that. We
can take you! By the Stone, anyone who's willing to

journey through Ortan thaig deserves some respect. We'll not send you back out there alone."

Rowan's eyes went wide in surprise. "You would do that?"

"We don't want to keep you from your dying, or anything," Maric said.

"Hah!" The dwarf clapped Maric on the back, just about knocking him off his seat. "To tell the truth, it gets a bit dull killing the darkspawn, day after day. There's always more of them. An endless sea of evil to drown ourselves in, yes?" He shrugged and belched loudly once again.

Maric paused, suddenly churning something over in his mind. "So you don't just fight darkspawn?"

"We cannot go back to Orzammar. What else is there to do in the Deep Roads?"

"You could probably survive out here a long time, if you wanted to," Rowan said.

The dwarf snorted. "We're dead men. What would be the point in that?" He waved his hand irritably. "There's honor to be found in slaying the dark-spawn, anyhow. If we're to find our peace, we'll do it fighting like true dwarves, fighting to take back what was once ours. Even if we never can."

Maric smiled slowly. "How do you feel about fighting humans?"

Nalthur looked at Maric curiously. "You mean up on the surface?"

"I imagine there's far more of us up there, yes."

"Under the *sky*?" The dwarf said the word as if it were terrifying.

"Unless we're already too late, we could use your help at Gwaren," Maric said earnestly. "I don't know what I could repay you with. I'm not King yet. I might never be. But if you and your men are looking for their deaths, I can at least offer you a glorious battle with something other than darkspawn."

"Deaths on the surface," Nalthur said without enthusiasm.

Maric sighed. "I suppose dwarves just don't go up there, do they?"

He snorted. "Ones without honor, perhaps."

Rowan arched an eyebrow. "Aren't you already exiled from Orzammar? What honor do you have to lose?"

The dwarf considered the idea, his face twisted into an unpleasant scowl. "We've none to gain, either. It's not our business what you cloudheads get up to, up on the surface. Down here we've darkspawn to kill, and the Stone to return to when we die. That's our business."

Loghain stood up. "Let's go, then. We'll find no help here, Maric."

"I don't know . . . ," Maric began.

"They're cowards," Loghain interrupted. "They're frightened of the sky. They'll find any reason not to come with us."

Nalthur leaped up, drawing his warhammer in a flash. He held it threateningly at Loghain, bristling. "You'll take that back," he warned.

Loghain didn't move, but eyed the dwarf carefully. The tension rose in the room as Rowan and Maric exchanged worried glances. Slowly he nodded to Nalthur. "I apologize," he said sincerely. "You've treated us well, that was undeserved."

The dwarf frowned, perhaps considering taking further offense, but then merely shrugged. "Very well." Abruptly he chortled with amusement. "And it's true enough, perhaps. That sky of yours is more frightening than an entire horde of darkspawn!" He bellowed with laughter at his own jest, and the tension in the room dissolved.

As he quieted, Katriel touched the dwarf's arm to get his attention. "There is one thing that Maric could do for you," she suggested. "Should he ever become King, he would be in a position to visit Orzammar. He could tell the dwarven Assembly how very valuable your help was to his cause."

"Oh? You don't say?"

"Your people treat human kings with great respect, do they not? The dwarves that assisted in the Siege of Marnas Pell during the Fourth Blight received many accolades at the word of a human king. One of them even became a Paragon."

The dwarf's eyes lit up with interest. "That's true."

Katriel smiled sweetly at him. "So there is, in fact, honor to be had on the surface. Honor for the houses you left behind. Honor that depends on Maric winning his battle, yes, but . . ."

Nalthur chewed on the idea. Finally he looked at Maric. "You would do this?"

Maric nodded, his look intense. "I would, yes."

Loghain glanced at the dwarf warily. "Maric may never be King. There is no guarantee he can do what you ask, you understand this?"

Nalthur seemed amused by the caution. "You don't seem to have much confidence in your friend. Are all you humans like this?"

"Just him, mostly."

"I am being realistic," Loghain muttered.

"I just ask one thing," Nalthur stated slowly, "that if any of us fall as we aid you, we will not be left up there. Return us to the Stone, do not bury us in dirt. Do not bury us under the sky." The prospect seemed to unnerve the dwarf, but his jaw was set.

Maric nodded again. "I promise."

"Then you have our help," he finally announced. Resolute, he turned and strode from the room out to the main cavern, where he immediately began shouting for the other warriors. The incessant ringing of the picks halted.

Those in the room stared at Maric, not quite believing this had just happened. "Well," Loghain said dryly, "it looks like we have our help."

Within the space of two hours, the Legion of the Dead was under way and traveling through the Deep Roads with all their equipment in tow. Loghain found himself quite impressed by the efficiency. Maric walked up front with Nalthur and the most senior of the warriors, all of whom listened grimly as Maric did his best to explain what they were likely to find on the surface.

The idea that the usurper might already have reached Gwaren and that they could be walking into an impossible situation they seemed to understand and accept quite readily. The notion that there would be no ceiling over their head, however, no comforting miles of heavy rock, just vast empty space that went up and up forever into an endless sky, made them blanch and fidget nervously. Maric had to explain several times that, no, no one had ever fallen up into the sky to be lost forever. Yes, there was indeed a hot sun in the sky, and, no, it had never made anyone blind nor had it ever crashed to the ground and set someone on fire. These things they had trouble with.

Loghain and Rowan and Katriel walked with the supply carts in the middle of the procession, the rear guard watching warily for any signs of darkspawn attack. As near as Loghain could tell, they had stripped down the outpost completely and had left nothing of importance behind save one: the great statue of the dwarven king that held up the cavern. As the dwarves efficiently went about their tasks collecting their supplies, each stopped in turn at that statue to respectfully touch its base. They closed their eyes, and Loghain wondered if they offered a solemn prayer to their ancestor. Perhaps they asked him to watch over them, or to send a speedy and honorable death. Perhaps they apologized for leaving him alone once again, to be defiled by dust and the darkspawn taint.

The few members of the Legion of the Dead who were not warriors, such as the cooks they had met earlier, pulled the carts quietly and stared at Katriel out of the corners of their eyes. Rowan asked one why they did so, and the answer was simple. They had seen few enough surface folk during their days at Orzammar, but not a one of them had ever seen an elf.

They made good time. The dwarves knew the Deep Roads well, and the farther they traveled, the more it became apparent that Katriel's idea of navigating the passages to Gwaren was unlikely ever to have worked. Even if there had been no darkpawn, it was likely they would have become lost. With little food and water, the chances that they would have made it out alive at all would have been slim.

But fortunately they had found the dwarves, Loghain reminded himself. Katriel's plan was going to succeed after all. He watched her as they traveled, saw her hover away from himself and Rowan and keep her gaze focused solely on Maric up at the head of the procession. Either she knew how Loghain and Rowan felt or she had guessed. Loghain supposed that they had not gone out of their way to keep their suspicions hidden.

He moved up to walk beside the elf, and she regarded him with sullen wariness. Rowan did not join him, but watched him go with mild surprise.

"I want you to know," he said to Katriel, "you've been a great help."

She narrowed her eyes warily. "Have I, ser?"

"You have. You obviously knew that the dwarves would value any help we could offer their relatives, no matter how remote the possibility."

She shrugged, looking away. Rather than being pleased by his comment, she seemed disturbed. "They become one of the Legion of the Dead," she said faintly, "because they have no other choice. They are broke, or ruined. The best the Legion can offer them is to wipe the slate clean, set the balance back to zero." She glanced back at Loghain, her look significant. "If they could do more than that . . . who wouldn't want to try?"

"Who indeed?"

She looked away from him once more, resentful.

Her chilly demeanor told him he was unwelcome, but he ignored it. Following her line of sight, he realized she was watching Maric again.

"Why do you stay?" he asked. "Is it for him?"

"Do *you* stay for him?" she rejoined coldly.

He thought about his answer for a long time. The blue lanterns swung overhead on their long poles, bathing the Deep Roads in their sapphire glow. They passed a dwarven statue that stood long-forgotten against one of the passage walls, now mostly a crumbled and silent guardian that watched them go by like they were intruders in this eternal darkness.

"No," he finally answered. "I stay for me."

It was a serious answer, and Loghain noticed that Katriel had turned to regard him with a thoughtful, almost melancholy look. "Maric is a good person," she said bitterly. "And when he looks at me, he sees the same thing in me. He sees the good I didn't think was even there. The longer I'm with him, the more it seems like it might almost be possible that I really am that person."

Loghain nodded knowingly. "Almost," he agreed.

His gaze met Katriel's, his icy blue eyes probing her strange green ones, and she was the first to turn away. She seemed oddly vulnerable all of a sudden, rubbing her shoulders and looking off toward Maric longingly. He almost felt sorry for her.

"He's not ready to be King yet," he said evenly. "He's too trusting."

She nodded silently.

"But he needs to become ready. And it'll be hard for him."

"I know." Her voice was hollow, resigned.

There was nothing more that needed to be said. Loghain returned to Rowan's side and the column continued its trek through the shadows.

Less than a day later, they encountered the ruins of what had once been the dwarven outpost under Gwaren. Several times the Legion had been forced to stop to clear away rubble from collapsed tunnels, and Nalthur grumped at the darkspawn tendency to sabotage even "solid dwarven engineering." Each time it was uncertain if there would be anything behind the rubble at all, but luckily each time they found more tunnels beyond.

The darkspawn were present. They lurked at the edges of the blue lights, watching. Always watching. Twice they surged out to make surprise raids, once from the fore and once from behind, but both times the Legion of the Dead assembled quickly and repelled them with bloody force. The calm precision with which the dwarves slaughtered a path through the monsters was uncanny, and sent the darkspawn scrambling to retreat back into their side caves.

Nalthur let them go. He said that even the Legion wasn't about to follow the darkspawn down into the side caves. Down there the darkspawn were on their home ground, and only death awaited. While death was something the Legion did not fear, they wished to go out while taking as many of the darkspawn with them as possible. Not ambushed and killed to a man.

After those two attacks, the darkspawn kept back. They hated the dwarves, that much was clear, but they also respected their numbers. For a time all anyone heard were strange high-pitched shrieks off in the distant shadows. The dwarves said that was another type of darkspawn, a tall and lanky thing with long talons that was incredibly fast. This made them nervous, as they said such creatures often brought the emissaries with them—darkspawn who wielded spells like mages.

The dwarves shrugged off the danger the emissaries represented, proudly proclaiming that their natural resistance to magic extended even to the sort wielded by the darkspawn. That didn't stop them from becoming extra vigilant, however. Their dark eyes became wider as they scanned the shadows, warily watching for the next ambush with their swords drawn.

It never came. As they got closer to the Gwaren outpost, water began to appear in the passages, dripping down from above and draining from stagnant pools into cracks in the wall. Crusty limestone piled wherever the water appeared, the smell of rust and salt thick in the air. Once the group encountered water that filled almost an entire portion of the passage, forcing them to wade through it with equipment held over their heads. Here the dwarves stared resentfully at the taller humans and the elf among them, but said nothing.

All the water made Loghain nervous. Did these tunnels go underneath the ocean? If so, then wouldn't the first cave-in fill the entire system with seawater? Nalthur dismissed the idea, but still Loghain kept thinking about it. He didn't know enough about dwarven architecture to be reassured.

The outpost, when they finally found it, was inside a great cavern mostly filled with seawater, an underground lake with a narrow path of rock that led around the water's edge. Stalactites hung down in multitudes from the cavern ceiling, each dripping water into the murky lake. The echoes of dripping water resounded everywhere, a cacophony of sound that greeted them as they entered.

The other side of the lake was too far off to see, the dark water disappearing into the shadows. Loghain wondered if it didn't perhaps meet up with the ocean, an underground "port" just as Gwaren above was? An interesting thought. The air was still in the cavern, if heavy and moist.

A great steel structure stood half submerged in the lake, just off the rocky shore and over a hundred feet across. It was now mostly crumbled from rust and covered with white streaks of limestone. Many long pipes reached from it into the rock walls, those, too, brown with rust and falling apart.

It was impossible to tell what the purpose of the structure might have been. The dwarves didn't say, and merely stood at the entrance to the cavern and hung their heads in reverence. The sounds of dripping were all they could hear. Nalthur eventually remarked to Maric that once there had been hundreds of pipes, that they wouldn't have been able to see the roof of the cavern for all of them. Now most of them had fallen, no doubt rusting beneath the water on the cavern floor.

Maric asked what it had been for, if it had been some kind of fortress, but Nalthur only looked at him in disgust. "You humans wouldn't understand," he muttered.

The way up to the surface required them to march along the precarious edge by the water until they found another door much like the one that Maric and the others had found all the way back in the hills. This one, while covered with lime and rust, was still closed. The lime was so thick on it, in fact, that they couldn't even see any evidence of a lock mechanism.

Nalthur immediately sent his men to work with their picks, chipping away at the lime and rust to see what lay beneath. The dwarf seemed unsure if it was going to do any good, however. "Even if we manage to get through," he muttered, "there's no telling what's at the top. You humans might have built over it, for all we know."

Rowan frowned. "I don't remember anyone mentioning anything about a passageway going down to the dwarven outpost."

"It would have been sealed centuries ago," Katriel said. "When the darkspawn took the Deep Roads, the townsfolk would have closed it up to keep them from attacking the town."

Nalthur sighed. "Then we'll have two seals to break, if we can." He glanced at Maric. "Otherwise you've come all this way for nothing."

Loghain stared at the cloudy water in the cavern, rubbing his chin thoughtfully. "If you swam out that way, would it lead out to the ocean? Could you swim up to the shore above?"

The dwarf looked at him incredulously. "If the sluice gate is open. And if you can hold your breath long enough. And if the pressure doesn't kill you."

"Maybe not, then."

The ringing of the picks went on for hours, until finally the great doors had been scoured enough that several older dwarves could take a closer look at the lock mechanism. One of them, Nalthur assured

Maric, had been a smith "when he was alive." After a time, the smith reported the bad news: the lock was rusted shut. They would need to burn their way through.

This process required the use of acid, which the dwarves brought forth from their equipment wagons in the form of small vials full of brackish liquid. They opened the vials with tongs and poured the acid into the lock. The result was a lot of acrid smoke and blue flame, and after three applications the smith finally declared the door ready to open.

Nalthur commanded the Legion to attach several large hooks to the door, each tied to a rope that five dwarves pulled on with all their might. They strained, gritting their teeth and digging their feet into the rock, and ever so slowly the doors opened. They groaned at first, letting out wrenching sounds that reverberated throughout the cavern. Then they began to give, parting by inches and generating an excruciating squealing noise as the rusted metal dragged along the rocky floor.

As the ancient doors opened more quickly, a great cloud of dust began to billow in, blown in by what was immediately recognizable as fresh air. As the dust made the dwarves cough, Loghain stepped forward.

Fresh air? His brows shot up. If there were fresh air, then that meant . . .

Suddenly a great form began to rush forward out of the dust cloud. It was a stone golem, over ten feet tall, and with a great roar it began to swing widely with its fists. The dwarves reacted with surprise as the creature charged into their ranks, its blows sending them flying into the air. Many of them slammed against the rocky walls, while others were flung into the nearby water.

The dwarves began to fall back in shock, drawing their swords as Nalthur charged toward them. "We're attacked!" he bellowed. "To arms, Legion! To arms!"

Coming from behind the golem, a crowd of human soldiers began to rush into the chamber with swords drawn, and they clashed against the dwarves that held their ground. The sound of steel meeting steel rang out, the golem continuing to swing its great fists. As the deadly melee spread, Loghain's eyes went wide in horror.

These were their own men. The standards on the soldiers that had surged out of the tunnel were Maric's own.

"Stop!" Maric shouted. He ran forward into the line of dwarves, heedless of the danger and waving his hands. "Stop fighting! For the love of the Maker!" Nobody listened to him as the fighting surged onward. Blood was being spilled. The stone golem swung a large fist dangerously near Maric, crashing onto the ground and toppling him.

Loghain and Rowan rushed forward immediately to Maric's side, drawing their weapons. They glanced at each other, wondering if they would need to engage their own men. The irony was that they might have traveled so far only to end up battling the very forces they had come to lead.

Loghain kicked back a soldier that had been about to strike Maric with his sword. "Don't be a fool!" he roared. "This is Prince Maric!" His words were lost in the shouts of battle and the crashes of the golem's fist against stone and armor. He looked about, hoping to spot the golem's mage amid the chaos, but saw nothing.

"Stop fighting!" Loghain roared again, Rowan pushing several men back beside him and trying to pull Maric to his feet. Nalthur saw what they were trying to do but he couldn't order the Legion to retreat. There was no room on the narrow rocky ledge, and trying to pull back would only end up with them being slaughtered or falling into the water and drowning.

The stone golem charged at Loghain, letting out a bellow of rage. It reared up over him, both fists ready to crash down on his head, and he held up his sword, bracing for the impact. . . .

"Halt!" rang out a new voice from behind the golem, and the effect was immediate. The golem went still.

The human soldiers paused in their fighting and looked around them in confusion. Nalthur took advantage and shouted for the dwarves to pull back, which they immediately did. A gap opened up between the forces, and while it looked like the human soldiers might chase after their quarry, they held their ground.

Like a sea had parted around them, Loghain was left in the clearing with Maric and Rowan beside him, the golem looming overhead as still as a statue.

"Who dares invoke the name of the Prince?" the voice demanded. The figure that walked around the golem into view wore yellow robes and possessed a pointed beard. Maric recognized him immediately.

"Wilhelm!" he shouted with relief. He jumped up and ran toward the mage.

Wilhelm's eyes went wide, and he stepped back as

Maric approached, staring at him in disbelief. Maric halted, and looked at the rest of the soldiers that likewise stared at him aghast. Nobody in the entire cavern said a word. The shocked silence was complete.

"Don't you recognize me?" Maric asked. Loghain and Rowan walked up quietly behind him, lowering their weapons.

Wilhelm's gaze flickered to each of them but went immediately back to Maric. His eyes hardened, and he held out a hand for the soldiers to stand back. "Be cautious," he warned. "This may yet be a trick, an illusion to deceive us."

He raised a hand, and bright power was summoned up from it. Maric stood still as the power surged toward him. He closed his eyes as it washed over him, and nothing changed. Wilhelm's eyes went wide, and he raised his hand again, summoning a different spell. This one crashed against Maric's form, and then another followed it.

Wilhelm's eyes went wide with disbelief. He sank to his knees, and actual tears welled up in his eyes as he stared at Maric. "My lord?" the mage asked in a tremulous voice. "You . . . you live?"

Maric walked cautiously up to Wilhelm and knelt before him, gripping the mage's hands in his own. Loghain and Rowan approached solemnly from behind. "It's me, Wilhelm. Loghain, too, as well as Lady Rowan. All of us are here."

Wilhelm looked back at the rows of soldiers that stared incredulously at them. "It is him," he said. "It is really him!" As if a wave of shock ran through them, the soldiers began to whisper to each other excitedly. Word was passed back in the ranks, and men in the passage began to run up a set of stairs to the town above. A babble of shouting could be heard up there.

One by one the soldiers followed Wilhelm's example, all of them falling to their knees and removing their helmets in respect. More soldiers crowded into the chamber, coming down the stairs behind the heavy doors, and as they laid eyes on Maric, they, too, fell to their knees. Some of them had tears running down their cheeks.

"We thought you were lost," the mage said to Maric. "We thought everything was lost. Rendorn was dead. The usurper declared you dead. We thought . . . we were sure this was another attack, and that this was . . ." His voice choked up, and he shook his head again as if he couldn't quite believe it.

Maric nodded gravely and stood, looking back at the row of silent dwarves behind him. Nalthur began giving orders to have those knocked into the water collected as well as the injured seen to. The dwarves scrambled immediately.

Maric turned back to look at the rows of soldiers in front of him, his own men. There were so many, crowded here into this dark passage and staring at him with the same hopeful expressions that he remembered when Loghain and Rowan had first brought him back to the camp in the western hills. There were more beyond, up on the surface. He could hear them shouting.

"We're not too late, then," Maric said. The relief was so overwhelming that tears rushed down his cheeks. "There's still an army, and you haven't disbanded. We made it? We actually made it?"

Wilhelm nodded, and Loghain put his hand on

Maric's shoulder from behind. "We actually made it," he said quietly.

Maric barely felt worthy. He walked toward the awestruck soldiers, almost unable to control his flood of tears as he looked at them all kneeling. They were hungry and tired and desperate. He could see it in their eyes. And yet they had endured.

Looking over them all, Maric raised a proud fist high over his head, and as one, the men of the rebel army leaped to their feet and responded with a re-sounding cry of jubilation that shook the very ground underneath them and rang far into the shadows of the Deep Roads.

16

Severan's hands shook as he read the parchment. His mouth thinned into a grimace, and when he finished, he quickly rolled it up. This was not good news.

The mage paused in front of an ornate mirror, smoothing his black hair and telling his heart to calm down. It was beating too fast for his liking, the sweat glistening on his forehead far too visibly. The King would see it and know what the news was even before Severan opened his mouth, and that just wouldn't do.

Meghren's moods were bad enough to contend with even when the news could be filtered properly. If he was to take it upon himself to fly into a fury, Severan would much rather he took out his rage on one of the servants as usual. A week earlier, it had been a slender elven serving boy who had failed to notice the cream he brought the King was soured.

His screams had brought the palace guard running into the royal chambers, only to stand there helpless as King Meghren beat the foolish boy within an inch of his life.

When the King turned his back, the desperate guard captain dashed forward to gather up the bloodied servant. It was a daring move, for Meghren could just as easily have turned his attention to the guard, his rage renewed by such outrageous interference. But Meghren had done nothing, seething and grinding his teeth as he stared out the window while the guards hastily retreated.

Frankly, Severan thought it would have been better had the fool just beaten the boy to death and been done with it. Instead, he had survived, and when he was returned to his wailing relatives with his tale of the event, there were riots in the alienage. The city garrison reported that it had needed to flee the quarter and lock down the gates, leaving the enraged elves to burn their own homes until a few days of hunger calmed them down. Meghren hardly cared about some rioting elves, but such problems did make things so very inconvenient for Severan.

But now there was worse news to deliver, and no convenient servant to pawn it off on. Severan wiped his brow with a silk handkerchief, a gift from a fawning Antivan merchant who had begged him to arrange an audience, and considered the possibility of not telling the news at all. He stared into his eyes within the mirror, frowning at the fear he saw there.

No, there was really very little choice.

He found Meghren down in the stables, being fussed over by a pair of burly smiths as they strapped new armor to him. It was gold-plated and specially crafted with the face of a lion embossed into the breastplate. It had many grooves, the metal glittering everywhere it wasn't covered by black leather, the kind of armor one could easily imagine a great king wearing, or even an emperor. Ever since Meghren had led the army at West Hill he had become practically obsessed with everything military-related. This despite many assurances from the commanders on the field that he had been nowhere near the action and mostly got to tour the carnage on the battlefield after all had been said and done.

Severan thought the armor looked impressive, befitting a great king. Naturally Meghren disagreed. He barely tolerated the smiths, constantly shrugging with discomfort and snapping at them for tying a particular strap too tightly or griping that the greaves pinched or that the gauntlets made his skin itch. Several servants hovered nearby, too frightened to make any effort to help the smiths. Indeed, the nervous aura even seemed to agitate the few horses in the stable. The beasts stomped their hooves and looked like they were about ready to kick down the doors to their berth.

He was about to enter when he noticed Mother Bronach seated on a stool against the far wall, observing the fitting. Why she was there, Severan had no idea, but she looked up and noticed him. The slightest smile played across her face.

It seemed she knew. Perhaps she had even come here to watch.

Meghren saw Mother Bronach's expression and turned to see Severan hovering in the doorway. "Oh, it is you," he sneered. "What is it now? I hope there is news from Gwaren. This business has gone on entirely too long."

The mage cleared his throat, which had suddenly become rather dry. He couldn't help but stare at the sword sheathed at Meghren's side. Ornamental or not, if the man decided to start flailing about with it, it could do more than a little damage. "Yes," he finally said. "There is news."

Meghren went cold, looking at Severan with narrowed eyes, and the entire room immediately picked up on the change in temperature. The servants all but scrambled out of the stable, and both the smiths stopped affixing the armor. They backed away, confused looks on their faces.

"What are you doing!" Meghren barked at them. "Why are you stopping?"

The smiths both immediately rushed back toward their king, so quickly that they bumped into each other and then nearly knocked him off his feet. Meghren roared in rage and kicked up with his metal boots, catching the nearest smith in the nose. Blood sprayed into the air as the man flew back, slamming into the stable wall.

"Get out of here, you fools!" Meghren roared.

The other smith stared at him with wide, terrified eyes, but only for a second. Running over to his comrade, who was kneeling by the wall in shock, covering his nose with bloody hands, he helped him to his feet and the two of them ran out of the stable.

Meghren watched them go, a disgruntled expression on his face, and then finally turned back toward Severan. "I would like to hear this news," he said, his voice low and unpleasant.

"I would like to hear it, too," Mother Bronach chimed in. She seemed awfully pleased with herself.

Severan tried to swallow, but found his throat constricted. So instead he cleared his throat. The sound seemed very loud in the silent room, with everyone staring at him expectantly. Even the horses appeared to be watching him.

"We . . . have taken Gwaren," he said simply.

Meghren snorted with derision. "And how is that not good news?"

Severan fingered the rolled-up parchment nervously. "It . . . is uncertain we will be able to hold it, Your Majesty. It was very difficult to take. There were . . . unexpected circumstances." A new bead of sweat rolled down his forehead. Severan prayed that Meghren did not notice it.

Thankfully, he seemed more occupied with his own annoyance. He tapped a boot on the wooden floor impatiently, his hands on his hips as he looked around the stable, perhaps in search of someone to commiserate with him. Finally his head snapped back toward Severan. "Unexpected circumstances?" he said viciously. "The remnants of those fool rebels, that's all that were left there, you said. I sent the chevaliers and half the men that took West Hill. More than enough, you said."

"Prince Maric is alive," Severan said. "He was in Gwaren." He immediately regretted it, as Meghren's eyes went wide with rage. Even so, he said nothing immediately. He merely stared at Severan, and the mage began to consider if he should retreat.

"Alive? How?" Mother Bronach asked. She looked truly shocked, Severan noted. So she had not heard that part, at least. He supposed he should take some small satisfaction from that fact. It would provide him a modicum of comfort should he be inadvertently skewered.

"Yes," Meghren snarled. "How is he alive? *Again?* And how could he be in Gwaren?" He pulled out his sword from the scabbard, his look menacing.

Severan frowned at him severely. "I will remind His Majesty that I said we had not found the prince's body at West Hill!" He slammed his fist down on a nearby wooden post, startling one of the horses. "How many times did I protest that we needed to be certain before you made your announcements? From all my reports, Prince Maric appeared in Gwaren just prior to the attack. The entire town thinks he rose from the dead! Raised up by the Maker!"

It was a gamble. Severan maintained his angry stare, the sweat continuing to pour down his brow, and after a moment Meghren sighed and pouted. "But there were so many burned corpses! You said any of them could be the boy!"

"I said they *might* be. I told you to give me time for our search parties to make sure! If you had at least waited until we had recaptured Gwaren . . ."

Meghren turned toward Mother Bronach, throwing up his hands. "Bah! This is your doing, woman!"

"*My* doing?" She stood up from her stool, gathering her red robes around her. "Prince Maric or no, how is it that we were not able to defeat a small group of rebels? The boy may have survived the battle, but he cannot work miracles!"

"We did defeat them," Severan said. "It was a close thing. They managed to get the help of dwarves from somewhere. Not a large number, but they were difficult to take down." His eyes glanced toward

Meghren nervously. "They were able to cleave through almost half the chevaliers. The casualty numbers have been . . . extraordinary."

"Half!" Meghren exploded. Then he closed his eyes, forcing himself to calm. "But you said they were defeated? The rebels, dwarves, and all?"

Severan nodded. "Our numbers were too great. They retreated into the Brecilian Passage, where we would have followed and slaughtered them all . . ."

"*Would* have?"

"That is when the riot began. Before the commander could regroup your forces and begin the chase, the people of Gwaren rose up. Swarmed the lines, I'm told, completely unexpectedly. Commander Yaris was killed, among others."

Mother Bronach took a step forward, alarmed. "That is no riot, surely."

"Rebellion," Meghren breathed. His eyes were wide with shock.

Severan held up the parchment, nodding. "The fighting in Gwaren has been bloody, and the town is aflame again. We're not sure what is happening now, but there is the possibility that the rebel force may have doubled back and attacked Gwaren once more."

"Can we not send more men?"

"It gets worse," Severan began uneasily. "Word has gotten out."

Meghren snorted. "So?"

"Perhaps you don't understand, Your Majesty." Severan strode toward Meghren and looked him straight in the eyes. "Word has gotten out that Maric lives. That he has returned from the dead, presumably to save these poor Fereldan fools from your rule. There was a riot in Redcliffe this morning, and the talk is spreading."

Meghren backed away. He spluttered indignantly, but at the same time he looked precariously uncertain. "What? Riots? How dare they!" He waved a finger in Severan's direction. "Send the call out! I want levies supplied! Every last member of the Bannorn will send troops this time!"

"They won't send men if they're frightened that their own lands are going to rebel underneath them. The Arl of Redcliffe has sent word asking *you* for assistance, asking you to send men to help him right away. He won't be the first."

"I am not here to help *them*!" Meghren stormed about the stable, outraged. "I want executions! Anyone who might even be suspected to be a sympathizer for those rebels, I want them hanged! These Fereldan dogs must learn who is their master!"

"Your Majesty . . . ," Severan cautioned.

"Do it!" Meghren roared. The horses in the stable reared up on their hind legs, whinnying in response. "They will see what it means to trifle with the might of Orlais! Them and the dog prince both!"

Both Severan and Mother Bronach stared at him, somewhere between shock and horror. Meghren looked from one to the other, as if waiting for one of them to speak. As if insisting on it, in fact. Neither the mage nor the priest knew quite what to say, however. The prospect of preemptive executions being committed throughout Ferelden might not have the effect he imagined. Even a beaten and cowed dog might still bite, if cornered.

"King Meghren," Mother Bronach began slowly, in the tone she reserved for those times she knew she was about to make him truly angry. "Perhaps now is the time to be merciful. Prove to the people you are the worthier king, and marshal your strength first before you—"

"Never!" he bellowed, spinning on her. His face was red, and Mother Bronach took a step back reflexively, stumbling against the stool behind her. "This is not a contest! I am the *only* king, and these others are . . . are malcontents! I will not let this spread further!"

With a step he was up close against her, his gritted teeth barely an inch away from her face. The Mother pressed herself against the wall, turning her face away from his in terror. Severan even thought for a moment that perhaps he should intervene; this was the Grand Cleric of Ferelden, after all. Even Meghren could not hurt her without consequences. But then he remembered that he didn't particularly like the woman. Let her squirm.

"You will tell them," Meghren commanded, his tone low and threatening, "that this dog prince is no savior, that he has not returned from the dead. You will tell them this, yes?"

She nodded, refusing to look him in the eyes. "I . . . I will say it was a mistake—"

"Not a mistake! He is a demon. A thing of evil risen from his grave."

She nodded again, quickly.

"That's not bad," Severan considered, rubbing his beard thoughtfully. "That might work."

"Of course it will work." Meghren stepped away from Mother Bronach, and she exhaled loudly. She composed her robes, beads of sweat running down her forehead. He turned toward Severan, much calmer now. "You will deal with the rebels, my mage. You can do this, yes?"

Severan nodded. "I will send word to the Emperor. He promised us two full legions in his last letter, if we needed. But he warned us that there would be no more after that, Your Majesty."

Meghren stared at the floor, considering. "Will it be enough?"

"Added to what we have left? Yes. It should be more than enough. We can finish the rebels and then turn our attention to any uprising. They haven't the strength to stand against you."

"Then do it."

Severan turned to leave, but Meghren grabbed him by the arm and spun him about. Meghren's stare was intense. "But this will be your last chance, my mage. That is clear, yes?"

Severan nodded, and he was released. *It may be your last chance as well, Your Majesty*, he thought to himself. He merely bowed low, however, and retreated from the room. A moment later, Mother Bronach did the same. She did not look pleased. Meghren was oblivious of them both, already wrapped up once again in an annoyed inspection of his golden armor.

As Severan crossed the long hallways back into the palace proper, thoughts whirled about in his head. If he was careful, this situation could still be turned to his advantage. Meghren had been forced to recognize that the situation was serious. A quick defeat of the rebels would make him most grateful—a better result even than defeating the rebels at Gwaren would have been.

Already most of the palace knew to look to Severan for their commands. The Orlesian commanders responded solely to his orders. The nobility came to him when they needed problems solved. Even the chamberlain came to Severan when it came time to determine Meghren's daily schedule, and they both made sure that he was kept busy doing what he did best: pleasing himself. Ostensibly all decisions were made by him, but anyone who was anyone important in Ferelden knew better. Without Severan, Meghren wasn't capable of finding his smallclothes.

He still had to handle Meghren with care. Severan hadn't yet gotten to the point where he could survive a direct confrontation, should the man get it into his head to realize what was happening. And with Mother Bronach still whispering into his ears, that was always a possibility.

With any luck, his rage against her tonight could be stoked. It was something to consider. For now, however, he had to keep his mind on the rebels.

A young page came around the corner and spied Severan approaching him, and responded by running up nervously. "My lord Severan!" he cried. The lad was out of breath.

"Another message?" More news from Gwaren would be welcome. If it was bad news, Severan at least had an excuse to avoid Meghren for a while yet.

"No, my lord," the lad gulped, nervous. "There is a woman. She sent me to find you. I've been looking everywhere!"

"A woman?"

"An elf, my lord. She told me to say her name is Katriel."

He paused. "Katriel, you say? Where is she now?"

"In your quarters, my lord."

Severan didn't wait for the page to reply, breezing past him quickly. Katriel had done excellent work at West Hill, but had then disappeared under suspicious circumstances. He had wondered if she had been killed, perhaps found out after she had finished her work. There had been several unanswered questions, which had begun to make him suspicious. If she was back, however, this boded well.

Provided, of course, that she could supply an explanation for her absence.

It took several minutes for him to reach his quarters, even moving at a steady pace. He considered briefly calling the guards, but decided that would be unwise. It was unlikely the guards would dare to question him, but rumors spread far too easily. Who knows what Meghren might happen to overhear?

Instead he paused at his door and cast an enchantment of protection over himself. As unlikely as it was, if she intended him harm, it was good to be prepared. Taking a deep breath, he opened the door and entered.

Katriel was as he remembered, golden curls down her back and majestic green eyes sizing him up. She wore dusty leathers and smelled faintly of sweat and horses. She had traveled here quickly, then, and had not stopped even to wash herself up? A good sign, then. His room was shadowed except for the flickering light of a lantern on his desk, and Katriel thumbed idly through one of his journals.

"I trust you have a good reason for your disappearance," he said evenly. "And why you haven't contacted me prior to your appearance here?" Severan didn't like to show off his magic, but he held out a palm and allowed a lick of magical flame to spin itself into existence. He imagined it drove home the point sufficiently.

"I do," she responded. The elf seemed far more solemn than he recalled. She closed his journal quietly and stared at Severan without challenge. He wasn't quite sure what to make of it.

"Good," he said. The ball of fire hovering over his palm winked out, and he stepped farther into the room. He kept a wary eye on her even so. "Are you still situated in the rebel camp with Prince Maric? Or did they lose you at West Hill, as well?"

"I am still with the Prince, or at least I was until their victory at Gwaren. Then I came directly here, though it was not easy to escape detection."

Severan waited for her to elaborate, but she didn't. He frowned, nettled. "Victory? Then their counterattack was successful? They are back in control of Gwaren?"

She nodded. "Yes. Though not before your men slaughtered half of the town. That will cause quite a stir when news of it gets out."

He waved away the matter, frowning. "That isn't important now. With your help, we can strike at the rebel force and finish it once and for all. I assume the prince in Gwaren is actually him? Not some pretender?"

"It is," she replied.

"Pity. Well, he will have to die. Thankfully you can make certain it is done properly this time." Severan paused as he felt a buzzing sensation in the back of his head. Uncertain what it was, he increased the magical aura of protection around him and watched Katriel more carefully. What was she up to?

The elf seemed oblivious of his discomfort, merely

shaking her head as she glided toward him around his desk. "No," she murmured. "I'm not going to do that."

"I see," he said stiffly, ignoring the buzzing. "And what about our contract? I was led to believe you bards held your honor above all else."

Katriel paused at his desk. "Let us assume for the moment that our contract was not canceled the moment you changed the plan at West Hill." She folded her arms, frowning. "I would need to remind you that my contract was to deliver Prince Maric to you, alive. Nothing more, nothing less." Her green eyes glinted dangerously at him.

Severan paused. The buzzing in his head got worse, and numbness crawled up his skull. He ignored it. "Would you bring me the Prince now, as we agreed, if I asked you to do it?"

She shook her head. "No. I would not."

"I see." He raised his palm again, and the ball of fire re-formed. It was brighter now, flickering blue at the edges. His eyes bored into hers, daring her to try to strike him with the daggers she surely had on her person. "Then we are going to have an issue, yes?"

Katriel didn't move. She merely stared at Severan expectantly, her arms still folded. He concentrated, but the buzzing only got worse. The ball of flame sputtered and then disappeared. He would have gasped in shock, but the numbness had spread to his face. He could only open his mouth and then click it shut again.

The room began to spin, and he reached out to grab on to a wooden bedpost to steady himself. He felt the strength in his legs draining out from underneath him.

Katriel gestured toward the door. "A contact poison, coated on the doorknob." As she slowly walked toward Severan, his hands slid down the post and he collapsed to the floor. Any attempt of his to cry out elicited only a painful wheeze as his throat constricted up tight, making it difficult to breathe.

The elf stood over him, looking down with sadness in her green eyes. She did not seem to be enjoying what she was doing, though that hardly brought him any satisfaction. His heart leaped madly about in his chest, just as his mind screamed at him to move, to find some way out of this trap of paralysis.

"I do not intend to kill you," she said quietly. "I should do it, but you are right on that count, at least. My honor, for what it's worth, forbids it." She crouched down over him, absently adjusting his robe so it did not bunch up around his throat.

Severan tried to reach out for his staff, propped up next to his bed not far away. His fingers flexed, the effort to do so making his face turn red and sweaty, but he could not move his arm. Katriel watched his effort passively. "Consider this, mage: if I had slain you, it would have been your pride that was your undoing in the end. If my time as a bard has taught me anything, it is that men with power can still be approached. The more power they believe they have, the more vulnerable they are."

He looked up at her, wanting to hurl furious insults, wanting to reach up and strangle her slender throat, but he could do nothing but wheeze and spit. Her eyes hardened as she stared down at him. "I am not your servant, mage," she said dispassionately. "I am no one's servant any longer. That is what I came to tell you."

Katriel stood up and moved toward the doorway, and he continued to lie there, struggling feebly against the poison in his blood. She opened the door and paused, looking back at him.

"If you are wise, you will abandon your plans and return to wherever you came from. If you continue here, you will die, of that I assure you." She looked off into the distance, her countenance softening for a moment before she shrugged off the feeling. "Consider that warning a courtesy."

And then she was gone.

Severan lay on the cold stone of his bedroom floor, trying with increasing success to reach out toward the staff. He supposed he should be glad for his life. He was a fool to let his guard down so completely, after all. As the beads of sweat rolled down his forehead, however, all he could truly think of was revenge.

For this indignity, she will suffer. Then the rebel prince after her and all the rest.

Oh, they will suffer.

17

Loghain watched Maric quietly from across the room.

They were all exhausted after the days of battle, finally resulting in Gwaren being successfully defended from the usurper's attack, but still Maric toiled away at his table, writing letter after letter. How many he had written so far, Loghain could only guess, but three riders had already been sent westward, carrying word into the Bannorn and other parts of the land.

Loghain was fairly certain that word of Maric's return would spread faster than any horse could, but Maric was determined to make a personal appeal to the Fereldan nobility while there was still time to capitalize on their victory. It had come at a heavy cost, after all. The number of dead within Gwaren had been staggering. The Orlesians had been brutal in their efforts to deal with the uprising, so much so that Maric had felt compelled to turn the army about even though they had been barely in fighting form and had been fleeing for their lives.

Maric felt responsible for those lost lives. Loghain could see that. He had stared at the streets full of dead men and women who had fought against mounted knights only because they believed in him, and Loghain had seen that a part of Maric's soul had shriveled up right then.

It had been a desperate situation when they had fallen upon the chevaliers in Gwaren only days after having been handed a narrow defeat by them, and luck had played into their hands. The usurper's men had not considered the possibility that they might come back, and their attention was wholly upon slaughtering the ungrateful populace. Maric had been filled with a righteous fury, and even when the enemy finally had been routed and fled the field, Loghain had been forced to hold him back from ordering them chased down. The rebel force had been decimated, and was in no shape to go anywhere. It had taken both Loghain and Rowan to convince Maric to stand down. They had to recover, and had many dead to burn.

And that was what they had been doing for days, now. Burning the dead. The air had been filled with acrid smoke that never seemed to go away. Only the Legion didn't take part in their rites. They grieved for their heavy losses but also seemed satisfied that their men had died in a glorious battle. Nalthur shook Maric's hand before the remaining dwarves took their dead back into the Deep Roads, promising to return soon. Loghain hoped they didn't meet their

end at the hands of the darkspawn after all. A sobering thought, to think that such creatures had existed
beneath their feet for so long, forgotten.

At first Maric had insisted on walking through
the streets of what remained of Gwaren, watching the
funeral pyres and joining in the prayers said by the
few Chantry priests that remained. But the eyes of
the people were upon him wherever he went. The
way they watched his every move and whispered
behind his back, the way they bowed low whenever
they spotted him and refused to get up even when he
begged them to; their worship disturbed him.

Returned from the dead, they whispered. Sent by
the Maker to free them from the yoke of the Orlesians at last. Despite the fact that Maric's mission
had not changed, suddenly it seemed real to them.
Suddenly it seemed possible, their loss at West Hill
forgotten. And Maric would kill himself to make sure
their belief was vindicated.

There were already tales being brought to them of
the people stirring in the west, and the usurper clamp-
ing down hard—supposedly the palace in Denerim
was lined with so many heads, they did not have
enough space to keep them all. Yet the patience of
the people seemed to be at an end. Their ranks were
swelling as fit survivors in Gwaren rushed to join the
rebels, and Loghain assumed that would only continue once they left for the west. Ferelden's champion
had braved death itself to come to their aid. So, despite their precarious position, Maric wrote letters in
an attempt to fan this blaze as if he could do so
purely through will alone.

Perhaps he could.

Loghain walked quietly across the room, mindful

of the fact that there were soldiers sleeping in the hall right outside. They had so few tents left, and no energy remaining to erect them. Most of their men collapsed out of exhaustion wherever they could, trying to get what little sleep they might. Most of them were still hungry. Tomorrow would bring only more of the same.

"Maric, we need to talk," he said gravely.

Maric looked up from his most recent letter, his eyes red and bleary from fatigue. There was a look in them that Loghain didn't like, a nervous energy that Maric possessed ever since they had emerged from the Deep Roads and seen just how little of their fighting force had made it back to Gwaren.

Outside the rain continued to fall, lightning occasionally flashing across the night sky. It was a welcome deluge, scouring the air clean of the smoke. Except for the single candle on his desk, Maric had no light to write with. Finding a proper lantern might have been difficult, as the chevaliers had sacked the manor almost completely and left it short of everything, so naturally Maric elected to do without. Really, he should have retired to his bedchambers long ago, and Loghain half wondered if perhaps he shouldn't demand that Maric get some rest.

But this discussion could not wait any longer.

"Talk?" Maric asked, blinking in confusion.

Loghain sat on the edge of the table, crossing his arms as he considered his words. "About Katriel."

Maric snorted, waving his hand angrily. "This again?" He picked up his quill to return to his writing. "I thought we settled this in the Deep Roads. I don't want to discuss it any more."

Loghain moved the parchment away from Maric.

In response, Maric looked up at him in irritation. "Nevertheless, we're going to," Loghain stated evenly.

"So it appears."

"Maric, what are you doing?"

Now the other brow joined the first, and Maric looked surprised. "What am I doing about what?"

Loghain sighed heavily, and rubbed his forehead in agitation. "You love her. I understand that, better than you think. But why? How is it that this woman, who showed up out of nowhere, can have you wrapped around her finger?"

Maric looked vaguely offended. "Is it so wrong that I love her?"

"Do you intend to make her your Queen?"

"Maybe." Maric looked away, avoiding Loghain's eyes. "What does it matter, anyhow? Who knows if I'll ever sit on the throne? Does it always have to be about the future?"

Loghain scowled, and glared at Maric until he reluctantly looked back. The fact that he could barely meet Loghain's gaze said plenty. "Arl Rendorn is dead." The words came out reluctantly, but Loghain said them anyway. "Rowan has no reason to keep your betrothal. Are you truly going to let her get away?"

Maric looked down. "She's already gotten away," he said gravely. "Do you think I don't know?" The words hung between them until Maric looked back up, and their eyes met. Of course he knew, Loghain thought bitterly. How could he not?

Loghain put a hand on Maric's shoulder. "Go after her, Maric."

Maric angrily jumped up from his chair, sending it skittering back along the floor, and stormed away from Loghain. When he looked back, his face was frustrated and contemptuous. "How can you ask me that?" he demanded. "How can *you* ask me that?"

"She is your Queen," Loghain stated firmly. "I have *always* known that."

"My Queen," he said the words distastefully. "How long ago was that decided for us? I don't know that's something she even wanted."

"She still loves you."

Maric turned away, distressed and shaking his head in exasperation. He turned back and started to say something, but then thought better of it, regret playing across his face. He looked up at Loghain accusingly. An awkward silence developed, neither of them knowing quite what to say next. Lightning flared once again outside in the night sky.

"You want to know why I love Katriel?" Maric spoke with a clipped, furious tone. "She sees me as a man. This gorgeous creature, an elf, she looks at me and she doesn't see the son of the Rebel Queen. She doesn't see me as awkward Maric, or the fellow who can't quite stay in his saddle or hold a sword."

"You aren't any of those things any longer, Maric. . . ."

"When I went to her rescue, she didn't doubt that I could save her. When she came to me in my tent that night, she wanted me. *Me.*" He held out his hands to Loghain as if pleading with him to understand. "No one . . . no one's ever looked at me like that. Certainly not Rowan." He looked pained thinking of her, his eyes drifting off. "I . . . I know she loves me. But when she looks at me, she sees Maric. She sees the boy she grew up with. When Katriel looks at me, she sees a man. She sees a prince."

Loghain frowned. "A lot of people see that. A lot of women, too." He snorted. "You must see the way they look at you, Maric. You can't be that big an idiot."

"Katriel is special. Have you ever seen someone like her? She's *saved* us, she guided us down in the Deep Roads, she's fought at our side." Maric pinched the bridge of his nose in frustration, shaking his head. "Why can't you see that? I don't *know* that she'll be my Queen, but would that be so wrong?"

"She's an elf. Do you think your people would accept an elven queen?"

"Maybe they'll have to."

"Maric, be serious."

"I *am* serious!" Maric stormed about the study, his ire building. "Why is everyone so set on telling me what decisions I have to make? How am I ever going to be a king if I don't make any of my own decisions?"

"You think this is a kingly decision, do you?"

"Why not?" Maric asked acidly. "Suddenly you're an expert on being a king?" Then he immediately regretted his words, holding up his hands. "Wait, I didn't—"

"You're going to need to make some hard decisions, Maric," Loghain interrupted, his icy blue eyes narrowing. "Ones you've been avoiding. You have an enemy to defeat, and while I may not know much about being a king, I do know what it takes to win a fight. The question is, do you want to win or not?"

Maric said nothing, glaring at Loghain incredulously.

Loghain nodded slowly. "I see." Part of him didn't want to continue. He felt his heart constricting, and wondered how it was that he had come to this point.

A few years ago he had been content to let his father lead the outlaws. His own decisions didn't affect anyone outside of himself, and he preferred it that way. Then Maric brought him into this world, and into the rebel army. Now with Arl Rendorn dead, there was no one else; the rebels lived or died based on everything they did. If they didn't make the right decisions now, the Orlesians won. The usurper won.

"Then there is something you must know," he said reluctantly.

"Not about Katriel, I hope."

"I had her followed." Loghain got up from the table and paced to the far side of the room. He felt uneasy. "She didn't go to Amaranthine, Maric. She went north. To Denerim."

Maric's eyes narrowed. "You had her followed?"

"Not easily. Maric, she went to the palace."

It took a moment for the implication to sink in. Loghain could see the connections being formed, even as Maric shook his head in denial. "No, it can't be true," he protested. "What are you saying?"

"Think about it, Maric," Loghain insisted. "Who could have destroyed us so completely at West Hill? After all the efforts we made to prevent the nobles here from getting word out, who could have arranged the trap so neatly? Who had your trust?"

"But . . ."

"Why did Arl Byron never mention such a skilled spy? He told us about others, Maric, and then he conveniently died, along with everyone in his command. Anyone who could have confirmed who she was."

Maric held up a hand, incensed. "Maker's breath, Loghain! We already went over this. Katriel saved our lives. If she'd wanted to kill me, don't you think she could have done that?"

"Maybe that wasn't her mission, Maric." Loghain stepped toward Maric, keeping his eyes level and his gaze hard. "Maybe her mission was merely to get into your confidence. Which she has done. And now she went to Denerim, to the royal palace. Why? Why do you think she would do that?"

The question hung in the air. Maric reeled from Loghain, looking anguished and sickened all at once. Outside lightning flashed, followed shortly by a peal of thunder.

"You don't know," Maric protested. He was grasping at straws, now. "She could have a reason, she could . . . It doesn't have to be what you think."

"Then ask her," Loghain said. "She's on her way here now."

Maric looked up at him, his eyes narrowed. The lightning flashed again outside the window, lighting Maric's face and making plain his suffering. "On her way," he repeated. "Then that's why you . . ."

"I needed to know. And so did you."

Maric shook his head in disbelief. He looked as if he were about to vomit. "I . . . what am I supposed to do with this? I can't just—"

"You are a king," Loghain said harshly. "You will need to make a decision."

The two of them stood there in uncomfortable silence. Maric leaned against a wall, folded over with his hands on his knees as if preparing to become sick. Loghain looked at him from across the room, keeping himself cold and reminding himself that this was necessary.

The candle on the table guttered dangerously as

the sound of rain increased outside. The winds were blowing in from the ocean, and bringing with them a freezing storm that would chill the entire coast before morning. The seasons were changing. By the end of the month, there would be snow again. Either the rebels acted before winter settled in or they would be able to do nothing until spring.

So they waited.

It did not take long. The door to the study creaked open, and Katriel quietly entered from the dark hallway outside, having maneuvered carefully past snoring soldiers. She was in traveling leathers and drenched from the rain, her blond curls clinging to her pale skin. Her long cloak dripped onto the floor.

Katriel paused, immediately becoming aware that something was amiss. The tension in the room was palpable. Her green eyes flicked from Loghain on one side of the room, glaring at her, and Maric on the other, standing up straight now and looking pale and ill. She stepped inside and closed the door behind her, her expression deliberately neutral.

"My prince, are you well?" she asked. "I would have thought—" She glanced back at Loghain suspiciously. "—you might be asleep. It is very late."

Loghain said nothing. Maric walked toward her, his emotions playing across his face. He was tortured by his torn loyalties; even Loghain could see that. Maric took Katriel by her shoulders and looked into her eyes. She seemed passive, almost resigned, and did not flinch away from him.

"You went to Denerim," he stated. It was not a question.

She did not look away. "Then you know."

"*What* do I know?"

Grief filled her, or was it shame? Tears streamed down Katriel's wet face, and she would have pulled away if Maric did not hold her there. She sagged as if the strength had drained out of her, but still she did not look away from Maric's fierce gaze. "I tried to tell you, my prince," she whispered, her voice thick with emotion. "I tried to tell you that I wasn't who you thought I was, but you wouldn't listen. . . ."

Maric's mouth thinned as he clenched his jaw, and his grip on her small shoulders became visibly tighter. There was seething fury in his eyes. "I am listening now," he said, each word enunciated carefully.

Her eyes swam red with tears. They said to him: *Don't make me do this, Maric. It doesn't have to be this way.* And he ignored them, answering with tears of his own. Loghain looked on gravely and did not interfere.

"I am a bard," she said reluctantly. "A spy. From Orlais." When Maric did not respond, she continued. "I was brought here by Severan, the King's mage, to find you, to bring you to him, but—"

"And what of West Hill?" Maric asked, almost too quietly to hear.

Katriel shrank as he towered over her, crying pitifully, but still she did not look away from him. "It was me." She nodded.

Maric let her go. He released her shoulders almost gingerly and stepped away, sick horror on his face as he looked at her. It was true. All of it was true. Maric turned from her and looked toward Loghain, twisted up with agony and tears freely streaming down his cheeks.

"You were right," Maric muttered. "I have been a fool."

"I'm so sorry," Loghain told him gravely. He meant every word.

"No, you're not," Maric gasped. But there was no venom in his words. He turned away from Loghain and made to walk away, his gaze falling on Katriel again. She stood there, vulnerable and shaking, crying as his gaze went from horror to disgust, and then calmed to icy rage.

"Get out," he spat at her.

She flinched at his words, but did not move. Her eyes were hollow and hopeless.

"Get out," he growled, more forcefully. Slowly Maric drew his dragonbone longsword from its scabbard, the glowing runes overpowering the faint candlelight and filling the entire room with an icy blue tint. He held the deadly sword before him in an overt threat. His whole body shook with a seething rage.

Ignoring the sword between them, her anguished eyes fixed solely on Maric, Katriel began to slowly walk toward him. "You said you didn't care who I was before, or what I had done."

Maric went cold, his eyes narrowing as he backed away from her. "I trusted you, I . . . believed in you. I was willing to throw it all away." His voice broke, and he gulped back a surge of grief-stricken tears. "And for what?"

Katriel nodded and continued to walk toward him. "If you believe nothing else, my prince," she whispered calmly, "you must believe that I love you."

"Must I?" He raised the sword sharply to bar her way. "You *dare*." He set his jaw firmly, refusing to retreat any farther.

She stepped forward again, her eyes solemnly fixed upon him. Letting out a scream of blind rage, Maric rushed toward Katriel with his blade raised high. The runes pulsated as he halted in front of her, sword poised over his head. She didn't flinch, didn't retreat, didn't attempt to stop his swing. She merely stared at him, tears coursing down her cheeks. He lowered the blade to his side, his knuckles white as his hands shook.

He couldn't stand to look at her, but couldn't look away.

Katriel closed the last distance between them to gently touch Maric's face. She said nothing. His whole body began to shake violently. With a cry of anguish and rage he threw off her hand and suddenly ran her through. His sword barely made a sound as it cleanly passed through leather and then flesh. Katriel gasped, clutching at Maric's shoulders as he embraced her, her blood gushing out over the sword's hilt and his hand that held it.

Maric stared down at her, his hateful expression dissolving into disbelief and horror. The moment stood suspended and still, Maric exhaling in a burst as he realized what he had done.

Katriel gasped again, and this time bright blood rushed out of her mouth, spilling down over her chin. She looked at Maric with eyes wide, tears flowing freely, and she slowly collapsed as the strength ran out of her. Maric caught her, still not letting go of his sword.

He looked over to Loghain. "Help me! We have to help her!"

Loghain, however, remained where he was. His expression was grim as Maric and Katriel continued their slow descent to the floor, but he made no move to approach them. Maric's expression of horror only grew as he realized Katriel was already dead, her lifeless eyes still staring into his.

He began to shake. Convulsively he let go of the longsword and scrambled away from her on the floor. Blood was already beginning to pool beneath her, and she folded forward like a limp doll. As her body covered the blade's bright runes, the room sank into shadow.

Maric shook his head. He lifted his hands and saw that they were covered in blood, dark and black in the dim light, and he stared at them as if he could not quite comprehend what he had done.

The door shook as someone pounded on it. Several voices could be heard outside, and the muffled voice of a soldier asking if all was well could be heard.

"Everything is fine!" Loghain shouted. Not waiting for a response, he crossed the floor toward where Maric sat. He put a hand on Maric's shoulder, and Maric looked up at him with wide, bleary eyes. "Stop," he said. His tone was firm. "She betrayed you, Maric. She betrayed all of us. This is justice."

"Justice," Maric repeated hollowly.

Loghain nodded grimly. "Justice that a king must dispense, whether it pleases him to or not." Maric looked away, but Loghain shook his shoulder roughly. "Maric! Think of the days to come. How much justice will you need to hand out, when you sit on that throne? The Orlesians have dug their fingers in deep, and you will need to pry them out!"

Maric looked dazed. He shook his head slowly. "You and Rowan both told me what she was, and I refused to listen. I should not be King. I am a fool."

Loghain slapped Maric, hard.

The ringing sound of the blow hung in the air, and

Maric stared at Loghain in shocked disbelief. Loghain crouched down, his face close to Maric's and his eyes intensely ablaze. "There was a man," he whispered in a bitter voice, "a commander among the Orlesians who sacked our farmhold. He told his men to take whatever they liked, and then laughed at our anger. He found it amusing."

Maric looked about to speak, but Loghain held up a hand. "He said that we needed to be taught a lesson. They held us there, me and my father, and made us watch as he raped my mother." He shuddered. "Her screams were . . . they are burned into my mind. My father raged like an animal, and they knocked him out. But I watched it all."

Loghain's voice became hoarse and he swallowed hard. "The commander killed her when he was done. Slit her throat and then told me that the next time we forgot our taxes it would be death for us all. When my father awoke he cried over her body, but it was worse when he saw me standing there. He left and was gone for three days. I didn't know until he returned that he had followed after the Orlesians and had killed the commander in his sleep.

"That was why we had to flee," Loghain sighed. He closed his eyes for a long moment and Maric simply stared at him silently. "He was a wanted murderer. He thought he had failed her, failed me, but not for one moment did I ever think that what he did to that Orlesian bastard wasn't justice." He gestured to Katriel's slumped corpse. "Tell me, Maric, that her treachery didn't call out for blood."

"You wanted this," Maric realized, his voice quiet.

Loghain looked him in the eyes, unrepentant. "I wanted you to see the truth. You told me you wanted to win this war. *This* is how it must be. The alternative is to be done in by treachery just as your mother was."

Maric looked at him reproachfully but said nothing. Absently he wiped his hands on the floor, and uneasily got to his feet. Loghain stood and watched him, but Maric only turned and stared helplessly at Katriel's body. It remained slumped where it was, a great red stain on her back where the sword pierced her, and a pool of blackness around her.

He looked sickened. "I . . . I need to be alone."

Maric stumbled to the door leading to his bedchamber and quietly went inside, shutting the door behind him. Loghain watched him go. Outside, lightning flashed again and lit up the darkness.

Rowan stood at her window, restlessly watching the lightning.

The patter of rain against the stone eased her nerves, but it couldn't make her want to sleep. Her muscles ached from the days of marching and fighting, and while her wounds were healing nicely, they itched under their bandages and threatened to drive her mad. She assumed that Wilhelm would want to see to her injuries personally at some point, but she almost wished he wouldn't. Some scars are deserved.

When the knock came at her door, she didn't respond at first. The chill wind blew in through the open window and tugged at her nightgown, and the lightning flashed again. She felt the rumble of thunder that followed in her chest, and for just a moment it filled up the emptiness. It felt good. It felt right.

The door opened, hesitantly at first, and then he

walked in. She didn't need to ask who it was. Taking a deep breath, she turned and watched Loghain as he closed the door behind him. His grim expression said a lot.

"You told him," she said.

He nodded. "I did."

"And? What did he say? What did *she* say?"

Loghain seemed uncertain, pausing for a moment to choose his words carefully. She didn't particularly care for that idea and arched a severe brow at him, prompting him to hold up a hand. "Katriel is dead," was all he said.

"What!" Rowan's eyes widened in shock. "She didn't return? Did the usurper—?"

"Maric killed her."

Rowan stopped short, stunned. She stared at Loghain and he stared back at her, his icy blue eyes unswerving. Certain things began to fall into place, and her heart went cold. "You told Maric everything, didn't you?" When he didn't respond, she marched up toward him angrily. "You told him that Severan has put out a price on her head now, that she must have—"

"It doesn't change anything," he stated firmly.

She shook her head in disbelief. Loghain was all ice and sharp corners now, staring at her like a man whom she didn't even know. She tried to imagine what must have happened, what Maric must have done. She couldn't picture it. "Loghain," she could barely get the words out, "what if she really loved him? All this time we thought she was just using him, we thought she could hurt him—what if we were wrong?"

"We weren't wrong." Loghain's look was intense,

and he set his jaw stubbornly. "She did hurt him. We thought she was a spy and we were right. We thought that she had been responsible for West Hill and we were right."

Rowan took a step back from him, horrified. "She saved his life! She saved *our* lives! Maric *loved* her! How could you do this to him?" Then she realized the part she had played in this. It was her scouts who had spotted Katriel sneaking away. She had conspired with Loghain to have her followed, had kept the information from Maric to prove that her suspicions were correct, and they had been. But Katriel had surprised her, too. Even so, she had let Loghain go to confront Maric alone. Despite everything that had happened, the thought that Maric might forgive her, that Maric might choose her . . .

"How could *I* do this to him?" she breathed, sickened.

Loghain strode toward her and grabbed her by the shoulders, his fingers digging in. "It is done," he snapped. He stared down at her, his face steel, and for a moment she was reminded of the moment at West Hill. She had rushed to him to make the decision she could not, and he had made it. They had abandoned their men and run to do what they felt they had to.

"Rowan," he began, his voice filled with anguish, but then he banished it completely. "It is done, and it can go one of two ways now," he stated. "Either Maric wallows in self-pity and is no use to anybody or he realizes that being a king and being a man are not always the same thing."

"And why do you come to me, then? It's done, as you said."

"I cannot reach him now," he said evenly.

It took a moment for her to realize what he was suggesting. "But I can," she finished for him. She stepped away from Loghain, her eyes narrowing at him, and he let her go.

"You are still his Queen." His voice could not hide the ache when he said the words, try though he might to hide it.

Tears came unbidden to her eyes. Grimacing, she folded her arms and stared challengingly at Loghain. "And if I do not wish to be his Queen?"

"Then be Ferelden's Queen."

She hated those eyes that bored into her relentlessly. She hated his arrogance, that he assumed he knew what it meant to be a king and what it meant to be a man, as if he knew anything of either. She hated his strength, the strength in those hands that had held her in utter darkness beneath the earth.

And most of all she hated the fact that he was right.

Rowan rushed at Loghain to pound her fist angrily into his chest, but he grabbed her wrist. She tried to punch him with her other hand and he grabbed that, too, and then she struggled with him and burst into furious tears. He just held her wrists, stoic and unmoving.

She never cried. She hated crying. She had cried once when her mother had died. She had cried a second time when her two younger brothers had been shipped off to the Free Marches to be kept safe from the war. Both times her father had stared at her, so mortified by her tears and so clearly incapable of assuaging her grief, she had sworn that she would never cry again. She would be strong for her father, instead.

She had also cried once in the shadows of the Deep Roads, she remembered. And it had been Loghain who had comforted her. Rowan stopped struggling and she rested her forehead on Loghain's chest, her body racked with sobs. Then she looked up at him and saw that he was crying, too. They drew together, about to kiss . . .

. . . and she pulled away from him. He regretfully let her hands go, his gaze searching for hers, but she remained resolved. It was done. Rowan turned away from Loghain and felt the chill wind blowing in through the window keenly. She waited for the thunder, but it didn't come. Somehow it seemed as if the storm should wash everything away. Wash it all away and start over.

"He's waiting for you," Loghain said behind her.

Rowan nodded. "Yes."

She found Maric in his bedchambers, seated on the edge of his bed. Neither the room nor the bed was truly his, all appropriated from its former Orlesian owner, and thus Maric had never been quite comfortable occupying it. He seemed even less comfortable now, as if shrinking in on himself could somehow remove him further from his surroundings.

The window was shuttered and closed up tight, leaving the air still. A lone lantern sat by the bed and threatened to extinguish as it used up the very last of its oil. Maric slouched and stared off into space, barely acknowledging Rowan when she sat down on the edge of the bed beside him. The silence in the room was deafening.

It took a while for Maric to realize that she was

there. When he turned to her, his eyes were sunken with grief. "It's just as the witch said it would be," he blurted out. "I thought she was just making no sense, but . . ."

"What witch?" Rowan asked, confused.

He barely heard her, looking off into the shadows again. "You will hurt the ones you love the most," he quoted, "and become what you hate in order to save what you love."

Rowan reached up with a hand and brushed his cheek, and he looked back at her again without really seeing her. "Those are just words, Maric," she said gently.

"There's more. Much more."

"It doesn't matter. Katriel loved you. Doesn't that count for anything?"

He seemed pained. He closed his eyes, reaching up to cover her hand on his cheek with his own, and it appeared to bring him comfort. There was a time she would have dreamed of this moment. Once she had thought of nothing but running her hands through his beautiful blond hair. Once it had meant everything to her to prove to him that she was what he wanted.

"I don't know that she loved me at all," he muttered. "I don't know anything."

"I think she did." She pulled her hand away from his. "We think she went to Denerim to cut ties with Severan, Maric. Whatever it was she was supposed to do, I think she changed her mind."

He chewed on that idea. "It doesn't change anything," he finally said.

"No. It doesn't."

Maric looked deep into her eyes. He was so full of pain, she could barely stand it. "She tried to tell me," he confessed, "and I didn't listen. I told her I didn't care what she'd done, but I was a fool. I've no business being on that throne."

"Oh, Maric," she sighed. "You are a good man. A trusting man."

"And look where it's gotten me."

"Look, indeed." She summoned a wan smile. "Your people adore you. The men in this army would lay down their lives for you. My father loved you. Loghain—" She stopped short and struggled to continue. "—all of them believe in you, Maric. For good reason."

"Do you still believe in me?"

"I never stopped," she said with absolute sincerity. "Never. You've come so far. Your mother would be so proud. But you can't always be a good man, Maric. Your people need more than that."

Maric seemed hurt by her words, though he said nothing. He hung his head low, weary and exhausted. "I don't know if I can give it to them," he breathed. Then he began to cry, his face racked by grief. "I killed Katriel. I put a sword through her. What kind of man does that?"

She wrapped her arms around him, patting his hair and whispering that everything would be fine. Maric cried into her chest, the desperate sobs of a broken man. It was a sound that alarmed her and filled her with incredible sorrow.

And then the lantern gave up at long last, and the room was blanketed in darkness. She continued to hold him, and after a time he quieted and they held each other in the shadows. Rowan lent him her strength, what little of it she had to give. He needed it. Perhaps this was what queens did. Perhaps they held their kings in the darkness deep within their castles and allowed them that moment of weakness they could never show to anyone else. Perhaps they gave strength to their kings because everyone else only took it from them.

Loghain was right. Damn him.

In the hushed darkness, Rowan leaned down and kissed Maric on the lips. He embraced her readily, eager for her forgiveness . . . and she gave it. He seemed so uncertain and hesitant, and that made it easier. His warmth and gentleness made her cry, but she couldn't let him see that. Tonight, for him, she was strong. Tonight she embraced the role that she had been born for, and while it was like nothing she had ever thought it would be, it was instead the way it had to be.

18

Maric waited quietly in the dark chantry, contemplating the marble statue of Andraste that towered above the holy brazier. The robes hung heavily on his shoulders, and he found the thick wool lining hot next to the brazier's flame, but even so he had to admit he liked them. Rowan had produced them from somewhere, claiming they would make him look more regal. And they did. The purple was a nice touch.

Rowan had been quite attentive since that night in Gwaren. She was always at his side, always ready to offer advice or even just a simple smile. This wasn't the Rowan he had known. It was a stranger, if a helpful one. When he looked into her eyes, he saw only a wall there, a wall she put up to keep him out. It had never been there before, and he supposed that was his doing. An unspoken agreement had been forged, and with it came a distance he could feel no matter how close they lay.

The army had been on the march for two weeks now, heading westward across the Bannorn and spreading the word of his return. The number of recruits that they were getting now was astounding, increasing every day. There were reports of violence all over the country as farmholders up and left their lands, as townsfolk pelted Orlesian guardsmen with rocks and burned Orlesian businesses. Attacks on Orlesian travelers had prompted the usurper to increase the guards on the roads threefold, and with each reprisal against the people, their resolve only stiffened.

The executions were brutal, he was told. There wasn't a single settlement in Ferelden where rows of heads didn't line the roads leading in as a demonstration of what defying King Meghren meant. The thought of them all haunted Maric. Yet still the people rebelled. They had had enough.

Already the banns were coming over to the rebels. Yesterday there had been two banns, old men who had not even come to his court at Gwaren. Two days before it had been an Orlesian, of all things, a young man who had fallen out of favor with the usurper and had begged to be allowed to keep his lands if he joined the rebels. He even promised to marry a Fereldan woman, offered even to change his name. The family that had once owned his lands was now dead, executed to the last child long ago, but Maric still wasn't sure what he was going to do about that.

It was all coming together so quickly. He reminded himself that if West Hill had taught them anything it was that it could fall apart just as fast. Still, this felt different. For the first time in his memory, the rebels had momentum. It was undeniable to everyone.

Outside, off in the distance, a bell began to ring.

It would be time for them to arrive soon, then. The flames in the brazier bathed the statue above him in a soft glow, while the rest of the chantry was left in shadow. The darkness made everything serene, he thought. Andraste looked down upon him kindly, her hands clasped in prayer to the Maker.

It was her most common depiction. Andraste as the prophet, the bride of the Maker, and the gentle savior. If the statue were more truthful, Andraste would have held a sword in her hand. The Chantry didn't like to dwell on the fact that their prophet had been a conqueror; her words had stirred the barbarian hordes to invade the civilized world, and she had spent her entire life on the battlefield. There had likely been nothing gentle about her at all.

And she had been betrayed, too, had she not? Maferath, the barbarian warlord, had grown jealous of playing second husband to the Maker. The more lands he conquered, the more the people adored Andraste, and he wished glory for himself. So he sold his wife to the magisters, and they burned her at the stake, and Maferath became synonymous with betrayal. It was the oldest story in Thedas, one that was told time and time again by the Chantry throughout the ages.

He wondered if Andraste won her battle in the end, even though she met her end in flames. But somehow Maric felt more like Maferath. The thought left a bitter taste in his mouth.

Footsteps on the stone alerted Maric to the fact that they had arrived. Slowly he turned about and watched as a group of men filed into the chantry one by one. The bright brazier was behind him, which meant that these men no doubt saw only his silhouette . . . and that was good, for he didn't want these men to see his face.

Bann Ceorlic was the first. The man had the good grace to look uncomfortable and keep his eyes on the ground. The four others that followed him were all familiar to Maric. Even though he had last seen them at night, in a dark forest, he knew them all too well. These were the men who had betrayed his mother. They had lured her with promises of alliance and then killed her where she stood.

All five of them shuffled in and stood before the altar, avoiding Maric's gaze. The altar was several stairs above them, and so Maric felt as if he loomed over these men. Good. Let them wait in the silence as he stared down at them. Let them see Andraste staring down at them, too, and let them wonder if she was praying for their forgiveness or offering them their last rites.

A bead of sweat rolled down Ceorlic's bald head. None of them said a word.

Loghain strode into the chantry shortly behind them, and the door was closed. He nodded across the chamber to Maric, and Maric nodded back. The tension that had grown between them was nowhere to be seen for the moment, but Maric knew it wasn't gone completely. They had barely spoken since the army had left Gwaren, and perhaps that was for the best. Maric didn't know what to say. Part of him wanted to go back to the easy banter they had once enjoyed, not this cool silence that had replaced it.

Part of him knew it wasn't going to happen. The way Loghain went stony silent and blank whenever Rowan was present, the way Loghain studiously avoided them both, told him that the night with Katriel had changed something between them. Perhaps for good.

So be it. There was nothing to do now but what had to be done.

"Gentlemen," Maric greeted the five noblemen coolly.

They bowed low. "Prince Maric," Bann Ceorlic said cordially. His eyes shifted about nervously, searching the shadows of the chantry behind Maric. Perhaps for guards? He could look all he liked, Maric thought, for he wasn't going to find any. "I must say," the man continued, "we were all rather . . . surprised when we received word of your proposal."

"You're here, so it seems you are at least willing to consider it."

"Of course we will." The Bann smiled solicitously. "It is not easy to see the Orlesians gorging themselves upon Ferelden's wealth, after all. None of us is pleased to live under the tyrant on our throne."

Maric snorted. "But you've made the best of it."

"We've had to do what was necessary to survive." The man had the good grace at least to lower his eyes when he said that. What he "had to do," after all, had been to kill Maric's mother. Maric stared down at the Bann, trying to control his temper. It was not easy.

One of the other noblemen, the youngest of the five present, stepped forward. He had curly black hair and a goatee, and slightly swarthy skin that spoke of his Rivaini mother. Bann Keir, as Maric recalled.

Maric didn't remember the young man from that night, but everything Maric had learned said that he had indeed been there.

"My lord," Bann Keir said politely, "you have asked for us to support your cause, to supply you with our men that currently march with the usurper's army, in return for amnesty." He traded a quick look with Bann Ceorlic and then smiled smoothly at Maric once again. "Is that all? Our forces are not insignificant, after all. To ask us to abandon the usurper's side solely in exchange for your . . . favor . . . implies that your position is stronger than it is."

He was charismatic, Maric had to give him that. Bann Ceorlic looked displeased, and Maric suspected that the young bann had hurried up and gotten to the point far more quickly than Ceorlic would have liked, but the other old men all stared at the ground in a manner that said they agreed. They wanted more.

"You killed Queen Moira Theirin, murdered her in cold blood." Maric said the words surprisingly easily. He walked down the steps toward them, regarding the young Bann Keir with a look that he hoped seemed neutral. "That is regicide, an unforgiveable crime. I offer you forgiveness anyhow, in exchange for doing what is already your duty, and yet you want more?"

"Our duty," Bann Ceorlic interjected, "is to support the King."

"An Orlesian king," Maric snapped.

"That has been put on the throne with the approval of the Maker." Ceorlic gestured toward the statue of Andraste. "We are in a difficult position, and the difference between a rebel and our future ruler could be small indeed."

Maric nodded slowly. He was among them, now, and he stopped before Ceorlic and stared him directly in the face. "And this was why you lied to my mother, lured her to her death with promises of an alliance that was never going to happen? Did you need to do that? Does the Maker approve of treachery, now?"

The nobles backed away uncertainly, Ceorlic with them. He looked at Maric indignantly. "We did as our King bade us to!" Ceorlic and the others beside him drew their swords, glancing at Maric and Loghain with obvious fear on their faces. Loghain drew his blade and stepped forward threateningly. Maric drew his own sword, glittering runes shining in the dim chantry, but did so only calmly and held out a hand to prevent Loghain from moving any farther.

Bann Keir did not retreat, however. He folded his arms and regarded Maric and Loghain contemptuously, not even bothering to draw his blade like the others. "There's no need to fear them, my friends. Prince Maric needs our troops. He needs them badly, or he wouldn't have called us here."

Maric turned toward the young man. "Do I?" he asked, his tone dangerous.

"You do." Keir shook his head at their swords as if they were only amusing to him. "You don't think we would have come here without telling everyone in the Bannorn where we were going? Invited to holy ground, on condition of truce? Do you really think the noble Prince Maric would kill us here, where everyone would know it?" He chuckled lightly. "What would people think?"

Maric smiled coldly. "They would think it was justice," he said, and barely taking a step, he spun around and lashed out with the dragonbone blade, cleanly severing Bann Keir's head at the neck.

It took a moment for the shock of the act to settle in.

Bann Ceorlic and the other three men stared, dumbfounded, as Maric turned calmly toward them. The pale dragonbone dripped bright red blood, Maric's eyes shining with an intense light of their own. Loghain slowly edged around the group, cutting them off from their exit.

"You're mad!" Ceorlic shouted. "What are you doing?"

Maric didn't remove his eyes from the man. "Isn't it obvious?"

"This . . . this is murder! In a chantry of the Maker!" another bann cried.

"Do you expect," Loghain snarled, "the Maker to come down and protect you? If so, then I suggest the four of you begin praying."

Bann Ceorlic raised a hand slowly, sweat pouring down his face. "You need our men," he said carefully, though Maric could hear the quivering in his voice. "Keir was right about that, you do this and our children will fight you with their last breath! They will tell everyone about this cowardly, dishonorable act!"

Maric took one step toward the four men, and all four of them jumped back, startled. Maric smiled coldly once again. "Your children will be given exactly one day to denounce the acts that you committed to earn your deaths here. If they agree, and join my forces without reservation, I will remember that your ill-considered acts were done for their sakes." He raised the longsword, the tip of the blade pointing toward Ceorlic. "And if they refuse, I will ensure your families die and your lands be given to men who know the meaning of words like *cowardly* and *dishonorable*."

The room was silent save for the crackling of the fire in the holy brazier. The tension hung thickly as the old men glanced from one to the other, their swords held before them. Maric could see their calculations. Two to one, they were thinking. They were not so young as their opponents, but they were skilled enough with their blades.

Let them come.

With a shout of terror, one of the elder banns made a break for the chantry door. Loghain gracefully swept low toward him and knocked his legs out from underneath him. The man went down hard on the stone floor. He gasped and opened his eyes wide in fear as he saw Loghain rise above him, holding the sword pointed down toward his heart.

Loghain made no expression as he thrust the sword down into the man. The blade penetrated with a wet, crunching sound and a single strained groan escaped the Bann's lips.

Ceorlic raced toward Maric with a war cry, his sword held high to strike, but Maric raised a foot and connected with the man's chest, pushing him back and slamming him against the wall. A second man rushed at Maric's side and swung his blade low, but Maric parried easily.

He turned and swung the blade in a wide arc at his attacker. The man raised his blade, but the magical longsword sliced through it. Sparks flew and the man screamed in agony as Maric's blade cut a deep slash across his chest. Blood spurted from the wound as Maric spun around again, slicing into the man's abdomen. The Bann fell heavily to the ground, clutching his chest as he died.

The third ran at Loghain, charging him at full speed as he shouted in a mix of rage and terror. Loghain frowned in annoyance at the man, quickly pulling his blade from the one he had just slain and thrusting it before him like a spear. The charging Bann practically skewered himself on the blade, rushing up half its length until he stopped, quivering, bright blood running from his mouth.

Ceorlic watched them from the wall, horror twisting his features into an ugly grimace. His eyes flickered from Loghain to Maric and back again, and he threw down his sword to the floor. It clattered there noisily as he sank to his knees, shaking in abject terror.

"I surrender!" he shouted. "Please! I'll do anything!"

Maric walked up to him slowly. The man cowered before Maric, and then lost what little dignity he had left as he bowed his forehead to the floor and crawled toward Maric's boots. "Please! My . . . my armies! I'll raise double the men! I'll say that . . . that the others attacked you!"

"Pick up your sword," Maric told him. He glanced toward Loghain, who only nodded coolly as he pushed the dead man off his blade.

Bann Ceorlic rose to his knees, looking up at Maric and putting his hands together in prayer. "For the love of the Maker!" he cried, tears running down his face. "Do not do this! I'll give you anything you wish!"

Maric bent down and grabbed the man by the ear.

He felt his rage bubble up, remembered how this man had run his sword through his mother, how he had raced through the forest while his men chased him. This man's treachery had started all of this, and Maric was going to end it.

"What I want back you can't give me," he said, shaking with rage as he thrust the longsword through Ceorlic's heart.

The man's eyes went wide with shock. Blood trickled from his mouth, and he stared uncomprehendingly at Maric as he gasped. Each gasp became weaker, and Maric slowly lowered him to the floor. When he drew his last breath, Maric gritted his teeth and yanked the blade out noisily from Ceorlic's chest.

The shadows grew longer in the chantry as Maric crouched there over Ceorlic. Five dead men surrounded them, their blood spreading and cooling on the stone and the statue of Andraste looking down from the dais upon it all. Loghain stood only a few feet away, but Maric thought he might as well have been alone.

"It's done," Loghain said evenly. There was a hint of approval in his voice.

"Yes. It is."

"There will be an outcry. They weren't wrong about that."

"Maybe so." Maric slowly stood up. His face was grim, and he felt as if something hard had settled within him, as if his heart had become a little more still. It was a strange feeling, peaceful and yet oddly disquieting. He had avenged his mother, but all he felt was cold. "But they can't pretend, now. They have to choose a side and suffer the consequences, and they have to know I won't forgive. Not now."

Loghain looked at Maric, those icy blue eyes piercing into him uncomfortably. Maric tried to ignore it. He couldn't tell what Loghain was thinking any longer. Was he pleased? This was what he had wanted. A Maric who did what needed to be done.

Loghain turned to leave, his black cloak swirling behind him, and then he paused at the door. "I had word shortly before we came. The two legions of chevaliers sent from Orlais will be crossing the River Dane in two days' time. That is where we'll need to engage them."

Maric did not turn to look at him. "You and Rowan will be leading the attack."

"You won't reconsider? . . ."

"No."

"Maric, I don't think the—"

"I said no." Maric's tone was final. "You know why."

Loghain hesitated only a moment, and then nodded firmly and left. The rush of wind through the chantry as the door opened was freezing cold, eagerly telling of the coming winter. The flame in the brazier fluttered wildly and then finally went out.

The die was cast. Maric felt the disquiet in his heart calm at last, leaving only an icy silence. There was no turning back now.

19

_____

A dragon had taken to the air.

Loghain had seen it first thing in the morning. He had been disturbed in his sleep by the strangest sounds coming from far off in the distance, and had gone out of his tent with the sun just barely a sliver of pink and yellow peeking over the western mountains. He had stood there in the dim light, frost clinging to his tent and his breath coming out in white puffs, listening for the sound again.

For a moment he had thought it might be the chevaliers arriving at the river crossing early, that their scouts had been wrong. When he heard the sound again, however, he knew immediately that it couldn't possibly be them. He couldn't identify what it was until he walked out past the tents and the sleeping soldiers wrapped in frosty blankets and stood at the edge of the valley. There he hopped up on some rocks and looked at the entire sweep of the land beneath him, the mighty River Dane cutting a twisting path through the rocks with the morning mist still clinging to the ground as if reticent to awaken.

It was a majestic sight, and even better was the dragon that flew over it. From a distance it seemed almost small, gliding slowly in the air with the snow-capped mountain range behind it. Had it been closer, it would have been a giant beast, large enough to swallow a man whole. As it was, when the dragon roared, he could feel the rumble in the ground even from this far away.

They had said there were no more dragons. The Nevarrans had hunted the beasts mercilessly more than a century ago, until they were said to be extinct. But here it was, gliding free in the morning wind. This was the first time it had come to the Fereldan side of the mountains, apparently, as for two weeks now it had been laying waste to the Orlesian countryside.

The Chantry had taken it as an omen. The Divine in Val Royeaux had declared the next age was to be called the "Dragon Age." Of all things.

The scout who had heard the news said that some were saying it was supposed to mean the coming century would be one of greatness for the Empire. But as Loghain watched the graceful dragon glide through the chill fog, its leathery wings spread wide, he wondered if that was really so.

He heard the footsteps crunching on the frost behind him, but didn't turn around. The entire camp was still and barely moving, but he already knew who would be up this early. He knew the way she walked, the sound of her breath.

Rowan stepped quietly onto the rocks beside him. Her brown curls fluttered in the crisp breeze, frost clinging to her armor, which had been newly polished for the coming battle. Loghain kept his eyes on the distant dragon, trying not to lose sight of it as it dipped low into the foggy valley. It could always turn and fly up here and feast on the men conveniently clumped together in the camp, but somehow he knew it wouldn't.

They watched in silence for several minutes, saying nothing. Only the wind rustling against the rocks could be heard, along with the occasional dragon roar far off in the mist.

"She's beautiful," Rowan finally murmured.

Loghain didn't say anything at first. It had been difficult to remain, to feel her anger when she looked at him. Rowan hadn't forgiven him; he knew that. Very likely she never would. But Maric had asked—no, *demanded*—that he put Ferelden first. And so he had done it. And now he would see this through.

"They say that Ferelden is in revolt," he finally said. "Denerim is burning, or so the last rider that joined us during the night told us. The usurper is paralyzed."

Rowan nodded slowly. "Considering what the Chantry said, I'm not surprised."

"What they said?"

She looked at him curiously. "You hadn't heard? The Grand Cleric of Ferelden herself, Revered Mother Bronach, declared that Maric was the rightful holder of the throne. She went as far as to call Meghren a dangerous tyrant, and proclaim that the Maker had sent Maric to save Ferelden."

Loghain's eyes went wide. "The usurper isn't going to like that."

"Evidently he has his hands full at the moment."

"You mean he hasn't put her head on a pike yet?"

"He'd have to catch her first, wouldn't he? Perhaps she shouted her pronouncement very loudly from the windows of her speeding carriage."

He smiled, but it wasn't very convincing. The Revered Mother had put the Orlesian bastard on the throne in the first place; more than likely she had merely detected which way the wind was blowing.

He suspected it might be a good move on her part. When news of their slaughter of Ceorlic and the others had gotten out, only a handful of the nobility had bothered to raise an outrage. Every single one of the families of those men had angrily sworn they would fight with King Meghren to the last, though it was doubtful they would have ever done otherwise, but for the others? Many seemed to hear the news, and they did just as Maric had predicted they would. The ranks of the army had swollen dramatically over the last two days alone.

Loghain realized that Rowan was staring at him, lost in thought. Off in the distance, the dragon roared again. The beast swooped low and disappeared off into the hills as the fog banks were slowly burned away by the rising sun. He tried not to stare back at Rowan, tried not to notice how she looked radiant in the wind, a warrior queen that the minstrels would no doubt one day sing about in awe.

"Are we truly going to go into battle without Maric?" she asked.

It was a good question, one he had asked himself. "You know where he is."

"I know where he should be. He should be here.

These men need to see him, they need to know who they're fighting for."

"Rowan," he said firmly, "he is doing what he feels he must."

She frowned, turning and staring off into the valley again. A strong breeze swept across the ridge, freezing them both, and she shivered in her armor. "I know," she breathed, her tone anxious, "I just fear what might happen to him. He could die, with no one with him to help. We've come too far to lose him now."

Loghain smiled at her, hesitantly raising a hand to brush her cheek. It was a small gesture, and she closed her eyes, accepting it . . . but only for a moment. Rowan's eyes fluttered open and she pulled away slightly, uncomfortably avoiding looking in his direction. It was enough. There was a gulf between them now, and it wasn't crossed so easily.

He let his hand drop. "He could die anywhere, even here."

"I know that."

"Would you refuse his chance to do this one thing alone?"

She thought about it, and then her eyes dropped. "No."

There was stirring in the camp around them now, and Loghain could see why. The sun was beginning to clear the horizon, setting the clouds ablaze, but more important there were signs of activity down in the valley. The vanguard of the Orlesian force, he suspected. They would have to move quickly.

He turned to tell Rowan, but she was gone. She already knew.

———

Not two hours later, the rebel army had assembled. They were gathered behind him now, a great unruly horde of riders and bowmen, knights and commoners. He barely could remember who most of them were; the small force they had left Gwaren with constituted only a small core of those who were present here. Standing prominently in front of them was a handful of dwarves, less than a third of the Legion of the Dead that had fought with them in Gwaren. Nalthur had been pleased to return just in time for the battle, and had grinned madly when Loghain had informed him of the odds they faced. He grinned still, watching Loghain from where he stood with his men, all of whom were given a respectful berth by the other soldiers.

Nearly a thousand men, all told. Far more undisciplined than Loghain would have liked, and even with the veterans such as the Legion they had had almost no chance to train together or work out ways to communicate strategy properly. It could potentially be a nightmare. Anything could go wrong.

But then he remembered the dragon.

The chevaliers were down in the valley and had already become aware of the rebel force assembling above them. They were scrambling to assume a defensible position and recall those horsemen they had already ferried across the river. It was either that or abandon them and retreat to higher ground, which they weren't going to do. Not yet. They would count on their superior mobility to pull them out of trouble if it came to that.

Which was why Rowan was riding with her

horsemen to the other side of the valley right now, to cut off any means of escape. They would crush the enemy here or die trying.

Loghain turned his horse to face the soldiers behind him, all of them waiting with steel gleaming in the light and breath blowing white in the cold. Loghain's black cloak billowed in the crisp wind, and as his stern blue eyes traveled over each of the men present, they stood a little straighter. He was wearing his old armor, the very suit of studded leather that his father had made long ago. For good luck, he thought.

"There was a dragon in the sky," he shouted to the men, his voice competing with the whistling wind. "I saw it myself, flying in the mountains. If dragons can rise from defeat, my friends, than why not Ferelden?"

The army howled its approval, raising swords and spears and shaking them until finally Loghain held up his hand. "It feels good to fight," he shouted, "to stand up to those Orlesian bastards and tell them *no more*!"

They howled again, and Loghain raised his voice even further. "Your prince is not here! But when he returns to us, we shall hand to him his stolen throne! Here at the River Dane is where the Dragon Age begins, my friends! *Today they will hear us roar!*"

And roar they did. If the Orlesian knights in the valley looked up at that moment, they shivered as they listened to the sound of a thousand men shouting with rage, the kind of sound that only those who demand freedom can muster. They froze in their saddles as they watched the rebel army spill over the ridge and come charging down the valley toward them.

And perhaps off in the Frostback Mountains, a

dragon lifted its head in a shadowy cavern and heard the rebels' long roar, and it approved.

Severan gathered his ermine cloak closer around him, cursing the Fereldan cold. It wasn't even truly winter yet, but already at this time of night the air nipped worse than it ever did in his own homeland. The cold air blew in from the southern currents and the wastelands beyond the Korcari Wilds, making every winter here a thing to be endured. One explanation, perhaps, for the land's harsh and unrelenting populace.

It was on moments such as this that he began to wish he had never come. Let Meghren flee back to Orlais and beg the Emperor to let him remain there and never return, as it was what he truly wanted anyhow. Let the Fereldans have their piece of dirt and their dogs and their cold. He would be better off returning to the Circle of Magi and starting over.

But then he shook his head. No, he had too much invested here. The revolts were far worse than he ever could have predicted, but once the rebel army was crushed, the locals could be pacified, one town at a time if need be. By the time it was all over, Meghren would be so utterly grateful and so utterly dependent on Severan that the mage would have free rein.

And then there would be some changes. Oh, yes indeed.

As it was, he was currently facing nothing but problems. He turned to glare at the young page cowering by the entrance to his tent, holding up the missive that the lad had brought to him and crumpling it in his fist. "Why," he seethed, "is my intelligence being insulted? Are you telling me that not a single one of our scouts has returned yet?"

"I don't know, Ser Mage!" the page protested. "I . . . I just brought the message?"

Severan scowled, and then tossed the crumpled paper at the boy. He squealed in fear, flinching as if he had been hit by a rock. Snorting in disgust, Severan waved his hand and dismissed the boy, who ran off gratefully.

There was no point in taking his anger out on anyone, much as he might like to. Severan had brought his army out to meet the legions of chevaliers arriving overland from Orlais, but currently the legions were nowhere to be found. Severan had been delayed by the riots at Highever, and then forced to send messages back to Denerim once he heard of Bronach's decree, and that had delayed him even further. Now he arrived at the rendezvous point only to find no chevaliers, and his efforts to gather intelligence from ahead were meeting with nothing but more problems.

Could it be the rebels? Could they have come this far west already? The last reliable report placed the rebel army at a village in the Bannorn, where Prince Maric had performed his surprising executions of Ceorlic and the others. That had been almost three days ago, however, and before that Severan hadn't had reliable intelligence for almost a week. It seemed unlikely that the rebels could seriously challenge two legions of chevaliers with the mishmash of forces they currently claimed, but doubt plagued him.

If only Katriel had not turned on him. How the thought of that elven woman galled him! Severan paced around his tent, kicking aside the silken cushions in agitation. He had already sent word to his contacts in Orlais, arranging a rather unpleasant surprise for her the moment she returned to her bard compatriots. He had paid good coin to arrange for her assistance, and now he had paid even more to acquire another, who unfortunately would not arrive for at least another week.

More delays, he fumed. He was tempted to storm out of the tent right now, kick the commanders awake despite the late hour, and demand the army march immediately. They could leave the rendezvous, head farther west, and perhaps intercept the chevaliers en route. But he made himself calm. He disliked having his hand forced, so he would school himself to be patient for now.

Severan shivered again, gathering the white ermine cloak tighter around him once more. He turned to the stove in his large tent, deciding that since the servants were not going to come and replace its coals, he had best deal with it himself. Then he stopped short, confronted with a man standing in the back of his tent by the rear flap. It was a blond man in brilliant plate armor and a purple cloak, holding a pale longsword before him that glittered with magical runes. The deadly glare of the man made his intent clear.

"Prince Maric," Severan commented. "How . . . unexpected of you to show yourself here, of all places." It *was* a surprise, truthfully. Was the rebel army here? Was it about to attack? Surely this fool didn't come by himself? Keeping an eye trained on his uninvited guest, the mage gestured with his hand, summoning a magical protection spell. A soft glow surrounded him, and the blond man warily moved into the tent, keeping his longsword trained on Severan.

"Your guards are dead," Maric told him. "I wouldn't bother calling for them."

"I could shout louder and bring my entire army here down upon you."

Maric smiled mirthlessly. "Not before I killed you."

Severan had to admit he was impressed. This young man looked every bit the King, and a warrior, too. How unlike the rumors about him; they spoke of a man entirely unlike the killer he faced now.

He stretched out his arm and spoke a single word, a command in the ancient Tevinter tongue, and Severan's ornate staff flew across the tent to land in his hands. He sneered at the young prince confidently. "Is that what you're here to do? You might find it a bit of a challenge, my prince."

Maric's face filled with fury. "Don't you call me that."

"My prince? Why ever not?"

Without response, Maric lunged at the mage, bringing his sword down even as Severan held up his staff and blocked the swing. White sparks flew as the weapons connected, as well as a flash of fire. Severan's eyes went wide as he realized the weapon's power.

Casting a quick spell, he held out a palm toward Maric, and lightning leaped out, striking the man and sending him flying back, screaming in pain. Maric smashed into a cabinet, knocking it over and nearly bringing that section of the tent down on top of him. Outside, the distant sound of alarmed shouts rang out.

Severan walked slowly toward where the Prince still spasmed in pain, jolts of electricity zapping throughout his armor. "Did you really think you could walk into my camp and defeat me, young man? How did you even find me?"

Maric rolled over, gritting his teeth in agony as he slowly got to his knees. "A present from Katriel," he hissed, looking up at the mage through slitted eyes.

"She told you?" Severan rubbed his beard in interest. "And where is she now?"

"Dead." The Prince stood, shaking with the effort and resisting the effects of the lightning with sheer willpower.

Again Severan was impressed. But impressive as he was, the man wasn't about to beat him with a sword. Holding out his staff toward Maric, he shouted several words again in the Tevinter tongue, and the entire tent flashed as a storm brewed within it. Chill winds suddenly spun within, instantly covering the fabric of the walls and the ground with frost and freezing Maric to the spot.

The silvery armor was quickly frosted up, and Maric doubled over in pain, trying to fight off the winds and snow. The skin on his face froze and cracked, bright blood welling from the wounds. "A shame," Severan sighed as he walked toward Maric calmly. "I would have preferred to kill the elven wench myself, after what she did to me. If you've spared me the effort, I imagine I'll need to practice the tortures I've thought up on you, instead."

The prince was back on his knees, cringing in pain as Severan stood over him. The mage held out a hand, preparing to cast another spell on his helpless target, when suddenly Maric flung his hand up.

Something flew from his hand at Severan's face, a cloud of dust or dirt. Severan wasn't quite sure, but either way, it stung his eyes and burned the inside of his throat, and he stumbled back quickly. Falling over an ice-covered chair, he cried out in pain as he hit the floor, instantly convulsing into a coughing fit as the burning sensation in his throat became even more intense.

He could barely see. Coughing madly, he tried to crawl away from where the Prince must still be, lest the man come running with his blade.

Maric picked himself up only slowly, however. The wind still blew wildly around the tent, flinging small pieces of furniture and books about and threatening to blow the tent itself away. More shouts could be heard through the wind, coming closer. Maric was covered in thick frost and bleeding from cracks in his face and hands, and gritting his teeth, he began to slowly limp toward the mage.

"Another gift from Katriel," he gasped through his pain. "She left me a letter. It told me who you were, told me how to find you and everything I needed to defeat you." As Severan's eyes began to clear, he saw tears running down from the Prince's eyes, leaving trails on his frost-white skin.

"You won't leave this place alive!" Severan shouted in rage. He scrambled back more quickly, but the Prince kept advancing. Finally, gathering his will, Severan held up his palm toward the man. His hand wreathed in a burst of flame . . .

. . . and then the flame guttered out. In the back of his head, a familiar buzzing roared into life, and numbness started to spread through his body.

"No!" he screamed in horror, realizing what the Prince had done.

Maric stood over the mage, snarling in fury as he held the longsword by the hilt and plunged the blade down. The point of the dragonbone struck Severan's protection spell and flashed bright sparks. Severan was not hit, but he reeled in pain as the magic blade cracked the energies of his shield.

As Maric raised the blade up high again, Severan screamed in pure terror. He put up his hands defensively, trying to summon another spell, but it was too late. The blade came down with Maric's full weight behind it. With a great flash of light, it shattered the protection spell, thrusting through it and plunging into Severan's heart.

The mage gasped, feeling agony exploding through him like white fire.

Thoughts raced through his head. *No! This cannot be how it ends! Not like this!* He tried to bring to mind a spell that might save him, a healing spell or even a rite to pull his spirit from his body and preserve it. But the numbness left him powerless, left him screaming in his mind as his pulse slowed and the lifeblood seeped from his wound.

Then the staff rolled from Severan's fingers and he was still at last, his disbelieving eyes focused on nothing.

The blizzard inside the tent vanished, disappearing as if it had never existed. The frost and ice it had deposited remained, coating the entire inside of the tent and the scattered furniture with a thick whiteness and a chilly mist that hung in the air. Confused shouts rang throughout the camp outside, some of them coming very close.

Maric looked down at the mage dead beneath him, the bright blood a stain spreading slowly in the frost. With a grimace, he yanked the sword up from the corpse. The mage did not move.

"Thank you, Katriel," he murmured, and felt the grief welling up inside him. He had found the letter and the tiny chest in her quarters the next morning, left by her out in the open, where he couldn't possibly miss it. She had known. She had known she was followed to Denerim, she had known what awaited her when she returned. She had written that there could be no forgiveness for what she had done, and then she had explained in detail how Severan could be approached and killed.

Without him, she had written, the usurper is lost. And then she had wished him well.

Maric cried. He hunched down in the ice-filled tent and the tears flowed freely for Katriel, for his mother, for the part of himself that he had somehow lost along the way. But it was done. He had sworn to his mother that he would find a way, and he had. All that was left now was to finish it.

Two soldiers burst into the tent, skidding to a halt as they saw their dead master on the floor and Maric crouched above him. One of them overcame his shock and ran at Maric, shouting an angry war cry as he raised his sword.

Maric stood and slashed his blade around in a wide arc at the same time. The longsword cut through the man's brigandine easily, leaving a deep gash that fountained blood. The man stumbled to his knees, and as Maric leaped past him, he stabbed downward into the side of the man's neck. The soldier died, gurgling.

The other saw Maric charging, and his eyes went wide in fear. He turned to run and began to shout for help at the same time, but Maric pulled his blade out of the first soldier and thrust it quickly into the chest of the other. The man's shouts died on his lips. Grimly and quietly, Maric stepped forward and finished running the soldier through.

There were more shouts nearby. The camp was in confusion, but the distractions he had planted would last for only so long. They would all be here soon.

Looking back at the dead mage, Maric paused. The man had paid for his arrogance. He had paid for helping the usurper keep his iron grip on the kingdom, and for whatever plan had brought him to Ferelden in the first place. If Maric owed him anything, it was for sending Katriel to him. For that, Maric had faced him alone. He had made it quick.

But now there would be no mercy.

I'm coming for you next, Meghren.

With that silent promise, Maric turned and stepped into the darkness outside and fled. Loghain and Rowan had fought a battle for him today, but the rest he intended to fight for himself. The stolen throne would be returned, and Ferelden would be free once more, and let the Maker pity any of those who stood in his way.

EPILOGUE

"But did they win?"

Mother Ailis smiled with amusement at young Cailan as he squirmed in excitement in his chair. For a twelve-year-old lad, he had listened rather intently to the tale, she thought. He was always fascinated with such tales, and loved the ones that involved his father the best. And why not? He wasn't the only boy in Ferelden who idolized King Maric, after all.

She smoothed Cailan's blond hair absently with a weathered hand and nodded. "Yes, they did win." She chuckled as the boy clapped his hands in delight. "As you must have guessed. If they hadn't, would you be here today, young man?"

He grinned. "Probably not."

"Probably not," she agreed. "Loghain led the army to a great victory, decimating the Orlesian army so terribly that Emperor Florian refused to send the usurper any more forces. We lost so many of our own. Nalthur and the Legion died bravely, as did half of our army. Even your mother almost died. But it was a great day for Ferelden, and that was how Loghain became known as the Hero of River Dane, a title that he still carries to this day."

Cailan flipped through the book in his lap, a fine book filled with delicate paintings that had been presented to the young Prince as a gift by the Orlesian ambassador. It had been the first representative sent since the crowning of the new Empress two years ago, and the man had been practically laden with gifts of all kinds. Bribes, Teyrn Loghain had called them.

Naturally, young Cailan loved the pictures of chevaliers and battles in the book, and if they fired his thoughts of Ferelden's victories rather than the Empire's greatness, the ambassador certainly didn't need to know. Cailan was surrounded by books, some open and half-read, others discarded or lovingly read a dozen times. Queen Rowan had worked tirelessly while she was alive to fill the palace with books, and she supposed the lad loved them as much as he had loved her.

Cailan looked up at her in confusion. "But what happened to the usurper? He wasn't at that battle, was he?"

Mother Ailis chuckled. "No, no, he was not. It was three more years of battles before your father brought him down. King Meghren refused to admit defeat right until the bitter end. At the last, he and the last few of his supporters barricaded themselves within Fort Drakon here in the city."

"The one inside the mountain?"

"That's the one. He held out there for six days,

until finally your father challenged Meghren to a duel. Teyrn Loghain was furious with your father for doing it, but naturally, the usurper couldn't help but accept. He was very sure he was going to win."

Cailin grinned widely again. "But he didn't!"

"No. That he did not." She paused, wondering for a moment if she should continue. But the King had said his son should know everything, had he not? Then he must know everything. "Your father dueled Meghren on the roof of Fort Drakon, and when he killed the man, he took off his head and placed it on a pike outside the gates of the palace. That was the last head ever to decorate this palace."

The boy nodded, accepting this news with equanimity. He returned his attention to the book in his lap, his long blond hair falling once again in front of his eyes. Mother Ailis watched him for a time, reaching out and brushing the hair aside again. There was little other sound in the library other than the rushing fall winds outside the windows.

"What are you thinking now, dear boy?" she asked him finally.

He looked up at her, his large eyes somber. "Did my mother and father not love each other?"

Ah. She took a deep breath. "That's not it at all, child." She smiled gently at him. "They became King and Queen of Ferelden, and that was of great importance to them both. There was much work to be done to rebuild this nation once it was freed, and they knew that they needed to stand united in order to do that."

Ailis saw that the boy didn't understand, and she sighed deeply and cupped his cheek in her hand. "They had great affection for each other, and in time, that grew into love. When your mother died," she broached the subject carefully, "it made him so sad that he stayed within his chambers for weeks. You remember, yes?"

Cailan nodded glumly. She remembered the time, as well. Months of wasting illness and not a thing even the finest mage of the Circle could do to help the Queen, and in the end, she had quietly closed her eyes and gone to sleep. For weeks afterwards, King Maric had shut himself off, staring into the fire or sitting at his desk. He said nothing at all and barely responded to anyone. He ate little, less with each passing day, and the entire castle had become alarmed. The nation mourned its beloved Queen, and they feared it might soon be mourning its King, as well.

Ailis had been at a loss for what to do. There had been no one she could turn to in the palace, certainly not Loghain. After the war, Maric had elevated Loghain to the nobility and made him the Teyrn of Gwaren. All of Ferelden had celebrated that day; the very idea that one of their own, a hero born of the common folk, could be raised to noble rank appealed to them greatly. Teyrn Loghain had married a fine woman and fathered a wonderful daughter, and yet despite the supposed legendary friendship between him and King Maric, he never once came to the palace.

Whenever Loghain's name was mentioned in front of the Queen, she had always become very quiet, and the King would glance sadly in her direction. The first time it had happened, Ailis knew. One could not help but know. And thus Loghain's name was not often spoken in the palace. The King would go to Gwaren on occasion, but whenever he did, the Queen would find reason to remain behind and Ailis would spend those days in the Queen's quiet company.

So she had sent a messenger to Gwaren, and Loghain had come. His face stone, he had gone into the King's chambers and shut the door and there he stayed for hours. And then, without warning, they had emerged. Without a single word to anyone, they had gone to the site where Rowan's ashes had been placed and they mourned together.

"I remember," Cailan sighed.

"What your father felt for the elven woman, Katriel, was very different. That does not mean that he did not love your mother, however. Never doubt that he did."

She remembered when Loghain had found her. She had been living in a small village north of the Wilds then and had heard of a man asking after the outlaws who had been slain years before by the usurper's men. He had been searching for his father. When Loghain finally spotted her in the hospice, he ran and swept her up in his arms, laughing with a joy that was so unlike anything she had ever seen in him.

And then she had brought Loghain to the place where she had spread his father's ashes, along with the ashes of so many he had tried to protect. It had taken her such a long time to put them all to rest on that hill. And there in the rain, she had held him like a child as he wept, and she wept with him. He begged her for forgiveness, and she told him he needed none whatsoever.

Gareth would have been proud of his son. She was sure of it.

Cailan closed the book, admiring the detailed embossment on the leather covers, and then he looked up at her quizzically. "Am I going to be the King someday, Mother Ailis?"

"When your father passes, yes. Let us pray that is not soon. I certainly doubt I will be alive to see it."

"Will I be as good a king as my father?"

She chuckled at that. "You are a Theirin, my dear boy. You've the blood of not only Calenhad the Great in you but also Moira the Rebel Queen and Maric the Savior. There is nothing you cannot do if you put your mind to it."

The boy rolled his eyes and sighed in exasperation. "That's what Father always says. I don't think I'll *ever* be as good a king as he is."

So much like his father, indeed. Ailis tousled his hair fondly and rose from her chair. "Come, young man. Walk with your old tutor, and let us find your father in the gardens. You can tell him yourself what a fine listener you were today."

Cailan leaped from his seat, grinning. "Do you think he'll tell me another story? I want to hear more about the dragons!"

"I think there is time for more stories later. But not today."

The young prince had to be satisfied with that, so he excitedly raced down the palace hall and was gone in an instant. Shaking her head in amusement, Mother Ailis picked up her cane and slowly began chasing after him.

TOR

Award-winning authors
Compelling stories

Please join us at the website
below for more information
about this author and other great
Tor selections, and to sign up for
our monthly newsletter!

www.tor-forge.com